A CONFIDENTIAL SOURCE

A CONFIDENTIAL SOURCE

JAN BROGAN

NEW YORK   BOSTON

Copyright © 2005 by Jan Brogan

Mysterious Press
Warner Books

Time Warner Book Group
1271 Avenue of the Americas, New York, NY 10020

The Mysterious Press name and logo are registered trademarks of Warner Books.

Printed in the United States of America

ISBN 0-89296-007-8

For Bill, for everything

ACKNOWLEDGMENTS

I couldn't have written this book without the help of my writers group, Barbara Shapiro, Floyd Kemske, Thomas Engels, Judith Harper, and Vicki Stiefel, who put up with my incredibly rough drafts and gave me such great advice and support.

A big thanks goes to Robin Kall, who helped with this book in so many ways: from teaching me about talk radio, to guiding me through Providence to educating me about the many idiosyncrasies of Rhode Island.

The following people were incredibly generous with their time and expertise: RI Attorney General Patrick Lynch; Retired Police Chief Augustine Comella; Deputy Chief of the Bureau of Criminal Identification at the RI Attorney General's office Pasquale Sperlongano; John Depetro, talk show host at WHJJ; Mitchell Etess, executive vice president of marketing at Mohegan Sun; Laura Meade Kirk, reporter at *The Providence Journal*; Pamela Hunt, assistant attorney general, Massachusetts Attorney General's Office; Cheryle Marcus, blackjack dealer at Foxwoods; Rachel Gould, production assistant at Waterfire; Linda Henderson, library director of *The Providence Journal*; and the folks at the Massachusetts State Lottery. Any mistakes are mine alone.

I'd also like to thank my early readers, Diane Bonavist, Hallie Ephron, Naomi Rand, and Laura Barry. I owe a huge debt of gratitude to Beth Kirsch for her incredibly generous and methodical editing.

I'd also like to thank Bill Clew for taking me to the casinos and teaching me the correct way to play the slot machines; Bill Santo and Bob Brogan for help with plot; Tom Brogan for help in legal issues; John Barry and Small House Studios for design and support of my website; Lannie Santo for help in site research; and Kim Swetchzkenbaum for showing me around the East Side.

Also, I'd like to credit as background sources "Vice and Virtue—The Two Worlds of Buddy Cianci," by Mike Stanton in *The Providence Journal*; and *Bad Bet* (Random House) by Timothy O'Brien.

Many thanks to my agent Dan Mandel at Sanford J. Greenburger Associates for his patience and guidance; and to Kristen Weber, my editor at Mysterious Press, for her support.

But most of all I want to thank my husband, Bill Santo. For everything.

A CONFIDENTIAL SOURCE

CHAPTER

1

I PUT MY glass of wine down beside the empty cereal bowl on the bar and turned the radio up a notch. Leonard of *Late Night* hated much of what was going on in Rhode Island, but nothing got him going like the referendum to legalize gambling.

"Bookmakers. We're turning into a state of bookmakers." His fury filled my apartment, intimate, even in outrage. I sat back on the bar stool and took a sip of wine. Leonard wasn't one of those radio jocks who argued just for the sake of it. You could feel his honesty, his indignation.

Dori from Warwick called in to say that if people wanted to gamble, they were going to gamble. She had a staccato inflection and added extra syllables. "Why shoul-d-n't the state getta cut?"

"Well, maybe the state should get in on prostitution and crack then," replied Leonard, without the slightest trace of any accent.

Dori must have been a first-time caller. She hesitated, perplexed. "Can we do that?" she asked.

Leonard played the "Tammy's in Love" theme song, which

officially designated a caller as a bimbo, and cut to a commercial.

I began to hunt for my cordless phone. You'd think it would be impossible to misplace a cordless in a one-bedroom apartment that doesn't even have a real kitchen, just a Formica bar that carves a galley-type kitchenette out of the main living area. But I'm not a particularly good sorter of life's materials. The mail, newspapers, and files from work all end up in stacks on the floor that I have to navigate around and search under. Finally, I found the cordless in the corner by the closet, on top of a carton of books I still hadn't unpacked.

As I returned to the bar stool, I wavered. I *had* called Leonard just last night. Thursday was Cinema Talk, and Leonard and I were both eagerly awaiting news about whether there would be another *Terminator* movie.

I call myself Mary from Massachusetts, even though I'm Hallie, now of Rhode Island. Working in such a small state, I feel I have to conceal my identity. Reporters, unless they have their own columns, are not supposed to have such loud opinions.

I put the wineglass down and dropped the phone back in its wall recharger. Tonight, I'd *listen*. I took my cereal bowl and spoon over to the sink, which still held my dirty cereal bowl and spoon from breakfast. I began washing the bowl, but got distracted when Leonard accepted a call from Andre of Cranston. Andre called even more than I did.

"Gambling destroys more people than drinking," he said for about the hundredth time.

I'd heard Andre talk about the violent fights his parents had had over gambling, about his father going bankrupt, even about loan sharks who threatened the family. The stories were so extreme I had to wonder if Andre was for real or some sort of plant in the calling audience.

Tonight, though, Andre was sticking to politics. "Obviously, if the city can't develop the Pier Project without legalizing gambling and opening a casino, it shouldn't develop it." Everything was always obvious to Andre.

I dropped the bowl and sponge back into the sink. Despite all the hype about the Providence renaissance, Rhode Island was in a financial mess, with a massive budget deficit. Couldn't Andre see how desperately the state needed some new form of revenue? The male listeners might have written off Dori of Warwick as a bimbo, but not me. There were casinos little more than an hour away in Connecticut and electronically available at home via the Internet. If people were going to gamble, they were going to gamble.

Suddenly, I was furious on Dori's behalf. The fuel of argument flowed through my veins, pulling me directly to the wall recharger. I grabbed the cordless, the station phone number programmed into my fingertips.

Busy.

I put the phone down on the bar and made myself take a deep breath. It's not as if there were any official rules about print journalists calling talk-radio shows, but reporters, in general, were expected to be objective, impartial, detached. The world was not supposed to know how they stood on the issues, unless, of course, they were experts. Then, the reporter was supposed to be the featured guest on the talk show. Not the caller.

If I just waited a couple of minutes, someone else would call and defend Dori of Warwick. To distract myself, I reached for my canvas knapsack, sitting underneath the bar. Hoisting the knapsack onto the bar, I pulled out a lottery scratch ticket from the inner pocket. A silly long shot, but it afforded a few moments of complete fantasy. I liked the $5 tickets, with the million-dollar cash prizes, so I could dream about paying off my debts and really transforming my life. Even in the dull light of the fifties-looking fixture that hung over the bar, anyone could see my life needed transforming.

The only furniture in the living area was a futon in an alcove that was clearly designed for a dining table, a twenty-year-old Haitian cotton couch, and an oak coffee table and bookshelf that I'd bought unfinished and never stained. I found a quarter in a cup of change on the windowsill to scratch off the ticket. If I won a million dollars, I promised myself I'd buy new furniture.

I tried to make myself think about exactly what kind of furniture I'd buy, but some new caller, another man whose name I didn't get, was now attacking the mayor of Providence. "What's he trying to do? Prostitute the city? Pimp for the entire state of Rhode Island?"

As legalized gambling's most powerful supporter, Mayor Billy Lopresti was Leonard's archenemy. A man of incredible charm, the mayor's personal popularity and hold on voters were not in the least altered by the fact that his top aide was under investigation for taking kickbacks. "Anybody planning to vote for this idiotic referendum has to turn the dial," Leonard was shouting now. "You are no longer welcome to listen to my show!"

I loved it when Leonard did that, ordering people not to listen to him. As if he didn't care about ratings as long as he made his point. Supposedly, it infuriated his talk-show competitors at WPRO and WHJJ.

I dropped the scratch ticket on the counter and reached for the phone. This time, I got through, and was put on hold.

Last month, when I had to cover a charity event, a bike-a-thon to raise money for the Veterans' Homeless Shelter, I met

Leonard in person. I'd expected a burly man, but he was an ardent bicyclist and had that kind of lean-muscled body. He was younger than I had thought, midforties, and quiet, as if maybe he didn't want to strain his voice. He'd told me all about his bike training, thirty miles every day. *You have to be religious about the mileage,* he'd said. I got the feeling Leonard was religious about everything.

Midway through the interview, I noticed him staring at my press badge. I tried to speak in a throaty timbre just in case he recognized my voice. I don't know if he thought I was trying to seduce him with my best Brenda Vaccaro or what, but when he lifted his eyes, he gave me a strange smile.

Another deep breath and a sip of wine. I'd learned from experience that I needed fortification when I was about to call and disagree with Leonard. That way, my voice wouldn't shake in those first few minutes when I realized I was actually on the air.

"I'm not switching the dial, Leonard," I said when I was put through. "You can't order me away!"

"Oh, Mary," he said, through the telephone line. "You're not going to give me that old argument about the innocent fun your mother and aunt have at Foxwoods, are you?"

"People need a little excitement," I said. "A little hope."

"False hope," he said swiftly.

I glanced at the scratch ticket, abandoned on the bar. "A little gambling doesn't hurt anyone. If it's in moderation."

"Oh, please," Leonard returned.

"There's no reason all that money—billions of dollars—should go to the Native Americans in Connecticut when God knows we need it right here in Rhode Island."

"You're right. The mob can always use more revenue," he replied.

"Oh, come on. This'll be run by the Narragansett Indians,

not the Mafia. And there's gonna be a special state commission—all sorts of safeguards—"

"You really, *truly* believe that *any* safeguard will keep things on the up-and-up in *Rhode Island?*"

I hesitated. Leonard's emphasis on *truly* combined with the probing resonance of his baritone made me stop and question myself. What did I really know about Rhode Island? I'd lived here only four months. "Why not?" I tried to make this sound like an answer instead of a question.

Through the radio, I heard the first few bars of "Tammy's in Love," the bimbo theme song. This was followed by Leonard's voice booming over the airwaves. "Oh, Hallie," he said, using my real name. "You are so naive."

I stood at the picture window of my third-floor apartment, looking down on my neighborhood, at the closed shops and wide sidewalks of Wayland Square. I listened to a distant siren downtown and the steady hum of the traffic on I-95, and wondered: How freaking small was this state, anyway?

Outside, it was an especially crisp autumn night. The bright moon somehow made me feel even more exposed, as if nature had conspired to put me under a spotlight. I went over the many things I'd said to Leonard and his listening audience in the belief that I was an anonymous voice—an informed and, I liked to think, intelligent opinion. I'd called about legalized gambling, Patrick Kennedy, and the pedophile-priest controversy. I'd called about bad movies, good restaurants, and the Pawsox. I covered my face with my hands. The truth was: I'd called about everything.

But how the hell did Leonard know who I was? From that one interview at the bike-a-thon fund-raiser? Was my voice, a bit raspy, that distinct? Or had I given myself away by quoting the newspaper too often?

I'd hung up as soon as he said my name. But it didn't matter; he'd cut to a commercial. Oh, why on earth did I always give in to my impulses? Why did I have to call every frigging night?

A thousand square miles of land is just too small for a state. Rhode Island should be annexed to Massachusetts. The cultures merged. Everyone in Providence could listen to Boston radio shows instead.

Finally, after several dozen vows to never call talk radio again, I decided there was nothing left to do but go to sleep. I flipped off the light switch and headed toward the bedroom, but moonlight still illuminated the apartment. And as I crossed the living room, my glance caught a little rectangle pushed to the edge of the kitchen bar: the evening's forgotten scratch ticket.

What the hell, I thought, maybe I'd win a million dollars and not have to worry anymore about being an idiot. I picked up the ticket and took it back with me to the moonlit window. The Green Poker game, a lime-green card with a leprechaun holding a hand of cards. Scratching off the latex was tough, as if the ticket had been hanging around on the store shelf for too long, but I stuck with it. The leprechaun, as it turned out, was holding a pair of queens.

I began scratching the hand dealt me. The first square revealed the number 3 with a clubs symbol under it.

It figured.

The second square, scraped swiftly, was an improvement, a queen of diamonds. Predictably, the next two squares were major duds, a five of spades and an eight of clubs. With little hope, I scratched off the last little square.

A queen of hearts. A match. A pair, or in the Rhode Island lottery's new Green Poker game parlance, a lucky lady two of a kind. It was only fifty bucks, but in that moment, a gigantic win.

Rhode Island could keep its statehood.

This time of year, when there wasn't any risk of hitting beach traffic, the bureau office in South Kingstown was about twenty-five minutes from my apartment in Providence. The office was in one of those sunny little strip malls where you can park your car so close to the plate-glass window that you have the occasional urge to drive through, right to your desk.

I was the first one in and had to hunt for the key in the bottom of my canvas knapsack so I could unlock the door. The *Providence Morning Chronicle*'s newsroom is in a big building in the heart of the city, but the paper has these modest little local bureaus throughout the state. The idea is that the community likes to see its reporters, likes to have somewhere nearby to drop off the PTA press release and the high school sport scores. The South Kingstown office, wedged between Surfside Realty and Poppy's Lunch, was a narrow alley of three desks and two computers in a room with bright-white walls and marbleized linoleum.

Some days, I wondered what the hell I was doing in this empty little insurance agency of an office, what I was doing in Rhode Island at all. After I'd left the *Ledger* in Boston, I'd told myself I'd never go back to reporting, never trust myself, my emotions, again. But after three years of drifting from public relations to insurance research to cocktail waitressing, here I was starting all over again at a small bureau, at a smaller paper, in what has turned out to be an incredibly small state.

I had a mountain of debt from this chronic employment instability, including a sizable loan from my mother I desperately needed to repay. But it could be worse, I reminded myself as I put the key in the lock and swung open the door: I could still be serving cosmopolitans.

From the pavement, I grabbed the stack of the day's *Chronicle*s and took them inside. I put them on the raised Formica counter that guarded the entrance. The stack could be seen through the plate-glass window, and often people walked in off the street asking if they could buy a paper. Oddly enough, because of union restrictions, we had to tell them no, directing them to Poppy's Lunch next door or the pharmacy at the far corner of the strip mall.

I went to my desk and threw my jacket around the back of the chair and my knapsack onto the floor. In the bottom-right-hand drawer of my desk, there was a piece of marble decorated with a bronze quill and an old-fashioned inkwell. It was an award I'd won for investigative reporting on the Tejian profile, the last big story I'd done for the *Ledger*. Most days, I kept the drawer shut.

I sat down with the phone and a notebook, calling local dispatchers to make the daily police and fire checks. Our office covered South Kingstown, Narragansett, and North Kingstown, which were all beach communities. It was generally pretty quiet in the off-season. The best I could hope for was a brawl at a keg party at the University of Rhode Island.

The big news of the morning was a Dumpster fire in the parking lot of the Ro-Jack's supermarket. As I was transmitting the five-inch story to Providence, the front door scraped open and Carolyn Rizzuto, my bureau manager and boss, walked in.

"Hi," she said, distractedly sorting through a stack of envelopes in her hand. She was often distracted in the mornings. Although she was only eight years older than I was, we were lifetimes apart. At forty-three, she'd had two marriages, two divorces, and two daughters whom she was now raising alone.

She stood over me, a bag of Poppy's bagels under her arm and a funny smile on her face.

"What?"

She dropped the envelope on my desk. "This was stuck in the mail slot, didn't you see it?"

I shook my head. Addressed to Hallie Ahern in Magic Marker, the envelope had no postal marking.

Carolyn breezed past me, taking off her coat, dyed-blue leather, which she hung up in a closet instead of tossing over her chair. Then she began slicing open two bagels on a cutting board beside the coffee machine. "You wanna peanut butter and cream cheese?" she asked, her back toward me as she began to forage inside our little ice cube of a refrigerator.

"No, just plain, please," I replied, tearing open the envelope. Inside was a handwritten note on WKZI stationery.

Dear Hallie,

Sorry I screwed up on your name last night. Please don't stop calling the show.

Leonard

I slipped the note into my top drawer as Carolyn approached my desk.

"That's why you look the way you do," Carolyn said, putting the bagel down in front of me on a paper towel.

She said this almost every morning and when I forgot to pick up cookies on the afternoon tea run. Carolyn was what you would call a full-figured woman, not fat, but with a good-size chest and hips that would not slim no matter how many aerobics classes she took at lunchtime. I ran every morning at dawn, which tended to keep the weight off, but I was still in need of full-scale renovation.

"Have you seen those new bras at Victoria's Secret? Very natural looking," Carolyn would say with a glance at my boyish figure. "Even under a T-shirt."

"Shoes can make a very big difference," she'd say, showing me a Nine West catalog. "And better jewelry." She didn't think the small silver half-moons I wore in my ears even counted as jewelry.

And then, just last week, as if she'd been giving this an enormous amount of thought, she'd said, "A little azure shadow at the crease and under the arch and you'd be amazed by how blue your eyes can be." She peered at me a little closer. "After you tweeze those brows, of course."

She was such a true believer in beauty, so committed to my transformation, that I couldn't get mad about it. And she was right about the eyebrows.

The phone rang and Carolyn picked it up. By the sound of the conversation, it had something to do with her older daughter's habit of forgetting her homework. I took a bite of my bagel and tried to chew. Leonard must have hand-delivered the note last night on his way home from the station. Why had he gone to such trouble?

"Okay, I'll drive it over at lunchtime," Carolyn said. "But this is the *last, the absolute last* time." She slammed the phone into the cradle and seethed in silence. Then she turned to me. "You are so lucky you don't have kids."

I nodded, noncommittally. There were only the two of us permanently assigned to this bureau, and sometimes, when I had to cover for her because the kids were sick or had to be driven somewhere, my child-free status worked in my favor. Other times, Carolyn seemed to resent me for it.

"That *friend* of yours coming to stay tonight?" she asked.

She meant Walter. He was my sponsor, a friend I'd met at substance-abuse meetings who'd helped me kick the sleeping pills my doctor had prescribed after my brother, Sean, died. Walter drove a cab in Boston but slept on my futon now and then when he had a late-night gig playing guitar in Providence.

"Yes." I felt it necessary to add, "He's engaged to a good friend of mine."

Carolyn shrugged in a manner that suggested that was no barrier. From what she'd told me about her personal life, I'd gathered that she hadn't hesitated to break up a marriage or two. Once, she'd fixed me up with one of her ex-husband's coworkers, who, it turned out, wasn't yet divorced. "Oh, please, it's just a matter of time. They're in couples counseling," she'd said afterward. "And you know how that goes."

There was really no use explaining again that Walter was a surrogate brother. Carolyn didn't seem to understand the parameters of a platonic relationship.

She dropped into her chair and booted up her computer. Even though she professed to despise all office politics, first thing every morning she dialed Providence and called up the newspaper's in-house gossip file.

The *Chronicle* used its bureaus much like major-league baseball used its farm teams. The occasional "star reporter" might get hired away from a smaller paper right into the downtown newsroom, but most new recruits were assigned to these little bureaus across the state, where they were expected to prove themselves before getting promoted into the city. Bureau managers like Carolyn were former reporters who had developed "management potential" and thus had to cut their teeth as bosses in a bureau before being taken seriously as candidates for a news-editor or department-editor job downtown. Just like in the minor leagues, some would never make it to the pros. And many bureau managers, like Carolyn, claimed an outright preference for the more autonomous hinterlands.

But whether it was involuntary or by choice, working in the relative isolation of a bureau helped whet an inordinate appetite for in-house gossip. Even the new reporters who hadn't met each other wanted to know who was getting married or having a baby. But more important, we wanted to know who was getting praise from the editors, who was getting the choice assignments, and who had the inside track into the city.

Today, though, I had more pressing interests. Opening my drawer to peek at the note, I could make out the big *L*, the hard slant of Leonard's signature on the bottom of the paper. I shut the drawer when Carolyn abruptly turned around.

"Susannah Rodman is leaving the paper for the *New York Times*," she said, looking fierce and sad and angry. Even though Carolyn swore she had no interest in a promotion to an editorial job downtown, let alone in leaving the state of Rhode Island, I instantly recognized what she was feeling.

"Big deal," I said.

"Big fucking deal," Carolyn amended.

We were silent, internally reeling from how big a deal it really was. From the *Providence Morning Chronicle* to the *New York Times*—not too many reporters made that kind of leap.

"It was her investigative work on the superior court judges a few years back," Carolyn said at last. "She was on that team that won the Pulitzer."

I had never met Susannah Rodman, couldn't tell you if she was tall or short, or maybe the nicest person in the entire world. But for a single moment, I hated her.

"You know," Carolyn said, giving me a sly, sideways look.

"They'll need someone to replace her downtown on the investigative team."

When I took this job, I'd promised myself that I'd devote myself exclusively to small-town community reporting, that I'd stay in a quiet little bureau, away from the kind of high-profile investigative stories that could chew up your life and force you into no-win decisions. But the truth was, I was bored out of my mind with school committees and garden clubs. And even though this wasn't the *Boston Ledger*, Rhode Island was a petri dish of bizarre stories. The investigative reporters who dug them up were awarded Pulitzers and sent off to the *New York Times*.

I choked back the ambition in my throat and tried to make it sound as if it were hypothetical. "You think they'd even consider me?"

CHAPTER
2

THE MAZURSKY MARKET was always busy at the dinner hour. Usually, I didn't mind. Working in South Kingstown in the off-season was especially lonely: the highway devoid of cars, the sidewalks and shops practically empty. Back in the city, I was often relieved to be standing elbow to elbow with other people.

But tonight, I was hoping it would be quiet so I could get a few minutes with Barry, the owner. He was always at the register when I stopped in at night and was the closest thing to a friend I'd made in Providence. He'd steered me to the Green Poker scratch-ticket game and would be excited about my $50 win.

I'd caught the tail end of the dinner rush. It was raining outside, and the store steamed with warm people. The line at the register was three deep and Barry was in rote mode, eyes fixed on price stickers as he scanned them into his machine. On really slow nights, he had two different newspapers in front of him, the radio playing in the background, and a lit cigarette in a makeshift ashtray. Knowing I worked for the *Chronicle*, he was always asking me what was the latest from

the mayor's office. He refused to believe I wasn't privy to inside information. "Just let me know when he's going to raise
my taxes," he always said.

On this night, he didn't even see me wave to him. So I
skirted around the people in line and headed across the store
to the farthermost aisle and the dairy case.

It was a good-size market, a deep rectangle with the register in front along the long wall, the deli in back, and six short
aisles that ran between them. The store had a nicely polished
wood floor and well-tended philodendron plants hanging
from ceiling hooks in front of the wall-length plate-glass
window that looked out on Angell Street. But all this taste-
fulness was undercut by the political posters taped on the
wall and the pornographic magazines on full display behind
the register.

Two guys, their backs to me, were blocking the milk cooler.
The shorter one wore an old navy wool jacket and gray wool
cap. Dark hair, thick like fur, ran from the base of the cap
down the back of his neck. The other one, at least six feet tall,
was wearing a khaki parka. On my approach, the one with
the parka turned abruptly and the jacket fell open: He was
enormous, with a shiny, square forehead, puffed-up chest,
and refrigerator shoulders. He looked like a heavyweight
fighter, or maybe a bouncer at a strip club.

"Fuck," he said, looking at me as if I'd just cut him off at an
intersection.

The smaller man in the gray cap never turned around; he
grabbed a pint of chocolate milk and headed down the aisle,
toward the deli counter. The guy in the khaki parka did not
seem to register his departure. His left eyelid drooped, bur-
dened by the weight of some kind of sty, but the right eye
glared at me.

"Sorry," I said, "I didn't mean to scare you."

I should have said *startle*. Apparently, he took my comment as an assault on his manhood. "You didn't *scare* me." His tone was mean and mocking.

The Mazursky Market had always been a friendly place. I stood there, stunned. Without another look at me, he pulled up the hood of his parka, turned, and headed down the aisle.

I was still standing there when someone touched my sleeve.

"You all right?"

It was a man about my age, and like me, his hair and business suit were drenched from the rain. Immediately, I was struck by the concern in his expression, the openness of a clear, kind face. I'd seen him before. We were often in the market about the same time at night buying takeout from the deli, but had never spoken. I smiled and made an effort to look as if I'd already shaken off the incident. "I'm fine."

He watched as I reached into the dairy case for a quart of milk. "Whole milk?" he asked with a glance at my quart. He reached past me to grab a quart of 1 percent.

"For coffee," I said. Actually, I drank it by the glass and had it with cereal, but most people seemed to be paying attention to fat grams these days.

"Ah," he said, as if illuminating an important point. He smiled and I could see he had a nice mouth and a dimpled chin. I have a thing about men's chins, and have been misled more than once by a strong jawline. But this guy's nose saved him from the kind of perfection I've learned not to trust in a man. It looked like it might have been broken, giving him a distinct round-the-block look. By this time, I realized that I was analyzing his face for a little too long and quickly turned away.

Once I got in the register line, I stopped thinking about the rude guy, who had left the store, and was thinking about the quart-of-milk guy who was now just ahead of me in line. He *had* been flirting with me, I decided. It wasn't my imagination.

I left the required distance between us, but I felt his presence as if I were standing much too close. At five foot four, I'm not very tall, and his height loomed over me. I found myself thinking about those high heels Carolyn said made such a difference. Get a grip, Hallie, I told myself, taking a small step backward. Don't let him see how desperate you are for a date.

I put my quart of milk on the floor by my feet and began scavenging through my knapsack for my winning lottery ticket. The line moved forward, and I was still in the midst of my search when I noticed that the quart-of-milk guy had turned around and was looking back at me.

"Can't find your wallet?" he asked.

"Scratch ticket," I confided. "Fifty-dollar winner."

I thought his eyes narrowed for a second, as if he thought scratch tickets were beneath me. But then he smiled. "Congratulations. I hope you find it."

And then I had one of those rare and wonderful moments when timing works in your favor. My right hand touched the smooth surface of the shiny lottery paper and I pulled it out, as if on cue, and validated myself with a little wave of the ticket.

He gave me that smile again, but the line moved forward and he turned to put his quart of milk, half a rotisserie chicken, and a plastic container of pasta salad on the counter. I tried to think up some sort of clever way to note that he appeared to be dining alone. *Chicken for one?* Would that be *completely* transparent?

"Hey, Hallie, is that a winner you got there?" Barry asked as he finished ringing up the order.

"Two queens," I said.

"Told you," Barry said, counting out change. He was just an average-size man, but he had been a marine, and had the kind of Popeye forearms that made him look formidable behind the register.

The quart-of-milk guy picked up his bag and hesitated, as if he, too, was trying to think of something else to say. "Don't forget your milk," he said, gesturing to my quart on the floor.

"I won't."

Another hesitation, and then: "You live in this neighborhood, right?"

I nodded.

"Me, too."

I smiled and gave him my best "small world" shrug.

"Since we're neighbors, you think sometime that you might want to go somewhere *else* for dinner?" He frowned down at his grocery bag for a second and then looked up with a hopeful expression.

Is it crazy to give your phone number to someone you just met in a convenience store? Maybe, but I liked this guy. It wasn't just that I have a weakness for strong chins; he had kind eyes—something about them seemed unclouded and true. So I nodded.

He told me his name was Matt Cavanaugh and asked me for my phone number. I tried to seem cool as I grabbed a pen from the counter and wrote it on his grocery bag, but my heart was fluttering. He put the grocery bag with my phone number under his coat to protect it from the rain. And then with a wave to Barry, he was out the door.

Barry waited until the door closed. "You think you should give your phone number out like that?"

"I've seen him here before," I said. "And he seemed pretty nice, don't you think?"

Barry shrugged and turned back to the register. "You want that all in cash?" He scrutinized my ticket for a minute before opening the register drawer.

I glanced at the blue lottery terminal beside the register. "Don't you want to scan it?" I asked.

He shrugged. "Terminal's down again. Piece of crap. Anybody else I'd make come back. You, Hallie, I trust."

My gaze traveled to the bright colors of the scratch tickets in the plastic dispensers over his head. "How many unclaimed winners left on the Green Poker game?"

"Like I said, terminal's down, but the game is getting old. I think the last report said there were only two or three prizes left."

"What the hell, give me three tickets," I heard myself say. It's not that I didn't know those were long odds for gambling, it's just that my life had been a case study of long odds, mostly in the negative sense. I was only thirty-five years old and I'd already lost my brother, my father, and almost an entire career. It seemed to me that if I was the kind of person unlikely *bad* things happened to, I must also be the kind of person unlikely *good* things happened to.

At the present, the world seemed full of possibilities. The last four months had been painfully lonely and now I had a potential date with a cute guy who wasn't wearing a wedding ring.

Barry shook his head. "Now that I think about it, there mighta been only one or two prizes left. The Caesar's Palace game just came out a couple of days ago. It's still fresh off the presses. Eight or nine prizes left. I'm telling you, I have a feeling about you and Caesar."

I shrugged, which he took as an affirmative. He began to reach up to peel off the Caesar tickets, and I realized it was only a $1 game. I glanced at the back. The top prize was only

$250,000, which in my current high-stakes mood didn't seem like much. Plus, I thought about how quickly I'd scratch off three measly cards. "Two of the Green Poker game, too," I added, impulsively.

Barry hesitated again.

"I've got a feeling about that leprechaun," I said. "It's my night."

Barry's eyes met mine. "You're in the mood for long odds all around?" This was another reference to my giving my phone number to Matt.

"Just feeling lucky, that's all," I said.

He handed me the five scratch tickets. "None of my business," he said, but he still didn't seem happy about it.

This surprised me. Barry and I had gotten into a number of long discussions about how hard it was to start over in a new city at this age. He was always after me to volunteer for one of his veterans' charities, saying it was a great way to meet people.

But now, he seemed unduly protective. I looked into my knapsack and zippered the inside pocket where I'd put the tickets. Barry rang up the milk and began to count out my change. He stopped midway. "Nothing for dinner tonight?"

The smell of rotisserie chicken hung in the air. The store had emptied. No one was behind me in line and the aisles were quiet. "Anything left in the deli section?"

"Some salads, I think."

"You mind if I run back?" I asked.

Barry gestured for me to go ahead.

I turned down the aisle. The deli section was closed, but I grabbed a prepackaged salad from the cooler on the wall near the last aisle. As I tried to decide between two different-size containers of Mediterranean salad, I heard the front door scrape open. I listened for the sound of conversation, but heard none.

And then I heard the gunshot.

The blast reverberated through the small store. For a moment, I froze in the vibration and time stalled. A loud thud. Instinctively, I got low, kneeling behind the aisle-end Italian biscuit display. I clutched the plastic container of salad still in my hand, and held my breath, waiting for what would come next.

An eerie silence. No wail of pain, no threats. Fear pumped in all directions from my brain to my heart. I pulled my shoulder in, dropped my head lower, trying to disappear into the floor. I heard rummaging. The register drawer opened. A loud clatter as something fell over. But there were no voices. No swearing. No threats.

Say something, Barry, I silently begged.

My entire weight rested on one shaking knee. I struggled to remain still, staring at the plastic container of Mediterranean salad in my hand, wanting to put it down, afraid to make a single move.

More rummaging and a second round of clatter, as if things were being pulled from shelves. I clutched the plastic container, staring into its jumble of colors. Oil leaked from the bottom and onto my hand. A wave of it, slick across my palm.

I put the container on the floor, plastic crushed—my fear condensed into a crumpled corner. I could hear shuffling, a couple of footsteps, then silence.

Somehow I found the courage to peek around the display and saw the back of a khaki parka and crumpled hair beneath a panty-hose mask. I pulled back behind the display and hit something with my elbow. The Italian biscuits. A swirl of orange and green fell to the floor.

I held my breath.

his lips and nose, I tried to feel air—even a slight movement. "Please, Barry!" I whispered. "Please!" How long could you go without breathing?

I sucked in the biggest breath I could with every intention of forcing it into his lungs. But as I lowered my mouth toward his, I stopped, unable to move closer.

Nothing flickered in Barry's eyes, nothing beat from his chest. I exhaled, releasing the last, strained hope. No emergency procedure could change the bullet hole in his forehead. No medic, no matter how well trained, no matter how high tech the equipment, could bring this man back to life. I searched again for the cordless phone Barry kept on the counter. I found it lying underneath the toppled magazines and dialed 911.

I did not cry or stumble over the words.

After remaining numb through two hours of intense questioning at the police station, I sat at an extra computer terminal at the downtown newsroom of the *Chronicle* writing with an oddly detached professionalism. As if I were watching myself at the computer, reporting a crime I hadn't witnessed. As if I weren't hearing the bullet blast over and over in my head. As if I hadn't felt my knee slide through his blood.

I sat at a U-shaped configuration of computer terminals that's called the Rim. In the daytime, it was occupied by a gaggle of copy editors clarifying and correcting the grammar of the day's events. But now, at nearly nine at night, the *Chronicle* was a lonely place with only half a dozen people scattered through the vast, open newsroom. I shivered in my jacket, separated by a dozen desks from a sole copy editor who wouldn't look up from his screen.

Barry was dead. I'd known it when I'd heard the thud, when I was still hidden behind the Italian biscuit display. The beat cop, a young guy who already had a seen-it-all expression, went through the motions of checking for vital signs. Medics eventually arrived, but they did nothing but cover the body with a sheet.

Providence—A man at the Mazursky Market was shot to death in an apparent armed robbery shortly after 7 o'clock last night. Police are pursuing a man wearing a khaki parka and driving a white midsize car.

"You sure you're up to this?" Dorothy Sacks, the city editor who was running the Desk, appeared beside me.

The Desk was another configuration of computer terminals, where half a dozen news editors made the final decisions on breaking news. At this hour on a Friday night, the Desk was empty except for Dorothy and another male editor whose name I didn't know.

"I'm okay." I looked across the vast expanse of bright-blue carpeting and flickering computers. Was I okay? Raised a Catholic, I hadn't gone to church for years, except for Christmas. Still, I had the urge to pray. But when you can't pray for someone to recover, what can you pray for?

"Sometimes it's therapeutic to write about it," Dorothy said. She was a tall, quiet woman in her late forties who was dressed in pleated jeans and what looked like an old, favorite sweater. Carolyn didn't like her. There was something steely and humorless about her eyes, and her lower lip curled in, as if she was trying to figure something out. But her tone was genuine enough.

I shrugged. The young beat cop had sequestered me in the back of the cruiser, even before Barry's body was carted away to the morgue. At the station, I was allowed to use the phone, and I called in the basic facts about the shooting to the newsroom. Dorothy had asked me to come downtown when I was finished with the police.

Now she leaned over my shoulder and read my copy from the screen.

Barry Mazursky, 57, was a father of three. He and his wife lived in Cranston, where he was active in several veterans' and community-action organizations. A Vietnam veteran, Mazursky was licensed to own a handgun, which was found on the floor. Police said it appeared that Mazursky had attempted to pull a weapon in self-defense.

Dorothy was squinting at the text in a way that wasn't good. Then she dragged a chair from an empty quadrant of desks and sat down beside me. Her head tilted thoughtfully as she reread the copy, deciding exactly what it was about it that she didn't like.

"It's not that this is bad . . . ," she began.

I was too numb, too frozen to reread my lead, to try to guess what was bothering her.

"It's just that anybody could have written it."

I was silent a minute, digesting her meaning.

"You can't pretend to be objective on something like this. You've got to put yourself into the story. A first-person account that tells the readers what it was like to be inside that store. How you felt when you heard the gun."

"I didn't witness the actual murder." I'd learned that from the police: From a strictly legal perspective, even if I could identify the guy in the parka, I could only place him in front of the dairy case ten minutes or more before the murder. No matter what my heart told me, I hadn't actually seen him commit the murder. I'd only seen the back of a khaki parka and a panty-hose mask fleeing the scene.

"Didn't you tell me you tried to give the guy CPR?"
Dorothy asked.

The shiver began at the base of my neck.

Dorothy must have seen it. "Maybe it's too much for you.
You're probably in some kind of shock. If you aren't up to
writing the kind of story I'm talking about, I understand."

She was right. I wasn't up to writing the kind of story she
was talking about. I hadn't wanted to think about what it was
like to hear the gunshot, or what it had felt like to see the bullet hole in Barry's forehead, to pound his chest and not be
able to help him. And I hadn't wanted to think about what
might have happened to me if I hadn't headed back to the deli
counter.

The shiver again. My fingertips were frozen and my wrists
ached. As I pulled my blue-jean jacket tighter around me, I
knew. This wasn't journalistic distance, but some form of
physical shock. The protective wadding of my numbness
would not last. No matter how I tried to block out the pictures, they were going to flash through my head. I'd see
Barry, the toppled magazines, and the cold, hard expression
of the man in the parka for days, maybe months. The tears
would come, whether I got a story out of it or not.

Dorothy was waiting. She caught my eye, trying to trans-
mit her patience, her understanding. She would accept my
decision not to write this story and maybe even be grateful
because she could go home earlier. But she'd think less of me
for it. There was a certain journalism machismo I'd be lack-
ing. A clarity in her mind's eye about why I'd left big-city reporting for public relations and cocktail waitressing. Why I
was now exiled to a bureau.

I thought of the opening on the investigative team and
reminded myself that I was only a low-level witness to
this crime, technically incapable of identifying the killer. I

thought about all the reporters who went to truly dangerous places: Vietnam, Iraq, Afghanistan. "Is this for page one?" I asked.

"Only if you're up to it."

"I'm up to it," I said, turning to the computer and forcing my fingers back to the keys.

> From the deli, I could hear the door swing open, but I didn't think much about it. My thoughts were on my stomach as I tried to choose a salad for dinner. Almost instantly, the sound of a gun blast blew away all those mundane considerations.

The hairline just underneath my temples throbbed with pain. I tried to rub the ache away and felt a trickle of sweat. Get it together, Hallie, I told myself, glancing at the clock. I had only forty-five minutes to write this story. I had to stay focused if I was going to make deadline.

I forced myself to reread my paragraph as an editor might. *Almost instantly,* what did that mean? I erased *almost,* began the next sentence, and halted. Who cared whether it was instantly or almost instantly; Barry was dead. An image flashed in my head: his eyes, frozen in alarm. The handgun on the floor. My fingers retracted from the keyboard, my hands balled into fists.

Another picture, this time: the big man in the khaki parka. The ugly look on his face when I'd apologized for scaring him. He would have killed me if I'd been at the cash register. He'd want to kill me even more if he read my byline, realized I'd been there. That I was the one who had called the police.

The shiver again. This time from lower in my spine. I wondered about the guy in the old navy jacket and gray cap, the hairy guy who'd never turned around. I wasn't entirely sure the two had even been together. And the level of sound in the store made me think the guy in the khaki parka had been alone. Maybe I should leave out the part about calling the police, about telling them about the broken left taillight and dented fender. Maybe I shouldn't write this goddamn story at all.

I told myself to calm down. I had a job to do. I couldn't let my brain spin in this direction, couldn't leave out details that would make this a better story. This was my chance. My chance to prove I still had the skills to be a real reporter. I was *not* going to let fear of some small-time crook stop me from writing a front-page story.

"I'm going to need that in about twenty-five minutes," Dorothy said.

She was standing over me again. The lights had been shut off in the back of the room. The copy editor's desk was now empty. Besides Dorothy and myself, only one news editor and one other reporter remained.

"Anything from police on an arrest?" I asked.

"Not yet."

What had I thought? That all this would be wrapped up neatly for me? That with all the criminals in Providence, the police would be able to reach out and pluck this one from the streets?

Dorothy walked away and I returned to my keyboard, forcing myself to describe the difficulty of trying to make out the getaway car through the rain. The shock of finding Barry on the floor. I could feel my adrenaline surge as I wrote about my desperate attempts to revive him, and then the dead feeling in my heart, the futility as I waited helplessly for the police to arrive.

I was exhausted when I finally finished. I had time to reread it only once and check for spelling mistakes before I had to hit the button that sent the copy to the Desk. Afterward, I walked over to Dorothy to tell her it was done.

Her eyes scanned the copy. She made a few clicks on the keyboard and looked up. Carolyn was wrong about her: Beneath the professional steeliness was real kindness. "You want to wait around and go for a drink when I'm done? Talk about it?"

"Thanks," I said, but it was already late. Walter would be showing up at my apartment in another hour or so—and he was probably the best person I could talk to at a time like this. "I'll take a rain check."

I turned and started away from her. But I suddenly thought of what would happen tomorrow after Walter went back to Boston. I'd drive myself crazy, hanging around my apartment, nothing to do but wait, hoping for an arrest. I turned back. "If it's all right with you, I'd like to come in tomorrow to make a few calls to police."

Providence police. As a South County bureau reporter, I was way out of my beat. Dorothy hesitated, her lower lip bitten as she weighed this. "The weekend reporter can make the calls," she said.

"Please."

She looked at me levelly so that I could see it in her eyes: There were more than twenty murders a year in Providence. This one did not warrant special follow-up coverage. "I can't authorize overtime."

I turned to go.

Either she liked the story I'd just handed in, or she figured my suffering earned me the right to follow this particular news event, because she tapped my arm. "But you could take a comp day next week, if you're sure you want to come in on a Saturday. . . ."

*   *   *

Memories kept rotating through my brain: the weight of Barry's head as I'd tilted it back, the thick smell of oozing blood, the scream of the police sirens getting closer and closer. I sat on the couch with a half glass of white wine and every single light in the apartment on, waiting for Walter to get here.

I thought of Barry silently scolding me for giving my phone number to a strange man. The look of worry, reprimand in his eyes: *How could I be so careless?* A door opens and he's dead. No more scolding, no more concern, no more electrical connections generating worry in his brain.

I closed my eyes and was back in the market, crouched behind the biscuit display. I saw the blur of dirty khaki as the man in the parka ran out the door. And then, as if he were running toward me down the aisle, I saw the man who swore at me in front of the dairy case, the sty in one eye and the glare of the other.

I started at the click of the lock. The door swung open. Walter stood at the doorway. He tossed his black felt cowboy hat on the bar, dropped his guitar case on the kitchen floor, and walked over. "Are you all right?" he asked. "What the fuck happened?"

I felt instantly soothed by the familiar roughness of his New York accent. He dropped to the couch beside me, and I told him everything—about the shooting, hiding in the back of the store, my failed attempt to save Barry.

Walter, who was originally from the South Bronx, used to be a cocaine dealer. Violence didn't shock him. He listened to my story with almost professional detachment and let me talk without asking any questions. When I'd finished, he got up, walked behind the couch to the window, and pointed in the general direction of the Mazursky Market. "Right there?" he asked. "I thought this was practically a suburban neighborhood." And then: "Christ, you're lucky the guy didn't see you."

He returned to the couch, began to sit down, saw my empty wineglass on the table, and reversed direction, taking the glass to the sink. Walter, who in his recovery had become something of a zealot, didn't even drink caffeinated coffee anymore, let alone do drugs. As my sponsor, he didn't approve of my drinking alcohol, not even a single glass of wine, but he didn't say anything about it. "Don't try too hard to sleep," he said, referring to the insomnia that had once led to my sleeping-pill problem. "I'll stay up with you."

He filled the kettle on the stove with water and wandered back and forth to the window while it heated. "Jesus, it looks like two or three unmarked cop cars are still parked outside there," he said, peering out at the square. "They must be tearing the place apart."

"They call it preserving the crime scene."

Walter didn't answer, but continued staring out the window, intrigued. He was right about Wayland Square. It was a few harmless blocks of upscale shops in a neighborhood that was only halfheartedly urban. Not a place where you'd expect this kind of violence. The kettle whistled. From the kitchen, he came back with two mugs of herbal tea and put one of them into my hand. Then he sat beside me on the couch and pulled off his tooled-leather boots, taking the time to pair them on the floor. Walter tended to dress in Southwestern gear, even when he wasn't performing. "He was kind of a friend of yours, wasn't he?"

I thought of how protective Barry had been, how he had worried about my welfare just minutes before he was killed. "Yeah. A real good guy." Walter put his arm around me and told me it was okay to cry. But I didn't cry. I sat there stone-faced, feeling emptied. "I think writing the story for the paper wiped me out."

Walter pulled away, leaned into the armrest, and folded his arms. "You went back to the paper to write about it?"

I shrugged. "I just reacted."

"Don't you think that's a little dangerous?"

"It's what reporters do."

"It's what ambitious reporters do." Walter's eyes met mine and held them. He was the only one who knew the real reason I'd quit the *Ledger*, that I'd done the worst thing a journalist could do, I'd had an affair with Chris Tejian, the subject of my prize-winning profile and a man charged with murdering his business partner. But Walter blamed it all on my vulnerability, my difficulty in coping with my brother Sean's death. He insisted that I had to learn to forgive myself. Let the past go.

"Maybe you should move outta this fucked-up neighborhood. Move back to Boston, where it's safe. Where they just rob convenience-store clerks, they don't have to kill them."

"What, and commute to South County?"

Walter made a face. "Quit. You know you hate that small-town stuff. And Geralyn says the *Ledger* would hire you back in a heartbeat."

Geralyn, an old friend of mine from the *Ledger*, was now engaged to Walter. Since, in the end, I'd written the tough story, a profile that exposed the manipulative side of Chris Tejian, no one ever suspected that I'd been in love with him. That I'd let equal parts love and hate cloud my judgment. "They wouldn't want me back if they knew I broke every journalism ethic there was."

He gazed up, as if addressing the ceiling. "Journalism ethics? Isn't that an oxymoron?"

"Come on, you know what I mean."

"I know that that dirtbag deserved what he got. That the world is a better place with Chris Tejian in jail. And I know that whatever amends you had to make have *got* to be made by now." He slugged back the last of his tea and rose from the couch as if the argument had been settled.

"I can't go back to the *Ledger.*"

My plaintive tone stopped him, made him sit back down. "Okay." The flipness was gone and Walter's eyes, a solid gray, looked tired, as if wearied by a lifetime of problems he had yet to solve. "But you know you haven't been happy here . . . even before tonight."

"There's an opening on the investigative team in Providence," I said.

He looked at me levelly. "Yeah?"

This was a probe. Was I going to put myself out? Go for it? I shrugged as if uncertain, but I knew then how badly I wanted it.

Walter said nothing, but began wrestling off his watch. Then he removed all his rings and, finally, he stood up to pull his wallet and keys out of his pocket and dropped them into the growing pile on the coffee table. If I wasn't going to elaborate, he wasn't going to wrench it out of me word by word.

What if I screw up again? I wanted to ask. But we'd already had this conversation so many times, I knew what he'd say: Walter thought I'd done the right thing in the end. That my story hadn't "convicted" Chris Tejian, that justice itself had done that. That whatever role I'd played was over and done with and that I should just move on, for Christ's sake.

"I'm afraid to trust myself with a big story like that again."

"I know," he said, sounding tired. "But you *know* you're not going to be happy until you prove to yourself that that loser in Boston was a onetime mistake." Then he took a few steps to return to the window to take one last look at Wayland Square. "And if you're determined to live in this fucked-up little state, you should at least be happy."

I woke up, startled, at seven A.M. I'd been dreaming about a parakeet I was trying to coax out of a cage. The light on my nightstand still shone and I was propped up on pillows, last week's *Newsweek* flat across my stomach.

I must have fallen asleep reading. After my father died last year, I was so worried about developing another sleep problem, I'd taken Walter's advice and started running every day. Now, not even a shooting could keep me awake all night.

But my brain felt gray. I winced at the dim light behind the window shade and scrambled out of the bedroom. I tiptoed to the kitchen to get a glass of cranberry juice, past Walter snoring on the futon. Out of the corner of my eye, I saw the colors of the bird I'd been dreaming about: the bright green and yellow feathers were the exact shade of the scratch tickets I'd bought at Barry's and thrown on the bar.

I returned to the bedroom and pulled on yesterday's running tights, jogging bra, a long-sleeved T-shirt, and my favorite sweatshirt and went to the closet to search for my running shoes. I didn't even stop to brush my teeth, but was outside on the sidewalk within minutes.

It was a clear, mild October morning, but my legs were stiff and I had run a short couple of blocks against traffic before I began to warm up. The streets were empty, but I found myself checking over my shoulder as I turned onto Butler Avenue.

I told myself I was being paranoid, that it was still too early for anyone to have read my story; the newspaper was just hitting the stores. No one would have figured out that this solitary figure running alone was the reporter. The one who'd called the cops.

I scanned the street, looking for hulking figures. The sidewalks were empty, the streets clear of cars. But it wasn't until Butler Avenue merged into Blackstone Boulevard that my breathing became even. Blackstone Boulevard was a leafy avenue of important-looking homes, with a wide, grassy park that divided the almost two-mile stretch. On weekday mornings, it seemed as if everyone on the entire East Side ran here before work. But this early on a Saturday morning, I was completely alone.

I ran north on the sidewalk, crossed to the park, and returned down the path in the shady central corridor, looking over my shoulder every time a breeze shook the leaves or I kicked back too much cinder. About halfway home, I finally found a soothing mental blankness, a certain peace underneath the changing autumn trees.

But it didn't last. Back at my apartment, the phone was ringing as I swung open the door. Walter was gone, the quilt folded on the futon. I'd hoped he could stay for breakfast, but he must have had an early shift driving cab today. The receiver wasn't in the recharger. Or on the bar. Or in the bedroom. The ringing continued, distant and muffled. A new round of adrenaline began to surge. I checked under the futon, but it wasn't there.

Finally, I found the receiver in the bathroom, ringing under a towel, and put it to my ear.

"I saw your story in today's paper. Jesus, you all right?" The baritone slid through me. No mistaking the voice.

"Leonard?"

"You all right?" he asked.

"Out of breath."

There was a pause.

"I was just out running."

A little beep sounded from inside the phone, warning me

that the battery was getting low. Was Leonard pretending to be concerned about me? Upset because I hadn't called in after the murder? Or did radio talk-show hosts in this little state regularly call their listeners at home? "I'm fine," I said.

Standing in front of the medicine-cabinet mirror, I saw myself: a small woman in sweaty running clothes, cheeks flushed, eyes brightly crazed. It occurred to me that I might have run too far, that maybe I was dehydrated and hallucinating.

"Did you get my note?" Leonard asked.

"Yes," I said. But it seemed so distant now. Sweat clung to me like steam on a shower curtain. I stepped into the bathtub to open the window for ventilation.

"Are you free this afternoon? Can I take you to lunch?" His voice was growing fainter with the weakening battery.

A lunch date with Leonard of *Late Night*, the man I called almost every evening, waiting endlessly on hold. Yesterday, I would have jumped at this offer, but today, all I could think about was going to work, calling police. "I'm on assignment."

"How about tonight? It's my night off. Any chance you're free to meet me for dinner?"

On his night off? What did that mean? "I'm not sure what time I'll be done," I said.

"We can do it near the paper. Eight o'clock, at Raphael's." His voice was getting faint. "Look, I know what this kind of trauma can do to people. I think it'll help you to talk about it." The phone beeped another warning.

I wondered if this meant the paper *had* run my story on page one. Was he going to pump me for more gory details? "What exactly is it you want?" I asked.

The phone battery was so weak I could barely hear him.

"What?" I asked. I was still standing in the bathtub and the question echoed.

Just before the phone went completely dead, I caught the tail end of Leonard's answer: "I used to know Barry Mazursky," he said. "And this is a *real* Rhode Island tragedy."

CHAPTER
4

On a Saturday morning, the newsroom was even lonelier than it had been the night before. Only a single reporter worked on Saturday, and he was huddled over a desk in the far corner of the newsroom. The copy editor must have been outside having a cigarette.

The reporter, a young-looking guy glued to the telephone, looked up briefly as I entered, then immediately shifted his attention back to his phone call. I headed upstairs to the cafeteria, where I grabbed a cup of coffee and the day's *Chronicle*.

Returning to the newsroom, I settled myself at a desk on the Rim and stared at the paper. My story was on page one, the lower-right corner. I swelled at the sight of my byline.

I flipped to the jump page. Reading my own version of the story, I tried to figure out what Leonard meant about Barry's murder being a real Rhode Island tragedy. Involuntarily, I saw the bullet hole in Barry's forehead again, the way the skin puckered, the dark red of his blood. I took a few deep breaths, trying to exhale the image away. How could murder *not* be a tragedy?

I wondered about Barry's family. I hoped that his wife had

kissed him good-bye that morning before he left for work. I
thought of how random, how tentative, life was. How in only
a minute, a bullet could blow all concerns, all thoughts, all
love out of your head.

A clunking sound startled me. I looked up to see a swivel
chair skidding into a desk. The reporter I'd noticed earlier was
clearing the path to my desk. He looked like he might be cap-
tain of the college wrestling team, with a small, square body
and a face full of blond freckles. There was a sense of mission
about him.

He dropped an envelope on my keyboard and leaned toward me conspiratorially, saying, "I can't believe my luck, but
Dorothy told me you'd be willing to do the follow-up today
on the Mazursky thing?"

I nodded.

He began to introduce himself, but before he got out his
last name, I realized that he had to be Jonathan Frizell, the
reporter hired away from the *New Haven Register*. With a
master's degree in journalism from Columbia and a relative
on the *Chronicle* board of directors, he was not a popular
guy.

"I'm being a good sport and covering that antigambling
demonstration in Kennedy Plaza. God, how I hate rallies.
Good story, today, by the way." He had an overconfident Connecticut intonation that immediately conveyed privilege.

He pointed to the envelope on the keyboard and thanked
me again for "being a lifesaver," before walking off. He hadn't
the slightest concern that I was wading into his turf, and I
wondered, was that because he felt there were enough murders in Providence to go around? Or that I wasn't serious
competition?

I slit open the envelope with my pencil, trying not to dwell
on the latter possibility.

Hallie,

*Could use Mazursky profile. First person. The man you knew.
But bring in other sources. Will lead Sunday metro page. No
more than 20 inches. Also, for Sunday paper call PD for details
about Gano Street car accident caught on scanner. Nothing
available last night.*

Dorothy

As soon as I asked the dispatcher about the accident, she
put me through to Major Holstrom, one of the detectives who
had questioned me about the shooting last night.

"What's going on with the car accident?"

He responded by asking if I would come to the station for
more questioning.

"Now?"

"That would be best."

There was weight to his voice. There'd been a development
since last night. Could they actually have caught this guy in a
car chase? I wanted to ask him for more information, but he
was a terse man who seemed even more stilted over the telephone. Instinct suggested I just get the hell up there.

It was a three-block walk from the newspaper to LaSalle
Square. I grabbed a fresh notebook from the supply closet,
threw on my jacket, and headed up Fountain Street to the
station, an aging building with duct tape over the outer-door
lock. The dispatcher buzzed me in, and I was ushered to the
second-floor detectives' office where I'd given my statement
last night.

The city was putting up a new $50-million public safety
complex a few blocks away, on the other side of the highway.
Returning to this old station by daylight, I could see it was
none too soon. The linoleum floors were cracked and dirty,

and the windows, coated with some sort of inner smog, let in only a dingy light.

Holstrom was at the doorway, waiting for me. He wasn't a particularly large man, and he was only a few years older than me, but he had an easily bristled quality that was a little intimidating. Even last night, when he was trying to be gentle in his questioning, he seemed to be containing his impatience—as if he sensed there were thought processes going on in my head that ran counter to his investigation.

He wore that same expression now. Was there some error in my story? Something I'd written but failed to tell the police last night?

He dropped into a chair behind a desk and gestured for me to sit on one of the straight-back metal seats that felt as if it was designed to torture prisoners. "You really shouldn't be writing this stuff in the newspaper," he said. "You put the case and yourself in jeopardy."

"I'm a newspaper reporter."

"You're a witness."

I raised my hands to the ceiling. "It's not like I planned it this way."

He looked as if he were about to argue with that, but decided it was futile. He sighed, as if he'd already wasted too many precious moments arguing with newspaper reporters, and that getting one as a witness was colossally unfair. "I want you to look at more pictures," he said.

"Don't you already have the guy?"

"That's what we gotta see."

He explained that the police had chased a white Toyota Camry with a missing taillight and dented fender up Gano Street to the I-95 entrance, where it had hydroplaned on a puddle. The driver lost control of the car, smashed into the cement abutment, and catapulted through the windshield. The suspect had been transported to the emergency room at Rhode Island Hospital and was now lying there unconscious.

I thought of the enormous man in the parka, the hard, evil look in his eyes, and felt a wave of relief: unconscious, as in lying helpless in a hospital bed. I offered a silent thanks for heavy rain and slick roads.

Because the accident had followed a police chase, it required an official review, which would make Holstrom and the department less than forthcoming. "Is there any kind of issue with the police chase? Any kind of internal investigation because it ended in a car accident?"

He looked slightly insulted. "There's always a review, but we have plenty of witnesses at the scene. The pursuing officers were well within the speed limit. The driver had an elevated blood-alcohol level and lost control of the car because of the rain. It's pretty clear-cut."

"Is he charged with murder?"

Holstrom shook his head. "Driving while under the influence of alcohol, driving to endanger, and resisting arrest."

"Did you find anything in the car? Cash? A gun?"

"Can't give you any details until the forensic report gets back from the URI lab."

"Can you at least tell me if this guy is a suspect in the Mazursky murder?"

"I just told you, we don't even have the forensics report back yet." Holstrom was growing irritated. "Right now, we've got no proof linking this guy directly to the murder." Then, he reached for a three-ring binder that was at his elbow. He picked it up, leafed through it, stopped, and pushed the open binder toward me.

I grabbed for it. More than anything, I wanted to give Holstrom his proof. I wanted to find the hulking frame, the mean eyes that I could still feel boring into me.

"Take your time," Holstrom said, leaning back in his chair with a *Sports Illustrated*.

I scanned the pages of mug shots, mostly Polaroids in plastic sleeves. They were all young men, all with the same black-and-white rawness to them no matter what race they were. Their expressions varied, from irritated to sullen to exhausted. Intelligence did not shine on their faces. I finished one book and started another.

"Anyone look familiar?"

I flipped over several more pages and moved on to a second book. Finally, in the back, in the right-hand corner of the second row, I saw him. He wore a T-shirt instead of a parka and looked like he might be a couple of years younger. But even though it was just a photograph, I could still feel the mockery, the sneer.

For just a second, my finger froze on the clear vinyl sheath. Then I was jabbing at the Polaroid, pushing the binder across the desk to Holstrom. "That's him. That's the guy I saw in the store."

"You sure?" Holstrom asked. "Take your time."

"I saw him—ten, maybe fifteen minutes before the shooting. He was in back, by the dairy case. I startled him. He looked me straight in the eyes. I got a real good look."

Holstrom made no comment. A detail man, he dutifully wrote it all down even though we'd gone through some of this the night before.

"Is that the guy you have in custody?" I asked.

Holstrom pushed the binder back toward me. "You recognize anyone else?"

I'd been so overwhelmed by the sight of the guy in the parka that I had forgotten about the other man in the dairy aisle, the smaller one in the navy jacket and the gray cap. I'd never seen his face, and wasn't even sure he'd been with the guy in the parka, but I dutifully scanned the mug shots again.

One guy on the bottom had dark, curly hair, but it was too much of a stretch to identify him on that one similarity. I flipped the page back to the guy in the parka. "No. Just this one guy." I pushed the binder back toward Holstrom again. "Was he in the car?"

Holstrom shifted his gaze upward, as if just noticing the ceiling tile that hung by a thread.

"Okay. Okay, so you can't tell me." If I wanted any information at all, I had to stick to the car accident. "But was the guy in the car, the white Toyota Camry—the guy driving to endanger—was he alone?"

Holstrom spoke carefully. "The guy in the car was alone."

I hadn't realized I'd been holding my breath until I exhaled. If the man I'd seen fleeing the murder was alone in the car and unconscious in the hospital. If it really was the same man . . .

I knew then that I had to see his face. I had to make sure that the guy I'd seen last night in front of the dairy case was the same guy who was now incapacitated in the hospital. Then I could breathe again, I could run on the boulevard without looking over my shoulder for hulking figures, without imagining threats in every shadow and on every street.

From my short foray into a hospital public-relations career in Boston, I knew that if this guy was a murder suspect, he would also be under police guard. But I also knew that most hospitals were short staffed on Saturdays and that the visitors' desk was often manned by a volunteer. It wouldn't be hard to sneak into the hospital, but what floor?

"You okay?" Holstrom asked.

"Fine." I smiled to show the appropriate gratitude, to let

him know I knew he was giving me information to allay my fears. "You said this guy was unconscious?"

He nodded. "Head injury."

"Did he need surgery?" If he needed surgery, I could limit my search to the surgical floors.

"Yeah. Something to do with relieving pressure in his cranium."

"Will he survive?"

"They usually do," he said, with a roll of his eyes.

I pulled out my notebook. It took only a few minutes to jot down the little that Holstrom had confirmed. I found myself wondering where exactly a police guard would be posted at the hospital—inside the room? Outside in the hall?

"Can you tell me the name of the guy? The *car accident* victim," I asked.

Holstrom gave me a look, and I realized I'd made a mistake by calling him a victim. This might again imply that the police cruiser chasing him was somehow at fault. "The reckless, driving-to-endanger guy. The one charged with resisting arrest," I clarified.

Holstrom rewarded me with an actual name: Victor Delria, twenty-four years old, of Central Falls.

"Prior arrests?"

"Simple assault and an unarmed robbery, two years ago. Driving under the influence, last year, too."

"But there's no official connection to the Mazursky murder?" Sometimes in reporting, you have to ask the same question over and over, just to clarify.

"The matter is still under investigation."

I scribbled this in my notepad to show that I would quote him verbatim. When I looked up, I saw another cop standing in the doorway. The man was dressed casually, in blue jeans and a ski sweater, and was holding a file under his arm, but I could tell by his posture and by the way Holstrom shifted in his seat that the new cop was of higher rank.

"I'm surprised to see *you* in today," Holstrom said.

"Just checking in on a few things." Holstrom introduced him as Detective Major Errico. He was a densely packed man with solid arms and a lined face. His eyes scanned mine, sizing me up.

"Reporter?"

"The one from last night. At the shooting," Holstrom said. "Hallie Ahern—new to the *Chronicle*."

"Ah," Errico said, as if that explained everything. He looked past me to the photo books on the desk. Holstrom tilted his head slightly. A response of some kind. A communication between them.

"Well, I think we're about done here," Holstrom said, standing.

I hesitated to take my cue, but Holstrom's face was suddenly stony. There was no question, this interview was over. I picked up my notebook from the table. At the doorway, Detective Major Errico acknowledged my departure with a polite nod, but his tense stance transmitted impatience. I glanced at the stack of files under his arm. On the outer corner, I saw some lettering.

He instantly tucked the file tighter under his arm. Outside in the hall, I heard the click of the door closing behind me.

With an extraordinary display of confidence, I told the elderly man at the visitors' desk that I was a social worker who had left a case file up on the surgical floor. "What floor is that again?"

He looked it up and even gave me a page of printed instructions, which first involved finding the elevator bank.

As I got off the elevator, I spotted a whiteboard with names and room numbers and scanned the list: V. Delria. 603 B. The elevator was in the exact middle of the floor, with two small nurses' stations on either side and hallways in almost every direction. I sauntered past the first nurses' station as if I already knew where I was going, turning the corner and heading down the first hallway. Immediately, I could tell the room numbers were going the wrong way, so I backtracked and headed down a hallway in the opposite direction.

As soon as I saw the police guard sitting on a chair outside the room, all my confidence vanished. Adrenaline started flooding my veins. What had I been thinking? That I would just barrel right past him?

I passed the police guard, walking purposefully. At the end of the hall, with nowhere else to go, I ventured into one of the rooms. An older woman was being examined by a man in scrubs. "Sorry," I said, turning around. "Wrong room."

If only I had a plan. A plan would be useful. I walked slowly back toward the cop. Someone had pasted Halloween decorations in the hallway. I halted outside a closet door with a witch on a broomstick flying over a full moon. Facing the door, I squinted, as if I needed perspective on fine artwork.

I decided that any attempt to cleverly divert the cop from his guard post would likely end up in my arrest. The thing to do was to identify myself as a brand-new reporter at the *Chronicle*, tell him it was my first big car-accident story and that I'd been assigned to check on the victim's current medical status. I had to hope that the room door was open and that I could catch a quick glimpse inside while the cop redirected me to patient information.

A peek, I told myself, all I needed was a peek.

I was heading slowly down the corridor, past several dirty breakfast trays, when I saw the cop rise from his chair. He folded his newspaper, put it on the seat, and started walking away from me, toward the elevators. Was he going to lunch?

Could a guard leave his post and go to lunch? Wasn't that some kind of major cop screwup? A miracle just for me?

Slowly, I walked past Delria's room, noticing as I did that the door was just slightly ajar. I was wearing a cotton sweater and black jeans and could feel sweat trickle from my armpits all the way down my sides.

I heard the elevator doors open and shut and walked to the end of the hallway and peeked around. The cop was gone. I turned, headed straight back to room 603 B, and put my hand on the knob.

I glanced over my shoulder, expecting another cop or a nurse to appear, to grab me by my sweater, pull me away from the door, curse at me for my audacity. But no one came. No one stopped me, so I swung open the door.

It was a private room, dim, with the blinds closed against the sunlight, and empty except for the patient, presumably Victor Delria, sleeping in the bed. He was lying on his back, hooked up to an IV. A pile of blankets blocked my view. I needed to see his face, the sty weighting the one eye. I took a single step inside the hospital room and froze, courage failing me. The room had a pungent odor, like bacteria in a flesh wound.

What if he woke up? What if he looked right at me? Even unconscious, he was terrorizing me. I told myself that the sooner I saw his face, the sooner I could get the hell out of here. On a chair by the window, I saw some kind of jacket bunched up inside a clear plastic bag. The color of the jacket was a muted green khaki.

As I took a step closer to the bed, I became aware of the sound of water running.

Directly to my right, a door clicked open and standing in the doorway of a bathroom was a tall man wearing a blue button-down shirt tucked into blue jeans and a sports jacket. Our eyes met. There was a moment of puzzled recognition.

It was the guy I'd been flirting with at Barry's, Matt, the quart-of-milk guy, with the dark eyes and nice smile. Only now he wasn't smiling. I was barely inside the room, but he quickly stepped in front of me, deliberately blocking my path to the patient's bed. "What are you doing here?" he asked.

What was *he* doing here? I might have asked, but there was an air of authority about him, something official, like maybe he was a plainclothes cop. It dawned on me that that was why the other cop could leave his post. He had backup. "I just wanted to check—check and see if this was the guy from Barry's—the guy from last night."

He looked at me for a long time as he processed all this. My heart started to pound, remembering my aggressive flirting the night before. God, this was awkward. Somewhere in his house was a grocery bag with my phone number on it.

"You're a reporter?" It was part question, part exclamation. I nodded.

"Jesus," he said, shaking his head. Then he put his arms out and backed me completely out the door, so we were standing in the hallway. He was square in front of me, blocking the door, making me aware again of his height, his shoulders. "How long after I left?"

"Five, maybe ten minutes."

"I'm sorry you had to go through all that." He had a nice voice, a warm tenor that made you want to believe he meant what he said. I had to make myself focus on the off-center nose instead of the unclouded brown eyes. I took a small step to the left, trying to position myself to see around him. He immediately shifted his weight in the same direction.

"So what are you doing here?" I asked.

As it turned out, Matt Cavanaugh wasn't a plainclothes

cop, but a prosecutor with the attorney general's office. "And you just happened to be at the Mazursky Market last night?" I asked.

"I told you, I live in the neighborhood."

There was a moan from the bedroom. Matt turned around, glanced at the bed, and then took another step, to back me farther down the corridor.

"Is that why they assigned you to this case?" I asked.

"One of the reasons." He looked down the corridor in both directions. We were still alone. "I'm sorry, but you've got to get out of here."

"I just want to get a glimpse of his face. Just a quick peek to see if it's him and I'll get out of here." I gave him my most beseeching look: hopeful eyes, pleading smile, air of can-do optimism. He stared at me for a moment, as if he needed a better read, as if there was something he didn't quite understand.

Then, I made the slightest gesture, not even a real movement, toward the door, just a change in posture, and his expression grew hard. Not only was Matt Cavanaugh not going to consider my request, but I'd really pissed him off.

"Are you out of your mind? Completely out of your mind? You're a potential witness. What if he woke up and saw you? Wouldn't his public defender *love* that?"

"I thought he was unconscious," I said, but it sounded feeble, even to me.

"I don't care if he's *dead*. This would taint your testimony." He stood there shaking his head, as if he couldn't quite believe that none of this had dawned on me.

"Hey, I'm a reporter, not a prosecutor," I said in my own defense.

"No kidding," he said, but he refrained from a blanket criticism of reporters as a subspecies. Instead, he reached behind him and pulled Delria's door shut so it clicked. Debate over. Subject closed.

I started to turn away, but I hadn't taken two steps when he touched my arm, forcing me to turn around. His anger, his annoyance, had abated. There was something else in his expression.

I waited, hoping, I guess, for something personal: a reference to our meeting at the Mazursky Market, or maybe an apology that he had to be so gruff. And for a moment, I saw warmth again in his eyes. He hesitated, as if there was something he wanted to say but couldn't.

"What?" I asked.

The warmth disappeared. Instead, I got a grim warning, cool and professional: "And don't write anything else about this in the paper. You're a potential witness, for Christ's sake. You're not only screwing up the case, you could be putting yourself in danger."

CHAPTER
5

FROM THE DATABASE, I learned that the Mazursky Market was a bigger operation than I'd thought. And that despite the way he acted at the register, Barry was no longer the owner.

He had been quite an entrepreneur in the eighties, buying and developing a half dozen markets across the state, but he'd sold out four years ago to a Boston conglomerate. He'd stayed on, working for the new owners, managing three of the Providence stores and acting like he still owned the joint.

The story didn't specifically give the dollar figure of the transaction, but it seemed odd that a successful entrepreneur would want to stay on afterward to work a cash register at night. I hit the button and waited for the printer to whir out a hard copy of the story. *This is a real Rhode Island tragedy,* Leonard had said, as if there were a lot more to tell me.

I reminded myself that Leonard was a talk-show host, prone to hyperbole. Maybe he just meant it was a tragedy that a guy like Barry got popped. Certainly there was enough glowing praise about Barry in the database for that story.

A clip from the early nineties cataloged Barry's impressive

civic activities. Two years before he'd sold the convenience-store chain, he'd received an award from the South Providence Neighborhood Association for making improvements to a city block where one of his largest markets did business. In the early 1990s, when a winning Powerball ticket had been sold from his Smith Hill market, he'd donated his 1 percent share of the winnings to a family that had been burned out of their home at Christmas. He'd also helped raise $250,000 for the Veterans' Homeless Shelter.

I gathered all my printouts from the machine and headed back to the newsroom. Screw Matt Cavanaugh. Trying to tell *me* what to write or not write about. Did he think that was the appropriate role of the attorney general's office? Or maybe he thought he had special powers over me because I'd been foolish enough to give him my phone number.

I got mad thinking about his warning. Of course he wanted to scare me into silence. The tighter control he had on the information, the easier it was for him in court. I could not let fear of a small-time, inept, and *unconscious* crook keep me from a story that could get me a spot on the investigative team.

I must have stomped across the newsroom, because after I dropped my files on the desk, I noticed that two copy editors, the weekend city editor filling in for Dorothy, and Jonathan, who'd just come back from his assignment, were all looking up from their desks.

"Trouble with the story?" Jonathan asked. All four men seemed to be waiting for my answer.

"No," I said, and sat down. I stared at the blank computer screen in continued fury. After their attention had drifted back to their computer screens, I turned back to Jonathan. "You know anything about Matt Cavanaugh?"

"From the AG's office?" His mouth twisted into a winking

sort of half smile. "Yeah, I've dealt with him a couple of times."

He wanted me to beg for information from his vault. "And?"

"Tight with the cops," he said. "Political, they say."

The twisted half smile, combined with the pause, gave the impression that he was just brimming with inside information. "Aren't they all political?"

He chuckled at my simplicity. "No. A lot of prosecutors are there just to get enough experience and connections to get something high-paying at a private firm. This guy is a career guy. Wants to move up the ladder. Got his eye on the big prize."

He meant attorney general, an elected position. Suddenly the reason for my interest dawned on him. "Cavanaugh handling the Mazursky murder?" He sounded surprised.

"Something strange about that?"

"Not like him to be handling a piddling little street crime like that." Jonathan had a very natural way of conveying disdain. Then: "But maybe he's stuck on the weekend shift. You know, like me, relegated to covering a fucking political rally."

Another reporter might have gone to Barry's home and tried to get a response from his wife or son, both of whom I'd seen around the store, or the older daughter I knew he'd adored. But after my brother, Sean, died suddenly of acute cardiac arrhythmia at age thirty-five, abbreviating a brilliant legal career, a brilliant life, I lost all heart for barging into a newly bereaved family's home and asking them how they "felt" about losing their loved one.

Just terrific? I mean, what were they going to say? You never got over it; certainly I'd never stop missing Sean, the older brother I'd looked up to, the friend I'd loved above all others, and it had taken me two years and a twelve-step program to finally come to peace with the abruptness of his death. But the next day? After a mere twenty-four hours of trying to believe the person you love, with your very DNA, no longer exists? Most of what Barry's family was feeling right now was pure physical shock.

Since it was Saturday, no one would be working at the offices of the YourCorner Corporation, the Boston company that had bought the markets from Barry. I found the name of the company's top officials on the company's website and tracked down the vice president at his Back Bay home. He told me Barry was a "great entrepreneur and a great manager," and said there were no problems or surprises after the purchase.

I drove to the Mazursky Market, which was still closed to the public, and hunted Wayland Square for a neighboring merchant who had known Barry. The woman who owned the bookstore where I'd bought my maps of Providence when I first moved was more than happy to talk to me. She was outraged that something like this could happen in a safe neighborhood and wanted to talk about what a great guy Barry was. "Such a good husband to Nadine, such a good neighbor."

A short-order cook behind the counter at Rufful's, a luncheonette where I often went for my BLT breakfast, recognized me from my preference for rye bread. "You knew Barry, right?" he asked.

I had a sudden picture of Barry the first day I'd walked into the market. His left arm was in a sling and he insisted on bagging my purchase with his one hand, all the while telling me about his car accident and treatment at the hospital. Then he leaned across the counter and extended his cast, an inky

maze of names. "I can tell you're gonna be a regular customer. You have to sign or it won't be complete," he'd said.

"He was a good guy," the cook told me. He was about my
age, but had an air of responsibility about him, as if he had a
stake in the business. "A good guy who did a lot for the community. And what thanks did he get?"

I used the quote for the last line in my profile: Barry
Mazursky, family man, entrepreneur, pillar of the community. I felt uneasy, rereading it, all that unmitigated praise. It
was hard to get anyone to say anything remotely critical
about a dead guy. I tried for balance, pointing out in my story
that although I was friendly with him, I didn't know him
well.

By five o'clock, Jonathan had filed his story on the
antigambling rally and gone home. I'd already sent my five-
paragraph follow on the car accident, Victor Delria, and police
refusal to name him as a suspect; but my story about Barry,
technically finished, remained open on my computer screen.

I picked up the phone and tried Leonard at the radio station, but the woman who answered the phone wouldn't give
me his home phone number. If he really knew anything truly
newsworthy, why would he share it with me? Wasn't I competing media?

I reread my profile about Barry one more time, closed my
eyes, and hit the send key.

My uneasiness about Barry's profile was short-lived. Roger,
the weekend city editor, loved the story, and pooh-poohed
my suggestion that we hold it a day so I could get to more
sources.

"This is perfect. He comes alive. A human," he said. "It's
like you can see him behind the cash register."

More important, it was a slow news day. Aside from the

antigambling rally, nothing had happened anywhere in the state. Originally slotted for the metro page, my profile of Barry was needed on page one. The adrenaline rush carried me through the copyediting.

Afterward, I still had a couple of hours to kill before I was supposed to meet Leonard. I was outside, headed to my car, when I noticed the throngs of people walking toward Union Station. Six o'clock was too early for it to be a dinner crowd.

Then I remembered WaterFire. It was a semiregular evening event in warm weather, and I'd heard there was an autumn performance scheduled for tonight: one hundred small, float-ing bonfires on iron braziers were lit up and down the river after sunset, with music piped into the air. It was something like fireworks, only classier. Carolyn liked to take her dates there in the summer to stroll along the riverside park in the crowd, and had been after me to check it out. Raphael's was spitting distance from the river. It seemed a good way to kill time.

It was unusually warm for an October evening. On the other side of Dorrance Street, police were shepherding herds of pedestrians through the intersection. By the time I cut through Union Station to the Wall of Hope, an underpass to the park, it was clogged with people stopping to admire the memorial of hand-painted tiles that decorated each wall of the tunnel. I was trying to politely maneuver around a fam-ily with two double strollers when I heard the striking of a gong.

Suddenly, music filled the air. A haunting opera gave me chills despite the cotton sweater I wore. I followed the people ahead of me into the park and pushed to the rail to look down on the water basin.

The river, which ran through the downtown to the bay, was narrow and still, so much like a canal that the effect was

Venetian, especially with the gondolas transporting tourists around. Five slim black boats slinked through the still water toward the wood-piled braziers, which were maybe ten feet apart, up and down the entire length of the river. Each time the people aboard these boats leaned out to light another brazier with a torch, a cheer erupted from the crowd. The lighting and applause created their own path down the river.

I stood there, watching the flames, embers escaping and reflecting on the water, creating a mournful orange glow. The music, piped into the air by unseen speakers, was moving and I felt the sadness of it in my bones. I missed Boston, and thought of all the times I'd gone to hear the Pops on the Esplanade. In Boston, if I looked into a crowd like this long enough, I could find someone I knew.

A young couple, arms slung around each other, stopped next to me along the rail to watch the procession of the boats. I thought of Matt Cavanaugh, the feeling of his hand on my shoulder, the way he'd hesitated, as if there was something else he wanted to say.

Chris Tejian had broken my heart, seduced me as part of his ill-fated public-relations campaign to win acquittal. It had very nearly destroyed me. After that, I never thought I could trust any man. Last year's disastrous one-month fling with a bartender, who turned out to be dating every other cocktail waitress in the bar, didn't do anything to restore my faith. But there was something steady about Matt's eyes, something genuine in the tone of his voice that I wanted to believe in.

A broad-shouldered woman, loaded with shopping bags like a pack animal, pushed her way up to the rail and slammed an enormous handbag into me. I caught it in my ribs.

The woman apologized, calling herself "the clumsiest woman alive." She leaned over the rail, beside me, pronounced the flames lovely and launched into a long explanation about how she'd wanted to put these shopping bags away in her car first, but her husband had taken off with the keys. This was what I liked about Rhode Island. With very little provocation, complete strangers were telling you the stories of their lives.

"He's just got to have it all his way, you know?"

I thought of Matt Cavanaugh and nodded to indicate that I shared the universal female understanding of the shortcomings of men. She seemed pleased. "Better go find him, I guess." She transferred her shopping bags to one arm and disappeared into the crowd. I stood there staring at all the couples and families strolling along the fire-lit river, lonely again.

Then, as if to help me out, the music shifted. The melody was no longer aching with love lost, but marching forward with a warlike progression. Screw Matt Cavanaugh and the way he had of looking so intent. He was a nonstarter. A prosecutor. A future politician, for Christ's sake. I pulled myself off the rail, away from the burning river with its ephemeral flames, toward the solid ground of the parking lot.

CHAPTER
6

I'D NEVER BEEN to Raphael's Bistro, in the renovated
Union Station, but I'd read about it in the paper. It was a fash-
ionable place where the mayor liked to lunch with his top
aides. Our living section had done an article on the restaurant's decor, which was very Manhattan, and said it was the
place to wear sleeveless black dresses and stiletto heels. I was
wearing jeans and a cotton sweater.

I got there a few minutes early. The restaurant, all blond
maple and uncluttered retro, was packed and I had to make
my way through a throng of people to find an empty place to
stand at the far end of the bar. I ordered a club soda with
lemon and scanned the room. Young couples mostly. A lot of
sleek twenty-something women wearing Wilma Flintstone–
type tank tops with only one shoulder. Their dates' wardrobes
varied, from casual to business suit, but all looked very Ar-
mani. I caught a drift of male cologne.

Ten minutes passed painfully. I felt awkward at the bar, and
tried for a moment to pretend I was back at Skipper's Landing in Boston, a fish place on Rowes Wharf where I'd finally
taken a job serving cocktails. Although the job was a disaster,

at least I knew everyone, from the bouncers to the problem drinkers to the distributor who tried to sell us more Mount Gay rum.

A man to my left looked at me as if I was getting in the way of his cigarette smoke. I stood on my toes to check the door so he would know I was waiting for someone. It was the life of a reporter to meet strange people in strange places, but I had a gnawing suspicion that Leonard wouldn't show up. That I'd dreamed the phone call this morning.

Directly to my right sat an older couple, a silver-haired man in a cardigan sweater and pleated corduroys who had a long, earnest face and looked vaguely familiar. His wife, sitting on a stool beside him, wore a full-length mink, despite the warm weather. She downed a martini and glanced at me with a dazed expression. For lack of anything better to do, I ate the lemon that had come in my club soda.

"How can you do that without wincing?" the man asked. His voice, a clear bass, was kindly.

I had to smile. "I like sour things."

"Then you'll like us," the wife said. She sounded drunk.

"Marge," the man said quietly, as if to steady her.

His voice was familiar, too, but I couldn't place him. I kept thinking he was someone's grandfather or uncle, but I didn't know anyone in Rhode Island well enough to have met a close relation like a grandfather or an uncle. "Do I know you from somewhere?" I asked. "You seem familiar."

The wife chortled.

The man gave me a moment to guess. Nothing came to me.

"Think Powerball," the wife said.

"Of course." I realized it was Gregory Ayers, who ran the Rhode Island state lottery. He was on radio and television all the time, awarding checks to the lottery winners and announcing new scratch-ticket games. In the television ads, people were always rubbing his arm for good luck. I felt oddly excited standing this close to him, like maybe he could affect my game.

"Go ahead," he said, offering his arm. "Everybody asks. It's okay."

"Ev-er-y-bo-dy," the wife echoed.

I touched his cardigan. Was that static or the zing of good fortune? I couldn't tell.

From the corner of my eye, I spotted Leonard working his way through the crowd.

"Sometimes it works, sometimes it doesn't," Gregory Ayers said, looking pointedly at Leonard.

"Very funny," Leonard said, and chucked Ayers's shoulder. "Nice to see you again, Marge." He kissed her.

It often amazed me how everybody but me seemed to know everybody else in Rhode Island. But now, it dawned on me that Gregory Ayers's lottery commercials played on Leonard's radio station all the time. And now that I thought about it, I remembered that Gregory Ayers, too, was an opponent of casino gambling, one of the only state officials to take a stand.

Leonard was only about five foot seven, but because of his lean build and the way he carried himself, he seemed taller. Unlike me, he was dressed to blend into the restaurant, looking effortlessly sophisticated in a gray turtleneck and casual black wool pants. He embraced me as if we were longtime friends. "Have you met Hallie?" he asked, turning to Ayers. "She's the reporter who wrote the story about the Mazursky murder."

I thought I saw Gregory Ayers stiffen at the word *reporter,* and I recalled that one of our columnists had recently done a piece criticizing him for "hypocrisy" when the "King of Lottery" came out against casino gambling. But instantly, his face softened. "What a story," he said, shaking my hand.

"I never shop in those little market stores," Marge offered. An enormous diamond-and-emerald ring on her finger knocked her martini glass askew, sloshing gin onto the cuff of her husband's cardigan sweater.

He grabbed a cocktail napkin, dunked it in a glass of water, and began dabbing it off. Then he glanced at his wife and shook his head sadly. "It's going to be a long wait," he said, and then with a very deliberate look at Leonard, he gestured to the dining room. "You might not want to stay."

Leonard turned toward the dining room and his expression grew dark. Following his gaze, I saw that while most of the customers looked like young twenty-year-olds on dates, there was an older, more boisterous group taking up three tables toward the back. In the center of this group, Billy Lopresti, mayor of Providence, was slugging back something in a snifter.

He was a funny-looking man, small and stocky, with olive skin, surprised-looking eyes, and hair dyed a shoe-polish shade of black. Years ago, he'd been a popular radio talk-show host at Leonard's station, and he was still quick with a wisecrack. He didn't just have voter support, he had fans.

As we watched, a young woman in a sleek black dress, sitting at a nearby table, stood up, walked over to the mayor's table, and planted a kiss on his cheek. The room cheered.

"Apparently, it's his birthday," Ayers said.

Billy Lopresti had been mayor forever—since the early 1990s—but I'd heard that it wasn't until last year, after he'd wept so openly, so disarmingly at his wife's funeral, that people had taken to calling him by only his first name. "You gotta give Billy credit for the renaissance, he really cares about Providence," a caller would say. "Billy's got so much compassion for the seniors." And what Leonard hated most of all: "If Billy thinks this casino thing is so good for the city, then it's a good thing for the city."

The mayor stood up, gestured to an elderly woman at a nearby table, pointed to his cheek. In a trained politician's voice that carried in a crowd, he said, "What? Don't *you* love me anymore?" The elderly woman blushed at the attention, the mayor walked over to her and kissed her square on the mouth, and the dining room roared.

It wasn't until the mayor sat back down that I noticed the others at his table: an older man with gray hair tied in a pony-tail, wearing blue jeans and a dress shirt, and a woman in a business suit. I'd seen both their pictures in our paper.

"That's the chief of the Narragansett Indians and Jennifer Trowbridge from Evening Star Gaming International," Leonard said with disgust.

The mayor whispered something to Jennifer Trowbridge, who leaned in close so she could hear what he was saying over the restaurant din. Then they both looked up at the bar and peered in our direction. The mayor raised his snifter and the three of them clinked their glasses in a toast. Instead of taking a drink, Billy Lopresti threw his head back and laughed.

I got the distinct impression he was laughing at Leonard. Leonard must have thought so, too, because when the host-ess came toward us to tell us our table was ready, he shook his head. "I lost my appetite," he said, and then to me: "Let's get the hell out of here."

We left Ayers and his wife at the bar and took Leonard's car, a Saab with one of those stand-up bike racks on the roof, over the highway to Federal Hill. This was Providence's famed Italian neighborhood and a source of endless restaurant possibilities.

Leonard, the man who talked nonstop on the radio every night, was silent, obviously injured, and I didn't know what to say to him. On the one hand, I was with a man I'd talked to just about every night for the last three or four months. On the other hand, all that talk had been on the air.

He said nothing until we were under the big, bronze-pinecone archway that was a gateway to Atwell's Avenue. He pointed to a building on his left. "You see that?"

I looked out the car window: a city block, restaurants, real estate office, private home, tattoo parlor. "What?"

He pointed to a small building right in the middle of the first block, with a low roof and a small sign that looked like it might advertise a lawyer.

"The one with the blue door?"

"My uncle was shot to death in that doorway," Leonard said. "It happened when I was a kid, but I never forgot it. They never arrested the guy, but everyone knew who it was. He worked for one of Patriarca's bookies."

"Your uncle had gambling problems?" I thought I was starting to understand Leonard's antigambling obsession.

He shook his head. "No. His father had gambling problems. They killed my uncle to impress upon the entire family that they were serious about getting repaid."

There was no appropriate response to the enormity of that revelation. I mumbled a vague condolence and wondered why he'd told me this. What did Leonard want from me? What did he think I could do for him?

We traveled another block in silence. I stared out at the crowds on the sidewalks. Couples, young professionals, and tourists hurried into restaurants. Valets stood in the street, eager to park each new BMW and Cadillac that pulled up. It

was hard to imagine anyone getting shot in any of these affluent doorways.

Leonard must have read my thoughts. "People like to think
the mob is a thing of the past," he said. "The FBI beat them
down with RICO, the old *omertà* loyalty gone by the wayside.
Junior Patriarca not the man his father was. That's what
everyone likes to think. But you know, Junior's grown up.
He's not so inept anymore. And this is Rhode Island. We don't
change that quick."

He looked at me with meaning, and I wasn't sure if this had
to do with the mayor, the casino-gambling referendum, or
Barry Mazursky's murder. I didn't get a chance to ask him to
elaborate, though. We'd pulled up to a restaurant with a faux
stone exterior and small neon light that said THE BLUE GROTTO,
and a valet was jumping for our car.

I followed Leonard inside the restaurant, where everything
was old-world formal. The waiters wore tuxedos and I could
hear the sound of a man crooning what sounded like some
kind of love song. Three middle-aged Italian men stood together at the bar drinking what I assumed was Sambuca.
After Leonard's introduction to the neighborhood, it was hard
not to think in stereotypes.

The host led us into a quiet and ornate dining room with
brass sconces on the walls and chandeliers with crystal
pinecones in them. We had to walk around the balding troubadour singing a mournful ballad to a young couple who had
their hands clasped together on the table.

We sat at a corner table under a framed tapestry of two
Roman-looking women. It was almost nine o'clock, and by
now I was starved for both food and information. "The
swordfish looks good," I said, snapping shut the menu and
folding my arms on the table.

"Hmm," Leonard said, studying his menu.

"You going to tell me what's going on?" I prodded.

"With the mayor?" He looked up and smiled, as if I would believe an encounter that had so clearly disturbed him was no big deal.

The balding troubadour was heading toward our table. I waved him away. "Yeah, with the mayor. With Barry Mazursky. With the mob history of Atwell's Avenue."

"Billy Lopresti wants me to think that nothing I say on my show can touch him," he said in a low voice. "That he finds my opposition to gambling amusing. That I'm an unworthy opponent."

He spoke as if this insult were just a part of the political game, something he'd already shrugged off, but I wasn't buying it. His eyes had lost confidence and I couldn't help thinking that he'd taken the mayor's laughter as a professional slur, one talk-show host snubbing another.

The waiter arrived and Leonard allowed himself to be diverted. As if to firmly establish the change of subject, he took his time ordering, fussing as he chose an antipasto for us to share, switching into Italian when he ordered the veal, and asking the waiter half a dozen questions about the wine before settling on a Chianti.

"I'm curious," I said, after the waiter was gone. "How did you figure out who I was? From that one interview at the fund-raiser for the Veterans' Homeless Shelter?"

"I'm a talk-radio guy, I listen closely to voices. They tell me a lot. You have a distinctive voice."

Clearly, I was supposed to feel flattered, but even though I knew he was single—divorced from a television news anchor who had left both him and the station for a bigger market—I didn't get the feeling that he was trying to hit on me. "So why have you gone to so much trouble to look me up? Because of the Mazursky story?"

"Because what I did was inexcusable," Leonard continued. "Please accept my sincere apologies for slipping up on the air."

He sounded so full of self-reproach that I might have believed him except that I knew there had to be more to it. He wasn't like Chris Tejian, trying to woo me, but radio talk-show hosts did not go this far out of their way to hunt down their listeners unless they wanted something pretty badly. And I remembered the music. "How about the bimbo theme song?"

"That, too."

He smiled again. Not so broadly. Not so professionally. It seemed real.

"So what is it you want from me?"

He put his finger to his lips as the waiter approached the table with our antipasto. Leonard pointed out olives I should try and speared the better-looking pieces of prosciutto and put them on my plate. I forked up a radicchio leaf in silence, impatient for the waiter to leave.

When he was finally gone, Leonard lowered the deep baritone to a bare whisper. "I've got a lead that can help me, help my show, but I need someone to do some legwork. A reporter."

"Doesn't the station have its own reporters?" I asked, but I knew the answer. Radio news stations reported news, debated news, but rarely unearthed news.

"Last fall, we cut back to two people on the news staff," Leonard replied. "They barely have time to read the *Chronicle*'s headlines."

I sipped my wine without tasting it. "Why me? You must know a lot of other reporters."

"Not like I know you; I've talked to you every day for, what, two or three months? I know your opinions, how you think. I mean, what? You think because all that conversation is on the radio, it doesn't count or something?" This wasn't rhetorical; his eyes were fixed on mine, a funny, insecure expression on his face as he waited for an answer.

I was startled by his wounded tone and heard myself almost apologizing. "It's just that . . . well, I'm new in Providence. Unproven."

"Oh," he said, smiling again and eager to comfort. "Don't say that. You're not unproven. I read your story this morning. You're a real good writer."

He sounded as if he might actually mean it, and I felt oddly embarrassed. As if he were trying to give me a little pep talk. Reluctant to trust anyone's flattery, I pushed back in my chair, determined to establish some distance. "If I did follow up on this lead, any news I dug up would have to be for the *Chronicle*. What do you get out of it?"

He smiled, as if delighted by my directness. "I get to suspect, on the air, that something's not right with the Wayland Square murder investigation. I can light up all phone lines for weeks with speculation. Then, when your story breaks, I look like a soothsayer. A genius."

"Your listeners already think you're a genius," I said. "At least Andre does."

"Andre?" He sounded surprised that I remembered another caller's name. "Yeah. Well. Late-night listeners maybe, but as you can see from the mayor's disdain, that's not exactly a power audience. I don't want to be *Late Night* Leonard forever. I want to be Drive Time Leonard. I want to be Nationally Syndicated Leonard. For that, I need to be more of a genius."

This surprising candor was both disarming and a little scary. Did he confess his ambitions to everyone? I wondered. Did he often refer to himself in the third person? "But I don't get how suspecting the deal behind Barry's murder does all that for you."

"Barry's murder is tied to gambling—"

"How?" I interrupted.

He held up one hand, a gesture for me to hear him out. "Trust me a moment, it's tied to gambling. The point is that our mayor will do everything in his considerable power to keep this quiet until after the referendum. He wants to make sure casino gambling passes, and he's going to lean on the Providence police. The investigation will be like molasses."

I thought of Sergeant Holstrom, his reluctance to answer even the most basic questions. And then of Matt Cavanaugh warning me not to write anything. "But how about the AG's office? The mayor can't slow them down, can't tell the state prosecutor what to do—"

"No," he interrupted. "But the prosecutors are overloaded. They've got a ton of cases they're working on and have to rely on the cops for information. They're not going to push too hard—it's not like the AG has come out against the referendum."

Silently, I processed this.

"Except for Ayers at the lottery commission and a couple of church groups, I'm pretty much alone in my opposition. And as you may have noticed, I never shut up about this particular subject. I've staked my career on it."

The ego in this was so overwhelming that I was suddenly grateful I'd never wanted a career in radio. Still, news tips often came in bizarre forms. And if Barry's murder really *was* tied to gambling, and the mayor really *was* trying to suppress it because of the referendum, it would be a huge story, maybe my shot at the investigative team. "So explain to me how Barry's murder is tied to gambling," I said.

"First you've got to promise me confidentiality. You've got to protect my identity."

Like you protected mine? I wanted to ask, but didn't. It wasn't unusual for reporters to promise to protect the confidentiality of their sources—and all sources, not just Leonard, had their own agenda in offering information. I nodded my agreement, but Leonard reached across the table and made me shake hands on our deal.

It was the moment he'd been waiting for. The moment he had set up, perhaps from the moment he'd let my real name slip on the air. Leonard released my hand and leaned back in his chair, settling in for a story. "You know I'm a board member of the Veterans' Homeless Shelter. Barry Mazursky used to be treasurer."

I nodded, recalling that from the database.

"About two and a half years ago, right after the big fundraising campaign, when Barry was treasurer, seventy-five thousand dollars mysteriously disappeared."

Barry embezzling from a homeless shelter? If I'd had anything in my mouth, I would have choked. Instead, I took a moment to mentally digest. "I didn't see any clips in the database involving embezzlement," I finally said.

"A prosecutor from the AG's office was called in, but Barry was never charged. One of the other guys on the shelter's board got wind of Barry's gambling problem and conducted his own little in-house audit. We gave Barry an opportunity. Repay within the month and we'd cover for him. The money reappeared the next week. No charges were filed, but I could get you the minutes from the board meeting."

I had a sudden vision of Barry's expression when I was impulsively buying more lottery tickets. One addictive personality to another. No wonder I had liked him.

"He was forced to resign as treasurer, of course. I felt bad for the guy. I always liked him. We went out for drinks and I asked him, If you had the money, why the hell did you do it?

"He was drunk by then, or maybe he wanted to ensure my sympathy, so this never came out. He told me he was broke. All the money from the sale of the stores was gone. Apparently, Barry had a real bad run at the blackjack tables at Mohegan Sun. He'd had to go to the street for the loan. They were threatening his family. He was scared shitless about how he'd repay them." Leonard stopped for effect, a pause so I could take it all in. Then, he asked, "You still think legalized gambling doesn't hurt anyone?"

I couldn't answer. The prosciutto I'd eaten was turning in my stomach.

"The boys on the street are a little less forgiving about late payments than the bank. You try to cheat them, they don't play nice like the boys on the board of a homeless shelter. The first couple of times they beat you up, they threaten your family. But Barry was an ex-marine, a tough guy who'd run out of options. He kept a loaded gun in the store." He paused. "I'm willing to stake my career on the fact that that wasn't any random armed robbery last night. That was a hit."

CHAPTER
7

I WASN'T EAGER to read my story about Barry Mazursky the next day. Not eager to see how naive, how incomplete it might be. But I forced myself to walk down to the square and pick up the Sunday paper at the pharmacy.

The sun was a little too ambitious for midmorning, a hard, bright light that made me wonder if I was hungover, even though I hadn't been drinking. I pushed my way past several young families with strollers and backpacks and toddlers who appeared to be on leashes, trying to feel unencumbered instead of alone.

The CVS pharmacy was four doors past the Mazursky Market, which still closed, the door locked tight. I tried to walk past it. I didn't want to see the cash register or the toppled magazines or even the hanging philodendrons thirsting for water, but I was drawn to the window despite myself. I pressed my face against the plate glass and peered into the darkness.

At first, I could see little beyond the yellow tape except the top of the cash register, the drawer still hanging open, and the handle of the broom Barry kept behind the counter. But as my eyes adjusted from the bright sunlight of the day to the dusty gloom of the store, I could see the phone I'd used to call the police, just where I'd dropped it onto the counter. For a moment, I was back inside, trapped in the minutes it took for the cruiser to arrive, pacing the store aisles, trying not to look at Barry, yet returning to the counter, to the body, again and again.

If Barry's murder was a mob hit, that made Victor Delria a hit man. Maybe that's what Matt Cavanaugh had been trying to warn me about. Maybe the mob didn't care if I didn't actually see the hit man's face. Maybe they'd kill me because I could ID the getaway car.

Behind me, car brakes screeched. I froze instinctively, pushing myself into the alcove of the market's front door, pressing against the smudged glass, waiting. I heard voices. "Fucking A!" someone shouted. I turned slowly. A Trans Am had skidded into a Volkswagen that was stopped in the middle of the street. "Fucking A!" the Trans Am driver shouted again. He jumped out of his car and headed toward the stopped Volkswagen. The cause of the accident, a golden retriever, stood in the middle of Angell Street, stunned by the commotion.

I took a breath to steady myself. I couldn't let myself get spooked, couldn't give in to the fear. If what Leonard said was true, if Barry had been killed because of his gambling debts and the mayor was deliberately delaying the police investigation because of the referendum, then this was a helluva story. This was my chance, maybe my only chance to get out of the bureau and onto the investigative team.

If what Leonard said was true. He was extreme in his opinions, hyperbolic on the radio, most of it a ruse to work up the audience. Could I really trust that what he said was true?

I thought of my past misjudgments, my colossal error with

Chris Tejian. But this was different: Leonard wasn't putting
the moves on me, and he wasn't pretending to grieve with
me over the death of my brother. His manipulations, at least,
were transparent. And Walter was right. I *wouldn't* be happy
until I proved to myself that Tejian was a onetime mistake.

I pushed onward to the pharmacy and bought the paper.
Then I turned the corner into Rufful's. Wayland Square was
an affluent neighborhood, a demographic for pretentious
bistros and European cafes. But Rufful's belonged to a simpler
era, with lumpy homemade pies under glass at the counter
and only one kind of coffee. The booths along the walls were
brimming with the young families of the sidewalk, the toddlers sucking on packets of jelly and twisting out of high
chairs.

I found an empty stool at the counter, where I settled in
with a BLT on rye and a large cup of coffee. The thing I liked
about this restaurant, aside from the clean, homey atmosphere, was the rye bread. Real caraway seeds. They made a
difference.

I bit into my sandwich and stared at a two-column photo
of Barry Mazursky. The newspaper had pulled a file picture of
him from the library, one that must have run on the business
page when he sold his chain of markets to YourCorner Corporation. He was only a few years younger, but his hairline
looked decades thicker, his forehead smoother, the jaw angled to the camera. There was no hint of debt or failure in his
expression, just triumph.

"Slain East Side Entrepreneur—Credit to the Community":
I reread the headline to my story. Had my sympathy for Barry
blinded me? Was he really a compulsive gambler who stole
money from charities?

"Gambling changes people," Leonard had said last night as
he drove me back to the *Chronicle* parking lot. "They get

themselves into all sorts of trouble." He'd sounded so sad about it, so uncharacteristically subdued. But should I really trust Leonard of *Late Night*?

The waitress, a woman who was either in incredibly good shape for her age or prematurely gray, walked over with the coffeepot. She glanced at the paper, and then looked past me to the young families sitting in the booths. "Can you believe it? In this neighborhood?"

I shook my head sadly.

"Before I quit, I used to buy my cigarettes there. Barry was so full of advice. He'd say, 'Livia, you sick of serving people coffee all day? You gotta get a job at one of those four-star restaurants like Al Forno where the tabs are high. Where people buy wine and cocktails. You gotta do better for your family, for yourself.'" She laughed dismissively. "But you know, they don't hire just anyone in those places. You gotta know someone. And besides, I don't wanna work till midnight waiting on a buncha tourists snapping at me because the wine isn't opened right."

I could actually hear Barry trying to sell her on the higher tabs and bigger tips, knew what words got the emphasis, which he swallowed. Underscoring it all was a dogged belief that with just the right move, everyone could be rich.

As the waitress walked away, I remembered something Leonard had said about Barry being a card counter who thought he'd had an infallible system to beat the odds. Blackjack had been his game. And he'd had a couple of favorite tables at the Mohegan Sun.

I told myself that the issue wasn't whether to trust Leonard, but whether his information could be confirmed. I had to find out for myself whether Barry had been a compulsive gambler.

My stomach began to churn the way it did sometimes late

at night, when I remembered an overdue bill I had to pay or a phone call I'd forgotten to return. Lying still in bed became a special kind of torture. I looked down at Barry's photo in the newspaper. His eyes spoke to mine: *Jesus, the taxes I pay, don't let them get away with this, Hallie.*

I tore both the article and picture of Barry out of the page and left the rest of the paper on the counter. I threw money on the check and went straight to my apartment to change clothes. An hour later, I was headed for the casino, in Connecticut.

I thought that on a sunny Sunday afternoon, most people would be raking leaves or watching football, but no. Most people were at the Mohegan Sun playing the slot machines.

I'd entered through what was called the Summer Entrance, where I was welcomed with a hopeful carpeting of cheery sunflowers. I'd never been inside a casino before, and I guess I expected it to be dark and glittery, with everyone wearing black and drinking a martini. But this was less Monte Carlo and more Disneyland Kingdom. There was a Native American theme played out in neutral earth tones, fake boulder formations, and an enormous wolf statue looking down on its gambling prey.

As I circled the perimeter of the coliseumlike casino, I stepped to a drumbeat of wailing Indian music and an incessant waterfall of clinking change. The casino reminded me, in turn, of both a shopping mall and an arcade. No one looked particularly sophisticated. In fact, most of the people at the slot machines were senior citizens in patterned sweaters and knit pants.

I could picture Barry here. But then, I could picture anybody here.

I found the blackjack tables, partially hidden behind

wrought-iron fencing with leafy designs. Like the slots, the
card tables were brimming with late-afternoon business, men
mostly, who sat with bottled beer to their sides and smoke
rings over their heads. The gaming was vigorous; dealers
swiftly went through their decks. I realized that I could not
just whip out a picture and ask if anyone around here knew
Barry Mazursky. I walked from table to table for about half an
hour just watching the play. Eventually, I returned to the
path around the casino perimeter and came upon an ATM
machine with my own bank's logo on it.

It seemed like some kind of omen.

It wasn't as if I wasn't aware of my troubled finances. Besides the $2,000 I owed my mother for the security deposit on
my apartment, I had another couple of thousand in credit
card debt and a mere $300 left in my checking account.
Somehow, I doubted the newspaper would reimburse gambling expenses, even if it *was* critical to research. But I'd
driven a long way to get here, and, suddenly, it seemed important to blend in. My card slipped easily into the machine.
I was conservative, I thought, withdrawing only eighty dollars. I quickly bought some chips and drifted between tables
to watch the game.

At last, I found a vacant seat at a friendly-looking table
with a female dealer, a couple in their midfifties, and a young
man who looked as if he'd had his twenty-first birthday yesterday and decided to drive over today and gamble.

"I have no idea what I'm doing," I said by way of introduction. I took a seat beside the man in his midfifties.

The woman smiled at me. "There's always beginner's luck."

Her husband had a craggy face, full of sorrow. "Worst thing
that can happen to you is that you win."

No chance of that. Within half an hour, the entire pile of
chips I'd bought was gone. But there was a pleasant cama-

raderie at the table. The dealer was a woman about my own age who offered beginners advice on when to hold and when to get hit; the married couple lived in the same neighborhood in Worcester where I'd grown up. The young guy, who wore tight blue jeans, a laundered white dress shirt, and an enormous silver pendant around his neck, turned out to own a chain of hairdressing salons in Bridgeport. He won his first four hands, tipped the dealer, and waved to the waitress to bring everyone a drink.

I withdrew another $100 from the ATM but decided to play more cautiously, lowering my bets and staying away from double downs, even when I had eleven. Dealt a ten of spades and a six of clubs, I clasped my hands on the green velvet table and held steady. I beat the dealer, winning a $25 bet.

I hit twenty-one twice, and later a real, true blackjack. My skin grew warm as I clutched the ace, my palms sweaty. I gulped my club soda with delight, not caring about the bubbles tingling my nose.

I won that hand, lost the next, but beat the dealer four of the next five hands. I was up a full $175 and feeling pretty good. The young guy, Will, his baby face aglow, cheered me on, lauding me for something he kept calling "basic strategy," and telling me that I was keeping the cards "in flow."

I had no idea what he meant, but it felt terrific, and when the dealer finished the deck and announced that there was going to be a shift change, I felt a sudden dejection, especially when she leaned over and told me to quit now, while the night was young and while I was this far ahead.

I didn't want to quit, but they were all looking at me, nodding their heads at the dealer's good advice. Ed, the husband from Worcester, was especially vigorous in his endorsement of this wisdom. The cocktail napkin under my drink was wilted and the corner shredded. I glanced at my watch and realized I'd spent an hour and a half playing blackjack and had failed to ask a single question about Barry.

"Before you go, can I ask you a question?" I asked the dealer as she finished tidying her shoe of cards.

She looked at me quizzically, and I pulled out Barry's picture. "Do you by any chance know this guy? Does he look familiar?"

Her expression was cool. I noticed everyone pull back just slightly from the table.

"He's a friend of mine," I said swiftly. "He died Friday. I told the family that since I was coming here anyway, I'd try to contact his friends."

The dealer's expression did not change.

"They're planning a big memorial," I heard myself lie.

More silence. Everyone was looking at me. I'm not sure if it was with sympathy or amazement. I had the feeling that you weren't supposed to talk about death or funerals in a casino.

"I've never seen him," the dealer said at last.

As soon as the new dealer seated himself at the table, the married couple excused themselves. They were going to dinner at the Bamboo Forest, one of the casino restaurants, and wanted to get there early. Will, the big winner of the evening, decided to move up to a high-stakes table and I was left sitting alone with the new dealer, a silver-haired man with a neatly clipped beard. He looked right past me, to the hall, for more players. I showed him the news clip of Barry. "I don't suppose you know him?" I asked. He didn't even look at the picture.

I'd cashed in my chips and was headed over to the food court to grab something for dinner when I came upon a cove of exclusive-looking restaurants hidden behind another boulder formation. At the end of the wall, I glanced at the glass display of menus and scanned one from Pompeii and Caesar, a fine-dining spot with expensive entrées. In contrast to the food court, which at six o'clock was clogged with lines of hungry retirees, the small, elegant restaurant was almost empty. It occurred to me that while the casino might be brimming with amateurs, the real gamblers, the high rollers like Barry, were probably a fairly small club. My mistake, I realized, was my random approach. The most likely place to find someone who might have known Barry was at a high-stakes table.

I purchased new chips with my winnings, made another $100 withdrawal from the ATM, and hoped like hell that rubbing Gregory Ayers's arm for luck really worked. Back at the blackjack tables, I found Will sitting at a crowded table where bets opened at $50. As I approached, he looked up from his cards with a curious expression and frowned when I took the empty seat beside him. "You sure you're ready for this?"

"Feeling lucky," I said in a whisper, knowing that saying this too loudly would certainly be a jinx. It was an all-male table, from the dealer, a wiry man who looked like he smoked a lot of cigarettes, to the two middle-aged men who sat to the left of Will and eyed me as I sat down, to the elderly gentlemen to my right. I noticed that they all sat at attention, guarding an imposed distance. A new tension filled the air and it took me a minute to figure it out. Will's eyes met mine and I caught an expression of resigned annoyance. And then I realized that I'd misread Will's fine features as youth, while all the men at the table understood that he was gay.

Not exactly an enlightened crowd, the men didn't seem pleased about me, either. They focused intently on their cards and talked to each other without looking at us, as if we were a distraction that would negatively affect their game.

I waited for the dealer to start a new shoe and played a $50 bet, the minimum, and held at sixteen. The temperature of my skin rose with the bet, my breath got caught somewhere above my stomach, and my palms were sweaty, but there was a tingling sensation in my shoulders, too—excitement rather than fear. Time was suspended as I waited for the dealer's hand.

When the dealer broke with two sixes and a ten, Will tapped my arm and smiled. Riding the luck I must have gleaned from Gregory Ayers's sleeve, I won the next two hands. Will seemed to enjoy my winnings more than his own, and the two middle-aged men sitting to his left started to pay attention. It was a heady feeling, this flow of blood, this run of luck. I proceeded to lose the next two hands, but was not discouraged. Everyone lost a hand or two, Will told me. And I could feel luck in my stomach. Feel that it was going to be my night. I won another hand, gained confidence and raised my bet to $75. I won four more hands and was up a net $450 for the evening; this was profit above the money I'd withdrawn from my checking account.

I was charged with luck, feeling both giddy and wildly competent. I had a kinship with the cards, a sense of what would be dealt, a knack I never knew for numbers. I could have played all evening, but when Will said he was going to the food court to get something to eat, I felt the rumbling in my stomach. It was already eight o'clock, and I'd forgotten about dinner. When the two middle-aged men beside him looked at each other and said they'd take a break, too, I knew I had no choice.

"Can I go with you?" I asked Will.

"Sure," he said, looking pleased.

I took my time, rounding up my knapsack and tipping the dealer to give the two middle-aged men time to get up from the table. They were a few yards behind Will and me, but we were all headed in the general direction of the restaurants. I slowed my pace to let the two men catch up. It was late, and I no longer cared if I was breaking casino etiquette. I whipped out the news clip of Barry, shoved it toward them, and repeated the story about rounding up his friends for a memorial service.

I got the same cool response I'd experienced earlier. The two men barely looked at the news clip before insisting that they had never heard of him. "He was a good guy. Experienced player," I said, making up new details in the hopes that this would jog their memories.

They shook their heads, determined not to even look at the picture.

I turned back to Will, expecting him to ditch me, too. But instead, he looped his arm through mine and asked if I'd rather go to the steak house or the Italian place for dinner.

Suddenly, I was more exhausted than hungry. "You know, maybe I should just call it a night," I said. "I've got to drive all the way back to Providence."

"Providence? I thought you said you were from Worcester."

"I grew up in Worcester. I live in Providence."

As it turned out, Will, whose last name was Poirier, had worked for a few years as a hairdresser in Rhode Island. He grimaced so I could see what a horrible experience that had been. Another thought occurred to him. "Is that where you know that guy from? The guy who died? From Providence?" he asked.

I nodded.

"Did he own some kind of convenience store?"

I looked at him with surprise. "He used to."

"Yeah, I think I know who he was," Will said. "A lot of people from Rhode Island gamble here. But this guy . . ." He took

the picture from me and for the first time really looked at it.
"This guy used to be around here a lot. Mostly blackjack,
some roulette. He liked to talk like he was a big deal, but you
could kind of see he was on a losing streak."

He returned the picture and stopped to study me for a moment. "So what's up? Are you a PI?"

I shook my head. "Newspaper reporter—but Barry really
was a friend of mine."

Will considered this for a moment, as if trying to decide
whether to believe it. "I'm sorry, then," he finally said, sounding sincere. "How did he die?"

"He was shot, working the cash register."

Will shook his head at the violence of the world, and then
grew thoughtful. "I would have figured a suicide."

Victor Delria was lying on the wooden floor in the Mazursky
Market, his face completely hidden in bandages. I thought he
was sleeping, and that I was safe. But as I stepped over him
to get to the register, I looked down. The gauze around his
face began unraveling. His eyes flew open. "You bitch," he
said, low and mean.

I sat up in bed. The low, mean sound was my alarm clock,
which growled its wake-up call. It was Monday morning, and
I was alone in a cold apartment.

I was tired from my trip to Connecticut and worn down
from the bad dream. As much as I didn't want to go running
this morning, I knew I had to get out there. It was the only
way to blot out the pictures in my brain.

I threw off my sleep sweatshirt and pulled on long tights, a
T-shirt, and a completely different sweatshirt—the one without stains. I found my running shoes, with socks still stuck inside them, right by the door.

It was colder than yesterday, with a gray sky that looked

like it would not provide sunshine all day. My hands were freezing, so I headed up Angell Street at a fast clip to try to warm up quickly. A few early-morning commuters were driving cars or waiting for buses, but it was still a half hour or so before rush hour, so the street was mostly mine.

In high school, I'd been on the swim team and had never even considered cross-country or track. That was probably a mistake, because I'm much faster on dry land than I ever was in the water. Maybe it's the adult anxieties that drive me; the faster I run, the harder it is for me to think. I cruised onto Blackstone Boulevard pretty quickly, breathing in cold air, breathing out fear.

Endorphins: the bonus prize for exercise. Sometimes I can run five miles and never feel that lightness of being, that goodwill toward men. Today, I'd run a marathon if it meant I could outrace the images, the unraveling gauze.

On a weekday, the run-before-work crowd starts at daybreak, and at seven A.M. I had plenty of company on the boulevard. Quickly, I gained on two women who chatted too much to achieve any real speed. I passed them and another single male runner. Instead of returning the same way I'd come, I decided to do a five-mile loop, leaving the cinder path and overhanging trees to continue north until Blackstone merged with Hope Street.

By the time I'd run through the mostly residential section and onto the commercial block, the city had awakened. I had to stop and wait for commuter traffic at each intersection.

But physical exertion worked its magic. My pace was even, my head clear, and I felt at peace with the world. I had $450 in winnings and a sense of leftover luck. I loved the East Side of Providence with its mix of funky shops, historic homes, and the occasional lavender two-family. This was my neigh-

borhood, I thought, drunk now with endorphins. I loved this
run.

I had just passed the CVS pharmacy and stopped at the red
light at the intersection of Rochambeau Avenue when the ul-
timate in civilization occurred. The light turned green and a
man driving a silver sports sedan waiting to turn left mo-
tioned for me to go first. I waved a brisk thank-you and
headed out onto the street.

I was halfway across. Out of the corner of my eye, I caught
a flicker of motion. The silver sedan. Was it turning? The guy
who had waved me on was coming right at me. A hunk of
moving steel.

I bolted forward in panicked acceleration. The car kept
coming, barreling through the turn. Didn't he have brakes? A
horn shrieked in my ear. I made a final leap. The car came
within inches, so close I could feel the air displaced, a rush of
pressure at my back.

I barely made the curb. I screamed at the driver. He looked
confused, but the car didn't stop. He didn't pull over to apologize. The silver sedan sped away. There was some minor
damage to the right-rear bumper, suggesting a previous accident. I tried to make out the license plate, but the only thing
I could see was that the last number was seven.

"Asshole!" I screamed.

The glint of silver disappeared at the end of the street.
Pedestrians emerged on the corner. The flow of traffic re-
sumed. I bent forward, hands on my knees, trying to catch
my breath. Was I crazy? Hadn't the driver waved for me to
go?

One of the pedestrians, a man with a bakery bag, stopped
at my side. "Are you all right?" he asked.

I couldn't answer, couldn't right myself or pull words out
of my throat. The sidewalk swayed beneath me; my head

throbbed with confusion. I tried to sort out events. The traffic light switched from red to green. I saw the driver wave for me to go. The car took the corner, the metal aimed at me.

"You're lucky," the man with the bakery bag said. "This is such a dangerous intersection. A twelve-year-old boy got hit trying to cross here just a couple of months ago. He died."

CHAPTER
8

I STOOD IN the shower longer than I should have, with my eyes closed, trying to let the hot water melt the clenched feeling in my bones. It was a dangerous intersection with a blind spot; cars and bicycles collided there all the time.

I replayed those words like a mantra as I dressed for work: *dangerous intersection, dangerous intersection, dangerous intersection.* I couldn't allow myself to think about Matt Cavanaugh's warning. I couldn't start believing that friends of Delria's were already after me. Delria wasn't even charged with the murder, for Christ's sake. All kinds of accidents occurred at that corner. All the time.

I reminded myself that I'd won $450 the night before, and that confirming Leonard's tip about Barry was good news, not bad. I told myself that the difference between good reporters and bad reporters was their level of boldness: If I gave in to fear, I'd spend the rest of my life in the bureau, resentful, like Carolyn. Or worse.

I arrived at the South County bureau office just after eight A.M., knowing I'd have to get the local police and fire checks out of the way before I could call Sergeant Holstrom to see if the forensics report had come back. I worried that if I didn't act fast, the city editor in Providence was likely to reassign it to Jonathan Frizell as a routine follow.

I was hoping Carolyn would come in early, too, but she was late, which was unusual for her. I'd checked police and fire in all three towns and written up three press releases by the time she arrived. Her eyes were swollen and she sneezed as she took off a lime-green ski jacket and fluffy purple scarf and hung them in the closet.

"You all right?" I asked, watching her pull a wad of Kleenex from the pocket of her jacket.

"You're the one who almost got killed Friday night," she said, sounding almost angry about it.

"I'm fine," I said. No need to worry her with the details of my most recent brush with death.

"Animals in this world. Animals." She flicked on her computer, sighed as it began the long process of booting up, and turned back to me. "That was a great story about that store owner yesterday. What's his name, your friend? What a guy, that guy. I cried when I read it. I actually cried."

"Barry," I said. "Barry Mazursky."

"Yeah, all that work for the veterans and shit. Why is it always the good guys who get shot in the head? Why don't they go try to rob my ex's auto-body shop and shoot him? Dirtbag population could use a little thinning. Why is it always the nice guys who stay with their wives twenty, thirty years—*they're* the ones who get popped?"

"Yeah," I said, in agreement, but I was trying to follow which ex-husband she meant and whether his murder would mean the end of the child-support payments she complained were too low. I got up and headed to our little kitchenette. "You want any coffee?" I called back.

Carolyn asked if we had any tea. I filled the Hotpot with water and waited for it to heat up. I was a little worried about the piece I'd written: Saint Barry Mazursky, innocent victim of random violence, the great husband who probably left his poor family with bad memories and staggering debts. But I told myself that there was no way I could have known on Saturday that Barry had embezzled from the Veterans' Homeless Shelter. And confirming that Barry was a gambler didn't necessarily confirm that he was an embezzler. Still, as the water began to bubble, I knew in my heart that it was all probably true.

In the same drawer where I found a sandwich bag full of Tetley tea bags, there was a small plastic container of honey along with packets of ketchup and barbecue sauce. I added the honey to Carolyn's mug and took it to her. "You probably should have stayed home today," I said, putting the mug on her desk.

"God knows, nobody downtown appreciates the effort I make to come in," she said as she sipped the tea and scanned her screen for the day's messages. She wore a good set of acrylic nails painted a dusty pink. They made a clicking sound on the keyboard.

I sat down at my own desk and leafed through the stack of public notices I'd meant to put up on the bulletin board. The South Kingstown Finance Committee was meeting this afternoon to weigh the school committee's plan to renovate the elementary school. It was the most controversial budget item in town, and I felt the dead weight of it in my chest. How could I possibly sit through a tedious municipal meeting this afternoon? How could I come back here and make a story of it? Try to sound as if I cared?

I kept thinking about what Leonard had said when he'd dropped me off at my car Saturday night:

"You break that story a week before the election and it's front-page news. That helps me, that helps you, and maybe that stops a few more people from ending up like Barry."

"Oh, they're praising you on the Today Show." Carolyn did not mean the actual network news program but the nickname for the *Chronicle*'s in-house daily computer file in which editors and reporters posted news, opinion, and out-and-out ranting.

I was instantly diverted by the mention of praise. "What does it say?"

"'Bold, front-line reporting. Kudos to Ahern,'" Carolyn read aloud. "That's from Nathan, the managing editor, and he's real cheap with praise.

"'Chilling story. Concise.' That's from Ernie Santos; he's a copy editor.

"'I mourned with the writer. What bureau does she work in, anyway? Does anyone know her?'" Carolyn laughed cynically. "That one's unsigned, but you can tell it's Nina Daggart; she mourns with the writer on every sad story."

I couldn't help but be pleased, but still, something was bothering me, holding me back, something I couldn't quite put my finger on.

"What's the matter with you, anyway?" Carolyn asked, her infected, uneven voice beginning to warble. "Even Jonathan Frizell, who always has some kind of snotty sideways comment, couldn't come up with anything negative to say."

"I got a tip Saturday night," I confided. "An anonymous tip—two hours past deadline, after I'd already filed my story—that Barry Mazursky was a compulsive gambler. Suspected of embezzling from the Veterans' Homeless Shelter when he was treasurer, and deep in debt to some loan sharks who finally ran out of patience."

"You mean, and knocked him off?"

I nodded.

"Loan sharks don't usually do that. It makes it tough to collect."

"Maybe the killer only meant to apply a little pressure and then Barry pulled his own gun. I don't know, but the compulsive gambling checks out. I took a ride down to Mohegan Sun yesterday where, apparently, Barry Mazursky was a regular."

Carolyn considered this. "So what's the problem? You got a good tip that checked out?"

"My story in Sunday's paper practically eulogized Barry as divine, for Christ's sake."

She waved that off. "So you quoted a bunch of people who wanted to canonize the guy. Like reporters here haven't canonized every single victim of every single tragedy that made the front page. Whoever died was Mother Teresa. No one wants to say the guy with the bullet holes deserved it. No one."

The knot in my stomach began to soften. Still, I told myself that there were turf politics to consider. As a South County reporter, I was supposed to stick to my own territory and report on Narragansett, South Kingstown, and North Kingstown. I had no intrinsic right to a Providence story requiring in-depth investigation, no matter what my prior experience.

Carolyn grabbed a tissue and began blowing her nose, but over the tissue, her eyes were watery and confused. The question I saw echoed in my head. What *was* wrong with me?

I knew, then, that it wasn't my story about Barry or turf politics that was stopping me. They were excuses. What was stopping me was the silver sedan gunning for my back, the fear that next time it might be a bullet hole oozing blood from *my* forehead.

"By the way, I heard Jonathan Frizell is after that job you want on the investigative team," she said. "You want that job, you better make your move."

"I'm planning on pitching this story downtown," I heard

myself say. "'Murder Tied to Casino Gambling'—two weeks before the referendum."

"You gotta." Carolyn sniffed, crumpled her tissue into a ball, tried to toss it into the trash and missed. Then a new thought occurred to her. "Hey, this is going to screw me, big time! I'll be stuck trying to cover this bureau alone. They better damn well send someone from West Bay out here to fill in while you're gone."

"Anonymous?" Dorothy Sacks asked. "You mean you don't know who is passing you this information?"

I immediately felt like an idiot. "Not anonymous, I guess. Confidential."

"A confidential source?"

"Yes."

"That you trust?" Something in her inflection told me to be wary.

I happened to glance down from the telephone and caught a glimpse of the bronze reporting award in the bottom drawer of my desk. I thought about what Walter had said, about proving that the Tejian story was a onetime mistake. "I don't trust anybody until the information checks out."

She gave a dry little laugh. "Meet me in the newsroom at four o'clock."

Although Providence is a smaller city than Boston, the newsroom of the *Chronicle* was larger and better furnished than the *Ledger*'s. It was the same open-office layout—a sea of desks in the middle, with private cubicles along two walls—but the carpeting was hotel grade instead of industrial, and the computers were brand new, with large, thin screens. Everything on the walls, even the bulletin boards, was expensively framed.

When I'd first interviewed here, this upscale and oddly

tasteful newsroom had comforted me, made me think that maybe my journalistic progression from the *Ledger* to the *Chronicle* wasn't such a big step down. And the editors had re-iterated that point: The *Chronicle* Company was one of the last remaining family-owned papers in the country, not part of a chain. It had standards. High standards. Reporters were expected to meet those standards.

Now, as I approached this newsroom, crowded and whirring with industry at four o'clock in the afternoon, I was determined not to be intimidated by the furnishings or the standards. I had been a member of the investigative team at a much larger newspaper in a much larger city. This was a good story. And timely. The referendum to legalize gambling was little more than two weeks away.

I found Dorothy Sacks at her desk in City, on the phone. She waved to me, as if to say to sit down. I looked around. Every chair was occupied by either an editor or a reporter deep in concentration before a computer screen, so I stood waiting in the perimeter corridor between the last row of desks and the wall.

I studied one of the bulletin boards. The *Chronicle* had something it called a writing committee, which was a group of reporters who got together to decide what was the best newspaper story of the month. The winner was posted on the bulletin board.

Carolyn had no use for the writing committee. She said it was made up of a bunch of artistes who put on French berets, drank espresso, and hid in the cafeteria pretending they were existentialists. I took this to mean that none of her stories had ever been nominated.

I studied last month's winner. Jonathan Frizell had gotten an in-depth interview with the mayor after his top aide was charged with taking kickbacks from a private tow operator who wanted city business. In response, the mayor had insisted that these kinds of spurious charges were always leveled at city officials, and that in America, "people are innocent until proven guilty." The story captured the mayor in all his colorful good humor, but it was clear from the tone of the article that the *Chronicle* wasn't buying any of it.

"We're meeting in there," Dorothy Sacks said. She was off the phone, standing and pointing in the direction of a small conference room. I followed her down the aisle between desks to the small room, glassed in on three sides.

Dorothy gestured for me to take a seat at the conference table. She glanced first at a utilitarian-looking Timex on her wrist, then over her shoulder into the newsroom. "Nathan and Marcy want to hear your idea. They should be here any minute."

Nathan Goldstein was the managing editor who had liked my story. Marcy Kittner was the state editor in charge of the bureaus, which made her Carolyn's direct boss. As I peered through the glass and into the newsroom to see if they were coming, I noticed several reporters leaning forward from their desks, trying to see in.

"Welcome to the Fishbowl," Dorothy said.

"Loved your story," said Nathan Goldstein. He walked with a slouch and muttered this praise without looking at me, tossing a notebook on the conference table. I wasn't even sure he was talking to me. But then, after seating himself at the far end of the table, he looked up suddenly, his eyes small, bright arrows.

He was waiting for my reply.

"Thank you," I said, probably too late.

Marcy didn't say anything. She had taken the seat next to me and was now writing something on a pad of paper. She was wearing a rose-scented perfume that was a little too much in this small, windowless room.

"Let's hear about your tip," Nathan said, with an expansive hand gesture that might have been an attempt to wave in some fresh air.

I told him about the charity embezzlement and about my trip to Mohegan Sun, which confirmed that Barry was a compulsive gambler. "My source says Mazursky told him he had to go to the street for loans to cover the embezzlement. He says Mazursky was a deadbeat and a cheat. And that his murder was a hit, a message to all the other deadbeats out there."

Nathan's way of not looking directly at you made his response difficult to read. Marcy was transparent. "Please?" she asked. This was a Rhode Island expression that meant, Excuse me? What? And in this case, Could I possibly be hearing right? "Didn't your profile about Mazursky talk about what a wonderful community volunteer he was?"

"It did," I said, striving not to sound defensive. "This tip came in a few hours after deadline. By someone who knew the other side of Barry—"

"Someone willing to go on the record?" Nathan asked.

I shook my head. "It's a confidential source."

Marcy gave Nathan a look. Theoretically, newspapers didn't like the use of confidential sources. In practice, the *Chronicle* stories quoted confidential sources all the time.

"If you read her original story about the shooting, a hit makes sense," Dorothy interjected. "Even when I was editing it, it struck me; it all seemed so fast. And police are being incredibly tight-lipped. They haven't even confirmed how much cash was stolen."

Nathan's head tilted slightly, an indication that he was listening, but his eyes had dropped to a note he'd written himself on a legal pad. "How much a part of the criminal investigation is she?" he asked Dorothy. "I don't want her reporting if she's the prosecution's key witness."

"I've been told I'm very low level," I said. "I was in the back of the store. Didn't see it happen. Can't make a credible ID."

That seemed to settle something for him. He made another note. "So what exactly do you propose?"

Unsure who he was addressing, Dorothy and I looked at each other. After a moment of confused silence, Nathan's eyes darted between us impatiently, as if wondering why the delay.

"I'd like to be put on special assignment to do an in-depth investigation," I began. "See if I can get my hands on a credit report and confirm Barry's debt problems. Interview his wife—if she'll talk to me, tell me if there were any threats. See if she's willing to go on the record about Barry's gambling. . . ."

Nathan scribbled something on his legal pad.

"How do we know this source of hers is reliable and not just stringing us along?" Marcy asked Dorothy.

"Well, you never really know, do you?" Dorothy replied. "You always take some risk that you might waste time traveling up the wrong road. It's called the newspaper business." To Nathan she said, "Hallie isn't some neophyte. She won awards for her investigative work at the *Ledger*. She knows she has to confirm everything independently."

"How much time will *that* take?" Marcy asked.

"The story would have to run before the referendum. So we're talking two weeks, on the outside." Dorothy addressed this to Nathan, who appeared to check this against the calendar in his Day-Timer.

On the other side of the dome of silence, I could see that several other reporters had gathered at the nearest desk and were unabashedly watching our meeting. I wondered how many of these reporters' pitches went on in a day, and if these spectators had a betting pool on who got the assignments.

Marcy was not about to concede. "Shouldn't Jonathan be following this? It's not like I have so much staff I can spare to take a reporter out of South County for a couple of weeks."

"I'm short staffed because of all the referendum rallies. And Jonathan's wrapped up in his own investigation." Dorothy and Nathan exchanged a meaningful look. Then she added, "Besides, Hallie was the on-scene reporter."

They all nodded at this, and I guessed this was some sort of *Chronicle* policy—something along the lines of finders keepers, losers weepers. Finally, Marcy wrote something on her notepad, ripped out the piece of paper, and pushed it across the table to Nathan. It appeared to be a list of names, possibly names of reporters already committed to various assignments. He studied it thoughtfully and turned to Dorothy. "Stateside does have a manpower issue."

"We all have manpower issues," Dorothy said matter-of-factly. "We still have to cover the news."

Nathan considered Marcy's list for another minute and slipped it into his legal pad. Then he capped his pen and used it to scratch vigorously behind his ear. "Frankly, I'm not sure I see the point in directing any manpower at all to this story." He addressed this to Dorothy. "We run the real risk of defaming a dead man. Upsetting the family. Possible libel. For what? Another story about a compulsive gambler? Who cares?"

Marcy practically gleamed in triumph. Dorothy looked struck.

I took a deep breath and could taste the rose scent of Marcy's perfume on my teeth. "Billy Lopresti cares," I heard myself say.

All eyes shot up at once. Nathan halted in the middle of an ear scratch and used the pen to gesture to me to continue.

"My source is convinced that Lopresti is exerting pressure

on the police force to stall this investigation until after the referendum vote."

Dorothy gave Nathan a piercing look, which did not escape Marcy's attention. She narrowed her eyes, knowing she'd been left out of the loop on something, and folded her arms, waiting for Nathan's response. He studied the pen for a minute, as if there were writing on the side he was trying to interpret, and then clasped it in the palm of his other hand. "Does your source have any proof of this?" he asked.

"No," I admitted. "It's just a tip. But as you know, Billy Lopresti has a lot riding on the referendum outcome, a lot of jobs and contracts to dole out with the Pier Project. I'd need to work with the city hall reporter to flesh it out. Or someone who can guide me to some good inner sources."

"She could work with Jonathan," Dorothy said quietly.

Nathan nodded, and I remembered what Dorothy had said earlier about Jonathan being already tied up with an investigation. I began to understand the meaningful looks. Frizell must already be working on something that tied into Leonard's theory about Lopresti's tight hold on the police department.

From the newsroom, I heard the whir of the copy machine and an editor shouting that he needed someone to write a cut line. Nathan checked his watch, his expression suggesting that this meeting had already taken up too much time. "The first thing I want to make clear," he began, "is that I don't care how many confidential or independent sources you have, this story doesn't get off the ground—not one word in print—until you get someone in Mazursky's family to confirm that he had a gambling problem."

I nodded to show I understood libel law and the very real threat of a lawsuit. Nathan's gaze shifted from me to Marcy and finally to Dorothy. His eyes remained on her, although the answer was meant for me. "All right, then. I'll give you one week."

CHAPTER
9

It was my mother's suggestion, actually. She'd been phoning me every day since I'd told her about the shooting, and she'd caught me just as I walked into my apartment, Monday night.

"You've got to go to the funeral," she said, referring to Barry.

"I'm not sure I can take a day off from work."

"The wake, then."

Sitting on a stool at my kitchen bar, I reached for the day's paper, which lay open over several stacks of mail, and began scanning the death notices. "It's tonight," I said, "the only viewing."

"You've got to go," my mother said. Elsbeth Ahern had never been much for psychology and she'd never utter a word like *closure*, but I knew, even if she didn't, that was what she meant.

But she also meant I had a duty to go. My parents had both been very active in the community in Worcester, and I'd been raised on mandatory attendance at wakes and funerals. My mother, a woman of both big heart and big grudges, kept a running list of neighbors, friends, and relatives who'd failed to show up for wakes or funerals that everyone rightly expected them to attend.

The Linnehan Ryan Settles Riordan Funeral Home was in the neighborhood, on Waterman, three or four blocks away. It was a clear October evening with a sky scrubbed clean by a cold front of Canadian air. I put on a funeral-appropriate winter jacket that I had to take out of last year's dry cleaner's plastic and walked at a runner's pace. I made it with twenty minutes to spare.

The parking lot was jammed with cars and minivans, so I'd expected a crowd inside—customers and curiosity seekers responding to the news event—but there were only about a half dozen people. Three I recognized as customers from the store.

I'd been to more than a dozen different funeral homes and they all looked the same whether they were in Worcester, Boston, or Providence. Neutral-tone rooms with high ceilings, dark, polished tables, and stiffly upholstered chairs that emphasized that no matter how casual the lifestyle, death was a formal affair.

I made my way to the coffin first, grateful that it was closed and I didn't have to relive the horror of Barry's expression or decide if the undertaker had adequately puttied the bullet hole. I kneeled before the gleaming mahogany box and found that I was pleased to see the neatly folded American flag. I wanted to remember Barry as the respected marine veteran, the successful businessman, and the man of strategy and vision. Not the Barry who embezzled from charities and turned to loan sharks for money. I closed my eyes and said three prayers: one for Barry, one for his family, and one for myself. I'd need a few miracles from God to pull off this story.

Afterward, I introduced myself to Barry's son, who I'd seen

a few times working in the deli section. He was in his midtwenties, with the same marinelike build as Barry. He had a similar brow, low and furrowed, as if he, too, worried too much for too many. He took my hand with a rough, unpracticed palm, thanked me for coming, and said he was Barry's son, Drew. His voice was the same tone as his father's, a hardened bass, eerily familiar.

When I told him my name, his brow lifted. A light of recognition flickered like halogen in his eyes. He interrupted his mother's conversation with a woman who looked like she could be a grandmother or a great-aunt to introduce me. "She's the reporter who was in the store," he said.

Nadine Mazursky might have been a beautiful woman. She had a trim figure, dark, gleaming hair tied back in a knot, and fine, even features. But today, her face was unnaturally pale, and I knew by her eyes that she was medicated. "Thank you so much for coming," she said without seeing me.

Drew wouldn't let it go at that. He put his face near hers, forcing her to look him directly in the eye, and spoke louder, more deliberately, as if to a child. "She's the one who wrote the story about Dad in the paper. In Sunday's paper."

Something wavered in Nadine's eyes. "Oh yes, of course. A beautiful story." She took my hand. "Thank you. Thank you so much."

But as I offered my sympathies, I could see her attention already drifting to someone standing behind me. I could feel her haze, could remember the numbness that followed both my brother's and my father's deaths. She'd never remember meeting me.

It didn't matter, really. The point was to come, pay my respects, and make a first step in putting the actual horror of Barry's murder behind me. I walked away from Nadine Mazursky and allowed a man standing behind me to offer the widow his sympathies. I moved down the line, expressing condolences to family members I was meeting for the first time: a daughter and her husband, a grandson, and two aunts. I did not introduce myself as the reporter who wrote the profile. I was one of Barry's customers, I said. One of his regulars.

Slipping out through a side door, I stood under a streetlight and took a minute to collect myself. *A real Rhode Island tragedy.* One minute, Barry had been giving me the odds on which scratch ticket to buy, and the next, he was dead on the floor. And all the police cared about was covering up the real reason for his murder until after the casino-gambling referendum passed.

In the dark, my wool jacket seemed insubstantial. I pulled it tight around me and headed up Waterman, the Canadian air now in my face. Out of the corner of my eye, I spotted a car driving down the street slowly, behind me. It was a block of residential-looking buildings that had all been converted into doctors' and dentists' offices, the waiting rooms all empty by now. I picked up my pace. The car followed, hugging the curb.

Instinctively, I began to scan the buildings for signs of life— a pediatrician with evening hours, an orthodontist working late—but the windows were dark. The only lights were in entry-ways, illuminated for security. The driveways were empty and there were hardly even any cars parked on the street. Why hadn't I driven? Realized how alone I'd feel at this hour of the night?

The car crept closer. I heard a window open. My rib cage tightened and I felt myself lean forward, ready to push off my toes if I had to run for it. A familiar voice called my name. I turned to see Matt Cavanaugh behind the wheel of a ten-

year-old Audi. He was wearing a dark-colored suit and looked
like he was coming from a courtroom. "Need a lift?"

"Jesus," I said, feeling both angry and relieved.

"Is that a yes?"

It was cold and late, and now I was a nervous wreck alone
on the street. I got in.

The car smelled of Windex and oranges and I noticed a roll
of paper towels in the back, as if he had just cleaned up some
kind of spill. A cell phone was charging from a cord in the
lighter and an empty Starbucks cup was stuck in the console
between us. A gym bag and basketball were thrown in the
backseat.

"You live in here?" I asked, as if my own car were clutter
free.

"When I'm working on a big case. Kind of late to be walking alone," he said as he pulled back into traffic. The warning
again.

"I'm a grown woman, I can walk alone on the street."

He didn't say anything, and I knew I'd been unduly harsh.
"I'm coming from Barry Mazursky's wake," I finally said.

"You were a pretty good friend of Barry's, right?"

I thought of the gambling, how little I'd ever known about
Barry. "Sort of."

He must have sensed the dark thought. "You probably
needed the closure, right? After the shooting?" His voice was
warmer now, full of understanding, as if he'd dealt with this
kind of thing before.

"The closure I *really* needed was seeing Victor Delria," I reminded him.

His shrug said he was not about to apologize, but his tone
was conciliatory. "I thought you understood about that."

"Not really," I said. But I did. As a prosecutor, he had a job
to do. I couldn't hold it against him forever.

"How's Barry's family holding up?"

He sounded as if he actually cared, and I found myself telling him about the wife being heavily medicated and how few people had turned out. "It was pitiful really, just a few other customers from the store. The son seemed to be grateful I came—" I looked at him sidelong. "They'd probably feel better if they knew someone was being charged for the murder. Police said the crime report still hasn't come back from the lab. Don't you think that's weird?"

"It can happen," he said, noncommittal. He turned up Wayland Avenue. "Besides, Delria's still unconscious. There's no rush."

No kidding, I thought, but I kept my mouth shut. I knew that in his own way, Matt was trying to mend fences, trying to meet me halfway. And in the closed car, I was becoming aware of his scent over the oranges. He smelled of some kind of soap that reminded me of warm laundry from the dryer. I found myself wanting to lean closer to him, to inhale a little deeper, but I stayed stiffly in my seat, determined to fight off this increasingly inconvenient feeling of arousal. We drove in silence until we hit Wayland Square. I directed him to turn left. "I live up at the corner, on Elmgrove."

"Really?" There was something funny in his tone.

"Yeah, why?"

He didn't answer until I'd directed him to my apartment building, which was on the edge of the square, in the first block on Elmgrove. He pulled into the parking spot behind my Honda, stopped the car, and pointed diagonally across Elmgrove to a large Victorian house about a half block from the square. It had a sweeping veranda that had caught my eye last summer because of all the hanging flower baskets and a real turret. "I live right over there," he said, with a half smile. "I've got the third-floor unit."

It seemed strange that I hadn't seen him on the street before. When I'd first moved in, my mother had come for a visit.
An avid gardener, she had actually climbed up onto that veranda across the street to examine one of the plants. "Since
when?"

"Last month." That meant he hadn't seen my mother root
and clip one of the hanging vines of the wild geranium and
stuff it in her canvas bag. "So you're a new neighbor, then?"

He nodded, with an amused expression, as if this were,
really, quite the development.

There was a long, awkward silence inside the car, and I got
the feeling he was waiting for something. It seemed to me
that maybe I should suggest something neighborly. Like inviting him to dinner or at least for a drink.

"You want to come up for a beer or something?" I heard
myself ask.

His eyes warmed to the idea and I felt a flicker of something
in the car. Surprise? Interest? Desire? He seemed to be
mulling it over, and I got the feeling that, like me, he dreaded
going home to an empty apartment. But then, something
changed in his posture, and his hands tightened on the
wheel. Immediately, I regretted my neighborliness. "Better
not," he said, shaking his head and looking away from me.

I knew then that Jonathan Frizell had been right about
Matt's career aspirations. It wouldn't be a good political move
for a prosecutor in the AG's office to get too neighborly with
a *Chronicle* reporter.

"Yeah, it's kind of late anyway," I said, making an effort to
sound relieved as I slipped out of the car.

I waited until two days after the funeral to approach Nadine
Mazursky for an interview, and even then I felt like a vulture.
Not surprisingly, the Mazursky phone number was un-

listed, so I hadn't been able to call ahead. I drove by the Mazursky Market first, hoping to find Drew working in the deli, but the market was still closed. I had no choice but to get on the highway and head to the Cranston address I'd found in the database.

My stomach grew tighter as I passed each exit. At Thurbers Avenue, I looked up at the Big Blue Bug, a ten-foot-tall fiberglass-and-steel termite that looks down on the highway from a pest-control building, and felt like *I* was the vermin. More than anything, I hated barging in like this on a newly grieving family, but I had no promise of a story, no shot at the investigative team until I got someone from the family to confirm Barry's gambling problem. On the record.

Christ.

A part of me hoped that the Mazursky family would slam the door in my face and I could be done with it. The other fantasized about Nadine inviting me into her home and championing me for my efforts to get to the bottom of her husband's murder.

Yeah, right.

I studied the small blue Cape on the corner lot of a middle-class neighborhood. The clapboard trim could have used a coat of paint and the lawn desperately needed to be raked. The shades on the windows were all drawn; there were no mums in planters or Halloween pumpkins on the steps to make the house look even remotely inviting. I couldn't bring myself to stop, but drove down the road to a dead end, where there was a small cove with a boat launch on Narragansett Bay.

I stared out at the water, gray like the sky and choppy from the wind, and steeled myself for the interview ahead. Some people found it cathartic to talk to reporters about their grief, I told myself. Maybe, the family, like me, was frustrated by the lack of information the Providence police had revealed about the investigation. Maybe Nadine Mazursky was pissed off that no one had been charged with Barry's murder and hoped a *Chronicle* story would spark action.

I turned, parked in front of the house, and forced myself out of my Honda. Because of the positive response I'd gotten at the wake, there was a good chance the family would let me in the door. But depending on how the interview went, it could be only a matter of minutes before they tossed me back out again.

I pushed the doorbell and waited. The wind kicked my hair across my face, and I tried to comb it away with my fingers. A couple of minutes passed. I rang the doorbell again. Another gust of wind and I had to grab my hair into a ponytail to keep it from flapping all over. Someone peeked out from behind a drawn shade. The inner door opened partway, and I saw Nadine herself peering at me. An outer storm door separated us.

"Hallie Ahern," I shouted through the thick glass.

I dropped the ponytail, and instantly, my hair was in my face again. I could see in her expression that she had no idea who I was. "The *Chronicle* reporter who wrote the profile of your husband in the Sunday paper," I added.

I'm not sure that made any impression either, but another figure appeared behind her. I heard her mumble something. The door opened a bit wider. It was her son, Drew.

He swung open the door. "Come in, please." I was taken again by the timbre of his voice.

As soon as I was inside the house, he closed and locked the door behind me. More creditors, I thought, but said nothing. I told them I wanted to ask just a couple of questions. They looked at each other for a long moment.

"Would you like a cup of tea?" Nadine finally asked. Her

tone had the same dull quality as her eyes, and I knew she was still on some sort of drug to deaden the pain.

We passed through a tidy living room and into a good-size kitchen with harvest-gold appliances that looked as though they had once been top of the line. There was no sign of Barry's daughter or her husband, or any of the older female relatives who had been at the wake, and the way Drew banged around in the cabinets, asking his mother where she'd moved the cups and sugar, I guessed he didn't live here anymore either.

I sat opposite Nadine at a long table made of hand-painted tile, while Drew filled a silver kettle with water from the sink. When I admired the table, Nadine told me that Barry had painted the tiles himself. "It used to be a hobby for him. He was planning on hand-painting furniture when he retired."

The kettle clanged loudly as it hit the grid of the stove. Nadine looked up at her son, who did not apologize. "He hasn't painted a tile in years," Drew said.

I left my notebook unopened on the table, so they would know I wasn't taking notes on their feud. It didn't seem to matter. Drew's gruff movements about the kitchen suggested he was still consumed by his mother's last comment. He lit a cigarette with a defiant air. Nadine gave him an annoyed look, but then she shrugged, as if to indicate that she was too exhausted to quibble with her son.

I pulled a tape recorder out of my knapsack and put it on the table. Nadine glanced skeptically at the small machine, which was why I normally didn't like to use a tape recorder for interviews. But Nathan's concern about a libel suit made me decide to be extra careful.

"What's this about?" she asked.

"Just some follow-up," I said, turning on the machine and

speaking into it. "I'm taping our discussion to make sure not to misquote you. Is that all right?"

At the mention of a tape recorder, Drew turned around from the sink. "You sure that's okay, Mom?" he asked.

"What are you going to be quoting me about?" she asked.

About your husband's gambling problems? No, I couldn't start there. "Just some questions about the investigation. If you don't want to answer them, or if you want me to shut off the tape at any point, I will. I just wanted to ask if you were bothered that there hasn't been an arrest yet."

I was hoping that after enough questions, Nadine would get so caught up in the flow of her thoughts, she'd forget all about the tape recorder. Now, her gaze remained fixed on the machine. "I have faith that the police are doing the best job they can," she said.

"Of course," I said. "But does it bother you that the police haven't released the results of the forensics report? That they won't even say whether Delria is a possible suspect?"

Nadine looked over her shoulder at her son, and I got the sense that even medicated, she could see right through my questions. "He's still unconscious, from what I understand. That limits what the police can do."

I asked a few more questions about the police handling of the case to try to convince her that this was the point of the interview, but her expression remained wary and her answers cautious. Finally, I shifted to a completely nonthreatening topic. "So how long was your husband involved in veterans' organizations?"

Nadine answered my questions without enthusiasm or elaboration. "Forever." When I asked if Barry had ever worried about crime in the neighborhood, she offered, "Not lately," and glanced up at a swirl of cigarette smoke that had drifted our way. The kettle whistled and Drew stubbed out his cigarette and served us tea. I'd swallowed the sugar that sinks to the bottom of the cup before Nadine finally warmed up to my effort to draw her out.

"When I was researching that profile I wrote, the owner of the Wayland Square bookstore made a point of telling me what a good husband Barry was."

Nadine gave me kind of a wry smile, her first real expression.

"And what a devoted father," I added.

Drew cleared his throat. She gave him a stern look. "Yes. A devoted father. A good husband. A good man." She told me how hard he'd worked in the stores. Then, with a deliberate look over her shoulder at Drew, she added that Barry had always been determined not to force any of his kids into the family business the way his own father had forced him.

Drew, who was leaning against the kitchen counter, shifted his weight and folded his arms in front of his chest. He stared back at his mother, refusing her demand for gratitude.

I pretended not to notice. "Is that why he sold the stores?"

"Partly," Nadine said, shifting her gaze back to me. The silent exchange with her son had sobered her. And now that she didn't seem so sedated, I could see that she was an intelligent woman. "And partly because in the early nineties, when all that crack was around, a cash business was more dangerous."

Drew cleared his throat again. But when I looked at him, he quickly looked away.

"So you believe his murder was random?" I tried to sound as if this question had just occurred to me.

Something flickered in her eyes. She glanced again at Drew, who stared back at her with his arms still folded.

"Or is it possible someone might have been out to get your husband?" I pressed.

"What are you trying to say?" Drew interrupted.

I met Nadine's eyes. She was waiting for an answer. I began to talk too fast, a wild race to persuade. "I've heard that your husband might have had a gambling problem, and I can understand how you wouldn't want to talk about that right now. But I have a confidential source who says your husband was in debt to loan sharks. And if his murder *was* caused by his gambling debts—if that was the motive—it's going to come out during the trial anyway. And it might be an important message to get out right now—*before* the state votes on whether to legalize gambling."

Nadine's once vague eyes were now full of focus, full of energy. "My husband didn't have any gambling problems," she said directly into the microphone. With a sharp look at Drew, she added, "And at the moment, I don't really give a damn about how the state votes on casino gambling." Then she reached for the tape recorder, turning it twice in her hand to find the button to snap it off. Then she stood up.

I stood up, too. I was a half inch taller than she was but felt dwarfed by her suddenly imposing figure. "I'm sorry."

"I'm well aware that my husband was not the perfect saint you wrote about in Sunday's paper," she said. "But he was not in any kind of gambling trouble."

Drew was suddenly behind me, his hand on my arm. "I think it's time you left."

I picked up my tape recorder swiftly, along with my notebook, and protectively slipped them both into my bag. "I'm sorry if I upset you," I said to Nadine, but she wouldn't look at me. Her gaze was fixed downward, at the table, the painted tile.

I let Drew lead me to the door, watching as he unlocked both the inner and the storm doors.

"Please," he said, as I stepped out into the cold air, "if you

were really ever any friend of my father's, don't write anything about him in the paper—good or bad."

I sat on the stool in my kitchen ignoring the half-eaten bowl
of cereal I'd poured myself for dinner and stared at the pile of
scratch tickets on the bar. They were the scratch tickets I'd
bought the night Barry was murdered, and couldn't bring
myself to play. It had seemed horribly wrong to try to win
money, to gain something from that evening. And yet, I'd
jumped at the lead Leonard had given me, was willing to use
Barry's murder, his gambling problems, to get myself on the
investigative team.

I picked up a ticket: the Caesar's Palace game. Barry had
said it was "hot off the presses." The left side featured little
roulette tables and the right side showed dice. You could win
by matching the winning number, by getting a seven or an
eleven in the dice, or by scratching a $$ symbol on the
roulette side. The odds suddenly seemed absurd.

I'd gone out on a limb, pitching a story I couldn't prove to
a bunch of editors who didn't particularly want to believe me.
What on earth made me think I could walk into the widow's
house and have her confirm her husband's vice?

I studied the bottom half of the card: the gray latex coating
that separated you from your good luck, from your losses. I
remembered the look of concern in Barry's eyes when I'd
bought all these tickets at once. The reckless impulse he had
recognized.

The image of Nadine Mazursky rose before me. The mo-
mentary clearing of her grief as she talked about what a good
husband Barry had been, followed by her outrage when she
realized what I'd really been after. Had I shown any sensitiv-
ity at all, or had I just barreled into the interview with my ac-
cusations?

I dropped the ticket back on the pile, unscratched. My big shot at the investigative team was finished. No way was I going to get anyone in the Mazursky family to trust me again. Maybe I should have stuck to cocktail waitressing. Maybe I should never have left Boston.

I stood up. My legs felt cramped and sore from running too many miles that morning, but I was too antsy to stay in one place. I wanted to be anywhere but alone in my apartment.

I thought of the instant camaraderie I'd experienced at the casino. The strange clearheadedness, the sheer energy of the air, the elation when the cards worked in your favor.

It occurred to me that it was Thursday. On the last Thursday of the month, my mother and aunt routinely took the bus from Worcester in the late afternoon and stayed at Foxwoods until about eleven. It was only six o'clock, and the casino was only about an hour's drive away. I told myself it was the perfect opportunity, a chance to combine daughterly duty with a much needed escape.

Foxwoods looked like it had come out of a crayon box: an inviting castlelike structure rising from the hills in unlikely shades of aqua and lavender. Inside, I was swept into a playland of brightly patterned carpeting, old-fashioned Victorian facades with candy-pink trim. Mixing into the crowd, I felt energized and grabbed what looked like a board-game map of the place from a woman at an information booth. I remembered that my mother liked one area of slot machines better than the others, but couldn't remember the name. Finally, after about a half-hour search through the main floor, I found my mother in what was called the Great Cedar Casino.

She stood between two slot machines, a bucket of change on one of the seats and her purse saving the other. She was feeding two quarters into each machine with a look of intense concentration.

A frugal woman of German extraction, Elsbeth Ahern had never so much as played church bingo until four years ago when she and my father took their first cruise together. My mother discovered that there was a casino onboard and on her very first quarter, she won $750. When my father died, after a year and a half in a nursing home, he left substantial debts. The only luxury my mother allowed herself were these monthly bus trips to the casino with my aunt.

My mother was not a woman who showed a lot of surprise. There was no double take or exclamation about this unexpected meeting at the casino. She accepted my explanation that I had research to do on a story and had timed my visit to see her, gave me a quick kiss, and returned her concentration to the slot machine. But she halted her play a moment later and looked at me suspiciously when I said I was going to head to the blackjack tables. "Since when do you play blackjack?" she asked.

I considered boasting about my beginner's luck, my winnings the week before. Instead, I heard myself say: "Barry, the guy who was killed, was a big blackjack player, and I've always wanted to give it a try."

Something in this answer alarmed her. Her eyes narrowed so intently on me that, for a moment, there was no clinking change or cheers of fortune—just a painfully protracted maternal silence.

"What?" I asked.

At seventy, my mother was an amazingly fit, strong-shouldered woman who commanded the space around her. Gamblers did not bump into her with drinks in their hands and no one tried to horn in on her machines. "Let me show you how I gamble." She opened her purse and withdrew two small cosmetic bags. One of them was filled with coins. The other was empty.

"I bring forty dollars each time I come," she said, pointing to the full bag. "If I win anything from the machine, it goes into that bag." She pointed to the empty one. "None of the winnings ever go back into the machine, do you understand?"

I was not in the mood for a lecture. But Aunt Cecilia, my mother's younger sister, was three machines away and stopped her play to give me a look: Don't argue with her, the look said.

My mother was an absolutist who lived her life efficiently by never considering shades of gray. But my aunt was right, it was best to nod and accept the black-and-whiteness of her rules. For one thing, she had an eerie way of being right. For another, she would not back off until you capitulated.

"I know. I know. Never gamble more than you can afford to lose," I said.

But this wasn't good enough. She shook her head vehemently. "You think that little slogan is going to help you? No. You can't make a decision about how much you can afford to lose when you're in the middle of the action. You have to set your limits *before* you start to play."

I nodded solemnly to show that I was not just following along, but was in complete agreement.

"You come with forty dollars or so, money you budgeted for entertainment, because that's what this is, entertainment. And when your original forty dollars is gone, you go home." She stopped for a moment and looked fondly at her slot machine. "Even if you win the jackpot."

My aunt, a younger, thinner version of my mother, shook her head vigorously in agreement.

"Of course," I said. "I can't stay as late as you guys anyway. I've got work tomorrow."

My mother smiled and all sternness disappeared from her face. She was a handsome woman with wide Teutonic cheekbones and a decided chin, the only thing I'd inherited in an otherwise Irish face. When she relaxed and let up on the rules, she was entirely lovable. I kissed her for luck and left the cacophony of clinking coins, headed for the gaming tables.

After chain-smoking beside me all night long, the man next to me had the audacity to give me a dirty look when I pointed to my hand and asked to be hit again.

"You sure?" another woman at the table asked.

I had thirteen and the dealer had two threes. By asking for another card, I was violating basic strategy, the mathematical equation that was supposed to reduce the favored odds of the dealer. Even the dealer looked at me as if it was a bad move.

In an hour and a half of play, I'd managed to lose almost the entire $450 in winnings from the week before. My last $25 was on the felt, the dealer was already at eighteen, and I desperately needed a win to remain at the table.

The dealer straightened her embroidered cuff, giving me a second to change my mind. Another waft of cigarette smoke from the man beside me blew into my eyes.

"Hit me," I said, with authority. The dealer flipped the card over slowly, as if to emphasize my mistake. A king. The guy next to me gave me a look of disgust, and the dealer swept my last $25 away.

I felt weak looking at the empty space where my chips had been. What had I done? I considered going back to the ATM, but I had just enough left to live on until my next paycheck.

Still, I did not want to leave the table, did not want to admit defeat.

I glanced back at the bright pink exit sign and saw my mother and aunt marching past the baccarat tables toward me. The night was clearly over. I summoned all the bravado I could find. "I'll be back," I said to my fellow gamblers. They did not look impressed.

"We're going for ice cream; do you want ice cream?" my mother asked.

I did *not* want ice cream. More important, I didn't want to detail to my mother, or even to myself, how much money I'd lost. "Early day tomorrow," I said, throwing my purse over my shoulder.

"Did you win?" Aunt Cecilia asked.

"Broke even," I said, taking a step away from the table so none of my fellow gamblers could hear me. I wasn't lying actually. I *had* broken even if you counted my total gambling experience with the Mohegan Sun winnings.

Luckily, my mother had scored $250 at her favorite machine and was beaming too much to detect any rationalizations. My aunt was preoccupied with the upcoming ice cream. They had finished gambling for the night. With a full hour to kill before their bus, they insisted on walking me to the elevator to the parking garage before heading back to Scoops.

My mother's handbag looked heavy, as if weighted with coin, and her walk, after a long night, was slower than usual. But I noticed that my aunt, who had nerve damage in her leg, hardly seemed to be limping. When I mentioned this, she responded, "Even when I lose, this place takes my mind off the pain. My doctor calls it my therapy."

"Therapy for old people," my mother quickly added as she pecked my cheek good-bye. "Not for the young."

* * *

By the time I crossed the border from Connecticut to Rhode Island, I was feeling better. I'd been stupid, let myself lose too much money, but I'd been tense from the beginning and distracted with my mother and aunt there. Who in their right mind could concentrate under those conditions?

The heat in the Honda had two settings, zero and sauna. I'd already flipped it on and off three times. So I couldn't make an extra payment on the loan to my mother, the way I'd wanted. It's not like she knew about the Mohegan Sun winnings. On a net basis, I hadn't actually lost anything from my bank account. It wasn't like I'd have to miss a car payment or anything.

I pushed the radio button preprogrammed for WKZI but couldn't make out anything because of the static. It was twenty more miles before I recognized the grandfatherly voice of Gregory Ayers, the lottery guy, who was apparently the night's guest on Leonard's show. "Legalized gambling will dramatically decrease lottery revenue from video slots and keno. When you figure the social costs of casino gambling, it's not a gain. It's a loss."

Hearing his voice, I felt cheated. What happened to all that good luck I was supposed to get from rubbing his sleeve? In one incredibly crummy day, I'd lost $450 and my shot at the investigative team.

I felt the pressure of the day building behind my eyes, and I had to focus hard on the road ahead of me. Jennifer Trowbridge, the woman from Evening Star Gaming International who'd been dining with the mayor, was Ayers's counterpoint. She had the confident, educated tone of someone who did a lot of arguing on national media. "How can you possibly imply that one form of gambling is okay and another is immoral?"

"It's not a matter of morality, but practicality," Gregory

Ayers replied. "The state retains more control over the games in a state lottery than in a privately run casino."

I didn't care about the referendum—the question wasn't about whether gambling was right or wrong, but who got to run it—the state lottery, or the Narragansett Indians. Why shouldn't the Narragansett, who'd been massacred so brutally in the Great Swamp Fight, be allowed to team up with Evening Star Gaming to run their own casino? As long as the state got its cut, why shouldn't the Narragansetts get as rich as the Pequots in Connecticut?

But I did care about why Barry was murdered, and that the mayor was trying to cover it up to make sure he got his waterfront redevelopment and the graft that comes with it.

Ayers began reciting statistics. "More than seven million Americans can be classified as problem gamblers. That's a five-billion-dollar drain on the economy. Around Foxwoods, the crime rate has increased three hundred percent—"

Leonard interrupted. "You mean the kind of crime we saw last week with that Wayland Square shooting? I've tried to get the attorney general on the air to talk about that murder, but he's not returning my calls. They're being very quiet about that case, have you noticed?"

Gregory Ayers had not noticed. Or more likely, he did not want to piss off the attorney general. "We don't need to speculate about cases we don't know are related," he said. "We have plenty of hard data about Atlantic City and Las Vegas and Ledyard—"

Leonard cut him off midsentence to repeat the station's phone number. "Lines are free, and we want to hear from you: Do you think Providence police are dragging their heels on the Wayland Square shooting?"

He was practically begging. I looked at the car clock. It was 10:30. Why wasn't anyone calling in? It occurred to me that there might be a PC basketball game on television tonight. Still, it was very quiet. Where was Tom of Woonsocket, or Eva of North Kingstown, or Andre of Cranston?

As I turned onto the Gano Street exit, I was suddenly hearing Andre's voice quite clearly in my head: *"Gambling destroys more people than drinking."*

Andre, who agreed with Leonard on every issue, but who got particularly worked up about gambling. Andre, who lived in Cranston, where Drew Mazursky had grown up, and who told heart-wrenching stories about what gambling had done to his family.

The car heat was on sauna now, and the dry heat penetrated through layers of clothing and skin. There was actual sweat on my forehead. Drew Mazursky's voice *had* sounded familiar, but not because he was Barry's son.

I raced back to my apartment and found my knapsack on the floor and began foraging through the notebook and the papers for my tape recorder. I rewound the tape, slid the volume to high, and clicked the play button. I paced back and forth in my living room with the tape recorder in my hand as I suffered through my awkward questioning and the slow pace of Nadine's responses. Then I realized I hadn't rewound far enough and started all over again. It was right at the beginning of the tape that I heard the voice I was waiting for: Andre of Cranston, in Drew Mazursky's kitchen.

"You sure that's okay, Mom?" he asked.

The WKZI radio station was not, as I expected, in an enormous building on a major highway with its call letters advertising itself. Instead, it was tucked away in a residential neighborhood in East Providence, an odd surprise at the end of a dimly lit maze of single-family homes.

I'd waited until the top of the hour to call Leonard, when I knew he'd be on a break for the news. He'd told me to come after midnight, when everyone else had left the station. So here I was at this ungodly hour, with only one other car in the parking lot and one light shining inside. It felt creepy, lonely, and a little far-fetched. But I had to check my tape against the show.

The outer glass door of the building was locked. I rang a bell and Leonard emerged from a back room to let me in. He looked older at this hour, the vertical line between his brows was a little deeper, his skin a rougher surface. But it made him seem less slick, more appealing. He must have cycled some distance that afternoon because I noticed that one knee looked stiff as I followed him down a narrow hallway to his studio.

It was a tiny room with huge microphones and tape decks everywhere. Jumbo Dunkin' Donuts coffee cups littered the desk and the room smelled as if the carpeting had absorbed the sugar and caffeine. The programming was automated, and Leonard turned off the studio volume of a syndicated behavioral therapist who was ordering her insomniac callers to turn on the lights and get out of bed. I sat in the guest chair, but Leonard remained standing. He only had to listen to about a minute of my tape to decide that the voices matched. "Andre of Cranston," he said, mostly to himself.

He walked out, beyond the production booth to another small studio or office. I heard the squeal of a file drawer opening, and then the opening and shutting of what sounded like a closet door. He returned with a shoebox full of tapes in his arms. "Andre of Cranston is in here," he said, handing the box to me. "Almost every night."

Inside the box, the tapes were labeled by subject and date. I saw at least a dozen marked "gambling ref." I picked one out at random and Leonard slid the cassette into a deck behind his microphone. Then he sat in his host chair beside the mike and leaned back, his hands clasped behind his head. Maybe it was the exhaustion of the hour, but he seemed more real to me tonight, as if he'd left the showman behind.

Considering how often Andre called, it was amazing how many tapes Leonard had to go through—many which contained my voice—before we got anywhere. Finally, on the fourth tape, Andre of Cranston's voice filled the room.

On the first segment, he spoke only of his father going bankrupt and the financial ruin of his family. After much fast-forwarding through tapes, we found another call in which he railed about gambling in general as a sickness. Leonard popped out that tape and put in another. Midway through the show, Andre called to discuss the crimes caused by gambling. He said he knew his father borrowed money from loan sharks because he'd seen these animals in his father's place of business. "Believe me, you can tell who they are from fifty feet."

"They have fins or something?" Leonard had joked.

"Yeah," Andre replied, somehow making it sound ominous. "Real big fins."

Both Leonard and Andre laughed at this, a cackle that now sounded harsh. The show cut to a commercial and Leonard snapped off the tape. His head was bent, and I couldn't read his expression.

"You going to use any of this on your show?" I asked.

"I know you don't quite believe me, but outing you was a mistake. If I start revealing callers, those lines will go dead." He pulled the tape from the machine and put it in my hand. The tape was still warm to the touch.

"This is your lead, not mine," he said, walking around the desk to drop into a second guest chair beside mine. It was almost two o'clock in the morning, and we were exhausted. Through the filter of Barry's murder, the talk-radio stories had a poignancy I didn't think either of us would be able to shake.

I held the tape by a corner and stared into its reel, feeling unexpectedly wary. This tape was exactly what Nathan had asked me to dig up: confirmation from a family member. You couldn't do much better than an audio confession by Barry Mazursky's own son.

I could take the tapes to a voice-recognition specialist to prove I had a match, that Drew Mazursky in his kitchen was Andre of Cranston on the air. But how would I explain to my editors that I happened to have an archive of taped talk-radio shows without giving away my connection to Leonard?

Leonard was leaning into my shoulder, peering at the label on the cassette. I noticed the date of the tape for the first time, in small, neat printing: May 14. The show had been taped more than a month before I'd even moved to Providence.

Our eyes met. Leonard might not know when I'd moved to Rhode Island, but he understood the risk of letting me walk out of the studio with that tape in my hand. Even the dimmest of editors would need about twenty seconds to fig-ure out that someone connected with the Leonard of *Late Night* had to have fed this to me, that that same someone was probably my confidential source.

I could see something simmering inside him, and I ex-pected him to get dramatic, to pull the tape from my hand and tell me this was, after all, the station's property. That giv-ing it to me could be the ruin of his career. But he didn't. In-stead, he stood up and walked to the shelf next to the cassette deck, where he'd left the two other tapes that held Andre's confessions.

"They say good reporters never reveal their sources," he said, sliding the tapes across the desk to me. "I'll have to trust you on that."

CHAPTER
10

W HAT DO YOU have?" Dorothy was standing over my shoulder.

I was downtown in the newsroom library at a bank of computer terminals designated for Internet use.

"A sad story," I replied. I'd gone to federal bankruptcy court and found that Barry Mazursky had quietly filed for personal bankruptcy only a year after selling his chain of convenience stores.

It was Friday morning, a week after the shooting. I'd gotten up at six A.M. to run and had come to work early. Few people were in the newsroom before eight o'clock and there was a feeling of peace before the day's storm. Here in the library, a long, windowless room in the front of the building, only one research assistant had arrived for the day, and she sat distracted by work at a distant desk. I'd been alone with the database until I'd looked up and seen Dorothy Sacks standing in front of me.

As the evening city editor, Dorothy often stayed until at least ten o'clock at night and didn't have to report to work until just before noon. Carolyn said Dorothy never went home. She said Dorothy was one of those women who should have been nuns, but instead devoted themselves to the religion of news. At various times, Carolyn had managed to hint that Dorothy was asexual, a lesbian, and a home wrecker who was carrying on a torrid affair with a copy editor named Harold.

I didn't quite get Carolyn's rabid dislike of Dorothy, except that years ago the two women had started at the *Chronicle* the same week. Childless and spouseless, Dorothy's career had catapulted her to city editor. Carolyn, who had married, divorced, remarried, had children, and divorced again, had stagnated as a bureau manager.

Dorothy dragged a chair over from another desk and sat down to better read from the screen. I noticed that she wore almost no makeup and did not have a varied wardrobe. It was always the crisp-looking jeans or corduroys and the worn office sweater. The sweater alone was enough to incense Carolyn.

"Doesn't actually prove he was gambling," I said.

"No."

"He could have been doing heroin," I offered.

"Or gone on a buying binge at the Home Shopping Network," Dorothy said. She had a very dry delivery.

Late yesterday, Victor Delria, who had been unconscious, had officially slipped into a coma at Rhode Island Hospital, and now, a week after the shooting, still no one was charged with Barry's murder. As each day passed in police silence, my theory that the shooting was more than just a robbery gained momentum. Nathan even sent me an interoffice memo saying that if I wanted to work on the investigation over the weekend, I would be compensated for overtime.

Dorothy and I both knew a personal-bankruptcy filing was a pretty good indicator that Barry had a gambling problem, but we also knew we couldn't print it. Not by itself. By itself, reporting the bankruptcy filing was an unnecessary invasion of a dead man's privacy.

It had to be coupled with an admission from a family member. If, say, a surviving son told us that loan sharks were actually seen at the store, threatening the deceased, now that could be decent copy. That could be enough to run with.

I thought of Leonard and the trust he'd put in me. Why? I wondered. My father used to do that when I was a teenager, emphasize his trust in me as a means of guilting me into responsible behavior. But that was an Irish-Catholic tactic. Leonard was Italian.

The library phone began ringing. The research assistant looked up briefly from her desk, but didn't move to answer it. Through the open door, I saw Nathan get off the elevator and begin walking briskly toward his office.

"He's in early," I commented.

"It's the investigative-team thing. Everyone on the reporting staff, almost, has asked for an interview."

I felt a rush of alarm. Had I missed something? Was there a list somewhere I wasn't on?

Seeing my expression, Dorothy said, "I take it this means you're interested in the position?"

I nodded and she wrote something on a notepad. With a glance at Nathan's closed office door, she added, "Don't worry too much about the crowd. By union regs, he's got to interview *everyone*. But he's getting the busywork out of the way first."

A second phone began to ring, a high-pitched yelp that cut the ear. The research assistant didn't seem to hear it. "Should we answer it?" I asked Dorothy, but she shook her head.

Just then, I saw Jonathan Frizell get off the elevator. He

and I had met twice about the Mazursky murder, and he'd said he'd nose around city hall for me, but so far I hadn't heard anything. Now, without a glance in our direction, he marched purposefully in the direction of Nathan's office.

Dorothy knocked her elbow into mine. "Stop worrying about the competition and focus on the ammunition. What else do you have?"

I rifled through my file folder to find the copy of the Veterans' Homeless Shelter board minutes Leonard had mailed me. There were printouts of *Chronicle* stories about the fund-raising drive and the official announcement of Barry's resignation, but where were the minutes? I was sure I'd dropped them into the file last night.

The first page of the minutes had detailed a conversation between the board chairwoman and the assistant treasurer calling for a full audit of the fund-raising drive because of "a $75,000 discrepancy." The second page, also missing, was of the following month's minutes, where the board had unanimously accepted Barry Mazursky's resignation, with the chairwoman noting, "It's for the best."

With a look of detached amusement, Dorothy watched me search through the file folder. The papers were nowhere in the folder. The high-pitched phone stopped, then started again. Why wouldn't the research assistant just answer it? Had I left the papers home on the bar?

Finally, I found them facing backward and stuck behind another set of papers in the middle of the file. Smoothing out one of the crumpled corners on her desk, Dorothy scanned the minutes, eyes lighting with interest. After a moment of calculation, the light faded, and I knew her conclusion. The minutes helped validate my source, but still weren't enough to justify a story that could libel a dead man.

Desperate, I plunged on. "I know this sounds a little far-fetched, but I'm pretty sure I recognized the son's voice on talk radio the other night. I'm pretty sure I've heard him talk on the air about his father's gambling problems before. I mean, he's on *a lot*. Andre of Cranston, he calls himself. I recognized the voice."

"Talk radio?" Dorothy asked.

I couldn't tell by her tone what she meant by this question. I continued anyway. "Leonard of *Late Night*. You think I should call the station, see if they have any of the old shows on tape?"

"You listen to Leonard of *Late Night*?" The expression in her eyes told me she was reassessing me.

"Sometimes," I admitted.

She considered this. What it meant about me. My lifestyle. My IQ. I found myself growing defensive. Okay, he was a little extreme. Especially about the mayor and casino gambling, but he had his reasons. I mentally began counting the number of our reporters who had appeared on Leonard's show: reporters who suddenly became experts, columnists who became celebrities.

"Is there a problem with that?"

She looked at me as if her mind had just been far away and had now returned. "I was just trying to figure out how you could use something like that in copy, even if you could track it down on tape."

"Oh."

"I mean, those callers are supposed to be anonymous, right? Isn't that part of the deal?"

I tried not to sigh audibly. "I guess."

"I think we better steer clear of talk radio."

I was in the cafeteria trying to get a cup of coffee when I spotted the *Chronicle*'s obituary writer, sitting alone with two doughnuts.

Somewhere in his midsixties, he was at least fifty pounds overweight and wore the vague and tired expression of someone who had burned out years ago. Trying to remember his name, I closed my eyes to picture the byline over the last big death in Rhode Island. An Italian last name: Martino?

This man had never once met my eye when I passed him in the newsroom, but now I remembered that Carolyn once told me that he'd been a highly regarded police reporter. DiMartino, that was it. His brother was still a sergeant on the Providence police force.

I stirred cream into my jumbo-size coffee and tried to remember his first name. Anthony? Joseph? Dominic? He was about halfway down the row of red-vinyl booths that faced the window, his head determinedly in the newspaper, as if to discourage anyone from attempting conversation.

I remembered that there was something incongruous about his name. That it didn't go together, didn't fit somehow. Out of an air pocket in my brain, the thought descended. It was a young name, a baby-boy-of-the-new-millennium kind of name: Justin, Josh, Jared? Evan, that was it. Evan DiMartino.

From Carolyn, I knew that DiMartino had been shoved aside a few years ago to make room for a young police reporter who'd since gone on to the *Los Angeles Times*. It occurred to me that he might instinctively resent all new hires. I decided to take my chances, buying a second coffee and heading down to his booth with two cups in my hand. "Evan?"

He looked so startled that I immediately heard myself apologizing. "Sorry to bother you, I . . ." I wanted to hand him the extra coffee, but suddenly it felt presumptuous, so I continued to clutch two hot coffee cups in my hand. "I was wondering . . . hoping I could talk to you."

Deliberately, he glanced at his watch.

"If you're not too busy."

He studied me for a moment, then a connection clicked in his head. "You the new reporter from Boston? The one who was there when the guy got shot in the store?"

I nodded and offered him the coffee. "I'd like to ask you a couple of questions. I don't know Providence police very well, and I could use your help."

Something in that plea softened him. The resentment disappeared. Curiosity took its place.

Without waiting for his invitation, I slid into the seat. "Mazursky was a compulsive gambler, in trouble with loan sharks. I have a source who says the mayor doesn't want that to come out before the casino-gambling referendum. That he's leaning on the police department to stall the investigation."

He opened the lid of his coffee and let out the steam.

"Do you think that if the mayor pressed hard enough, the chief would stall a murder investigation?" I asked.

"Who's your source on this?"

"A confidential source."

"Inside the police department?"

I shook my head.

He examined his doughnut as if it had just fallen onto the floor. "Then that's just speculation. A lot of things can hold up a murder investigation."

I nodded with a vague sense of disappointment.

"But that's not to say the mayor doesn't have influence." He brushed the sugar from his doughnut off his fingers and onto his lap. "Whether the chief would agree to hold up a murder investigation until the vote? Who knows? It's only—what, a week and a half? Almost doesn't count as real corruption."

Then he focused on something behind me. I turned and saw that three of the youngest male reporters on the investigative team had walked into the cafeteria together. Two of them carried stacks of files and the third had a laptop with him.

My gaze must have lingered too long. Evan noticed, saw my yearning. "You after Susannah's job?" he asked.

I shrugged, trying to look only moderately interested, but Evan wasn't buying it. "Of course you are. And you think this Mazursky thing is going to get it for you. Move you to the A-list, right?"

"I'm hoping it'll give me an edge, yes," I admitted. "But I'm still new to Providence, and I don't have any sources inside the police department."

The three investigative reporters marched past us to a far booth, their eyes focused on the goal ahead, as if we weren't there. Their voices rose from the table where they had re-grouped, sounding loud and just a little too self-important. I had a flashback to my high school cafeteria.

"They *need* someone old enough to have a driver's license," Evan said, leaning forward. "Otherwise their mothers have to drive them."

I smiled to show that I appreciated his disdain, and for the first time, he smiled back.

One of the cafeteria workers came out from behind the counter to erase yesterday's lunch specials from the black-board. The chalk squeaked as she began to list today's soup of the day: "M-U-S-H-R-O-O-M."

Evan grimaced. "I hate mushrooms. You ever see where they grow?"

I had never seen where mushrooms grew.

"Usually in a pile of crap." For a moment, he looked dis-turbed, and I wondered if he was seeing the mushrooms rising from dung on the forest floor. But his attention had already shifted. "So who's involved in this case?"

I told him about the patrolman, who'd been the first to ar-rive at the Mazursky Market, and about Sergeant Holstrom. As an afterthought, I mentioned that Major Errico had come to the station the following day.

"Errico? On a Saturday?" There was nothing vague or tired in Evan's expression now. "You sure?"

I described what he looked like, and the way Holstrom had snapped to attention. Evan nodded to indicate that this meshed. "He say anything?"

I shook my head. "But he came in with a bunch of files under his arm. Files he didn't want me to see. There was some lettering on the side."

"What kind of lettering?"

"Two initials, I think."

"OC." This was an answer, not a question.

"Yeah. I think so."

Evan looked over his shoulder at the guys on the investigative team, and lowered his voice to a gravelly whisper. "Organized crime. They usually keep those files in a locked cabinet in Errico's office. He's the OC guy. He knows who's who in the organization. Can pick up the phone and get through to capos if he needs to."

The squeak of the chalk punctuated this last sentence. Evan turned to make sure no one was within earshot. He waited until the cafeteria worker walked behind the counter, watching her the whole time as if she were some kind of spy. Then, he continued, "Errico doesn't come in on a Saturday to talk about some little convenience-store holdup. He doesn't get interested in a case unless they're pretty damn sure it involves organized crime."

CHAPTER

11

I HADN'T EXPECTED TO see Drew Mazursky the next day. I'd gotten up early, run, and was now across the street from my apartment trying to buy coffee at Starbucks. I was still wearing the enormous gray sweatshirt I'd run in, along with a pair of baggy old blue jeans I'd pulled from the laundry and an old pair of running shoes with the laces missing. Standing in an incredibly slow-moving line, I was killing time by looking out the window onto Angell Street when I saw the door to the Mazursky Market open. A woman carrying a small grocery bag emerged.

I abandoned my place in the Starbucks line and headed outside. Sure enough, two more customers walked out of the market door. It had reopened. I crossed the street and peered into the store through the glass window. I could see Drew Mazursky working the cash register.

Drew's plea for me to back off the story now struck me as ironic. The devoted son who demanded discretion had called talk radio almost every night to broadcast a litany of his father's sins. If I had so easily recognized his voice, hadn't other people? Like his mother? His sister? His aunt? And I was the one who was supposed to feel guilty?

On Saturday mornings, the Mazursky Market always had doughboys to sell alongside the doughnuts. Enormous puffs of fried dough, they were delivered fresh by a Federal Hill bakery. People came from all over the neighborhood to get them while they were still warm. Even standing outside, I could smell the grease and powdered sugar.

From my vantage point, I could see the spot on the floor where the blood had been. The wood had been cleaned and polished and the toppled magazine rack righted. I closed my eyes and saw the wound in Barry's forehead oozing. Suddenly, I felt nauseous.

I ran a couple of fingers through my mostly uncombed hair. Why go in? It wasn't like I was prepared to cross-examine Drew Mazursky. Like I had an actual plan. The best thing to do would be to go home and come back when I'd showered and had a chance to think about what I was going to say.

The glass door swung open. A man leaving with three coffees in a tray leaned his back into the door to hold it open for me. There was a line of people at the register, and I could slink in behind them without Drew seeing me. If I didn't go in now, I might never get up the courage.

I ducked into the store, heading to the deli section in back, where the U-Serve coffee stand was set up. Crowded with people, the store was completely safe this time of day, I told myself. The least likely place in the world for a murder.

A woman I'd never seen before was working the deli counter, and another line of people waiting for her to make egg-and-bacon breakfast sandwiches had formed. Once these customers got their sandwiches, they had to go up to the register to pay for them. It could be ten minutes before there was a quiet moment in the store to talk to Drew.

I poured myself a large, vat-size coffee and was searching among the lids to snap on the right size when I saw another woman, this one wearing a shirt with a "YourCorporation" emblem on it, bring out a stack of premade salads.

I stared at the square, lidded containers, again feeling the plastic crushed in my hand. Time stopped and I felt as if I were coated in film. Customers chatted with each other, but I couldn't hear them. I saw them through a thick windshield. I was separated from everyone in the store, stuck in place, alone, waiting.

The moment stretched. My fist tightened on the plastic coffee lid. Someone coughed, breaking the sound barrier. And I realized that I'd been waiting for a gunshot.

My eyes darted back and forth, scanning the aisle. I looked for someone suspicious, with thick features or slouched posture. I couldn't help but think of the guy who'd been with Delria, the guy in the gray cap, with the thick, dark hair running down his neck. But there was no one thuglike in the store today: just a father in rumpled blue jeans and a baseball hat with a two-year-old at his side and, beyond them, two teenage boys with skateboards, heading toward the register.

I turned down a middle aisle, hoping to hide among the Italian canned goods and packaged breads until the crowd of customers thinned. I pretended to search among the variety of anchovy pastes, trying to slow my breathing, to get a grip and clear the bad programming from my brain.

I knew that I couldn't let myself give this fear its own life, allowing my imagination to invent a monster. I wasn't even completely certain that the man in the gray cap had even *been* with Delria and now I was letting him terrify me.

I put the anchovy paste back on the shelf. Clearly, it wasn't good for my mental health to hang around this market for too long. Memories were feeding the monster, nourishing the panic.

I needed to go to the register and pay for my coffee. If there were too many people around, I'd just say hello to Drew, reestablish myself as a regular customer, and get the hell out of there. I could come back later, when I was calm.

As I turned up the aisle to the front of the store, I halted at what had become a gridlock. Customers, coming at the register from all directions, clustered together, forming an uncertain line. I found myself pushed back, to the corkboard on the wall where Barry had pinned community notices. Among them, I saw a "VOTE NO on PROPOSITION #3" flyer in the trademark red and black colors. I could tell by the way the red lettering had faded to orange that the flyer had been hanging there exposed to the sunlight for a long time. For a moment, I was struck by the irony of Barry Mazursky, of all people, coming out against legalized gambling in Providence. Then I realized that Drew must have put it up.

I thought of his talk-radio passion. Andre of Cranston might be a loudmouth, but he'd been honestly devoted to stopping the casino-gambling referendum. If I could resurrect this passion in Drew, I might be able to get him to cooperate with my story.

At the register, Drew was bagging an unusually large order and didn't notice me until I put my coffee down on the counter and pointed to one of the remaining doughboys.

Throughout the transaction, he kept his eyes level with mine. His expression read: What do you want now? But he didn't speak except to ask me for two dollars and fifteen cents.

"Can we talk, later?" I asked, handing him the money.

"I have nothing to say." His eyes were now on whoever was standing behind me.

"There's been a development," I said.

His eyes returned to mine. "What kind of development?"

I struggled to think of something that had changed. I leaned forward and whispered, "Victor Delria is in a coma." It was lame, already reported in the newspaper.

Drew raised his voice so that all the customers could hear. "So?"

A woman standing behind me coughed impatiently and shifted her basket of groceries from one hand to the other. "So there may never be an arrest," I continued to whisper. "Especially not before the referendum election."

For a moment, I thought I saw a flicker of interest in his eyes, but maybe I imagined it. "Nothing I can do about it," he said in a disinterested voice.

Having overcome my anxiety, forced myself into the store, and waded through my panic in the anchovy aisle, I was not about to surrender now because of Drew's withering tone. "No, but I think getting out the real story could have an impact on the vote."

For a second, his eyes narrowed, as if he were considering this or trying to gauge my sincerity. But just as quickly, his face grew hard; he wasn't going to fall for this kind of crap from a newspaper reporter.

"Right." He redirected his gaze to the woman behind me, gesturing for her to move up in line. She began unloading her cart on the counter, forcing me to step aside.

Two other people moved into line behind her, and all three of them looked at me. I became aware of my oversize sweatshirt and uncombed hair. Drew's gaze shifted from me to his other customers, a deliberate eye movement that said he didn't really know me, but could tell I was a nut.

I racked my brain for something else to say, something that would make him want to deal with me. I leaned forward on the counter as if to say something confidential, but knocked a box of Jell-O with my elbow. It flew off the counter and onto the floor.

Drew coughed a derisive laugh.

"Excuse me?" the woman with the groceries said. She was wearing a tennis skirt over warm-up pants.

"Sorry." I bent down to retrieve the Jell-O. "Just one minute," I pleaded as I handed the woman the box.

"You're holding up the line," Drew said.

I leaned forward again, more carefully this time, attempting to get close enough so I wouldn't have to shout, but he backed away, practically into the magazine rack. "I have a better description of him now," I heard myself say.

"Better description of who?" a man in back asked another customer. Drew threw up his hands as if he had no idea what I was talking about. He looked at the other customers for sympathy; he couldn't believe all that he had to endure.

Blood flowed to my face. This writing me off as a nuisance, a nut, was infuriating. I wanted to make Drew take me seriously, make him understand. "Don't you want to know the description?" I asked.

"Not really," Drew said.

"He looked like a fish," I said, in a voice loud enough to include all the customers in line. For emphasis, I repeated: "A fish." Fully convinced of my insanity now, the woman in the tennis skirt put her hand over her mouth to quash a snicker.

I smiled a bit crazily as I strained to remember how Andre had said it on Leonard's show: "Not just any fish. He looked like one of the big fish who eat the little fish."

"There's lots of *those* around," someone behind me remarked.

"I heard a guy on *talk radio* describe him as a shark."

The other customers looked both baffled and amused, but

the alarm sounded for Drew. His expression froze. His breath may have stopped.

"A shark you could spot from fifty feet," I said. "A shark with *real big fins.*"

"Later," Drew had said between clenched teeth. "Later, we can talk."

We agreed on three o'clock. I waved to the other customers, who looked confused by the exchange, and I headed home to shower. I went to the newsroom, made a few phone calls to the police, borrowed a staff recorder to make a copy of the tape, and got back to the market in the lull of midafternoon.

The store was practically empty. Drew was sitting on a stool behind the cash register, smoking a cigarette and watching a hockey game on one of those tiny portable television sets. He stubbed out the cigarette as I opened the door.

I handed him a copy of the tape of Leonard's show. He took it nervously, the evidence of all his passion, and gazed for a moment at the inner reel. He turned it over, as if it might look different on the flip side.

"I realize you're still in shock," I continued, "and you don't want to talk to me now. But do me a favor and just listen to the tape. Think about how much you wanted to stop casino gambling—and about the ammunition you have now."

Suddenly, the young boy I'd seen in Drew was gone. He looked aged by conflict and compromise. He reached over and snapped off the television set. The store was completely silent.

"I lost my brother a few years back. I know it's hard when you lose someone so suddenly—"

He shook his head as if to correct me. As if to say that he'd been expecting something like this to happen for years. "My father's been in a lot of trouble."

I said nothing, hoping that if I remained absolutely still, he would continue. Drew shifted his gaze beyond me, into the aisles of the store. Clearly, he had an inventory of painful memories stocked on those shelves.

As I flipped the notebook open, Drew stared at the clean page. "The guy from the attorney general's office keeps telling us not to talk to anyone but him."

Was that my imagination, or was there resentment in his tone?

"You're talking about Matt Cavanaugh?" I asked.

He nodded and pulled back from the counter. "Everything I say to you, everything that gets put in the paper, hurts *his* case later down the road."

There was no mistaking the meaning. Drew resented that Matt was so focused on *his case.* I had to be cool. I had to make sure I didn't sound completely focused on *my* story, my shot at the investigative team. "I don't know what the AG's office is up to, but I have a source who tells me that Providence police will deliberately stall this investigation until after the referendum vote." I kept my tone level. "Do you want that?"

Drew met my eye. "You know from that tape I don't want that."

Pressing him now would be a mistake. He'd see through any self-serving claims I made about this being an opportunity, a chance to effect his politics. Instead, I walked to the wall where I'd found the faded "VOTE NO on PROPOSITION #3" flyer. "Did your father put this up, or did you?" I asked.

I didn't hear his answer. Behind me, a door opened. Startled, I whirled around, an automatic response, a memory, a flinch. I heard the door shut and the shuffle of feet. I looked up. It was only an elderly man. He gave Drew a puzzled look and headed down the aisle.

"You all right?" Drew asked me. There was recognition in

his expression, and I knew he'd flinched a few times in his own life.

"Yeah." But my heart rate had not returned to normal.

He glanced down at the tape I'd given him, sitting on the counter. I could see him wondering exactly which stories it told, how much I already knew about his father. Maybe he decided it didn't matter. When he looked up, his expression was not one of defeat but of resolve.

"You've got to promise to leave out the part about talk radio."

"You haven't adequately addressed the cover-up angle," Dorothy said. The assistant editor working the Saturday shift had called her at home, and she'd come into the newsroom twenty-five minutes later.

"But I've got two sources saying that Mazursky was killed because of gambling problems. One's a family member—just like Nathan asked." We both had a copy of my story in our hands.

"Nathan also made it clear that there was no point running this kind of story unless we can prove the mayor's deliberately stalling the investigation for political reasons."

"Jonathan hasn't been very helpful," I said.

There was complete silence. Dorothy knew, as I'd learned, that Jonathan was not known for being a "team player." He was working his own investigation, which involved some woman who said she'd paid a cash bribe to Lopresti's right-hand man to get her son into the Providence Police Training Academy. Clearly, Jonathan didn't want to waste any time on a competing corruption story that might upstage his.

"I got a confirmation from the son, for Christ's sake."

She didn't answer. She was standing at my desk with the printout of the story still in her hands. She grabbed a Bic pen that was stuck inside the spiral ring of my notebook, oblivious that it was severely chewed, and began poring over the draft for about the fifth time.

I tried to relax. Tried to tell myself that if the story got held another couple of days, it wouldn't be the worst thing in the world. But my adrenaline had not stopped charging since I'd left the Mazursky Market. Getting this information out of Drew Mazursky was a major accomplishment. A part of me worried that Matt or maybe Nadine Mazursky might get to him. That the phone would ring and it would be Drew trying to take back everything he said.

"What are police saying?"

"Holstrom's not in today. The guy filling in, Antonelli, said he couldn't comment, but Evan DiMartino is working on getting me a source inside the police department."

"But nothing yet?"

I shook my head.

"I don't know, Hallie. I'm not sure how I feel about this."

It was not a good idea to push her. But this was such a high-impact story; it *had* to lead the Sunday paper. "Maybe you could call Nathan."

"I already did. I got his machine."

"I know it's risky," I said. "But this is a big murder. Police haven't made an arrest, and we have two sources—one the freaking son—saying Mazursky was in trouble with loan sharks. Feared for his life."

Dorothy pursed her lips in that odd way of hers and began walking back to her desk, rereading my copy the whole way. I picked up the phone and dialed the cell phone number Evan DiMartino had given me.

He was at the dog track with two guys from production. The connection was full of static, and I could barely make out that it was him. I told him I was on deadline and asked if he'd gotten any information for me. There was more static, followed by silence. For a minute, I thought our connection had gone.

"I left you two messages on your cell phone last night," he said, sounding irritated.

I had a habit of not recharging the battery. It was completely dead inside the glove compartment of my Honda.

"What?"

"How the hell you think you're gonna be an investigative reporter when you don't check on your information?"

"I'm checking now. Please, Evan . . ."

There was another silence. Then he relented. "I got a good source who says the day you saw Errico, that Saturday, he put in a call to Sideways Carpaccia. You know who that is?"

"No."

"Look him up in the database. He's a capo for Junior. Runs Warwick. Anyway, word is that Errico put in a personal call to him to find out if Mazursky's murder was sanctioned."

"Was it?" I reached for a notebook on the desk.

"No definitive word, but the next day, Holstrom was taken off the case and it was moved into Errico's office. You remember what I told you about Errico?"

"He only handles organized-crime cases." I was scribbling furiously, scrambling to keep up.

"Okay, that coupled with the e-mail I sent you, you owe me coffee for a month."

E-mail I couldn't have missed. Whenever you logged on to a newsroom computer to write, the message alert blinked like mad until you read all incoming e-mail.

"I didn't get an e-mail from you."

"Not on your computer. I put a hard copy in your mailbox, or don't you check that either?"

"The copyboy didn't know I was working downtown. He's been forwarding all my mail to South County."

"Then drive down there." Evan's voice was hard and impatient. "Now."

Dorothy called Jonathan Frizell in on his day off to help verify the authenticity of the e-mail. With the help of one of his sources, as well as the systems department of the *Chronicle*, we were able to confirm that the e-mail, sent to the police chief, came from Billy Lopresti's home server.

Tom,

Release nothing on Mazursky murder until you hear from me. Imperative no leaks. We need to keep a tight lid until Nov. 6 for obvious reasons. Counting on you.

W.A.L.

I wondered if it was Evan's brother, inside the department, who had such access to the chief's personal e-mail, but Jonathan said that it could have been anybody, a secretary, a janitor, someone in the systems department. "Tommy boy's not a real popular chief. He's an old friend of Billy's—from the neighborhood. Missing a few key management skills."

Jonathan was able to get through to his source inside the mayor's office. She told him that Lopresti had taken an unusual interest in the Mazursky investigation and had called both Police Chief Thomas Linnehan and the attorney general. "He was really worked up about it," the source said. "Over the top."

The phone at my desk rang at about eight o'clock, and I practically jumped out of my chair. The mayor was away this weekend at a four-day mayoral conference about casino gambling that was being held in Las Vegas. After several attempts to track down his press secretary, I finally got the name of the hotel where Billy Lopresti was staying and left an urgent message with the front desk that he return my call. I'd been waiting for more than an hour.

"Jesus, these conferences are dull," said the mayor, without introduction. "I've only got about five minutes before I got to go to the banquet. The food is not so great out here either."

I explained that I was working on a story about the Barry Mazursky murder. He was quiet, as if to imply that he couldn't begin to fathom why I'd have questions about this for him, so I played along. "The murder in the market in Wayland Square. Last week."

"I know which one it was. Senseless. You're from the *Chronicle*? How come I've never heard of you before?" He made it sound like an omission on his part.

"I'm new."

"How new?"

"Four months."

"Ah," he said, as if this filled in some very important blanks.

I launched into an explanation for my call, telling him that I'd been in the market the night of the shooting, that it had been especially quick, and that Barry Mazursky's son was charging that his father's murder was tied to casino gambling.

The reply was quick. "So you think I shouldn't be going to conferences, then? Scrap the referendum. And the Pier Project. What the hell? Whose idea was this, anyway?" He was chuckling into the phone.

The sarcasm in this was at just the right level, not so sharp as to be insulting, but not so subtle as to be misread. It had the intended effect of unbalancing me, making me question myself as to how best to proceed.

"I'm sorry about Mazursky," he said, his tone suddenly respectful. "Horrible thing."

People who were good at the charm thing didn't ooze it, they dribbled it so that the personality didn't overwhelm you so much as catch you off guard. I found myself suddenly liking the mayor and feeling bad about reading his private e-mail.

"But I think whatever questions you have are best answered by the chief," Lopresti said. "Don't want to miss the canned fruit cocktail."

"Just one more question," I sputtered, reaching for the hard copy of the e-mail memo on my desk. I read from it verbatim. Told him it would be used in a story we were running tomorrow and that I had called to offer him the opportunity to explain.

He muffled the receiver and said something to someone in his hotel room. Whatever he said had the same cadence and number of syllables as "Jesus fucking Christ." Into the phone, Billy Lopresti said, "I'm not going to comment on a police investigation."

"Would you care to comment on your e-mail?"

"It has nothing to do with the referendum."

I read the last line of the e-mail to him again, reminding him that he'd actually specified the November 6 date. There was silence on the other end of the phone line. After a moment, he said, "That wasn't a reference to the referendum election."

"Then what is the November sixth date a reference to?"

"This has nothing to do with the referendum," he repeated.

"Just a coincidence with the dates? Then tell me, what other meaning does November sixth have?"

Lopresti did not like to be grilled. "What department did you say you worked for?"

"South County bureau."

"Then how did you get hold of my personal e-mail? That was a confidential memo, not a press release. That little piss-ant Frizell, I bet he had something to do with this."

He muffled the phone again, consulting with someone else in the room. The words were unintelligible, but I could hear the emotional rise in Billy Lopresti's tone as he argued with whatever advice he got.

When a source got heated, you had to respond with excessive calm. "I used to be an investigative reporter with the *Ledger*, in Boston," I said, in one of those even, public-radio tones. "And as I said before, I was in the back of the store when Mazursky got murdered. I know it wasn't an armed robbery."

"What? That makes you a homicide detective now? Wrong. You're a reporter who's got half the story. A reporter trying to get on the front page with some new conspiracy allegation. Well, it's going to blow up in your face. I'm telling you, that e-mail had absolutely nothing to do with the referendum."

"Then tell me, what does it have to do with? What?"

But halfway through this question, I realized he'd already hung up the phone.

The Providence Morning Chronicle

Local Businessman's Death Tied to Gambling
By Hallie A. Ahern
Chronicle Staff Reporter

Barry Mazursky, the man shot to death at the Wayland Square store last week, was a compulsive gambler who feared for his life, according to his son.

"He wasn't a victim of a random armed robbery," said Andrew Mazursky of Cranston. "My father was a victim of compulsive gambling."

Barry Mazursky had been beaten up twice in the last eight months by thugs associated with loan sharks and was determined to defend himself the next time he was assaulted. "That's why he had that gun in the store," the younger Mazursky said. "For self-defense."

More than a week after the shooting, Providence police still won't confirm whether the man they have in custody, Victor Delria, of Central Falls, is a suspect. Delria was thrown from the windshield of his car following a police chase and is in a coma at Rhode Island Hospital.

Police have said they believe Mazursky was murdered resisting an armed robbery, but have not released the results of forensics reports. But off-the-record sources inside the Providence Police Department say that the investigation was transferred to the organized-crime unit after mob sources were queried about whether Mazursky's murder was a sanctioned hit.

A confidential source aligned with the antigambling forces charged that the mayor was stalling the results of the investigation until after the November 6 referendum election. The *Chronicle* yesterday obtained a confidential memo from Mayor Billy Lopresti, a proponent of the casino-gambling referendum, to Police Chief Thomas Linnehan, asking that the matter be kept quiet until after November 6.

Lopresti denied the memo had anything to do with the referendum election, but would not offer an alternative explanation of the November 6 date.

Opponents argue that both compulsive gambling and personal bankruptcies will rise dramatically, and that the Mazursky murder is typical of the kind of crime that will escalate if Providence becomes home to a new casino.

"Casinos bring violent crime. They bring organized crime and they bring white-collar crime," Marjorie Pittman, chairwoman of Citizens for a Stronger Rhode Island, said yesterday. "For obvious reasons, the mayor doesn't want anyone reminded of *that* a week before the referendum election."

According to a confidential source, Mazursky, a regular at both Foxwoods and Mohegan Sun, got into trouble with loan sharks two years ago, shortly after an alleged $75,000 discrepancy was found in accounting books when he was treasurer of the Veterans' Homeless Shelter Foundation in Providence.

Board minutes confirm that the issue was raised at two separate meetings, and Mazursky resigned his position as
See Gambling Ties, page B-24

CHAPTER
12

Sunday morning at six a.m. it was so dark that I turned over to go back to sleep. But then, an ignition clicked, the engine turned inside, and thoughts began to rev: My story was running page one today.

It was too early to buy the paper, so I found my thicker running tights in an unpacked box of winter clothes, put a turtleneck underneath my sweatshirt, and searched for my running shoes. Dressing for a cold-weather run was tricky. You had to wear enough warm clothing to get yourself outside, but not so much that you wanted to throw it all off by the time you reached the boulevard.

I was met by a bracing wind just outside my door, but for the first quarter mile, it was at my back, an extra push going my way. My brain was still fuzzy from sleep and my feet drifted across the sidewalk without detailing the distance or effort of my legs. There was nothing quite as satisfying as a story that would run above the fold. With a 24-point headline. On an issue that would galvanize an entire city. Hell, maybe an entire state.

The miles seemed to pass quickly, painlessly. By the time

I'd turned onto the boulevard and begun the trek homeward, my muscles had warmed up so nicely that my stride grew long and fluid.

Another pleasant thought occurred to me: Carolyn had told me a couple of days ago that there was actually a step-wage increase of almost $150 a week for reporters on the investigative team because they worked longer, more irregular hours. Six hundred dollars a month would go a long way to help me pay off the loan to my mother and some of those credit card bills.

If only I hadn't blown all my Mohegan Sun winnings that night in Foxwoods. But I didn't like thinking about losing, so I fastened my gaze on an enormous maple tree in the distance, increased my speed to a sprint, and silently vowed never to gamble anywhere near my mother again.

Soon after I passed the maple, endorphins began to take over. I entered a state that's called the zone, a place of pleasantly narrow focus that obliterates the periphery of all possible agitations. I'm not sure how long I remained there before awareness crept in and I again felt my legs lifting, lungs expanding, heart pounding. And then, in an instant, I became aware of the world, of another presence, of the faint sound of other footsteps displacing the cinder on the path.

The cinder crackled in the distance. Whoever he was behind me, he was increasing his speed. Turning slightly, I spotted a man hooded in gray sweats on the path, running fifty yards back. Men hated it when you ran faster than they did, and always tried to catch up and pass.

The morning was stubbornly dim, as if the sun would never fully rise, and the gold and red leaves were already beginning to look muted. I looked over my shoulder and made out that the other runner was tall. Long legs would give him an advantage.

Something about the long legs made me turn a third time. It wasn't just another runner. It was Matt Cavanaugh in gray sweats. I shifted up a gear. I was feeling particularly light today, and if there was anybody I'd like to leave in the dust, it was Matt Cavanaugh.

I was running into the wind now, and the cold air was a force to be reckoned with. I kept my head down, fighting the resistance. I wondered how much of a runner Matt was—I'd never seen him running on the boulevard before. Of course, a lack of experience wouldn't stop him from trying to prove he could beat me. I focused on my elbows, bringing them behind me faster to increase my foot speed.

The path ended and I plunged onto the asphalt of Butler Street. In the distance, I could make out a single car, stopping for the traffic light on Angell Street. My side was beginning to ache and my lungs felt tight. I glanced over my shoulder again. Matt was only about fifteen yards away. The needle in my side began to shoot pain down my legs. Stay cool, Hallie. Focused. Sprint speed.

Crossing the road, I headed to the sidewalk. I had to slow down to slip my body sideways between two parked cars. I cleared the hedge of metal and jumped onto the curb.

Gnarled tree roots had grown through the cement, and I stumbled on a crack. Throwing my hands in front of me, I struggled for balance. Please, God, don't let me fall on my face in front of Matt Cavanaugh. I caught myself and righted to center. As if in slow motion, the earth settled underneath me.

"Hallie!" The hood of Matt's sweatshirt was pushed back, revealing the dark eyes and the off-center nose. Sweat had collected on his forehead and he wiped it with his forearm. Bending forward, he put his hands to his knees, as if to baby a cramp. "Jesus, you're fast," he said between breaths.

My heart was still running the race, but I sucked in measured amounts of air and tried not to sound winded. "Well, I wasn't going to let you *beat* me."

He was standing erect now, taking me in, the whole picture: racing tights, sweatshirt, ponytail. He seemed to find something about it amusing.

"What?" I asked. "Don't you ever race people on the street?"

"Just a little competitive?" he asked, but he was smiling and sounding appreciative.

"I guess." I made an effort to sound casual, but I was pleased. He was looking at me with sincere admiration, appropriately impressed with my foot pace. I bent down as if to check a shoelace and played with the knot an extra minute to get my breathing fully under control. He stood over me, waiting. His legs *were* really long.

I took another breath and stood up. "You run a lot?"

"Every day," he said, "but usually in the evenings."

"That's why I've never seen you before. Didn't know you were a runner."

"If you did, would you have stopped?" he asked. "Or run even faster?"

At first I thought he was still joking, but then I noticed that his tone had changed. He was looking at me with meaning, a meaning that eluded me. Flushed with new heat, I looked down at my sneakers, unsure of what he meant by this or how I should respond.

And then: "How come you didn't call me?"

He made it sound so plaintive, so personal, that for one brief moment, my thinking blipped: Had I missed a cue? He was the one who'd taken my number, not the other way around. But luckily, I kept my mouth shut, resisted the temptation to blather. Because when I looked up from my sneakers, I saw that he'd shifted his posture and crossed his arms. I realized that we were talking business.

Another flash of understanding: Matt must have the *Chronicle* home-delivered to his apartment. He'd already read my story about Barry Mazursky. Obviously, he wasn't happy about it.

I crossed my own arms. "I didn't call you because it was Saturday," I said.

"I work Saturday," he said.

Should I have called the attorney general's office? On a *Saturday*? Just to get another *no comment*? "Why should I call you? You never answer my questions."

"I would've liked a chance to respond to this . . . this . . . *conjecture* before you put it in the paper."

Conjecture. He meant bullshit but was trying to be professional. Suddenly, I was angry. "No comments" like Matt Cavanaugh never wanted to trust you with anything close to real information but always wanted a chance to muck up your story afterward.

"Barry Mazursky's murder had nothing to do with loan sharks," he said, sounding so earnest that I almost believed him. Or at least I almost believed that he believed what he said. "Honest."

Maybe there was too much earnestness, or too much in him that I wanted to trust, but I knew I had to check myself. Matt Cavanaugh, the flirt at the dairy case, the master of sincerity, was a political animal. His job demanded that he work with Providence police day in and day out. If they wanted to stall—or let's just call it postpone—an investigation for a couple of measly weeks, what difference would it make to him? Justice was slow, anyway.

He was still staring at me, eyes level, determined that I believe him.

Was he trying to charm me? Was I supposed to melt into his sincerity and print a retraction? When I had the victim's son telling me otherwise? When I had it all on tape?

I returned the same deep, heart-to-heart look and said, "You want to tell me about it? Give me the real reason Barry was murdered? I'll be happy to do another story. Let's go back to my apartment; I'll get my notebook."

I don't know what I expected from him, anger or more amusement. I got neither. Instead, he shook his head and in a regretful tone that I wouldn't be able to get out of my head all day, he said, "Try to believe me, Hallie, the more I tell you, the worse off you'll be."

Leonard was all accolades. He called later that morning after I'd already bought the paper and reread my story several times. I'd moved on to more mundane matters, and when the phone rang, I was sitting on my bedroom floor collecting the dirty laundry from the bottom of my closet and sorting it. Not by color, but by urgency.

"My phone lines will be jammed all night!" Leonard's voice boomed with enthusiasm. "You think I could book you as a guest?"

A guest? The towel in my hand dropped into the nearest pile. "Really?"

"You doing anything tonight?"

My heart was suddenly pounding like a piano. A guest? On Leonard of *Late Night*? I knew enough to wait until the song settled, to force myself to hear the low, cautionary notes. I didn't want to make any wrong moves, blow my chances for the investigative team now. "I'll have to check with my editor."

"Check," Leonard said. "But they can't stop you. Not by contract. We have this issue with the sports reporters all the time. And it's good advertising for the paper. Just call me by five o'clock, and promise me you won't do interviews with any other stations, radio or TV, first. Okay?"

Any other radio or television stations? Was he serious? I was soaring somewhere over the apartment building, above Providence, Rhode Island. It might not be Boston or New York, but suddenly, it was a spectacular view.

"You promise?" he pressed.

I gave him my word and threw all my laundry back into a single, unsorted heap on the floor. Then I got dressed in the only clean shirt and pair of jeans I had left and headed down to the newsroom to find someone who knew where I could find Dorothy Sacks on a Sunday afternoon.

Dorothy had no husband, no family, no life outside the newspaper, according to Carolyn, but on this particular Sunday in late October when I desperately needed to talk to her, she didn't answer her home phone, her cell phone, or her pager.

"Sometimes," said Roger, the weekend-shift editor who had given me Dorothy's phone numbers, "sometimes she comes in Sunday night with leaves all over her jeans, wearing these big, ugly hiking boots."

"Maybe I should try Nathan at home."

Roger, an extremely thin, lanky man who had worked nights and weekends forever, looked alarmed. "On a Sunday? Nathan? You kidding? He'll freak."

I tried Dorothy's pager again and read the entire Sunday paper from cover to cover waiting for her to respond. It was almost five o'clock when Roger looked over and noticed that I was still there.

Roger was an official of the union and didn't like it when he thought anyone was working off the clock. "I'm telling you. They can't stop you, by contract."

I must have looked unconvinced because he added, "You want to do it, do it. The publisher won't mind."

"Really?"

"Why would he? You're reminding everyone that the *Chronicle* broke another story. It'll sell papers."

With embarrassing admiration, Leonard introduced me to his producer as "the reporter who broke the Mazursky murder."

Robin, the producer, was in her early twenties, with short, curly hair and about twenty earrings. She cocked her head slightly. Was she supposed to be impressed? With an amused expression, she guided me to a seat in the studio directly facing Leonard and instructed me on the correct way to use the microphone.

There was nothing haggard about Leonard tonight. He was wearing the latest in microfiber warm-up suits, and his face was flush with color, as if he'd just jumped off his bicycle. "After that story of yours this morning, the phones are gonna be lit up like Christmas," he said, brandishing a copy of the *Chronicle*. And then, as if it were some kind of mantra, he repeated it to Robin. "Lit like Christmas! Lit like Christmas!"

She offered a nod to his good spirits as she ducked back into the production booth. With the show about to begin, the microphone before me seemed suddenly ominous. "What if I stutter or something?" I heard myself ask.

Leonard grinned. "Stutter? You didn't stutter once in the three months that you called in, you want to stutter tonight, go ahead and stutter. People don't care. They'll forgive a stutter. Just don't go on and on like some kind of windbag."

"That's *his* role," Robin called over her shoulder.

Leonard nodded good-naturedly. "Yes, that is my role." Then, catching some kind of cue from Robin, his expression changed. A look of intense concentration came over his face as he listened intently to whatever was coming through his headset. He began introducing the show. The topic. His guest: *Hallie Ahern.*

He left out the part about me being the bureau reporter in South County. Instead, he spouted off every award I'd ever won in Boston, startling me with his research, and making me sound like such *a big deal.* "Welcome to the show, Hallie."

My throat tightened. "Thank you," I said, barely getting it out. "I'm glad to be here."

Still standing, with several microphones of various sizes before him, he started reading directly from my *Chronicle* story. His voice was deep, grave, reverential. Had I really written all that? It sounded so powerful, so earth-shattering, so conspiratorial with all those pauses and added emphasis.

"Didn't I tell you something wasn't right in the Wayland Square shooting? Didn't I tell you cops were dragging their heels, covering something up?" he asked. "Listen to this . . ."

To Leonard's right, mounted on the wall, was a computer monitor. Within minutes, text began appearing with identifying bits of information about each of the callers Robin had typed in. The lighting was a dim fluorescent. I squinted to read:

"Magda of North Scituate: 'Gambling will ruin the state.'"

"Corey of Providence wants state police instead of Providence police to investigate the murder."

"Ed of Tiverton says the *Chronicle* blows everything out of proportion."

My stomach tightened on that last remark, but Leonard decimated Ed of Tiverton in about two minutes, calling him one of "Billy's groupies." With a mischievous smile, he concluded the call with the first few bars of the "Tammy's in Love" song.

Leonard flailed his arms like a conductor, waving people on

in their outrage at the slowness of the police investigation, cutting them off when they voiced doubt that there was a deliberate conspiracy. "Billy will do anything, anything to get this gambling referendum to pass," he said. "You've got to believe he doesn't want us thinking about the mob being alive and well on Atwell's Avenue. He doesn't want us thinking about a successful businessman like Barry Mazursky losing it all, even his life, because of casino gambling. Right, Hallie?"

I was growing uncomfortable. I'd only lived in Providence for four months. Spoken to the mayor only once on the phone. How was I supposed to know what Billy Lopresti thought? "Well, I have heard him admit that compulsive gambling comes with the territory."

Leonard gave me an exasperated look, and I could see that evenhandedness was not a part of the program. "You don't have to set aside a special fund for compulsive gambling if you don't create more compulsive gambling in the first place. Legalizing a casino is just going to mean more Barry Mazurskys. Gloria from Warwick, welcome to the program."

Gloria from Warwick began by gushing about how great Leonard was, how he alone really cared about Rhode Island, and about how he was going to save the state from corruption. Leonard rolled his eyes as if embarrassed, but I noticed that he didn't cut any of it off. Through the glass window, I could see Robin, in the production booth. She put her finger to her temple in a gesture to Leonard that said: If she had to listen to much more, she'd shoot herself.

"What I wanna know," said Gloria, finally getting to the point, "is how many other people steal from these charities that are always hitting the rest of us up for money? How come they let board members just put the money back? How come they don't get arrested for that? Doesn't anybody in this state care about the little guy who sends in the donation checks?"

Praised or not, Leonard didn't want to talk about Barry Mazursky's crimes. He immediately started scanning the computer monitor for new callers. "Compulsive gambling does crazy things to people, Gloria. Remember, Barry Mazursky was a victim, let's let him rest in peace." He hit another button and clicked her off the line. "Tony from Providence, welcome to the program."

"How did this reporter find out the mayor was involved in this?" Tony asked. "I mean, how do newspaper reporters get their hands on the mayor's personal e-mail, anyway? Isn't that a violation of privacy? And how do we know for sure that Providence police aren't just screwing up by themselves?"

"Sources have their own reasons for leaking information to the newspapers," I began. "As a public figure—"

"Because who else but the mayor has his entire career riding on this?" Leonard said, cutting me off. "Who else glides around town with casino executives and has this kind of influence with the police department? You think Billy wants to bite the bullet and reduce his bloated budget? Oh no. He needs cold, hard cash to keep pushing the renaissance and promoting himself. He's like a slot machine himself, he *craves* casino revenue."

"So how did the *Chronicle* find out?" Tony asked.

I opened my mouth to answer, but Leonard waved me silent. "Our guest, Hallie Ahern, is the reporter who was actually there in the store when Barry Mazursky was murdered. She's been saying from the very beginning that this wasn't just an armed robbery. That whoever killed Barry Mazursky that night came in with the express purpose of shooting him.

That police are not being aggressive enough in this investigation."

"I didn't actually say that—"

"Oh, I read that story," Tony said. "You stepped in the blood, right?"

"Uh, yes, but—"

"Thank you, Tony, we have time for one more call before Hallie Ahern from the *Chronicle* has to leave. George on a cell phone, you're on WKZI with Leonard of *Late Night.*"

"I want to talk to the reporter—" I thought I heard him say. But his voice was low, and static cut off the last part of his sentence.

"George, we have a bad connection," Leonard said.

"—*Chronicle,*" was all I could hear.

"George, you must be in a dead area," Leonard said. "Maybe you should call back tomorrow night."

"I'm not calling back tomorrow," George said. "I'm just calling today to tell that *Chronicle* reporter—" His words dissolved, and for a moment, there was complete blankness. But I'd caught something hostile in his tone. Through the glass window of the production booth, I could see that Robin, too, had gotten the drift. She stood up and gestured to Leonard with a slice across the neck to cut off the caller. He ignored her.

"We're running out of time here, George, and this static is terrible," Leonard said. "News is up next. Quickly, George, what did you want to say?"

Robin was waving at him, but Leonard didn't sever the connection, didn't hit the button to disconnect the phone and cue the news. He gave George another second, another chance at the last word.

There was more static and then startling clarity. "I'll give you news to report," George said. "You tell that *Chronicle* bitch, she's next."

The station had a five-second delay and Robin edited the threat from the air. "Just some nut," Leonard said.

Robin agreed. "Usually, they threaten to kill Leonard."

But I was completely rattled, and they both knew it. Leonard offered to follow me home if I was scared, but I declined. I wasn't about to spend the night alone in my apartment wondering if George-on-the-cell-phone would make good on his threat. So instead, I called my mother from the station and told her the heat in my building wasn't working. Then I drove to Worcester in under forty-five minutes, watching my rearview mirror for lights the entire ride.

My mother still lived in the same modest colonial I'd grown up in, and she'd left a door to the garage open. I crept in, immediately locked the door behind me, and set the alarm before I climbed the stairs to my old room.

The quilted bedspread was turned down and my mother had put the day's *Worcester Telegram* on the nightstand, but I took no comfort in the welcome. I pulled down the blinds of both windows and left the light on in the closet. Just like when I was a kid, only now the monsters weren't in my head, they were threatening me on the radio.

Fully clothed under the blankets, I slept fitfully, waking up with a lurch at three A.M., wondering where I was. I sat up, hand on my heart, as if I could control the panic from the outside. Finally, my eyes adjusted to the dark and I made out a pleated lampshade on the bureau and three trophies lined up, side by side: high school swimming; sophomore, junior, and senior year. I was at home in my bedroom in Worcester. Safe.

But it took a full hour of talking to myself, reminding myself of how fear expanded at night, before I could pull my hand off my heart and trust myself in a horizontal position. Eventually, I drifted back to sleep.

Luckily, my mother had a garden-club meeting in the morning, so she had only a few minutes to scrutinize the dark circles under my eyes before she had to head to the senior center. "You're not sleeping again?" she asked, gathering her files and a foil-wrapped loaf of her apple bread.

My mother, who considered Walter her own personally canonized saint for having helped me through my sleeping-pill problem, would still never stop worrying about my insomnia, no matter how many years had passed.

I blamed my dark circles on the "buzz" of working late. In the old days, this would have elicited a lecture about my unhealthy "obsession" with my career, but ever since my hiatus from the business, my mother had decided I was happier and healthier obsessed. Luckily, it never occurred to her that I could write a story that might prompt a death threat.

In the middle of the night, it had seemed absolutely clear that someone was out to get me. If Barry Mazursky's murder was a hit, it meant there was an organization behind it: an organization that would want to protect its members from being identified in court by a witness. But in daylight, with the sunlight streaming into my mother's orderly kitchen, I was more inclined to believe Leonard and Robin. Surely it was a crank call. I mean, would a real, true mobster bother to tip you off ahead of time? On the radio? Wasn't that just a *little* unprofessional?

"Come back tonight if that landlord doesn't fix the heat," my mother said. "I'll make your favorite stuffed cabbage leaves with caraway seeds and we'll get a movie."

I nodded and she turned to go. But as she did, a pamphlet fell from one of her folders and slid on the floor. I picked it up and saw that it was from a real estate company. It was an assessment of how much my mother's house was worth.

My mother grabbed the pamphlet from me a little too swiftly and I got a strange feeling in my stomach. "You're not thinking about selling the house, are you?"

"It's getting to be a lot of work," she said matter-of-factly. "And they say those Briarwood condominiums are very nice."

Briarwood, an elderly housing complex? I was incredulous. "You're going to leave your gardens?"

She shrugged to express that at a certain age, one must accept such things. But there was something about the way she avoided my eyes and turned to the door. Something nervous and out of character. A lot of work? My mother could spend three solid hours wheeling piles of dirt from one garden to another and then come inside and cook a turkey dinner. She was also deadly suspicious of condominium fees, and I'd heard her say several times that she'd rather die than live anywhere surrounded by a bunch of old people. And then, I realized: My mother, a woman who never lied, was lying to me.

As she took her taupe-colored trench coat from the closet, my mother's usual steady movements were rushed. The belt to her coat fell to the floor and she scrambled to pick it up.

"What's going on? Why are you selling the house?" I asked.

"Hallie, please, I'm going to be late for my meeting." With obvious agitation, she crushed the cloth belt into a ball, stuffed it into a pocket, and put her coat on. She yanked her purse off the hook by the door, and heaved it over her shoulder.

I thought suddenly of that night at Foxwoods, how all those slot-machine coins had weighed down her handbag.

"Oh my God, Mom. You haven't gotten yourself into trouble gambling, have you?"

She stopped, clearly stunned. But when she turned, it was not with the expression of someone who'd been found out. It was with the expression of someone who couldn't believe her own daughter could be so stupid. "How could you possibly suggest I'd be so irresponsible? Didn't I show you the cosmetic bags?"

"Then what? What on earth would make you want to move?"

My mother had something hard and tight inside her that rarely yielded to interrogation. But now, she sighed. "It's very expensive maintaining a house like this, Hallie."

This wasn't it, and we both knew it. My mother and my father had paid off the mortgage years ago. And it was clear from the chronically slow drain in the upstairs shower and the aging stairway carpeting that my mother didn't lavish a lot of money on home maintenance.

She met my eyes, challenging my disbelief. My mother was fierce about her independence, and I wouldn't have been surprised if she'd turned on her heel and stormed out the door. But she didn't. An expression of futility crossed her face and she sighed again. "You have no idea how many medical bills I still have to pay from your father's illness."

She gestured toward the metal file cabinet she kept in the kitchen. "Sixty-five thousand dollars for treatments insurance wouldn't cover. The accountant suggested I take out a mortgage." She added, "You know how I hate mortgages." A wisp of hair escaped from a bun she wore at her neck and she swiped at it. "I'm too old for these kinds of problems. So I thought, why not just sell the house? Get out from under?"

She said this in an apologetic tone, as if she were letting me down. I wanted to cover my face with my hands in shame.

How long had she been struggling with this burden? How clueless and self-centered had I been? But I couldn't make it worse by letting her see how guilty I felt. So instead, I hugged her and told her that any decision she made was fine with me. "Just don't rush into anything, okay?"

"I never rush," she said, pulling away and recovering a bit of her fierceness. She lifted herself into her shoulders and headed to the door. And then, as if our conversation had never taken place, she turned and pointed to the frying pan of scrambled eggs she'd left on the stove, letting it be known that it would be a personal insult if I didn't finish them.

When she was gone, I stood staring out the picture window at the gardens, lovingly mulched with a thick layer of straw to protect root systems from frost. My mother needed money to pay my father's medical bills and I couldn't help her. I was thirty-five years old and still nothing but a drain.

After quickly wolfing down the eggs and thoroughly washing the pan so my mother wouldn't rewash it when she got home, I told myself that the only thing to do was to head to the newsroom. This was not the time to cower in fear, but to capitalize. I'd just broken an important story; I'd been on the front page, above the fold, and a guest on talk radio. I needed that job on the investigative team and that step-raise. In deliberate mimicry, I lifted myself into my shoulders the way my mother had and headed upstairs to change.

Midmorning, the newsroom was always a hive of high energy, desks full, phones ringing, keyboards clicking. But something special was going on, I could feel it as soon as I got off the elevator.

It was like going from an air-conditioned room into the heat. A story of some sort was fueling the room. About a dozen reporters gathered around the city desk, attention riveted on the three televisions that were hung on a shelf suspended from the ceiling. I saw Evan standing, arms folded, in the outermost part of the ring.

"What's going on?"

Evan looked at me twice. I'd gone home first to shower, and since I had almost no clean clothes left in my closet, I'd been forced to put on a cotton oxford shirt with a button missing at the wrist and a wool skirt I wore only for sober events like funerals. It was a bit more formal than my usual reporter attire, but it seemed better than asking for a promotion in yesterday's blue jeans.

"A bunch of people are at city hall protesting the mayor's support of the referendum."

"How many?"

"They're saying a couple hundred." The way everyone was looking at me, there was only one implication.

"Because of my story?"

"And the radio show," he said and gestured to the televisions. "Didn't you see the press conference this morning?"

"The mayor?"

"And Providence police."

There was no way I could have anticipated a rebuttal press conference only twenty-four hours after the story first hit the street. Still, I wished to God I hadn't let my fear run me out of town. "I slept at my mom's last night, in Worcester," I explained.

"Nathan's looking for you." Evan gestured to the front of the newsroom, toward the Fishbowl, which was standing room only with editors and assistants. "You've created quite a stir," he said, in a dry way that could have been either a compliment or a criticism.

I glanced one last time at the television. The camera had shifted to three women carrying placards.

NO MORE VICTIMS
NO MORE BARRY MAZURSKYS
VOTE NO ON PROPOSITION #3

Creating a protest had to be a good thing, right? Galvaniz-
ing the public, wasn't that what journalism was about? Still,
I wished to God I'd seen that press conference.

Marcy Kittner stuck her head out of the Fishbowl, looking
for someone. I waved to her, and by the way she started
waving back, I knew she'd been looking for me. Everyone
seemed to be watching me make my way up the newsroom.
As I approached the Fishbowl, Marcy practically grabbed me
by the arm and pulled me inside. She glanced briefly at my
blue skirt. "Apparently, you were on *Late Night* with Leonard
last night?"

There was no missing her tone, but I refused to cower.

"I tried to call you," I said to Dorothy, who was sitting directly across from Nathan.

"I know," she said sadly.

"Didn't anyone tell you to stay away from that lunatic?"
Marcy said. "He tries to lure in new reporters."

Lure in new reporters? What did that mean? "Roger told
me it was okay to do the show. That it sold papers."

"Oh Christ," Nathan said, without looking at me. He wrote
something down on a piece of paper.

"It's true, the publicity can be good," Dorothy said. "But
you've got to be able to hold your own."

I was ragged from lack of sleep, but what had I missed?
Leonard might have extrapolated a bit, but I hadn't said anything that was so horribly wrong. "I held my own."

There was another exchange of looks. Now I was starting
to get mad. "Did any of you actually listen to the whole
show?"

"I listened to most of it," Marcy said.

"Anybody else?" Were they relying on Marcy's interpretation?

"I didn't listen to the radio show," Nathan said. "But I got the call from the mayor's office this morning, and I saw the press conference this morning in which they denounced the *Chronicle* for 'shoddy reporting.'"

"I didn't expect the mayor to be happy with my story," I said quietly. "Providence police either."

"We didn't expect them to be happy with the story," Nathan said, "but we didn't expect them to be able to refute every single thing in it."

In fact, the police did not refute every single thing I wrote in my story. But it didn't matter. They refuted enough of it to make me look like a complete incompetent.

The basic revelation was this: Because of Barry Mazursky's gambling history, police detectives had investigated that angle as a motive, but it had proved false. Not only was there "no concrete evidence" that his murder was a sanctioned hit, informants concurred that Barry Mazursky had paid off all his illegal loans.

Nadine Mazursky had even made a public appearance at the mayor's press conference this morning to say that her husband had successfully overcome his problems through Gamblers Anonymous. "I can't believe the *Chronicle* is dragging this up and making an issue of it." Marcy said she'd even wept.

Billy had taken the microphone to explain that his internal memo "leaked by some malcontent" had nothing to do with the upcoming referendum. He claimed city attorneys had urged caution about releasing information because of the potential liability of the high-speed police chase. Neither the mayor, the police chief, nor the Fraternal Order of Police wanted any details released to the press until an internal report, due November 6, could rule out "reckless driving" by the pursuing police officers.

Instinctively, I knew this was a lie. "If that was the real reason, why didn't police just explain that from the start? Say that no information would be released until after the investigation into the high-speed chase?"

"Did you even ask about it?" Marcy asked.

"In fact, I did," I replied. Holstrom had brushed off the issue of internal investigation the very first day. "Sergeant Holstrom said the pursuing police officers would be cleared easily because they had witnesses and because of Delria's blood-alcohol level."

"Apparently, the chief had a different idea," Nathan said.

"And the internal report just happens to be due November sixth, the date of the referendum election? Isn't that kind of a coincidence?"

No one answered.

"And if the report was due on that date, why didn't the mayor tell me that last night?"

"He says he did."

"That's bullshit." Blood rushed to my face. "I asked him at least twice to give me another explanation for that date. He blew me off both times." I could tell by Nathan's expression that he didn't believe me.

The injustice of this was staggering. "I'm telling you, they're lying. Mazursky's own son says he was threatened by loan sharks as late as September. He's certain his father was killed because of his gambling."

"Yes." Nathan and Dorothy exchanged a glance.

"What?"

"Apparently, his mother claims he has stability issues," Dorothy said.

Stability issues? What was that supposed to mean? He was a paranoid schizophrenic? "He's not hallucinating this one. I saw Barry myself with a broken arm just four months ago. And I have another source, too, who says Barry couldn't get out from under the loan sharks."

"Is that the same source who told you about the embezzlement?" Nathan asked. He wasn't looking at me, but reading from the Sunday newspaper, where my story had gone on to detail how Barry had first turned to loan sharks to cover the missing $75,000. "At the Veterans' Homeless Shelter in Providence."

"That's right," I said.

Dorothy was shaking her head. "Did you check that out with anyone else on the board?"

"I had a photocopy of the minutes," I said, but I got a cold feeling, an iced shell around my stomach. I'd spent a week checking and confirming that Barry Mazursky was a compulsive gambler, I'd called police three or four times, double-checked all the statistics on crime and legalized casino gambling, and given the mayor a chance to refute. But I hadn't gotten anyone else from the Veterans' Homeless Shelter to talk about the embezzlement. Leonard was a board member, for Christ's sake. For confirmation, I'd relied on the photocopies, the meshing of the dates, the fact that news stories reported Barry Mazursky's unexplained resignation from the board a month after the embezzlement. A bad tingling started to move upward into my throat as I tried to formulate my answer. I couldn't explain that Leonard was a board member without giving his identity away. And I couldn't say that I'd been so focused on confirming the gambling and the police delays that I'd thought of the embezzlement, the alleged embezzlement, as only a minor detail of the story.

Even before I saw Dorothy's brow knot up in my extended silence, before I read the supreme disappointment in her expression, I knew I'd screwed up. It was always the lesser details of a story that tripped you up.

"I trust my source on this," I finally said.

They all looked at Nathan. As editor, he could demand that I reveal my source to my supervisor. My breathing stopped. What would I do? I'd promised Leonard. Besides, it was obvious that they all thought Leonard was some kind of huckster, a showman never to be trusted. If I said Leonard's name out loud to anyone, my career would be over. For the first time, it occurred to me that I could even be fired.

Nathan glanced at my story again, as if trying to decide something. Then he looked across the table at Dorothy, who lifted her gaze to his. Her eyes were steady, certain, a hint of morality in them. You have to trust your reporters, her expression said. He looked at Marcy, who shrugged. Marcy would turn on anyone. That was clear to me. Maybe it was clear to Nathan. Maybe it was the deciding factor. He glanced back down at the notepad, and I breathed again. I knew he wouldn't ask.

Another minute of painful silence passed. Finally, Nathan said, "Lawyers for the Veterans' Homeless Shelter called the publisher first thing this morning. They say that there was never any embezzlement from the fund. That Barry Mazursky resigned because of his own private financial problems, and they didn't want to embarrass him by making it public."

The agitation raised the combined body heat in the Fishbowl to near suffocating. I wanted to run out of the room, open a window and breathe. But I knew it was important not to sound rattled. "I'll *find* another source to corroborate my information," I proposed.

"I'll need it by deadline today," Nathan said. "Because the Veterans' Homeless Shelter has threatened that if we don't run a retraction in tomorrow's paper, they're going to sue the *Chronicle* for libel."

CHAPTER
13

I HAD TO give myself credit, I sounded convincing. Nathan didn't say anything, but he met my eyes, which was a feat in itself. I took this as an acknowledgment that there was a possibility I could pull this off. Marcy was mercifully speechless and Dorothy, clearly relieved. But as soon as I retreated to an empty table in the library and hid myself behind stacks of Providence Veterans' Homeless Shelter annual reports, the rat-a-tat of fear and doubt began to throb in my heart and head.

The shelter's motive for denying the embezzlement was clear; they didn't want donors thinking board members regularly pilfered from the till. So what were the chances of finding another renegade board member? Someone who would contradict the party line?

Shit. Shit. Shit. I flipped open an annual report, but stared at the page unseeing. The throbbing in my head was so intense that I felt the veins at work through my hair. Whatever made me think it was a good idea to do a story using a confidential source? Whatever made me think it was okay to go on that confidential source's radio show?

I became aware that my face was pressed into my hands and immediately withdrew them. I forced myself to sit upright, look confident, to see the actual words written on the page. The news librarian walked by with newspapers for the counter files, which were still bound in print form even though you could get them electronically: the *New York Times,* the *Wall Street Journal,* the *Boston Ledger*—prestigious publications that would never want to hire me. I made myself smile at the librarian and say hello.

Breathing helped. In, out, in again. The implications of this size screwup were too big to contemplate, and I had to think in small steps. I had to tell myself that this was nothing like the Tejian story. My judgment hadn't been clouded by either love or grief.

Leonard might be manipulative on the air, but he'd been sincere about Barry Mazursky. I was sure of it. And Drew hadn't come to me with the stuff about the loan sharks; I'd forced it out of him. Besides, I'd seen Barry in that arm cast when I'd first moved to Providence, and that was only four months ago.

Tell that bitch at the Chronicle, *she's next.*

Irrationally, hope surged. Maybe it wasn't some nut. Maybe it wasn't some crank call. If that threat *was* real, it meant my story had been right. It meant the mayor and the police and even Nadine Mazursky were lying and that I would be vindicated.

With some effort, the words on the annual report came into focus. "The Veterans' Homeless Shelter in Providence, founded in 1973 to serve Vietnam War soldiers suffering from war experiences, seeks to provide food, shelter, and mental health services to all veterans in need." I turned the page. There were pictures of volunteers with long, smudged aprons and netted hair, looking noble as they served food from tubs to men who sat together at tables, drinking coffee and warily eyeing the camera.

Flipping the report to a back page, I found the listing of the twelve board members, which I compared to the current annual report. I was looking to determine which board members had left since the embezzlement. They were the only ones who might not have been coached to hang up on me.

There were three. The first was Peter E. Halkias, senior vice president of the Compass Rose Bank and Trust. Bankers were not known for their openness with members of the press, but I tried him anyway. His secretary said he was at a conference in New York.

The second was a man named Clifton L. Snickers. Looking him up in the database, I learned that he was a lawyer and a state representative, which meant I'd never get the truth out of him. I moved on to the third board member, Laura Ann Mocek, who was the CEO of one of the largest costume jewelry companies in Rhode Island. Maybe that meant she was the creative type, a freethinker, a tells-it-like-she-sees-it kind of person. The vein in my head was still throbbing. I dialed her number and sat there, practically twisting my earring off as I waited.

When I told Mocek my reason for calling, she was immediately put off. "I thought this was about our new faux pearl line," she said.

"I'm sorry, no."

"Does that mean you didn't even *get* our press release?"

"I'm not a business reporter."

"And you're *not* covering the New York trade show next week?"

"Not me, but maybe someone else. Someone in the business department," I offered. "Maybe it's already been assigned."

"I doubt it," she said, darkly.

"I'm calling about your two years as a Veterans' Homeless Shelter board member. I'm trying to confirm information I received from another board member, concerning an attempted embezzlement from the fund two and a half years ago."

There was complete silence on the other end of the phone, but I considered that a good sign. If it hadn't happened, or if she didn't know anything about it, I would have heard an exclamation of shock.

The silence continued. Had she hung up? "I've been following the murder of Barry Mazursky. Trying to establish the motive."

"I know," she said. "I've been reading the paper."

Again, the silence, but this time, it was a better silence, as if she were actually contemplating what she should say.

"Please help me," I said. "I'm trying to get to the truth."

There was an intake of breath on the other end of the phone. And then: "Who do you know on the business staff?"

Laura Ann was shrewd. She wanted to trade and I had nothing to offer. Even if I were still at the *Ledger*, where my best friend was the business editor, it wouldn't do any good. Business reporters were extremely touchy about taking story suggestions. "I don't know anyone personally, but if you want to fax me the press release, I can at least walk it over to the right desk."

There was another intake of breath, a long pause, and finally, a request for my fax number. "You were way off track today in the paper," she said.

"Set me straight," I replied.

"There was an incident . . . money was missing . . . or I guess we thought it was missing. Barry was accused . . . it was awful, actually. One of the other board members knew about his gambling problem and accused him of screwing with the books. But it all turned out to be a clerical error—more of an embarrassment than anything else. Especially to the board member who was doing the accusing. Of course we apologized to Barry. I personally went to him, pleaded with him to stay on the board, but he was really upset. He resigned, like, the very next day."

"But there was no embezzlement?"

"No, it was a completely false charge. A terrible mistake."

Leonard lived in Bristol, an East Bay community less than a half hour from Providence. I'd heard it was a quaint waterfront town, but I never got to see any of it. He lived on the outskirts in one of those enormous apartment complexes on a less-than-scenic highway. I spent fifteen minutes trying to navigate the irrational logic of a dozen or so buildings labeled by number and letter, a system that seemed purposely designed to hide the residents. Finally, I found a groundskeeper who led me to a building superintendent who in turn steered me to the right lobby.

By that time, I was so frustrated that I leaned on the buzzer without mercy. Leonard answered the door in biking tights and a short-sleeved nylon T-shirt, his hair looking sweaty and smashed by a bike helmet. He ran his fingers through his hair and smiled, as if pleased by this surprise visit.

"Tell me about the embezzlement, Leonard," I said, barging past him into the living room.

It was clearly a bachelor's pad, with big pieces of tan furniture that looked like they could have been won behind door number three on *Let's Make a Deal*, lots of electronic equipment, and no knickknacks. I marched past an enormous stuffed chair and pivoted. "Because I have until deadline to prove it wasn't complete and total bullshit."

"Calm down," he said, combing his hair with his fingers for

a second time. "Just got back from my workout and I haven't even showered or had a cup of coffee yet." He walked in the opposite direction, through the doorway to a kitchen with spotless white cabinets, shiny appliances, and a counter that had nothing on it but a Rolodex and a bike helmet emblazoned with a WKZI emblem. A glass door that went to a small balcony was partially open. An expensive-looking bike with thin wheels was chained to the wooden rail. It was an iridescent red that screamed for attention.

"Did you lie to me, Leonard?" I followed close behind him.

"No, I swear to God, just got back from the workout. I'm religious about it. Thirty miles. Up through Barrington." He feigned innocence, as if I'd fall for this pretense of misunderstanding.

"Not about your workout, and you know it. About Mazursky. Did you set me up?"

"Set you up?" More innocence. "Are you kidding?"

"Because I have a source on the board who is telling me it never happened. That another board member, probably you, accused Barry of embezzling money from the charity, but it turned out to be a big mistake."

"That's not true," he said, reaching for the handle of the refrigerator. A photograph of a woman standing with her arms around two young boys slipped from a magnet and fell to the floor. He picked it up slowly. "My sister, Ellen," he said, as if I cared. Then he took his time returning the photo to its original position and securing it with two magnets. "She and the boys moved to Connecticut. Horrible state. Terrible restaurants." He pulled out a pound of Starbucks, inhaled the aroma of the coffee with obvious pleasure, and put it on the counter. "Who did you call on the board?" he finally asked.

"It *was* you, wasn't it? It was *your* mistake?"

He turned back toward me. "It *wasn't* a mistake," he said,

raising his voice for the first time. "Fucking Mazursky. I couldn't prove it, though. Mazursky was quicker with the accounting shit than I was."

"But he wasn't forced to resign, like you told me."

"I'm not sure I even said that."

"You're not sure you said that? Well, let me help you out." I reached into my knapsack, pulled out my notebook, and turned to the pages I'd reread just a half hour ago. "'He was forced to resign as treasurer, of course. I felt bad for the guy. I always liked him.'"

A cloud of something crossed Leonard's face. Was it guilt? Remorse? "He *was* forced. I mean, he knew I knew what was going on. That knowledge alone *forced* him out."

"He never confided in you about the loan sharks, either, did he?"

"I *knew* he was going to loan sharks."

"But he didn't confide in you, did he? The part about going out for drinks and him getting drunk and spilling his guts, that wasn't true, was it?"

"It was metaphorically true."

"'Metaphorically true'? What the hell does that mean? It was true in a fucking poem?"

Leonard had the gall to look indignant. "I knew he was in over his head. He knew I knew. He didn't have to tell me over drinks in a bar, because I knew."

"So I reported some kind of psychic communication between you two?"

Leonard looked at me for a long moment and then shook his head, as if I'd never understand. Then he turned back to the bag of Starbucks on the counter, and began measuring tablespoons into the coffee filter.

"You made it all up, didn't you?"

He moved to the sink to fill the coffeepot with water. I

watched as he filled the pot, rejected something about the quality of the water, and poured it down the sink.

"Did you ever think that I could lose my job over this? That the *Chronicle* could get sued for libel?"

He sighed heavily and turned from the sink. "That's all bluster. The shelter won't sue the *Chronicle*. They don't have the legal budget for that. And they can't suffer a dry period of no press coverage. Believe me, it's an empty threat."

"Believe you? Because you thought it all out before you lied to me? Believe you?" Was he insane?

He put the coffeepot on the counter as if it were the heaviest carafe he'd ever carried. "Barry Mazursky was a compulsive gambler, in over his head with the mob. You found other sources saying that, not just me."

"But you were my only source on the embezzlement."

"Look, I know he took money from the fund. He could fool everyone else, but he couldn't fool me. I knew how desperate he was."

"How do you know? Your psychic powers again?"

Leonard didn't lash back, didn't return my caustic tone. Instead, he said, "Listen, Hallie, I didn't mean for this to get you into trouble. I consider you a friend."

"Friend?" I was both dumbfounded and outraged.

He ignored the outraged part. "Yes, a friend."

Was I supposed to feel honored? He was a shameless con man. All that crap about trusting me to be a good reporter. I felt a surge of blood rise to my cheeks. "Do you always lie to your friends?"

"I didn't lie." Then he looked away, a moment of internal consultation, and back again. His voice grew quiet. "Did you ever wonder how I got to be so against casino gambling? Why I'm so determined to stop that referendum?"

Did I ever care? "Because it made good radio?"

He did not respond to my cynicism. Instead, he gave me a long, meaningful look, as if to say: Think, Hallie, think.

The meaningful look was followed by a meaningful silence. A second later, I got my first glimmer. Something about the all-knowing tone, the lines in his face, all that holier-than-thou passion. I'd seen it before. "Oh, Jesus Christ," I said.

He nodded his head to affirm my conclusion. This was why he had been willing to trust me with the tape, willing to risk his career. He was one of the reformed. A zealot.

"Did you gamble alongside Barry or did you meet him at a Gamblers Anonymous meeting?" I asked.

He didn't answer.

"Okay then, if Barry Mazursky confessed to you that he embezzled from the charity, if it really happened, I need you to go on the record. I need you to save my reputation at the paper. I need a former board member I can quote, someone who can stand up to the shelter's denial in print."

"I can't go on the record. I can't talk about anything I heard at a meeting. It's anonymous."

I didn't tell him I knew all about the rules of twelve-step support groups. That I'd spent two years going to substance-abuse meetings in Boston. I didn't want him to know there was anything we had in common or to think for one moment that I cared. If he'd told me the truth in the first place, I would have known I couldn't put it in the paper. "I commend you on your integrity," I said, with as much sarcasm as I could wring from the words. "But you *owe* me this."

The demand hung in the air. An hour seemed to pass in the minute that he stood there, pretending pain as he mentally calculated his choices, his debts. His eyes met mine. For a moment, I thought I saw some sort of compromise. But then his expression changed. He wasn't offering compromise, but seeking it. "Please try to understand."

With that, I turned and walked out of the kitchen and headed toward the front door.

"Hallie, everything I told you today was off the record," he called after me.

I wheeled around. "Off the record? Because you told me in confidence? Or off the record because it's complete and total bullshit? Jeez, with you, Leonard, it's hard to tell."

"Hallie, you can't print anything I just told you," he said.

There was just enough authority in his voice to infuriate me, and for a moment, I considered scaring the living crap out of him by telling him I was going to run a bold headline on page one. "Leonard of *Late Night*: COMPULSIVE GAMBLER."

But it would be an empty threat. Leonard would fight back, call the paper before I got there and talk to an editor. I couldn't risk anyone suspecting that I'd had anything to do with Leonard of *Late Night*, that I'd been stupid enough to rely on a guy who specialized in exaggeration.

So instead I said, "Because of you, I have to go back to the *Chronicle*, throw myself at the mercy of my editors, and beg them to forgive me. Because of you, I have to go back to the newsroom and write a retraction. Because of you, I'll probably spend the rest of my life in a bureau writing up school lunch menus. So don't worry, Leonard, your secret is safe with me. I will never, *ever* print another word you say."

CHAPTER
14

Chronicle Reports in Error

Because of a reporting error, a front-page article in Sunday's *Chronicle* incorrectly stated that Barry Mazursky, the victim of a Wayland Square market shooting a week and a half ago, had embezzled money from the Veterans' Homeless Shelter in Providence when he was treasurer there.

The Veterans' Homeless Shelter yesterday released a statement that confirmed that Barry Mazursky was treasurer and board member of the fund from 1995 to 1999, but said at no time did he or any other board member misuse funds from the charity.

"The Providence Veterans' Homeless Shelter has an exemplary history of using charitable donations for charitable work with very little administrative overhead," lawyers for the organization stated.

Interviews with current and past board members confirm that *Chronicle* reporter Hallie A. Ahern used inaccurate information in the story.

The *Chronicle* deeply regrets the error.

Generally, the *Chronicle* ran its corrections on an inside page. Only a screwup of this magnitude could bump a correction to the front page. Everyone knew it.

I folded the paper on its crease, then in quarters, and pushed it to the far corner of my desk. I was back in the South County bureau, off the Mazursky murder forever. Staring out the office window, I felt heat burning deep in my eye sockets. I wanted to crawl under one of the cars in the parking lot and let someone back over me.

Carolyn sat at her desk sorting through a stack of mail: one letter pushed to a must-do pile on the desk, one to a maybe-later pile on the computer keys, three dropped directly into the trash. Now, she turned, breaking her rhythm. "We all make mistakes," she said.

Yes, reporters all made mistakes, and newspapers ran some form of correction every day. But each correction was a stain, and a correction like this—on the fundamental facts rather than a minor detail of a story—was like a gallon of grape juice that would never wash out. I would forever be known at the *Chronicle* as the reporter who'd royally screwed up the Mazursky murder.

"You don't want to work for her anyway," Carolyn said. "She's a real bitch." She meant Dorothy Sacks, who had been the one to officially send me back to the bureau. The one to reassign the Mazursky murder follow to Jonathan Frizell.

"She isn't a bitch." Dorothy had gone out on a limb for me. I was the one who screwed up. I was the one who put my trust in a loudmouthed talk-show host.

Carolyn shrugged and turned back to her computer screen. She'd been struggling all morning, trying to come up with something that would comfort me. Now, when bad-mouthing the downtown editors didn't help, she was thoroughly frustrated. "You want more coffee?" Without waiting for an answer, she started toward the kitchen area in back. "Because I'm going to make another pot."

From the kitchen, I heard her banging around, opening drawers. Water ran as she filled the carafe from the sink. She switched on the radio and I heard the cutting off of songs as she flipped stations. Finally, she settled on something that sounded like news.

After a couple of minutes, she came back with two mugs of coffee. She'd left the radio on and the volume increased as it shifted from news to a commercial. I heard the familiar jingle of the lottery advertisement first, and then a promotion for Leonard's show. I'd let myself be used. Used by a man who cared more about ratings than the truth. And worse than that, I'd let Barry down. I put my hands over my ears.

"You all right?" Carolyn asked.

I dropped my hands to the desk. "Fine."

She put the coffee on my desk. "You might need some extra caffeine today. Final round of the middle school spelling bee starts at three-fifteen. Marcy wants a full feature for Thursday's regional education roundup. I'll need you to cover."

I was afraid that if I said anything, my voice would crack, so I just nodded an okay. Carolyn couldn't bear to meet my eyes but moved quickly past me to her own desk. "It shouldn't go much past four-thirty or five o'clock," she said, in an apologetic tone, as she picked up the pile of mail from the keyboard and began typing the photo assignment into the computer.

Something about the keystrokes got to me. The throbbing in my head started again, and I had to force the tears back into my eyes with the heel of my palm. It was no good. Carolyn looked up. "You sure you can do this?"

"Sure."

Carolyn opened her mouth to say something, but sensing that sympathy would just make the moment worse, she stopped herself. Soon she began typing again, the pink acrylic nails clicking on the keyboard, officiating the assignment on the day's news budget: "Spelling Bee at the Middle School." My life had come to that.

I don't know why exactly, but I drove to the casino right after the spelling bee. It might have been the word that tripped up the last of the finalists: *catastrophe*. Misspelled with an *f* instead of a *ph*. I sat in the front row of the auditorium spelling it correctly over and over in my head, knowing that seventh-grader Jocelyn Rascher had the bee in the bag. That she would, with complete confidence, spell catastrophe with the *ph*, and that the headline for the story would have to read: "Seventh-Grader Wins by Catastrophe!"

Somewhere in the middle of all that spelling, it came to me: I couldn't go home alone. I couldn't face the emptiness of my apartment, the failure of my furniture, or the radio that I wanted to throw across the room. There was only one way to avoid the reality of my own personal catastrophe. A win at the casino. Even a small win would help turn my mood. And a big win, say, a $50,000 win—and I've heard that it happens—would let me pay off my mother's loan and quit the bureau. I could say *fuck you* to all the editors at the *Chronicle* and tell Nathan that I never really wanted a spot on his stupid investigative team.

But I think, mainly, I wanted to forget about Barry, about the swiftness of the gunshot and the feeling in my gut that told me that his murder *had* been a hit. That despite Leonard's other lies, there was some truth at the core of it all, some truth that would never come out because of my own screwups.

Where better to get away from yourself than inside a casino? I wanted to be inside that atmosphere of opportunity. I wanted to feel that promise as a tingle in my skin, an excitement that traveled upward from the pit of my stomach. I wanted to concentrate on the numbers. I wanted to concentrate so hard that I couldn't think of anything but how many face cards had been dealt and how many were left in the shoe.

I avoided Foxwoods and the bad luck I'd had there and drove the extra twenty minutes or so to the Mohegan Sun, where I'd had my good fortune. I borrowed $500 on my MasterCard and went to the exact same blackjack table where I'd learned to play the game and had won $450.

There were two older women who both looked like grandmothers playing against the dealer. I decided that grandmothers were good luck and sat beside the one in the white cardigan sweater who was cradling a quilted handbag. She did not smile at me indulgently, in grandmotherly fashion, or even look up from her cards. "Hit me," she said to the dealer, who complied.

I had to wait until the new shoe was being dealt; I began cautiously with a ten-dollar bet. I won my first hand with seventeen. The dealer broke at twenty-five. I considered this the best possible omen.

Neither grandmother looked at me. One was preoccupied by the vodka and sodas she kept ordering. The other, the one with the handbag, was on a losing streak, and by the way she kept her shoulder angled to me, I guessed she blamed me for the turn of her luck.

But I didn't care because I stayed hot for the first dozen hands, winning twice as much as I lost. A middle-aged man who said he was from New Jersey joined us. He drank Manhattans, smoked small black cigars, and kept licking the tips of his fingers before he touched the cards. At first, I thought he might bring the table bad luck, but I won three hands in a row after he sat down and so did the grandmother with the quilted handbag. She even smiled, first at the man with the cigars, then at me. When he left, about an hour later, she got up to go. I worried that my luck would change. I was up almost $350 and determined not to get carried away by my euphoria. But God, it felt good to feel good. To feel competent.

The dealer at the table, a woman with a bored expression who kept looking beyond the table as if searching for more exciting players, was not big on offering advice, but I remembered what my very first dealer had told me: Quit while you're ahead. I decided I needed a break, a moment to come down from my winning high and think strategically. I grabbed the hamburger-plate special at the food court for dinner, found an empty table, and made myself chew slowly instead of gobble.

I washed my hands thoroughly in the bathroom in case chopped meat and fried potatoes was too pedestrian to bring fortune. I had this contented feeling in my stomach that had nothing to do with just having eaten. My destiny was before me. This was going to be a good night in my new life.

I took one walk around the four seasons of the main hall and scouted several high-stakes tables. When I spotted Will sitting at one, eyes narrowed, chin lifted, back straight in his chair, I considered it another omen. He looked confident, decisive, street-smart. And when I noticed that he was wearing the same lucky silver pendant around his neck, I took the empty seat beside him and began emptying chips out of my knapsack.

"Hey," he said, with a smile. "Barry's friend."

"Hallie," I said, reminding him of my name.

He smiled again, but in a distracted way. He had a big pile of chips beside him and bet $50 on his hand. I took a breath and followed suit.

I won my first two hands and was convinced I'd read the table right: Will was clearly a source of good luck. But then I lost five hands in a row and gave back $150. Still, I knew that the trick was to wait out a run of bad luck. Will ordered a club soda with lemon that he sipped during my next round of losses. I was now down $200 and thinking about going home.

But what was at home? An empty apartment? I couldn't even listen to late-night radio anymore. If I heard Leonard's sanctimonious call for statewide morality, I thought I might smash the radio into bits. So, even after I'd lost the whole $500, I decided to go back to the ATM machine and borrow another $500 from a different credit card.

It didn't seem like such a big deal. Will was down $3,000, but confident that if he stuck it out, his luck would turn. "Basic strategy," he kept saying to me. "You just have to wait it out and play basic strategy."

It occurred to me that if Leonard and Barry had gambled together, Will might know Leonard.

"How many years ago?" he asked.

"Two or three."

He shook his head. "I've only been coming here for maybe two years. It's all fuzzy of course, but I think Barry was usually alone."

It occurred to me that Leonard could even be making up the part about his own gambling, and suddenly the reality of my idiocy was back upon me. How I'd been so touched that Leonard had trusted me with tapes from his show. How he'd counted on that. How I'd let Barry down.

I couldn't go home a loser. Not tonight.

The dealer, a twenty-something guy named Henry who had his already thinning hair shaved into a whiffle, didn't reply when I said I'd be right back. An Asian man at the other end of the table suggested I might want to take a dinner break.

"I already ate," I said.

When I got back to the table with the cash, I won three hands in a row and the euphoria returned. I won $200 and had $700 in chips at my side when I noticed that Will, too, had a growing pile of chips.

"Sometimes all you need is a little patience," he said.

That line became my refrain, especially when I lost the entire $700.

The young, balding dealer began to shuffle a new shoe of cards. It was almost midnight and I was exhausted, but I couldn't go home down $1,000, with the feeling of loss in my stomach. So I took $500 more from another credit card that had just extended my credit line. Sometime after one o'clock in the morning, I grabbed another $500 from the machine.

I was down to my last $50 when I saw Will yawn. I looked over and noticed that all his chips were gone. He shook himself off and got up from the table. "You're not leaving, are you?" I asked.

He looked at his watch and then at me. "It's almost two A.M.; don't you have to work?"

"I'm trying to be patient," I said.

He let out a low, sarcastic chuckle, and I wasn't sure if he was laughing at me or at himself. "Go home," he said. "Don't chase bad luck."

"What about being patient?"

"Nobody can be patient at two in the morning. It's too late to think straight anymore. Call it a day."

Collecting the spent cards in front of me, the dealer met my eye and nodded sagely. The air smelled of stale smoke, but the glass ashtray at my elbow had been wiped clean. It was then when I realized that everyone else had gone home.

CHAPTER
15

MORE THAN JUST about anything in the world, I wanted to stay in bed, sleep until noon, facedown, with the pillow over my head. But my mind clicked awake at six A.M. with a rush of worries that felt like insects in the mattress. I kicked off the covers and sat up. An eerie, early-morning light reminded me that it was Halloween. October 31. Rent was due tomorrow.

I wished this hangover were from alcohol so that I could throw up. I wanted to empty my stomach, my entire life, into a toilet, watch it swirl away into a sewer somewhere. But vomiting into the toilet was too small a penalty. And I wasn't likely to feel better afterward. Because afterward, I still would have lost $2,000.

Standing, I felt as shaky as if I *were* hung over—$2,000. That wasn't even counting the $450 I'd lost at Foxwoods. What the hell was I going to do? Even if I didn't spend a single cent from my next two paychecks, I wouldn't be able to make rent.

I'd cleaned out my checking account and maxed all my credit cards. I had a strange, hot feeling in my stomach, along with a case of the chills. Even in my darkest days, when I'd been fired from bartending, I'd always been able to make rent.

I stumbled over my running shoes on the way to the kitchen counter. I couldn't run this morning, couldn't risk seeing Matt Cavanaugh. Not today. He'd look at me with those sincere brown eyes and I'd feel his judgment like something sticky that wouldn't scrape off. Even if he didn't say a word about the front-page retraction, I'd hear it all too clearly: *I tried to tell you, Hallie, but you wouldn't listen.*

I dropped to a stool at the bar, put my head on the counter, and stared at the little flecks in the Formica, like stars in a very small, very limited universe. I thought of the spelling-bee story I had to write today. A low moan escaped.

When I finally lifted my head, I saw that the light was blinking on the answering machine. It occurred to me that I'd never gotten back to my mother about the stuffed cabbage.

I didn't want to think about my mother—my frugal mother—and what she would say. Two thousand dollars. The same amount she'd taken from her savings account and loaned to me, trusting me to pay her back, like a responsible adult. I winced in a way that included my entire body. After a while, I decided that I couldn't afford take-out coffee and rose to make myself a cup of the despised instant. Staring at the swirl of sludge-colored liquid, I listened to my messages. There were three: one from my mother wondering if my heat was back on, one from Walter telling me he had a gig playing in Newport on Thursday and needed to crash at my apartment, and one from Leonard.

The one from Leonard must have come late last night because his voice sounded hoarse, as if he'd been screaming for many segments. "Pick up," he said. A pause. "I know you're there, and I know you must have listened to the show. Pick up! Pick up! I need to talk to you."

And just hearing Walter's New York accent made me feel guilty all over again. He'd managed to pull *his* life together after losing a girlfriend to a drug overdose without veering back to the dark side. Not in almost five years. What was wrong with me? Had I not listened to one word he'd said?

Knowing my mother would be out, I quickly called and left her an upbeat-sounding message about how warm my apartment was now and how I'd try to come see her next week. Then I forced myself to swallow half the cup of instant coffee before flinging it into the sink. I don't know how long I stood there before the burning in the back of my throat finally stopped. Before I stopped hearing Marcy Kittner's voice repeat like a mantra in my head: *He tries to lure in new reporters. He tries to lure in new reporters. He tries to lure in new reporters.*

I headed to the shower, trying to wash this refrain away. I stood under the water until it went cold, hoping to rinse off all traces of myself. The woman with poor judgment. Chaser of Bad Luck. Loser by Catastrophe! But when I toweled off, I felt no better.

All my laundry was still sitting, unwashed, in the bag, so I hunted through my closet until I found an old jeans skirt I never wore because it was too short and a turtleneck shirt I had intended to turn into a cleaning rag because of a chocolate stain on the sleeve. Looking at myself in the mirror was a mistake. At thirty-five, I still looked immature, with clothes that didn't fit, hair that was too long for my face, and eyes that would never be shrewd.

My stomach was mostly empty, my legs still shaky, and I was exhausted from lack of sleep, but luckily, I'd left a twenty-dollar bill at home in my bureau drawer. So I stripped the sheets off both the bed and the futon, gathered the towels from the bathroom, and stuffed them into my already full laundry bag. The good thing about being back in the bureau, I told myself, was the convenience of the strip-mall Laundromat and the abundance of slow news days. I'd clean and dry every piece of clothing, every towel and every bedsheet I owned. It seemed critical, all of a sudden, that I had clean clothes to put on, that my life, at least, had that much order.

By eleven o'clock, I'd finished the spelling-bee story for Thursday's regional education section and skipped out of the office to start my laundry. I was alone in the bright, canary-yellow Laundromat with hurtling hot water sanitizing my underwear and the rhythmic churning of my sheets and towels in the dryer.

There were ten minutes left on the dryer, and normally, I'd go back to the office, but I was tired of putting on a happy face for Carolyn, tired of pretending I was a perfectly competent person whom she could trust. I dropped to a seat on the plastic bench. Listening to the rhythm of the machines, I stared blankly out the glass window onto the vista of the strip-mall parking lot: the South Kingstown Apothecary, the Peddler's Five, and Fraser's Liquors, the storefronts of my small, getting-smaller, world.

I wondered how I was going to manage. Peanut butter sandwiches from home instead of take-out Greek salads from Poppy's. I could put off electric and telephone bills and pay the minimum credit card payments. Still, there was no way I could make rent. I tried to pull the numbers out of my head, but I couldn't. I kept multiplying my take-home pay by weeks, subtracting the cost of gasoline, car payments, and groceries and falling short for another month and a half. When I'd moved in, Hal Andosa, a landlord who often came to the door *personally* to collect, had emphasized the importance of prompt rental payments. I'd been quick to assure him that I'd never in my life been a day late with the rent.

If my father were still alive, I could go to him for a loan. My Irish father, who in his own day had thrown away a few dollars in the pub, would've given me the required lecture on responsibility but quickly conspired to keep it from my mother. I winced again remembering her detailed advice about good gambling that night at Foxwoods.

I tried to concentrate on the comforting rhythm of the machinery, but I was distracted by two men in the parking lot getting out of a Chevy Lumina and heading toward the liquor store. They had the swift, purposeful movements of people who knew for sure they needed a drink. Wearing jackets of the sporting variety, big leather arms and some sort of football- or hockey-team logo on the back, they looked like the kind of guys who called radio sports programs and argued passionately about bad trades. I always wondered what kind of people bought liquor in the mornings.

The same kind of people who played blackjack at a casino until two A.M., a voice inside my head said. The same kind of people who called Leonard of *Late Night* every single night.

A dryer stopped abruptly with a grunt. I looked around, almost expecting to see my sheets spit out onto the floor. Two thousand dollars in a casino. What was I going to do?

Never go to a casino again, the little voice continued. Had I listened every night to Leonard's show and not picked up that gambling was addictive? Or had I assumed, for some unknown reason, that the addictive part didn't apply to me? I knew now that I had to give up all forms of it, even the little scratch cards and the Powerball tickets. I had to face what I'd known all along: Moderation wasn't one of my personality traits.

I had a vision of Drew that day at the market, standing be-

hind the register and staring off into those aisles of bad mem-
ories. His father's gambling had caused him so much pain.
Leonard might have been lying about the loan sharks, but not
Drew. That had come from his heart.

I took a deep, cleansing breath of soap-scented Laundromat air and tried to exhale those thoughts from my system.
There was nothing I could do to make it up to Drew, or to
Barry. I was off that story, forever. The practical side of me
had to accept that or I'd be completely lost.

Laundry was constructive: a good first step, a simple task I
might be able to accomplish. But as I began emptying the
dryer, I realized I'd overloaded it again. Everything from the
sheets to my sweat socks was still twisted and damp.

The change machine was out of order, so I decided to go to
the liquor store for more quarters. I passed the two sports-
radio guys in the parking lot as they practically danced their
way back to the Chevy Lumina. I heard the first bars of a
heavy-metal song before the doors slammed and the car tore
out of the parking lot.

Opening the door to the liquor store triggered a computer-
chip gizmo that belted out a throaty "Ha!Ha!Ha!" from a sin-
ister goblin. Mrs. Fraser, who was on her knees unpacking a
case of wine into a wrought-iron rack, looked up from the
floor. She was a divorced woman in her early fifties with tight
gray curls and defined biceps. She wore a short-sleeved
T-shirt over three-quarter-length leggings, and the kind of
high-top aerobics sneakers that went out of style in the eighties. Because it was Halloween, she'd added a black velvet
witch's hat.

I waited for her to finish heaving the last of the bottles into
the rungs before asking if she could make change. The last
time the Laundromat change machine was out of order, Mrs.
Fraser had begrudgingly parted with her quarters. This time,

she popped back behind the cash register and opened the drawer with a big smile on her face. "See those guys who peeled out of the lot?" she asked without waiting for an answer. "I almost didn't sell one of 'em a scratch ticket 'cause I thought he was underage. But the big one in the Bruins jacket had ID. Wouldn't you know, he bought a winner? Five grand."

That got my attention. "Five grand. Really?" I took the quarters. "On what game?"

"Caesar's Palace Two. Just got it in this week. You played it yet?" She could barely contain her excitement. "They're promoting it like crazy on the radio. Pays up to one million dollars. Been selling like mad."

"On a one-dollar ticket?" I heard myself say. Buying a scratch ticket *was* gambling. I knew that. Buying one would be like betting on horses instead of on cards. Still, I now had two dollars in laundry coins in my hand.

"You wanna try one?" she asked. "Maybe the goblins and ghosts will bring you good luck."

Ghosts. Barry had sold me an earlier version of the Caesar's Palace game the night he died. One of the tickets I couldn't find in my apartment. *"I'm telling you, I have a feeling about you and Caesar,"* he'd said.

Barry would have considered this a message. Maybe it was Barry himself sending me the sign. Signs didn't show up too often. They had to be followed.

I cupped the quarters she'd just given me. Two dollars. A voice urged me to save the change for the Laundromat. Another voice said I could just toss the damp clothes from the dryer into my car's backseat and let the sun finish the job.

Mrs. Fraser pushed a Halloween bowl of Tootsie Rolls and Red Hots on the counter toward me. "Sometimes I think the odds are better with these new games."

That was exactly what Barry had said about the new

games. If I won $5,000, all my financial problems would be over. I could repay my mother and my credit cards and have something left to celebrate. And it wasn't like the casino, it wasn't like I could lose it all. I'd only be risking a couple of dollars.

Mrs. Fraser was gazing at me with the pleased look of someone who knows she has just sold something. I got a good feeling, as if she knew just how badly I needed a shot of good luck. One last scratch ticket, why not?

But then the throaty "Ha!Ha!Ha!" of the front-door goblin startled me, as if deriding my thoughts. A man about my own age, wearing plaster-splattered overalls and a painting hat, walked in. He wanted to know if the store carried Narragansett beer and whether there was any cold. With that same sales smile, Mrs. Fraser pointed to the cooler in the back of the store.

Her eyes returned to mine. Although she didn't say anything, I saw her disapproval of the man's on-the-job drinking, something about the level way she looked at me and didn't blink. I felt myself retract, my chest drop into my stomach, my fingers clench the quarters in my palm. Alcohol, gambling, compulsive calls to late-night radio—it was all the same. When Mrs. Fraser stood on her toes to pluck a ticket from the plastic dispenser, I stopped her.

"Not feeling all that lucky today." I dropped the quarters into my skirt pocket and forced myself to walk out the door.

When I got back to the office, my phone was ringing. Carolyn gave me a skeptical look. "How much laundry did you have, anyway?"

"Too much," I said, taking off my jacket. She gestured toward my phone. "Answer it. It's been ringing on and off for the last half hour. Driving me crazy."

I knew who it was. Leonard had already left two voice-mail messages: one before I'd gotten here this morning; and one when I was at the Laundromat putting in my first load of clothes. He kept saying the same thing: that he'd gone overboard because the cause was so important, that he felt a "personal responsibility" to stop casino gambling in the state. If I picked up the phone and heard him claim the moral high ground one more time, I was going to slam down the receiver. I didn't want to have to explain to Carolyn who deserved that kind of treatment.

The ringing stopped. I left my jacket on the hook and slipped into my chair. The silence was large and welcome. Carolyn looked at me closely now, studying my relief. "Whoever it is isn't going to give up, you know. They hang up when they get the voice message. They dial again like they've got nothing better to do."

"How obnoxious," I said.

"Yeah." Her eyes did not leave me.

The silence continued, and after another minute, I grabbed a stack of press releases and began typing: "South Kingstown elementary school teachers are urging all students to bring in their excess candy to school the day after Halloween. The candy will be donated to the women's shelter in Newport."

Carolyn shifted her attention to her computer. I knocked off a second press release about a weight-loss clinic at the University of Rhode Island. The phone rang again.

Turning around, Carolyn said, "I don't know what boyfriend you're trying to ditch, but you can't work at a newspaper office and *not* answer the phone."

I could pretend it was a wrong number. I could announce that this wasn't the features department, but the South County bureau, a common misdial, a digit apart. "South County, Hallie Ahern," I said, businesslike, into the phone.

But it wasn't Leonard. It was Matt Cavanaugh.

My stomach did an emotional pivot. Carolyn was still watching me. "AG's office," I mouthed.

"I was wondering if you'd heard the news," Matt said. His voice had a warmer quality than I would have expected given my current standing with the law-enforcement community. "About Victor Delria."

That he was not a hit man? Or in any way associated with organized crime? It was a little late in the day for Matt to be rubbing my face in it. "What news?"

"He died about an hour ago. Rhode Island Hospital. I thought you'd want to know."

I was struck silent. Not by Delria's death. He'd been in critical condition for some time, but by the gesture. Despite the complete and total idiot I'd made of myself, Matt Cavanaugh had called me first with the information.

I didn't tell him that I had to pass this tip on to the city desk, where Dorothy would assign it to a reporter she could trust to get it right. He must have assumed that I had to get right to work on it, because he didn't go into what it meant for his case, or for my role as a witness.

"Thank you for tracking me down," I said.

There was a pause, as if this gratitude confused him. Or maybe he was about to say something, but changed his mind. "No problem," he said, and swiftly hung up.

At home, there was another voice message from Leonard pleading with me to call him back. The second was from Walter, who explained that his gig the next night was early and that he'd be at my apartment around midnight. It occurred to me that I might be able to borrow money from Walter, who now owned three cabs in Boston and was generous by nature.

Of course, I'd have to confess to him about the gambling, and that could be worse than telling my mother. But worse in a different way. With my mother, I'd feel like a failure as a grown-up. With Walter, I'd get the spin on how failure was human, but I'd have to make all sorts of promises that my conscience would force me to keep.

I knew I'd screwed up, but Walter was a rabid twelve-step disciple. Secretly, he felt *everyone* was in need of some sort of program. The idea was that you were always vulnerable to everything, and even if you weren't, you were supposed to go to meetings to provide inspiration to those who still were. He'd be on the phone in seconds scouring Providence for Gamblers Anonymous meetings that I'd have to attend.

I reached into the kitchen cabinet and pulled out a can of Campbell's tomato soup and a box of elbow macaroni. I pictured myself walking into a church basement in Providence and telling a group of people I didn't know that I had no control over anything in my life. I decided it might be better to just starve for a month.

I brought the soup to a slow boil, threw in a handful of macaroni, and turned on the television. I didn't normally watch television news, but now that I was boycotting the radio, I needed a new source of background human voices.

The moral victory of not buying the scratch ticket was not as satisfying as I'd hoped. I found myself wondering if I'd blown it. If that one scratch ticket was *the one*. What if there'd been a $10,000 prize waiting for me under the latex? I knew I was working myself up, but I couldn't seem to stop. One negative thought chased the other, a race with no finish line. What if I'd thrown away that one chance in a million—the only chance I was ever going to get—by walking out the liquor-store door? Maybe that's what the front-door goblin was "ha ha ha-ing" about.

I heard a knock on a door somewhere on my floor. This was followed by laughter and welcoming voices. A second knock that sounded a little farther down the hall made me realize that the families in the building must be taking their children trick-or-treating. I had a momentary panic wondering if I had any Almond Joy bars stashed in the cupboard, any kind of treat to hand out, but I couldn't find any. It didn't matter. No one knocked. Feet shuffled down the staircase. No one considered coming to my door.

The macaroni had congealed into a single lump on the stovetop, but I didn't care. I'd lost my appetite. There was only one thing that was going to make me feel better and it wasn't in a soup pot. The scratch tickets I'd bought the night of Barry's murder. The ones I'd never played. Once upon a time they'd been on the bar. I searched under a stack of newspapers and under the basket of vitamin pills, but they were gone.

Finally, I got a grip on myself and went back to the stove to stir the soup. Too much water had evaporated and it looked like one big red macaroni. I was trying to decide whether or not I should just toss the whole thing in the trash when I heard the newscaster report Victor Delria's death at Rhode Island Hospital. I shifted my attention to the TV.

The camera was on a middle-aged Hispanic woman with a toddler on her lap. She was introduced as having once been Delria's foster mother. She told the news reporter that Delria had been orphaned when his parents died in a car accident when he was fifteen. Then suddenly, there was an insert of a family portrait and the camera zeroed in on a photo of a boy identified as Victor Delria-Lopez when he was fifteen years old.

The boy was very slight, with a narrow face and a wide, lantern jaw. The screen changed to a single photo of Victor Delria-Lopez as an adult. I dropped the spoon in the soup and

moved into the living room to get closer to the television. This
man didn't have the height or the anger to terrify me or keep
me awake worrying if he had friends who might come after
me. This man didn't have any viciousness at all.

This was not the man I'd picked from the photo lineup, because this was not the face that had scowled at me in front of
the dairy case.

I stood there, immobile, watching the photo dissolve from
the television screen. The camera shifted back to the studio,
focusing on a bright-blond newscaster with a ruffle at her
neckline. She wore a sad expression and spoke in a slightly
nasal tone. "Delria, captured in a police chase immediately
following the murder of Wayland Square store owner Barry
Mazursky, was cleared today of any connection to that crime.
Police said that although his car matched a witness's description of the getaway car, the forensics report and DNA testing
produced no evidence linking Delria to the crime scene."

The newscaster pursed her lips, as if she needed to disci-
pline her vowels or concentrate on not dropping her *r*s. "Police said sneaker impressions left at the crime scene did not fit
Delria's footwear and that DNA analysis of hair roots and
saliva on a panty-hose stocking mask recovered near the
crime scene did not match Delria's DNA.

"Police now believe that eight hundred dollars in cash
found in Delria's car did not come from the robbery, but may
have come from a recent drug sale. Trace amounts of heroin
powder were found in Delria's trunk, according to the forensics report. Police have not named any other suspects in the
murder of Barry Mazursky."

The camera shifted to a weather map, and I snapped off the
TV. Police might not have another suspect, but I sure as hell
did. The man in the parka who was out there running free.

I went to my apartment door and double-checked the lock.

Both the doorknob lock and the double lock were firm, but I knew from experience that the outer door, downstairs, was always left open. I moved to the window and scanned Elm-grove. I watched a couple head into Starbucks, but there were no children in costumes prowling about in groups with their parents. A lone man walked past the Mazursky Market, hands clenched in his pockets as he headed purposefully down Angell Street.

I watched him until he got into a car and drove off. If Victor Delria-Lopez wasn't the man in the parka, it meant that Barry Mazursky's murderer had been free the whole time in Providence. He'd been the one barreling through intersections and calling talk radio, intent on killing me.

CHAPTER
16

A SCRAPING SOUND was coming from my bedroom. I stepped away from the window into the alcove and stood behind the futon, trying to hide in the relative shadow. Every muscle in my legs and arms tensed as I listened. Another scrape, followed by a ping and a hiss. Steam heat. The radiator.

I needed more light. I reached for the floor lamp, but couldn't find the switch. I groped the bulb, the neck; how did you turn this thing on? Giving up, I walked across the room to the closet, opened the door, and flicked on the light. A sputtering of fluorescence illuminated a few extra square feet with a grim light.

I turned the dimmer up on the fixture over the bar as high as it would go and snapped on the lights over the sink. I became aware of an awful chemical smell. Metal burning? I ran to the stove and turned off the burner where I'd left the soup, the liquid now boiled off and the macaroni scorched into the bottom of the pot.

Throwing the whole mess into the sink, I was forced to inhale the new burst of steam. I wished to hell Walter was coming to stay here tonight instead of tomorrow. I wished to hell that I didn't have to wait out the night in this goddamn apartment alone.

Alone, without even the radio for company. I could taste metal in the back of my throat. When I went to crack the window, I found myself staring across Elmgrove in the opposite direction of the square, trying to make out the lights at Matt's house. The Victorian had three floors, maybe four if there was an attic unit. I saw lights on the bottom and the top.

How long had he known that Victor Delria was not the man I'd identified to the police? Not the man in the parka. Not the man who killed Barry Mazursky.

I couldn't remember which floor Matt said he lived on, but it was almost seven-thirty and there was a good chance that he would be home. I desperately wanted to be with another human being, and he *owed* me an explanation. I put on my jacket, carefully double-locked the apartment behind me, and headed downstairs. It was a cold night, and even in the stairway, I could feel the ambush of frigid air.

On the ground level, there were two outer doors, and I pushed through the first into the even colder corridor of mailboxes and discarded flyers, a limbo before the street. Pulling my jacket around me, I hesitated at the door, peering through the glass panes in both directions to make sure no one weird was hanging around. Finding a complete absence of human form, I bolted across the street, not stopping until I was on Matt's porch, shivering.

There were three mailboxes. Cavanaugh was marked as number 3, which meant he lived on the same floor I did. If he stared hard enough, he could probably see my shadow through my front window. I hit the buzzer with force.

He didn't answer at first, so I buzzed again. The wide front porch was more rickety than it looked from the street, with several floorboards that needed to be replaced. Fallen leaves collected around an enormous pumpkin placed beside the door, the back side of which had been gnawed by squirrels.

Slow steps made their way down the staircase. Eyes met mine through the leaded-glass side light, and he opened the door. Barefoot, Matt was wearing an old T-shirt, washed so often it was threadbare, and tattered sweatpants. There was a bag of Butterfingers in his hand. "A little late for trick-or-treaters," he said.

"I've got to talk to you," I said, suddenly embarrassed about the intrusion. The T-shirt was tight and ripped underneath the neckband and along a side seam. I found myself wondering what kind of workouts he did and what he looked like doing them.

I made myself focus on his eyes. They seemed amused. Was that a smile on his lips? He backed into the small vestibule, allowing me entrance. He studied me for a moment, and it struck me that he should have been a little more surprised by my visit. A little less amused. He touched my shoulder. "You all right?"

Although it was just his fingertips that touched me, I was aware of the bare chest that I'd been picturing underneath the T-shirt: the pectoral muscles that were defined but not bulky, the shoulders that were narrow, but solid. Christ, what was I thinking? "No. I'm not all right," I said, pulling away. "How long have you known that Victor Delria was not the guy I saw in Barry's that night?"

He looked swiftly up the stairs. The vestibule was a common area; anyone standing on one of the landings could overhear. "Come upstairs," he said, "where we can talk."

I followed him up two flights of stairs, my eyes fixed on a third tear in the T-shirt, this one just above his left shoulder blade, at the seam. I could see skin underneath that still looked tan, and I wondered if he ran without his shirt on in the summer. The bare feet on the carpeting were not tan at all.

He guided me into the apartment, which was big, with a high ceiling, bare wood floors, and a lot of corduroy furniture. Dropping the bag of Butterfingers on the coffee table, he reached for a sweatshirt that was tossed on the couch and turned away from me to slip it over his head. I felt embarrassed again, as if he'd caught me trying to peek through the T-shirt holes.

The Simpsons played on television: the episode about Homer joining a gun club. Matt snapped it off, removed a dirty glass from the end table, and gestured for me to take a seat on the couch. He started to head for a La-Z-Boy, but didn't sit down. Instead, he turned back to me, his eyes scanning for something. It took me a minute to realize that he was looking for my notebook.

I might have told him I wasn't there as a reporter, but as a witness, a witness scared out of her mind, but I didn't. Let him worry, let him wonder, let him feel a few knots in *his* stomach muscles. "I identified a completely different man to Sergeant Holstrom and you know it. Police must have known for almost two weeks that Victor Delria was not the man."

Unconsciously, Matt returned the dirty glass to its original spot on the end table and took the seat beside me on the couch. Between the couch and the fireplace was a rough-hewn coffee table that looked impossible to destroy. He put his left foot on the table and leaned forward, resting his elbow on the raised knee, his head resting on his hand. His right knee swiveled toward mine and I had to force away thoughts of the tanned back I'd followed up the stairway.

"Holstrom told me the IDs didn't match. You said right

from the start that you never saw the guy's face when he came back into the store. All you saw was the back of the parka and the mask. So at first, we figured you might have had the wrong guy."

"The *wrong guy?* I might not have seen his face, but I saw how tall he was. I *told* Holstrom he was a big guy. Over six feet. That parka would have been around Delria's ankles."

"Delria was not that short."

Was he going to argue every point? "I saw him on television. I saw what he looked like."

"Me, too. He was actually taller in real life. About five feet eight."

He sounded as if he was rattling off the statistics of a college ballplayer, deliberately focusing on extraneous details. "You know," he continued, in that same detached tone, "witnessing a murder is an emotional thing; it can affect your perceptions."

"No shit."

He ignored this, but continued in that infuriatingly detached tone, as if he was a social worker and I was a case number. "It affects the way you remember things. It affects the way everyone remembers things. And you said you were looking up at him while you were squatting on the floor."

Discrediting me as a witness, was that the ploy? And then I realized that Matt was bullshitting me. Looking at me with those sincere brown eyes and spouting absolute bullshit. I gave him a cold stare so that he would know I knew it, but he did not shift his gaze.

"And the forensics report? That had to have come back at least a week ago, and it confirmed that the sneaker imprints weren't Delria's." Anger began pumping into all kinds of veins I didn't realize I had, and I couldn't stand staying seated on the couch beside him any longer. Rising, I began pacing,

setting off in the direction of a small dining area with an
antique-looking oak table. It was stacked precariously with
legal pads, files, and newspapers in various stages of being
clipped.

Beyond, a bow window overlooked the street, providing a
clear view of my apartment building. Matt must have known
that once I'd figured out Delria was not the guy in the parka,
I'd cause trouble. That's why he'd called me at the office; it
was a calculated effort to establish trust. Maybe that was his
assignment at work today. Maybe that's why he hadn't
looked so surprised when I'd shown up on his doorstep.

I pivoted back to Matt, who was now standing. "Why keep
it secret? Why not announce it Monday at the same press
conference where police tore my story to shreds? Why not
clear Delria then?"

He leaned against the back of the couch, arms folded in the
nothing-can-really-get-to-me way, but there was more tension in his expression now, as if he was watching a very close
basketball game that his team could lose. "Your story was
wrong, Hallie. Loan sharks wouldn't kill Barry. They'd kill
someone close to him. Or burn his car, his building. Not kill
him."

The certainty with which he said this put new fury into my
heels. I paced back to the living room, stood directly in front
of him, in his face now. "You didn't answer my question.
Why not clear Delria at the press conference if police weren't
deliberately stalling, trying to keep the press off track until
after the referendum?"

Now, the soulful brown eyes burned with insult. I watched
him wrestle with that anger, swallow so that his Adam's apple
dipped and rose. The fold of his arms grew tighter, his sentences shorter.

"Look, there was some confusion, that's all. Conflicting evidence. Delria's car was a good match. Cops found eight hundred dollars in cash on the backseat. That was about the same amount the son figured was taken from Mazursky's cash register."

"The trace amounts of heroin must have shown up right away."

"Like junkies never rob convenience stores? It took a little police work to find out Delria was a dealer coming from a sales call in Fox Point—which is probably why he freaked when police started chasing him. And it took a while to get the DNA results on the mask."

"Two weeks? On a priority case?"

Matt ignored the incredulity in my tone. "DNA can take longer than that if the lab's backed up. Besides, whether Delria was the guy or not had nothing to do with the referendum or the fact that your story was wrong."

I had no idea how long it took to process DNA results at the URI lab, but I had a gut feeling that Matt was lying. Something about the way he glanced away after he said it. And he was spending too much of his energy trying to convince me that my story, already retracted on the front page, was wrong.

The couch faced an enormous marble fireplace, and I stared at the stacks of law books on the hearth. Matt Cavanaugh was stonewalling me. Was under instruction to stonewall me, or worse, gain my trust and deliberately misguide me. "And what's being done to find the guy in the parka? The real killer?"

"The case is still under investigation, Hallie." The careful, clipped sentences, again. The professional distance. And I knew for sure then, felt it in my heart. He was an integral part of the plan. He must have seen it on my face, because he tried to recover, tried to warm up his voice and return to the personal plea: "Why don't you just let us do our jobs? Leave it alone—just for another couple of weeks."

Until the referendum election was over? Or until the guy in the parka could kill me? I was shaking, physically shaking, and I wasn't sure if it was fear or anger. Was everyone in this godforsaken state connected? The attorney general's office in league with a corrupt mayor?

I stormed away from him, no choice really but to head back to the dining room, where I had the urge to kick the legs out from under the antique table. Instead, I continued moving as far away from him as I could get, to the bow window, overlooking the street and my building. I could see my bare window, and beyond, the bright light of the fluorescent ring in the fifties-style fixture above the bar. The apartment looked so harsh, so empty, even from here.

I walked back to the couch, reflexively searching for my knapsack under the coffee table, kicking aside a stack of *Sports Illustrated* magazines, not caring that they toppled. But I hadn't brought the knapsack or a notebook. Why had I come here, anyway? What made me think that Matt Cavanaugh would ever tell me the truth? I headed to the foyer, but the outer door had an elaborate locking system I couldn't figure out. I flipped levers and tugged at the door. Matt followed behind me, putting his hand on my arm to stop me.

I spun around, not caring how high my voice was raised, how shrill I sounded. "That night you drove me home from Barry's wake. That night you *had* to have known. Why didn't you tell me that the guy in the parka was running around free? Don't you think you owed me that courtesy?"

He stepped back, looking stunned. As if he couldn't understand why all this anger was directed at him. As if he'd been so generous with me and now I was here with a gun in my hand sticking him up for his wallet.

But he was not a man to surrender his cash and credit cards. Recovering, he shook his head, slowly at first, and then with more velocity as he began to add up my offenses. "Jeez, why do you think? Could it be because everything we tell you, and crap that we don't, ends up in print? Could that be it?"

We stared at each other, a mutual "fuck you."

"Could it be," he continued in that same tone, "that the more stories you write warning this guy that we're looking for him, the harder he is to catch? And maybe, just maybe, there's more incentive for him to come after you, because you never seem to tire of reminding everybody in the paper and on the *radio* that you know what this guy looks like."

I didn't run the next morning. I told myself that my right hip, which was sore to the touch, needed a rest. That I needed a few days off from the pounding of the pavement. But it was not like me to baby an injury and I knew, even as I stepped over my running shoes to get to the bathroom, that Matt's anger and sarcasm had done its damage. I wouldn't be running alone on the boulevard, or anywhere else at six A.M., as long as the man in the parka was free in Providence.

I didn't want to hang around my apartment either, especially since it was the first of the month and my landlord was likely to knock on the door for the rent. I showered, got dressed for work, and ended up at my desk in the South County bureau by a quarter of seven, doing police checks with my jacket on because the heat hadn't warmed up from the overnight setting.

It was going to be a long day. I drilled through a stack of press releases on leaf-collection day and the Rotary Club's turkey shoot, and fielded a call from an irate high school football coach who took issue with a sports reporter's criticism of his failed offense. I called the town clerk's office to get the week's meeting agenda and learned that the most controversial issue coming before any of the boards this week was whether or not to give the Young Women's Club a one-day beer-and-wine license for its holiday fund-raiser.

Carolyn arrived late, having come from a meeting of regional bureau managers downtown, and by that time, I was overwhelmed with the minor details that had defined the morning. She'd picked up two frothy-looking coffees and handed me one with what looked like caramel on the top. I sensed that it was some sort of consolation prize, like the ice-cream cones she bought her daughter when her soccer team lost a game.

I frowned at the froth, afraid to take a sip. "You hear anything downtown about who made the investigative team?"

"Nothing definitive," Carolyn said, hanging her lime-green ski jacket in the closet as carefully as if it were one of her furs. Then she spotted something on the floor of the closet she didn't like and kicked it to one side.

"What does that mean?"

"What is all this crap in here?" Carolyn said, digging into the closet and pulling out two large pieces of poster board. She turned them around and displayed some badly glued red and yellow construction paper cutouts that had suffered from their closet storage. It was one of her daughter's elementary school art projects. "Oh," she said to herself.

"Carolyn, tell me," I persisted.

She stuffed the poster board back in the closet and sat down at her desk reluctantly, picking up a stack of interoffice mail and dropping it in her lap. She seemed wearied by her trek to the city, the turf battles she'd had to wage, the expenses she'd had to defend.

"Tell me."

She sighed, swallowed some coffee, and relented. "Nothing official. But I heard that Jonathan Frizell has been assigned on a temporary basis. Some big story of his is running in to-morrow's paper." She met my eye, offering me her full sym-pathy. "You don't want to hang out with those idiots in Providence, anyway. I mean, why do they all have to walk around carrying laptops when the newsroom is filled with word processors?"

I shook my head to indicate that I didn't know. I didn't care. I was obviously destined to spend the rest of my days in laptop-less exile. I tried the coffee, but it was already tepid, the caramel melted into a swirl of oil. Carolyn's phone rang and she answered it. I could tell by the long silence and the roll of her eyes that it had to be Marcy Kittner.

"Can't you get someone else from city to cover, if it's so important?" Carolyn asked.

And then: "You're not being fair."

And finally: "I've got a life, you know. I can't work morn-ing and night."

There was more silence as she listened, lips pinched, re-sentment building. "I'll see what I can do," she said in a clipped tone. "Bitch," she added after she'd already hung up the phone.

Frizell, who was supposed to cover an antigambling rally at the University of Rhode Island that night, was putting the fin-ishing touches on the final copy of his big investigative piece. So Marcy wanted Carolyn to cover the rally instead.

It seemed like an odd request. Never in the four months that I'd been here had I seen Carolyn work a night shift. In fact, I'd assumed that was the major perk of being a bureau manager. But I could see from Carolyn's expression that she was in some kind of a corner.

"I can cover it," I offered. I'd begun to dread my empty,

pinging apartment. And even if only ten people showed up, a political rally was a decent-size story in South County. At worst, it would make the cover of the zone page.

Carolyn didn't jump on this, a disturbing response.

"I'm free. Why don't you let me cover it?"

"That's okay." Carolyn turned away from me, one hand on her keyboard, the other flicking on the machine.

"Really. You'd be doing me a favor. I'm short of cash this month and could use the overtime. Besides, you know me. I have no other life."

"Let me think about it," Carolyn said, watching the computer boot up instead of turning back to me. Her posture was off, too, spine uncharacteristically stiff. The *Providence Morning Chronicle* logo came up on her screen and she failed to make her usual derisive comment.

And then I knew. "You mean they don't even trust me to cover a public event?"

With a sigh, she turned back to me. She hadn't wanted to tell me, but was damn glad I'd figured it out. "Those assholes. They're still pissed off about the correction." It all came out in an angry torrent. "And Marcy's always been vindictive."

"A public event? Journalism 101?" My voice raised in insult.

Like most people in journalism, Carolyn shouldn't have been made a manager. She was no good at containment or diplomacy. If I'd wanted to set fire to the office, she'd have handed me a can of gasoline. "Those assholes!"

Seeing her worked up like that toned me down. I became practical. "How are you going to work tonight? Who's going to watch Deirdre and Katie?"

"I'll have to drop them with Tom." He was Deirdre's father and always late with child support. She spit this solution.

In the heat of this us-against-them fury at the downtown

editors, I felt the last of my anger dissipate. One of us *had* to remain levelheaded. Solution oriented. And, more important, I wanted this assignment more than ever now. "You don't want to drop the girls off with Tom, and you don't want to work until eleven tonight," I said firmly.

Carolyn was not inclined to disagree.

"You could . . ." I drew this out and watched her closely to gauge her receptiveness. Seeing enough, I plunged on. "You could call Marcy at around two o'clock and tell her the school nurse sent Deirdre home *deathly* ill."

I saw a distinct glint in her eye, a consideration of the idea, and a calculation of risk. "You know I can handle this assignment," I pressed. "You *know* I won't let you down."

I'm not sure if it was belief, pity, or simply a rejection of anything that imposed on her family life, but Carolyn didn't take long to weigh the morality of my suggestion. She brightened at the thought of besting Marcy and jumped right into the subterfuge. "I'll wait until four o'clock to call her," she said with a conspiratorial smile. "That way it'll be too late for her to get anyone else."

One of the tasks of reporting a public event is counting the crowd. The tendency is to exaggerate in either direction. If almost no one shows up, there is a pathetic failure to call attention to. If it's standing room only, it becomes a bona-fide news event.

I was pleased to see that there was no need to exaggerate tonight. The Edwards Auditorium, a rich, old-world hall with tall Palladian windows, was crammed with people. I counted chairs across and multiplied by fully occupied rows. Added fifty for the people sitting in the balcony and another twenty-five for those standing in the aisle. Three hundred, I estimated in my notebook. A decent headline.

Making my way through the crowd to the front, I found a place to lean along the wall. Reporters from two Providence television stations and their cameramen were gathered in front of me. Behind me, a young girl with a notebook announced that she worked for the college paper, the *Good Five-Cent Cigar*, and asked if I was from the *Chronicle*.

I nodded and she made a notation in her notebook, as if participating media were somehow relevant. It occurred to me that since news was always scant in the Saturday paper, this story might have a shot at the front page. I scanned the crowd, looking for the *Chronicle* photographer who was supposed to meet me here. Without a photograph, the rally, no matter how well written, would get relegated to a less prominent position—below the fold, or even worse, an inside page.

Gregory Ayers, the lottery executive director whose arm I had rubbed for luck, was just stepping up to the podium. Onstage, there was an aura of television fame about him, a certain celebrity to his gait, and maybe even a film of hair spray over the silver hair. As soon as he took the microphone, an immediate hush fell over the room, as if he were about to announce the Powerball number.

"We all want to be winners," he said, with his warm, uncle-like familiarity. The audience applauded with a force that took him aback. It made Ayers shift at the podium, rearrange his index cards, and take a sip of water while the clapping subsided. I realized, for the first time, the power of his personality. He was the guy who gave away money on television, who called out winning numbers and handed out life-altering checks.

"But what I want to talk about today—" There was more clapping and Ayers had to stop again and wait. "What I want to talk about today are all the ways in which we Rhode Islanders are going to lose if this casino-gambling referendum passes."

The Citizens for a Stronger Rhode Island had packed the hall with gambling opponents who clapped like mad at this. But there were rows of senior citizens—I recognized a few bingo players from South Kingstown—who remained still in their seats, and a row of businessmen whose arms began to fold over their chests.

Ayers began detailing lottery revenues, which were staggering, and where the money went: arts, education, local aid. People clapped after each number, many looking up at him with awe. He was the man who drew winning tickets, the man who gave them an illusion of hope.

Excitedly, I began to formulate headlines for my story: "Lottery Chief Mesmerizes Antigambling Audience." "Lottery Chief Plays Antigambling Card." "Casino Gambling Referendum's Luck Runs Out."

"What's going to happen to that revenue if a casino opens in Providence? With that kind of competition, the lottery will face declining electronic-game receipts, the revenue the state needs most."

Someone shouted an unintelligible answer from the audience. Ayers pretended to understand.

"Sure, casinos bring in revenue, but for each dollar the state receives in gambling revenue, it costs at least three dollars in increased criminal justice and social welfare expenses. Is that a net gain for Rhode Island?"

"No! No! No!" Ayers's supporters shouted somewhere on the left-hand side of the auditorium.

"What a hypocrite," the college reporter said. She looked and sounded like she was about fifteen, with a rose tattoo showing in the small of her back above her low-slung jeans, purposefully messy hair, and a bored tone of voice. "As if there aren't plenty of uneducated people addicted to those scratch-card games."

I felt myself bristle. Hadn't she taken the class on how journalists were supposed to remain detached and objective?

Where was the photographer? I searched the doorway again, hoping to see a familiar figure weighted with cameras stroll in beneath the red and black "VOTE NO on PROPOSITION #3" banner. Instead, I caught a glimpse of Drew Mazursky standing in the crowd of people carrying "VOTE NO" signs and looking around, as if he, too, were searching for someone.

Seeing Drew gave me a guilty feeling. He'd confided in me. My story, my inaccuracies, had let him down, and God only knew the fight he must have had with his mother. But when his eyes found me across the auditorium, he didn't look away in disgust, or glower. He tilted his head, a greeting of sorts. An acknowledgment of something.

He looked away, resuming his search, scanning for someone else, leaving me with something new in my stomach: curiosity and maybe even a semblance of self-respect. I turned back to the stage, standing a little straighter. Drew might believe that I'd been right, after all.

Gregory Ayers was peering into the audience as if he was trying to make out exactly who was out there. "The casino lobby has tried to bribe seniors for their vote, promising all of you that the money will go strictly to senior programs. But I think we can all see through that. You're all too smart for that."

A low booing began in the back of the room. When I turned around to see where it was coming from, I practically smacked my face into Leonard's. "Shit," I said.

He took a step backward and smiled. He was wearing a turtleneck jersey and gabardine pants that looked as if they

had been pressed. For a moment, I wondered if he was scheduled to go onstage and speak. "What are you doing here?" I
asked.

"How come you didn't return any of my phone calls?"

I looked over my shoulder to see if anyone was close
enough to hear me tell him to buzz off. The college reporter
was looking at Leonard with curiosity.

"Busy," I said. For the benefit of the college reporter, I af-
fected a professional tone. "I didn't see your name on the program. When are you going on? After Ayers?"

A look of disgust settled on his face as he shook his head.
Apparently, the organizers had failed to invite him. "I
wouldn't stand on the same podium as Gregory Ayers."

This threw me. "But he's on your side. You had him on
your show as a guest just last week."

His bottom lip curled. "Mistake."

The college reporter elbowed me in the side and whispered,
"Did you see the six o'clock news? The lottery threatened to
pull its advertising from his station unless he tones it down.
He was all over television." She pointed to Ayers at the
podium. "He called Leonard irresponsible."

"He's just figuring that out now?"

The college reporter grew bolder. "Apparently, Leonard
said that Ayers ran the lottery like a compulsive gambler, *addicted* to action."

"That's not what I said," Leonard said. "That's what they
said I said."

Leave it to Leonard to attack his only ally a week before the
referendum vote.

"I heard Ayers was getting airtime rebuttal on your show
tomorrow night," the college reporter said.

Leonard grimaced. "The station caved in." I took this as an

involuntary confession that Leonard actually had said what he'd just denied saying, and turned from him in disgust.

Suddenly, there was a shift of attention away from the stage and I followed the turned heads to see that Billy Lopresti had arrived. Was he supposed to speak? I flipped my program from one side to the other looking for his name. A quick check of the stage to gauge Ayers's expression suggested that this was a surprise visit.

The mayor was a short, burly man who clearly enjoyed a plate or two of pasta, but he was amazingly light on his feet as he bounded up the aisle on the other side of the auditorium. The television reporters, crew, and the college reporter all headed across the room. I was about to follow them, but Leonard grabbed my arm.

"I've got new information," he said. "Bigger than anything you've ever written. The *real* reason Barry was murdered."

We were alone now, standing together along the wall. "Why would I want to hear anything you have to say? Why would I ever trust you again?"

He leaned forward, a whisper directly into my ear. "I know you have no reason to ever trust me again. But you don't *have to* trust me. Mazursky is supposed to meet me here, and he has proof."

I needed to get to the other side of the room, get close enough to the mayor to catch his reaction if Ayers ejected him from the stage, but I remembered Drew's scanning eyes, his search for someone. Despite myself, I stayed another minute to ask: "What kind of proof?"

"An audiotape. His father made it. Apparently, he'd left it in his glove compartment the day he died. Drew came to borrow the car or something. But he didn't find the tape—one of those microcassettes—until this morning, stuck inside a cigarette pack."

My thoughts began to race: the police's reluctance to clear Delria until he was dead, the stalled forensics report, the voice inside that told me Matt had been trying hard to keep me off the story. It all fueled an interest I refused to let Leonard see.

"Look, I could just play this thing on the radio. I'm giving it to you first because I owe you. It's my apology. My amends."

Our eyes met. I wanted to believe him, but I had to be wary. Why would Barry make a tape? And if Drew found it, why would he give it to Leonard? But my heart rate kicked up a notch because I knew the answer: Drew didn't trust the police or Matt Cavanaugh any more than I did.

Leonard saw me waver. "This is Sunday's front-page story, Hallie. Something I owe you. The vindication you deserve. I was wrong about *why* Barry was murdered. But it wasn't an armed robbery, and the cops have known it all along."

CHAPTER
17

BACK AT THE bureau, I took the precaution of locking the door behind me and closing the blinds so that not everyone who stopped at Fraser's for a six-pack could watch me typing at my desk. But I was too charged up, too in gear, too single-mindedly focused on my story to have much room for concern. It was as if I were in the final mile of a 6K run: Fixed on the finish line, I lost sight of the road directly in front of me.

Vindication. I told myself that I had to be wary of any information that came from Leonard. That I couldn't believe anything he said until I'd actually heard the tape. But if he wasn't jerking me around . . . if there actually was a tape with evidence on it . . . a tape I could play for my editors . . .

I forced myself to focus on the story at hand. To be given a chance at redemption, I'd need to win back the editors' confidence by doing a good job on this rally. Clear angle, uncluttered language, accurate details.

As it turned out, there wasn't a lot of leeway on the lead for the rally story. The mayor's surprise appearance had seen to that.

Narragansett—An antigambling rally turned ugly last night when Providence mayor Billy Lopresti crashed the event and ignited a fight between senior citizens.

A South Kingstown woman was arrested and a West Warwick woman was injured following the emotional debate. More than 300 people, mostly senior citizens, packed the audience at Edwards Auditorium at the University of Rhode Island.

The clock in this office was old and the humidity had gotten behind the number plate, so that the minute hand scraped as it struggled across each increment of time. I glanced up. It was almost nine-thirty.

Lopresti, an avid proponent of the referendum to legalize casino gambling, was not invited to speak at the event. In a surprise visit, he marched up to the stage shortly after lottery executive director Gregory Ayers concluded his speech.

The audience, which had been cheering Ayers's antigambling rhetoric, grew quiet after Ayers allowed the mayor to take the podium.

"This isn't about the morality of gambling. Or even the revenue. It's about fiefdoms," Lopresti began. "When you go to the polls on Tuesday, don't do what's best for the lottery commission, or what's best for the state, or even what's best for Providence. Do what's best for you, the voters!"

The audience remained silent, except for one person in the back who began to clap. A woman sitting in the second row with members of the antigambling organization Citizens for a Stronger Rhode Island immediately rose to her feet. Turning to address the anonymous person clapping for the mayor, Marilyn Caruso, 75, of West Warwick, shouted, "Don't believe a word he says. He's a crook!"

Lopresti folded his arms but appeared largely unaffected by the insult. But Hildagard Vettner, 81, of South Kingstown, who was sitting in a wheelchair near the wall, took off her shoe and threw it at Caruso.

"You learn to behave," she called out, shortly before her shoe hit Caruso in the face.

Campus police immediately removed both Mrs. Vettner and Mrs. Caruso from the audience. Mrs. Caruso was treated and released for minor injuries at South County Hospital. Mrs. Vettner was taken to the Narragansett police station and released in the custody of her son, Anthony, a probate lawyer in Washington County.

I finished the first ten inches of the story and printed it out to get an idea of length. In an urge to be thorough, I circled everything that had to be double-checked and was in the midst of verifying the capitalization of the antigambling group's formal title when I heard a car door slam outside.

It sounded unusually loud, as if it were just on the other side of the office door. With a tight feeling in my stomach, I found myself thinking about Matt and his warnings. I got up and checked the window, peeking between the louvers of the blind.

But it was only a Ford Taurus parked in front of the liquor store with the engine running. A man sat behind the wheel, and after a minute, a woman appeared in the doorway of Fraser's and gestured to him. He got out and helped her carry out a case of wine.

I stood there feeling like an idiot as I watched them put the case in the trunk and drive away. Returning to the desk, I vowed to put all thoughts of the man in the parka from my mind. A minute later, the phone rang. It was Dorothy Sacks, who told me the story was slated for page one.

I felt a little boost of confidence, which was swiftly deflated.

"I'd like to see the copy as early as possible," Dorothy added. This might seem innocuous, but I knew her real meaning. She wanted to see the copy as early as possible so she could catch all the factual errors my story was likely to contain.

I struggled hard to keep any strains of resentment out of my voice. "Ten minutes."

"Fine." Her tone was distant, professional, as if we'd never worked together or previously felt a rapport. "Oh, and make sure to include a reaction from all camps," she added.

Was she kidding? That was standard event reporting 101. Nothing an intern wouldn't know. "Of course."

As she hung up, I realized that if the story was going Page One, it wasn't because of any confidence in me, but because of the art. The photographer, who'd finally shown up, had gotten a shot of the shoe in flight, just before it hit poor Mrs. Caruso's face.

In an interview following the debate, Lopresti called the incident unfortunate and blamed it on gambling opponents who have made the issue "so damn emotional."

Asked for his reaction, Ayers suggested that Lopresti limit his speaking engagements to progambling events, but added that no public speaker should be subjected to verbal abuse.

Marjorie Pittman, chairwoman of Citizens for a Stronger Rhode Island, criticized Lopresti for "crashing our rally" and said she hoped that he had learned a lesson about "turning up uninvited."

She added, however, that Caruso was not an official of the antigambling organization and had attended only one meeting. "We don't condone name-calling," Pittman said, "even in politics."

It took me a couple minutes longer than I thought it would to decipher my notes and double-check Marjorie Pittman's title. I was deep into editing the final copy when I was jerked to attention by the phone ringing a second time.

I picked it up, expecting it to be Dorothy asking what was taking me so long. It was Leonard. "Don't come to the station tonight," he said.

I felt an unpleasant stab of suspicion. Was this some kind of trick? "Something happen to the tape?"

"Nothing's wrong with the tape. Some car's been following me since I left URI. It's been hanging around in the parking lot all night."

"Is it still there?"

"Yeah, but now the lights are off. I'm not taking any chances. I'm going to leave with the rest of the staff tonight. You want to meet me at my place after work? If you get there before me, there's a key hidden in the molding over the door."

I was not about to drive to Bristol and wait hours alone in an empty apartment for Leonard to get off from work. Especially when he thought someone was after him.

"Okay, okay. How about we meet tomorrow for coffee? Somewhere public. A restaurant, near you maybe."

"Rufful's at ten o'clock?" I suggested, but I was struck both by how worried he sounded and by the need for us to meet in a public place. Suddenly I was grateful that Walter was coming to stay at my apartment tonight.

I didn't want to be alone tonight, tomorrow, or the next day. God, when was this going to end? I couldn't even run by myself in the morning anymore and that was my only form of relief. Involuntarily, my back arched, remembering the car that had almost hit me on Rochambeau Avenue. "What does it look like? The car?"

"Nothing special. It circled the parking lot for a while before it parked. It's some kind of sedan."

There were a zillion sedans. Christ, practically everything that wasn't a minivan or a sports car was a sedan. But I couldn't help think of the silver sedan. "What color, could you make it out?"

"Yeah, it was sort of a silver gray. You could see a little damage to the right-rear bumper."

At home, I found a note the landlord had slid under the door: "Missed you today. Be by tomorrow. Hal Andosa."

One day late. One day and I was already getting overdue notices. I crumpled the note and threw it on the counter.

I'd have to ask Walter to loan me the money. I'd have to tell him the whole story, steady myself for all that compassionate understanding, and agree to find myself a twelve-step meeting. Sometimes I wondered if the real reason Walter came to stay at my apartment after his gigs was to keep an eye on me. Make sure I wasn't floundering.

Well, I was floundering, all over and in a completely new way; I'd have to own up to it. But Walter would give me the money, I was pretty sure of that. And I wouldn't have to spend the rest of the month trying to duck Hal the Landlord.

I threw off my jacket, made myself a bowl of tomato soup, buttered some saltines, and sat at the counter, forcing myself to eat. I listened for the door, wondering when Walter would arrive. I both dreaded his arrival and was impatient for him to show. More than anything, I just wanted to get the confession over with.

I tried to take consolation in the fact that there'd been no sign of any silver sedan in the strip-mall parking lot, and that no car had followed me home. But I didn't feel consoled, I felt panicky. I needed a distraction.

I moved a stack of bills on the counter, hoping to find the scratch tickets I'd bought from Barry underneath. Where could I have put them? If they'd been inside the apartment once, they had to still be here, somewhere. Matter could not just disappear.

This was more a theory for me than a conviction. Letters, news clips, files, a desk at the *Boston Ledger*. All of that stuff had been matter in my life. All of it had disappeared.

I emptied the contents of my knapsack onto the coffee table and searched the inner pockets. Nothing. I flipped over a pile of newspapers on the floor, next to the couch, knowing full well there was no way the lottery tickets could have ended up there. But still, they had to be somewhere, right?

In the midst of this, the phone rang. I stepped over the scattered newspapers on my way to grab the cordless on the bar. It was Leonard checking to make sure I'd made it home safely. He said that the sedan was gone before he left the station and that no one had followed him home. "I keep thinking about that whack job who called and threatened you the night you were on my show. You got a security alarm or anything where you live?"

"I have a friend coming to stay with me tonight," I told him. "I'll be okay."

"Maybe I'm overreacting," he said.

"What's on the tape?" I asked. "What's got you so freaked out?"

"Are you on a cordless?" he asked.

"Yeah, so . . ."

"So I really don't want to talk about it on a cordless. You can hear it all for yourself tomorrow morning." There was a pause, and then he added, "Don't worry, Hallie, I promise you that I'm not going to let you down again."

He hung up and I put the phone on the counter. *Amends.* I was starting to believe he was sincere, but still, it was frustrating. I wanted to know what was on that tape and I didn't feel like waiting until the morning. I began pacing the living room again, kicking up newspapers. What kind of evidence were we talking about? What kind of story did I have? Where could I have put those scratch tickets?

I didn't even hear Walter's key in the lock, just the door swinging open. "You been ransacked or something?" he asked, glancing at the newspaper mess I'd made on the floor.

"Very funny." But I didn't elaborate or try to explain. Walter looked like he'd had a hard night, his eyes red from the cigarette smoke, his lips chapped and bitten.

"Tough crowd?" I asked.

"The worst. At least three requests for 'Leather and Lace.' As if I could sing that sappy duet alone."

Not the best time to ask for money, I decided. Let him relax first.

Besides his two guitars, Walter also had a small amplifier and a PA system that he didn't want to leave overnight in his cab, so he had to go back down the stairs to get the rest of his equipment. I made a quick search for the tickets when he was gone, hoping to scratch myself a winner before he finished unloading. No such luck.

At least the panicky feeling had begun to subside. Walter wasn't a huge guy, but he was smart and street savvy, and the silver bracelet he wore looked like it could hurt somebody. I felt safer now that he was in the apartment.

Walter was about to fling his cowboy hat on the bar, but spotted my bowl of tomato soup. "Fine dining again?"

It occurred to me that this was the perfect opening to ask to borrow money, but I decided to wait. Let him relax. Have a cup of tea. Put his feet up on the coffee table. I dropped to the bar stool and picked up the spoon. My long-ignored tomato soup was now completely cold. "Want some?"

He shook his head. He was working an early cab shift tomorrow morning and was going straight to bed. He took his overnight bag with him into the bathroom, which meant he'd be in there for a while.

I sat there, mindlessly stirring the cold soup as I prepared my speech. *Walter, I've had a setback, and I was wondering . . . Walter, I know I should have listened to you and found a meeting first thing when I moved here, but . . . Walter, I've learned the hard way that I really have to stay away from casinos. . . .*

My stirring grew agitated. When I looked down, there was a puddle of red broth encircling the bowl. Grabbing a sponge from the sink, I returned to the bar and lifted both the bowl and the place mat to wipe up. Five scratch tickets were lying underneath, about a quarter inch from where I remembered putting them.

A miracle. A symphony. A shaft of sunlight streaming through my ceiling. It was as if the tickets were some kind of gift from heaven and not something I'd misplaced all along. I scooped up a Caesar's Palace ticket, the one Barry had recommended, found a quarter in a teacup on the counter, and scraped off the latex. It was a complete dud. I slipped it back under the place mat and listened for the sounds in the bathroom.

Sometimes when he had to get up really early, Walter showered at night. Often, he sang songs from his show, mid-seventies Eagles, Jackson Browne, Steve Miller. But tonight, not a peep. Not a good night to ask for money. I started scratching the next ticket. So much for Barry's good advice: The second and third Caesar's Palace tickets were duds, too.

The last two tickets were Green Poker Game tickets, the ones Barry hadn't wanted me to buy. But the leprechaun who had been lucky before came through a second time. I won $50 on the fourth ticket.

Gratitude rose in my chest. Thank you, Barry, I said softly. But luck was a greedy thing. I couldn't possibly stop here.

Fifty dollars was not enough. The gray latex on the last ticket was especially stiff. I scraped relentlessly. The green leprechaun was holding a flush. I had to match diamonds.

I scraped off my first two boxes: a king and a deuce, both diamonds. The bathroom door opened, but I didn't even bother to look up. The third and fourth boxes both revealed diamonds and I slapped myself in the head.

Walter walked toward the bar, draped in a towel. "What are you doing?"

I didn't answer. I had one box left. The quarter, now coated with bits of latex, had lost its edge. I had to put all of my weight into it, angling the coin into the cardboard.

Walter was looking at me with a curious expression, trying to figure out what I was doing; why I was gasping without taking in air, why I kept smacking my forehead, and opening and closing my eyes.

I didn't try to explain it to him, I just pointed to the scratch ticket, begging him to read me back the cards, to verify what I saw. To make sure I was awake. Because unless I was dreaming, I'd just won $10,000.

CHAPTER
18

THE LOTTERY OFFICE was an impressive one-story brick building with intensely manicured shrubbery and mulched gardens. It also had an enormous parking lot that was empty at seven-fifteen in the morning.

It was a cold day that promised a clear sky. I parked in the space closest to the building and sat in my car, doors locked, heat on, staring alternately from the ticket to the front door, waiting for it to open. Walter had been happy for me—nothing like a winning scratch ticket to squelch a lecture on gambling—but he'd had to leave at six A.M. for his cab shift. So once again, I was alone, completely alone for what had to be one of the single biggest moments of my life. But I didn't care. Every time I glanced at the ticket in my hand to make sure it was still there, I won all over again. I could feel elation in my fingers, my elbows, my toes.

I was afraid to put the ticket down on the console, or even zipper it inside my knapsack for fear it would disappear, dissolve, or self-destruct in some way uniquely tragic to me. A winner. A little piece of cardboard worth $10,000. Still here, still safe.

Thank God I'd found the scratch tickets. Thank God I hadn't thrown them out in an antigambling purge. As I fingered the cardboard ticket, I daydreamed about driving to Worcester tonight and handing my mother $2,000 in cash. I imagined the look of surprise on her face, which would be followed by an instinctive, suspicious concern about where the money had come from. This would be followed by relief, then joy. She'd love the story about finding the winning scratch ticket under the place mat and would be at the senior center in no time telling her friends about it.

Two Toyota Camrys pulled in and parked next to each other about a hundred yards away. Two middle-aged women got out of their separate cars and I could tell by the familiar way they walked together toward the building that they were employees. One of them looked over her shoulder at my car and said something to the other. I guessed I wasn't the only winner who'd arrived at the lottery office at the crack of dawn.

I checked my ticket again, making sure it was still a winner. The five red diamonds were still there, no mistaken heart smuggled in. The cardboard was getting damp from my palm, but I didn't care. I wasn't going to put it in my pocket or in my knapsack. I sat there holding the ticket as the cars filled the employee spaces and the digital clock in my car finally snapped to eight o'clock. Still clutching the ticket, I checked to make sure no one suspicious was walking around the parking lot, turned off the car, and ran to the door.

Out of breath, I entered a reception area with a polished marble floor and a bottled-glass floor-to-ceiling window that let in a flood of morning light. I felt as if I were walking into a stage set where the director had cued the sunlight. Soon there would be music as the camera followed me, recording this momentous event.

Beyond the reception area was a tall counter, walled off, with a protective glass shield, like a bank. No one stood at any of the terminals. I wondered if Gregory Ayers was back there. Maybe he'd come out from some office to award me my check in person. I felt myself getting giddy. Maybe he'd want to do it on TV.

The reception desk was empty, too. A door to the walled-off bank area opened and a man walked out. He glanced at the empty desk. "She's probably in the ladies'," he told me. "Just be a minute." I forced myself to settle down, check out the framed photographs of previous lottery winners that adorned the walls: Raymond Olson of Cranston, $100,000 in Powerball. Norman Picard of Cumberland, $47,000 in Lot-of-Bucks. I glanced back at my ticket. Hallie Ahern of Providence, $10,000 in the Green Poker Game.

"Can I help you?" a kindly voice asked. An older woman was putting a coffee mug down on the reception desk. She wore enormous glasses with a rhinestone star in one lens.

"Yes," I said, waving my ticket.

The reception lady saw my scratch card and smiled. The little rhinestone star caught the light and glittered. "Your lucky day?"

"You bet," I said, smiling back.

She pointed to one of the terminal windows far to the left. "That's the validation area, right there. You go ask Tina to help you. She'll give you a claims form."

I stood at that window for a couple of minutes before a woman appeared from one of the back offices. Tina was about thirty years old, with large breasts revealed by a dress that fit her like a dance leotard. She had a very large, Mick Jagger mouth and the whitest teeth I'd ever seen.

"Oh, wait a minute." I'd remembered the $50 ticket, which I'd stuck in my pants pocket. She looked surprised when I passed it to her. "Guess it really was your lucky day," she said, handing me two claims forms and a pen.

I returned to a table in the waiting area and began copying the serial numbers from the tickets onto the forms. When I'd finished adding all the pertinent data and digging my photo ID from the bottom of my purse, I returned to the validation area.

For a moment at the counter, I felt nauseous. I didn't want to let the tickets go. Didn't want to pass them under the glass for fear my luck would disappear. Tina saw my hesitation and laughed. "Don't worry, I won't eat them."

Reluctantly, I surrendered the tickets. Glancing at the leprechaun's hand of cards, Tina said, "I always tell my husband I got the best job in the world. All I do all day is deal with winners."

The nausea disappeared. I was a winner. Not a newsroom reject. Not a talk-radio junkie. Not a lonely woman without family or career.

Tina scratched off something from the bottom of the first ticket and glanced up at me a second before feeding it into what looked like the base of the terminal. The machine beeped. She did the same thing with the second ticket, and the machine made the same high-pitched sound.

"Something wrong?"

"Lawrence!" she called over her shoulder to offices in the back. Her voice sounded shrill, but when she saw my expression, she caught herself. Leaning forward, she explained, "I'm gonna need him to cut you a check!"

I was overwhelmed with relief.

Lawrence walked over with an air of managerial authority. His suit must have been too warm for the sunny office because he already appeared to be sweating. He took both scratch tickets from Tina and studied them carefully. She handed him my claims forms with my Massachusetts driver's license. He studied the license as if Massachusetts didn't count. "We like to have two photo IDs," he said slowly. "You got anything else?"

I dug into my knapsack for my *Chronicle* ID. My hand swam over the familiar shapes of my keys, my notebook, lipstick, pens, wallet. I dove deeper into the knapsack for the thick plastic square. It occurred to me then that it might still be on the kitchen table where I'd overturned my knapsack last night. My hand began to flail in panic. I squatted to the marble floor to empty the entire contents onto it. Nothing. "I must have left it at home."

Tina smiled at me in an apologetic way, but her voice sounded strained. "We're always extra careful with the big winners."

"State police have to review any payoff over a grand. It'll be a few minutes," Lawrence said in a practiced way. He pointed to a row of upholstered chairs against the wall. "Make yourself comfortable."

I gathered my possessions from the floor and stuffed them back into my knapsack. In the waiting area, I found a *People* magazine. I had no idea who the celebrity was on the cover, but sat down, prepared to flip through the magazine without being able to read a single word. What was taking so long? Finally, Tina reappeared from a back room followed by a state trooper. I heard a buzzing sound and the state trooper left the glassed-in area and headed toward me.

He was an older man, early sixties, but still very much in shape. He hadn't lost any of the state-trooper swagger and he held the scratch tickets tight enough to inflict permanent damage. "Where did you get these?" he asked.

I noticed he said "get" instead of "buy" and I had to squelch a panicky feeling rising in my chest. "I bought them. In Providence. The Mazursky Market."

The kindly reception lady was shaking her head as if she'd seen it all. The state trooper asked me to come into the back office to answer a few questions.

"Why? What's wrong?"

The state trooper pulled a magnifying glass from his pocket and waved it over the bar code on the bottom of both scratch tickets. "What's wrong is that you have two winning scratch tickets and *both* are counterfeits."

There was an empty hole of time while I stared at the scratch tickets that could have changed my life. My heart started pounding with a ricochet effect in my brain. Instantly, all major body systems were in distress. All my stupid hopes, my new furniture, my noble plan to pay back my mother. Counterfeit?

As we walked through a hallway to a private office in the back, the state trooper scraped a fingernail along one of the cards and stopped to show it to a secretary. "They did a helluva job duplicating the latex," he said.

In the office, I wound up sitting at someone's desk, staring at a framed picture of two children poking their heads out of a leaf pile. I tried to take deep breaths to slow the whirlwind inside me. I'd missed a question. "What?"

The state trooper asked me when I'd bought the tickets, and then, why I'd taken so long to cash them.

I thought of the scramble in my apartment last night, the thrill when I'd found the tickets under the place mat. Counterfeit? A heavy feeling settled over me, a feeling of futility and depression. "I misplaced them for a couple of weeks, that's all."

He gave me a look that said he didn't believe me, but I

didn't care. He asked me if it had struck me as unusual that I'd had two winners from the same game. What did it matter? I wanted to ask. I was a loser after all.

And then the state trooper asked me if I'd bought scratch tickets at any other stores.

"Fraser's Liquors in South Kingstown."

"How about Mazursky's Smith Hill Market? Or the one in South Providence?"

Slowly, the murky, heavy feeling began to lift. I could see through the devastation to my first positive thought. "Why? Have you come across counterfeits from those stores?"

He didn't answer.

"Is there an investigation into this?" As I heard myself ask this question, the sky above me opened and the light hit. *I was wrong about why Barry was murdered. But it wasn't an armed robbery, and the cops have known it all along.* Barry had been selling counterfeit lottery tickets. This was why he was killed. And Drew Mazursky had proof of it. On tape. "Have you come across counterfeits from the other Mazursky Markets?"

The state trooper's eyes narrowed. "What did you say you did for a living?"

"I'm a reporter for the *Chronicle*."

He pulled himself up from his chair. "That's it. We're going to headquarters."

"What?" It was nine-thirty. I had to meet Leonard in half an hour. "I didn't do anything wrong. I paid for those scratch tickets. Bought them at a convenience store. A registered lottery agent. I can't go to headquarters. I've got to go to work."

This only seemed to strengthen his resolve. "I have to ask you to come in for questioning."

"What if I say no?"

"Then I'll have to take you into custody."

*   *   *

State police headquarters was a complex of buildings at the end of a long, circular driveway hidden in the woods. I was escorted into the first building, past the dispatcher and into a spartan room with a desk and a small conference table.

The state trooper, who'd finally introduced himself as Corporal Linsky, asked me questions I had already answered at the lottery offices: how long I'd lived in Rhode Island, who I knew in Providence, the restaurants I frequented, and the other places I hung out. But now he also wanted to know if I was claiming this winning scratch ticket for someone else.

"You think I'm working for someone else? Passing counterfeits?" I was insulted by the implication. "Hey, I'm the victim here. I told you, I paid good money for those things. Could I just use the phone?" I needed to call Leonard, tell him where I was and what was going on. I wished to hell I'd been able to pay my cell phone bill and hadn't canceled my service.

"Give me a minute," said the state trooper, getting up from his desk. "I've got to call the detective sergeant."

He disappeared through the door before I could ask how long *that* would take. After several minutes passed, a female state trooper entered and asked if I wanted coffee. She was short, with a wide Slavic face and purplish-red hair tied in a ponytail. I told her I wanted to make a phone call instead. She said she'd go find Corporal Linsky.

The room was colorless, with cold, hard chairs and very little sunlight. There an abundance of fluorescence, though, and I felt my nerves begin to cook, as if I was under a warming light. I needed to call Leonard. And Carolyn, and maybe a lawyer.

I rubbed my right hand. The small bones just beneath the knuckles ached in a strange way, and I realized it was from the way I'd been clutching the counterfeit scratch ticket. But

I couldn't let myself think about all that early-morning hope, all those solutions to my problems. I was broke again. That was it. I had to focus on the opportunity, the story: Barry Mazursky had been selling counterfeit lottery tickets, and someone had killed him because of it.

I heard footsteps in the hallway, and straightened. If I wasn't under arrest, they couldn't keep me here. I could demand to leave. Demand to be driven back to my car, at lottery headquarters.

The footsteps stopped, and for a moment I heard nothing. I felt like a race car stuck on a track. White-hot fuel replaced blood in my veins. I had a front-page story. Maybe another shot at the investigative team. I had to get out of here and meet Leonard before he gave up on me. I paced back to the door and stared into the hallway. I couldn't get out of the building without the dispatcher buzzing me through.

"I want to get out of here!" I shouted down the hall. The female state trooper returned and guided me back into the room.

"Just another minute or two." She had the faintest accent, as if she'd immigrated here as a teenager. "Detective Sergeant Randall should be here any minute . . . problems with the little one at home, I think."

"I don't care about his problems at home," I said. "I'm late for work. You can't hold me here!"

"You are upset," she said soothingly, as if to validate my anger. Raising a finger that asked for another minute, she backed out of the room. "I understand. Very upset. I'll see what I can do."

I paced the small room for the next five minutes waiting for her to come back. The police couldn't actually charge *me* with counterfeiting. I'd paid money for those things. And if they weren't going to arrest me, they had to let me go.

Finally, I went back to the conference table, grabbed my knapsack from the floor, and swung it over my shoulders. If they wanted to keep me prisoner, they were going to have to physically subdue me. Police brutality. Wait until I wrote about that on the front page.

But I didn't get far. Just as I reached the door, it swung open. It wasn't Corporal Linsky, the female state trooper, or the detective sergeant I'd been waiting for. It was Matt Cavanaugh holding his hands up in front of him as if to protect me from ramming into his chest.

I stepped back awkwardly. "I want to get out of here," I said.

Matt was dressed for the office, but in rumpled clothes: a pair of chinos, button-down shirt with the sleeves rolled up, and loosened tie. He was carrying one of those vat-size cups of coffee and he had dark circles under his eyes. He looked both wired and weary, and for a moment, I felt for him. But when he shut the door behind him and gestured for me to take a seat at the table, I got pissed off all over again.

"I've got to get out of here," I repeated.

"Just a few questions and I'll drive you back to your car, I promise." His eyes met mine. The offer seemed genuine. I felt relief. A way out of here. A way back to my car.

"How long ago did you buy these tickets?" he asked.

"The night I met you," I said, sitting down again. "The night Barry got shot."

Something clicked in his eyes, and I knew he remembered me waving my winning scratch ticket at him when we stood together at the register. He shook his head again, as if awed by the chain of events. "What are the odds of this happening?" he asked, mostly of himself, as he dropped to the chair beside me and put his coffee cup on the table.

"To a reporter working on the story? Pretty long odds, I'd say."

He looked physically pained by this remark. And then his expression grew determined. "You can't write about this incident, Hallie. You've got to promise not to write about this."

"Are you kidding?" Nabbed as I tried to cash in scratch tickets purchased at a convenience store where the owner was mysteriously murdered? Without one word of confirmation from Matt, without any other connection at all to Barry's murder, I had a front-page story.

He took a moment to regroup. The tone became more personal. "Couldn't we work together on this? Couldn't you wait just a couple of days?"

"For what?"

He refused to answer. But he looked away, as if he was just too tired to deal with me, and I sensed an opening.

"Oh yeah, you expect me to trust you, but you won't give me anything to work with. Why should a couple of days make a difference?"

He turned to me with an open look of exasperation.

"What am I waiting for?" I repeated.

"I just need time to get a search warrant, all right?" he said in frustration. "That's off the record, by the way. Completely off the record."

"Search warrant? For what? What are you looking for?"

He shook his head to indicate that there was no way in hell he was going to part with that information. But I had a pretty good idea what he must be looking for: the tape Leonard had promised me.

"Maybe," I began, "maybe, if I knew what the hell we were *working on* together. Maybe if I knew who was doing the counterfeiting, who really killed Barry."

"No way." He had the weary, determined eyes of a man

who has been working too hard and too long on something he wouldn't see destroyed. And then, the boulder moved in my brain and cleared the path again, and I knew: Matt wasn't part of a cover-up, he was part of an investigation. A long-term investigation into the sale of counterfeit scratch tickets, which was probably why he was in Barry's that night in the first place.

"So could you just give me a couple of days?" he asked, sounding so tired and so frustrated that I felt an unexpected tug on my heart. A part of me wanted to agree, but if I gave him this promise, I'd be stuck with it. Leonard might give me first crack at the story if he was sincere about making amends, but he wasn't going to wait for *days* before breaking it himself on late-night radio.

Matt was watching me closely, reading my calculations. He began to say something, but stopped himself. Then his expression grew cold. "It could take a few hours to get you out of here."

That asshole.

"If I have to get the newspaper's lawyers involved to get out of here, it'll be sure to make the six o'clock news," I returned.

We faced each other, our mutual threats. Finally, he just shook his head at me. The look of disappointment cut deeper than anything he could have said.

The drive back to the state lottery offices was long and silent. There were a few names he would have liked to call me, but he was too professional. He pulled up beside my Honda and stopped the car.

I swung open the door, not really caring if I scraped my own paint. But then I hesitated. Matt was staring directly ahead of him at the lottery building, refusing to even look at me. "I'm sorry," I said.

But he was not about to forgive me. "Go ahead. Knock yourself out. Get yourself killed over this one. But you might want to ask yourself first: Is a front-page story really worth it?"

CHAPTER
19

By the time I got to Rufful's, Leonard was nowhere in sight. I asked Livia, the prematurely gray-haired waitress, if she'd seen a man waiting alone. She pointed to a booth that now held what looked like a college-age couple. "Almost an hour; he kept watching the door."

I went back to the newsroom to use the phone. Sitting at an empty desk in the sports department, I tried Leonard's apartment and got no answer. On his cell phone, his voice mail picked up: "Your call may or may not be important to me. Leave a message and let me decide."

It was noon, and even though it was a raw, windy day, Leonard was probably out riding his bicycle. Religious about the mileage, he'd told me, something like thirty miles this time of day no matter what the weather. I wasn't sure of the exact route Leonard took, but I thought he'd mentioned something about Barrington. I was too fidgety to hang around the newsroom. Even if it was desperate, I had to try to go find him.

I headed to the elevator. If I couldn't find him on the streets, I'd wait for him at his apartment complex, be there when he got back. Just as I reached the lobby, I felt someone touch my arm.

It was Dorothy Sacks. "Good job on the story today." I turned. She was looking at me with a funny expression, as if pleased that I'd actually come through. I might have been offended, but I knew she meant well. "I had someone call in sick; I was wondering if you'd consider working for me tomorrow? The last WaterFire is tomorrow night."

I stared at her dumbly. WaterFire was the outdoor performance-art event along the river at sunset. It was usually an arts assignment.

She read my confusion. "Arts is short staffed, so it got transferred to my budget. You don't have to do any artsy critique or anything, just cover it as a news event."

I intended to be writing a major exposé of Barry Mazursky's murder by the end of the day. I expected to be too busy with the follow to write a sappy WaterFire feature tomorrow. But I wasn't ready to tell Dorothy this yet, so I stood there, not sure of what to say.

"You'd be doing me a huge favor," she said, in a tone that suggested she would be grateful to me forever. Because I couldn't come up with an excuse, I still didn't respond.

She decided to take this as a yes. Reading from some kind of schedule, she told me I needed to be there at the 4:48 P.M. sunset tomorrow, and suggested I work daylight savings into the lead.

"You headed to South County now?" she asked, gesturing to a sealed manila envelope in her hand, one of those interoffice communications meant for Carolyn.

"I worked a double yesterday, so she made me take the day off."

She cocked her head, as if to ask what the heck I was doing in the newsroom on my day off. I knew I should tell her about the counterfeit scratch-ticket story, the hours spent at the state police barracks. The reporter in me wanted to spill all, pitch it to the editor and sell it to tomorrow's front page. But I hesitated. I didn't want to write half the story; I wanted the full tie-in to Barry's murder, the story that would exonerate me, prove that my suspicions had been on the right course all along. "I just came in to pick up the paper," I said, lying.

She glanced at my hands, which were empty.

I shrugged, as if embarrassed by my own distractedness. "I got waylaid by a phone call." I walked over to a stack on the floor, picked up a copy, and glanced at the photo of the shoe in midflight across the front page. Above my story was one with Jonathan Frizell's byline: "Feds Investigate City Leases, Lopresti Denies Favoritism."

"They officially hire him on the investigative team yet?" I asked.

"Not yet," Dorothy said. I could tell by the way she looked away that she felt it was just a matter of time.

I was stuck in traffic, somewhere on Route 114 in Barrington, a onetime country road that was now crammed with small, upscale shopping plazas. It felt leafy and rich, a suburb with impeccable sidewalks and quaint street lanterns that would never consider widening its thoroughfare. The fuel gauge of my car pointed toward an increasingly dire need for gasoline, but I couldn't see a station anywhere, just more stores hawking such essential items as tea cozies and teddy bears.

It was the kind of gray November day best spent under an afghan. A gust of wind picked up fallen leaves from the ground and churned them. I heard the wail of a siren. Maybe it wasn't just the shoppers causing the traffic snarl, maybe a tree was down.

There had to be some kind of accident drawing attention

because the cars only inched forward. Leonard's apartment complex in Bristol was little more than five miles away, but it might as well have been across the bay. On the other side of the road, where there was nothing but a cemetery and a medieval-looking town hall, traffic heading north moved freely, but in this southbound lane, Volvos, Mercedes, and Land Rovers were backed up in parking lots trying to make their way in.

The needle of the fuel gauge slipped another notch. I tried not to look. Warning indicators were notoriously alarmist. There was always more gas in the tank than it seemed. I spotted a cyclist in the distance, pulling out of a plaza parking lot. He was about Leonard's size. The bike also had thin racing tires just like Leonard's.

I squinted, trying to will Leonard into view, but as the cyclist got closer, the details started to give way. The man's jacket was a shade of orange Leonard wasn't likely to wear and his legs looked especially scrawny in biking tights. The absence of the WKZI emblem on the bike helmet also confirmed that he wasn't Leonard.

The cyclist began weaving through the stopped cars to the other side of the street. As his wheel bounced across a fancy brick median strip, a bottle fell out of a metal holder on his bike frame and began to roll. The wind and gravity took it onto the northbound lane, where it was crushed under the wheel of an oncoming car.

But on this side of the road, traffic still wasn't moving. I wished that I was on a bicycle that could weave between the stalled cars, that I could ride on the shoulder or climb up the curb. I glanced at the fuel gauge again. There had to be at least one or two gallons in a special reserve.

There was probably a gas station in the next block, but the green SUV in front of me made it impossible to see anything beyond it. It was one of those enormous vehicles that should be reserved for military use but instead was driven by a lone woman. It probably had three full tanks of gasoline.

Behind me, a car honked. I flipped on the radio to see if there was a news report about the traffic snarl, but there was nothing. Instead, I caught a public-service announcement about the season-finale WaterFire tomorrow night and wondered whether I should have just told Dorothy the truth.

Better to wait until I had all the information, not just pitched, but proven, I reminded myself as I nudged the nose of the car a foot closer to the SUV. The woman driver looked up, in her rearview mirror. I was being obnoxious. She twisted around in her seat so I could know that she was glaring at me.

The engine made a funny sputter, as if trying to suck every last bit of fluid from the tank, but I ignored it. Finally, we were beginning to move and I could see a gas station in the next block. The SUV slipped through the next traffic light, but I got caught at the red light.

First in line at the intersection, I could see what was causing the problem. A police cruiser and an ambulance were up on the curb of the cross street. The back doors of the ambulance were open and there was a huddle of people around a tree.

Three women stood across the street together on a postage-stamp lawn, watching. I searched for signs of a banged-up car, but couldn't see anything. Then I caught a glimpse of mangled bicycle next to the tree. Bright, iridescent red, just like Leonard's.

My breathing stopped. I told myself that I was overreacting, forced myself to exhale. Nine out of ten fancy road bikes were probably painted that same shade of red. Because of the bike path in the area, cyclists came here from all over the state. It could be anyone. Anyone but Leonard.

I pulled into the side street without waiting for the light to change. Parking on the corner, I walked swiftly to the accident site. "I'm sorry to bother you," I said to a cop who was standing near the tree, clutching a clipboard. "I saw the accident and I was supposed to meet a friend who was out biking. Just wanted to make sure—you know—it wasn't him."

The cop was young, barely out of the academy, with straight brown hair cut in a pageboy under her chin. She was about my height, but stockier, and I could picture her in a field-hockey uniform. Her badge said "Toland." "We don't know who it is, the guy's unconscious and we can't find any ID." She sounded irritated, as if she'd already answered too many spectators' questions.

I took a closer look at the bike, hoping to see the thicker tires of a mountain bike. But they were thin road tires just like Leonard's. I averted my eyes from the bent metal frame. "It's probably not him."

Toland wasn't listening to me; she was watching the three EMTs, who were now moving the stretcher toward the ambulance. "How old is he? Your friend?" she asked.

"Forty-five maybe. Forty-six."

Her eyes returned to me swiftly. I saw a glimmer of something I didn't like and her tone became friendlier. "Maybe you could take a quick look, just to make sure. It would help us if we could identify this guy."

"I doubt it's him," I said, as if repeating it could make it true. But she had already turned, already lifted her hand trying to get the attention of the EMTs. Her pace toward the ambulance quickened. I scrambled after her.

"How bad off is he, this guy?" I said, matching my pace to hers.

"Unconscious, a couple cuts. But otherwise the injuries don't look too bad. Be good if we knew who he was, though, so we could call his family."

Another gust whipped up leaves under the tree where the bicycle lay. I pictured Leonard hurtling through the air. I thought of his phone call last night, of the silver sedan that had followed him into the station parking lot. I flinched, involuntarily, remembering the silver sedan that had gunned for me in the street, the way it had nearly crushed my back.

The cop looked over quickly. "You all right?"

"Fine. Did a car hit him?"

Gripping the edges of her clipboard to keep the paper from fluttering, she shook her head. "No skid marks and the woman across the street didn't hear any car brakes. But she didn't see it happen. No real witnesses to the accident, right now . . ." She began waving her arms. "Joe! Joe! Wait a minute, I got someone here who maybe can do an ID."

The EMT's back was toward me. The stretcher was already beyond him, inside the ambulance. He turned, a solid, square man in some sort of uniform. A firefighter, maybe. He waved me over, an impatient gesture. Let's get this over with, quickly.

My legs suddenly stopped. I stood there feeling like this was a big mistake. Here I was wasting precious minutes because of a premonition, a bad feeling in my stomach that probably had to do with hunger. The EMT waved again, with thick, square fingers. Officer Toland gestured for me to get moving. I was wasting time. As I stepped closer to the open back doors of the ambulance, two EMTs parted, giving me room to see. I looked into the sterile cavern, down at the man who lay there bundled into the stretcher. His eyes were closed, a deep cut bled over the brow, and spatters of red spilled onto the chest of the nylon bike jacket.

The world spun in my peripheral vision, leaves blew around my feet. "Leonard Marianni," I said softly.

She asked me to spell it for her. I also gave her the phone number of the radio station, which I knew by heart. I turned back to the EMT. "He's going to be all right? Right?"

"We're doing our best," the EMT replied. Not a prognosis, just something he'd said a hundred times before. But he took a second to give me a hopeful look that made me think it might all work out. Someone else snapped the back doors shut and I was left standing with Officer Toland on the sidewalk as the ambulance peeled away, its lights already flashing.

After a failed attempt to get through to a human at the radio station, Officer Toland asked if I knew of any other way to contact Leonard's family. I was numb and cold, and wanting to do something that could help. Remembering the pictures of the nephews on Leonard's refrigerator and the Rolodex on his kitchen counter, I offered to show her where he lived in Bristol.

"You have a key to his apartment?" Toland asked.

I remembered what Leonard had said the night before about the extra key hidden in the door molding and nodded.

Glancing at her watch, she asked me to wait a minute, went back to her cruiser, and consulted with someone by phone. When she returned, she asked if she could follow me to the complex. By the miracle of my reserve tank, we made it there.

The apartment complex looked lonelier than I remembered: plain brick buildings with very little landscaping and almost no grass. I guided Officer Toland through the maze of buildings to the alleyway that led to Leonard's building. On one of the second-floor balconies, someone was drying towels on a makeshift clothesline. They flapped like crazy in the wind.

A lone woman carrying an Apex shopping bag was walking out of Leonard's building and held the outer door for us. Inside, I stood on my toes and felt above the door frame for the key, trying to act like I let myself into Leonard's apartment all the time. Luckily, I easily found the key behind a loose piece of molding.

I took Officer Toland directly into the kitchen. Through the glass slider, I spotted the U-shaped bicycle lock still clinging to the corner post of the balcony. An image of the mangled bike rose in my head and I had to stop, take a breath, and tell myself that Leonard was going to be all right. He would probably be conscious by the time I got to the hospital.

But then, as I turned to the refrigerator, I saw that the photograph of the nephews and the sister was gone from the door. The Rolodex had been knocked off the counter, and half of the little cards were scattered all over the floor. When I bent to pick them up, I found the photograph underneath the kick plate of the refrigerator.

Behind Toland, I saw that one of the counter drawers had been left slightly open, and I got a tight feeling in my chest. Had someone been in the apartment? Toland's expression suggested that she didn't notice anything odd.

"You can kind of tell he's a bachelor," she said, with a roll of her eyes.

"It was a lot neater the last time," I said, my eyes scanning everything now, trying to remember how it had looked the last time I was here. My impression had been of pathological cleanliness that bordered on sterility, but maybe that was just in contrast to my own apartment. Maybe I was overreacting. So far, there'd been no signs of forced entry.

I decided to check the rest of the apartment before I said

anything to Officer Toland. "I'm pretty sure his sister's name is Ellen, and he said she lives in Connecticut," I said, handing her the photograph and a stack of address cards from the Rolodex and excusing myself to use the bathroom.

As I walked through the living room, I saw that one of the decorative pillows was on the floor and one of the back cushions was pulled away from the couch. A wide-screen television system, DVD player, and several additional shelves of expensive-looking electronics were untouched in an elaborate wall system, but a magazine had been knocked off the coffee table. I started down the hallway. I'd never seen the master bedroom before, but something told me Leonard would not leave his nightstand drawer hanging open. I made a quick check of the bedroom windows. They were both locked tight.

In the spare room, done up as a study, the desk drawers were all pulled open and there were folders and notebooks scattered on the floor. A bronze wastebasket was upside down, with crumpled papers beside it and tape sticking to the carpeting.

My stomach made a quarter turn. Someone had been searching for the cassette.

Looking down, I saw my name on a crumpled piece of paper on the floor. I picked it up.

"Hallie, listen to this carefully. You'll forgive me."

The next line was crossed out. Then:

"If this doesn't nail"

The note broke off here, unfinished. I put it in my pocket and scoured the floor for another, more complete version, but found none. I thought about Leonard's phone call last night: *Don't worry, Hallie, I promise you that I'm not going to let you down again.*

"I think I got it!" Toland shouted from the kitchen. I

walked softly into the bathroom. Then I flushed the toilet and closed my eyes, struggling to breathe slower, think clearly. If someone had found the tape and read this note, they would know Leonard had been intending to give me the story.

"You said she lives in Connecticut?" Toland asked.

"Yes!" I shouted through the door.

I ran the water in the sink, trying to figure out what to do. Should I tell Toland that I thought the apartment had been searched? What would Leonard want me to do?

I still hadn't seen any signs of forced entry. No open windows, cracked storms, or broken screens. And the electronic equipment hadn't been stolen. If I told the police that the apartment had been ransacked, they'd start asking me all sorts of questions. Like what intruders had been searching for. Where Leonard had gotten the tape. Why critical evidence was being withheld from the police. I was pretty sure that was considered its very own crime. I decided that the best thing was to go to the hospital first, see what kind of condition Leonard was in. If he'd regained consciousness, I'd ask him what he wanted me to do.

Back in the kitchen, Toland had an index card in her hand that she wanted to show me. Leonard had written "Ellen," with no last name. Several addresses were crossed out and a Connecticut address scribbled in. Four different phone numbers suggested a close, communicative relationship. "I'm pretty sure that's her," I said.

Although anxious to get to the hospital, I had to wait for Toland to finish her call. Pacing the small kitchen with the receiver pressed against her ear, she looked uncomfortable waiting for someone to answer, and I was struck again by how young she looked. But I was surprised by how mature and experienced she sounded once she got Leonard's sister on the phone. Keeping an even, no-nonsense tone, she suggested that family members get to the hospital as soon as possible, but she did not speak in a way to incite hysteria.

I gave Toland my phone number, in case she had more questions, and left her to lock up. Racing to my car, I slammed my key into the ignition, twisting it so fast that it locked midway. Calm, I told myself. Control. I turned the key again. The engine turned. I forced myself to back out of the space slowly, carefully.

The world around me grew sharper, clearer, as I forged ahead. Adrenaline pumped me to the closest gas station where I bought $5 worth of fuel. As I waited for the tank to fill, I said a prayer that Leonard would pull through. Then I snapped the gas cap back on and drove as fast as I could to Rhode Island Hospital.

For such a big hospital, the emergency room waiting area was small and looked as if it had been set up to discourage contact. Receptionists were practically hidden within smoked-glass booths and patients were called into closetlike offices with thick oak doors that shut behind them. At the far end of the room, I spotted a nurse standing at what looked like a triage desk, but it was behind an observation window. The door to this area was locked.

I knocked on the glass to get the nurse's attention, startling a man nearby lying on a stretcher. Frowning, the nurse walked to the door and opened it a crack.

"Is Leonard Marianni conscious yet?" I asked her.

"Are you his wife?"

"A friend."

"I'm sorry. I have to wait for the family. It shouldn't be too much longer." She gestured toward the rows of chairs in the waiting room and backed away from the door, letting it lock.

I hung at the window for a few more minutes, scanning the faces of patients on stretchers, none of them Leonard. A teenage girl propped herself up on her elbows and twisted toward the window, looking beyond me for someone in the waiting room. She looked bored, irritated to be here. How I hoped Leonard's injuries were like hers, an annoyance: stitches over the brow, a cast for the ankle or forearm.

I sat down in the middle of a row of chairs, staring intermittently from the television set to an illuminated ad for the hospital featuring several competent-looking doctors and nurses standing together in team formation. The slogan read: "It Isn't Just Our Technology That's State of the Art." I felt a yearning somewhere in my stomach, wanting to believe those doctors and nurses were all determined to save Leonard, to wake him up, make him well. With a little good technology and good care, he'd be home in no time.

There were a couple of phones near the entryway door and it occurred to me that I should call the paper and tell Dorothy about the accident. Accident? I found myself scoffing at my own choice of words. My heart began beating rapidly. I kept imagining that silver sedan lying in wait for Leonard, following him from his apartment, driving him into the tree. I didn't care whether there were skid marks or not.

I was standing at the phone searching my bag for a quarter when a small, dark-haired woman with a lot of jewelry walked in with an elderly woman who had been crying. Even from this distance, I could see the resemblance. Leonard's sister and mother.

I turned, openly staring as they approached the first window. The receptionist stood up and gestured for them to continue to the other door, where they were whisked into the treatment area. The paper could wait. I sat down on the nearest seat. About ten minutes later, they reappeared. Both women were crying and clutching each other.

I knew that expression, which had been on my own face twice in my life. I couldn't bring myself to approach them, to verify, or to offer sympathy. But I knew. I felt it in the same hollow space that had yearned so badly for everything to be okay. There was no more point in yearning, or praying, or putting desperate faith in a hospital billboard. It was over. Leonard was dead.

I returned to my car and sat there behind the wheel, unable to move. Across the parking lot and a mass of construction, I could see the entrance to the emergency room and found myself staring at the four ambulances parked side by side. Others would be rushed in, unloaded on stretchers. Others with much worse injuries, with cardiac arrests and hemorrhages, would be whisked behind that glass window. They would be treated by those competent-looking doctors in the ad and would survive. Why not Leonard?

The nurse had not wanted to answer any of my questions, but I could tell by her expression, her hand gestures, her silence that she considered it strange, medically baffling even, the same way my brother Sean's death had seemed. Minutes dissolved into a thick, gray background. I finally became aware of how cold it was in the car. When I looked up, the afternoon had become a grim evening and my fingers were numb on the steering wheel.

I started the car and turned on the heat, waiting to feel blood in my feet and toes. Slowly, anger began to heat through the shock. Leonard's death wasn't a freak accident. Someone had murdered him. Probably the same someone who had followed him last night in the silver sedan. The someone who had searched his apartment. The someone who'd threatened to kill me.

On Eddy Street, I stopped at the first gas station that had a phone booth. After a few transfers, my call finally reached Dorothy. She told me the East Bay bureau reporter had already gotten the details on the accident from police.

"It wasn't an accident," I said.

"How would you know?" she asked.

I offered her the abbreviated explanation: When I'd interviewed Leonard Marianni at the vote-no rally in Narragansett, he'd told me about the audiotape from Drew Mazursky. The tape spelled out the reasons for Barry's murder.

There were a couple of seconds of silence then. "You know, Hallie, Leonard has always been known for blowing things sky-high, for trying to manipulate the news."

"I know. I know, but there's more." I told her about the counterfeit scratch ticket I'd bought at Barry's, about my suspicion that Matt had been involved in a long-term investigation involving the market.

"Why didn't you tell me about this earlier today?"

I explained that I wanted to have all my facts together, that I was on my way to meet Leonard and then had stumbled upon the accident scene. I added that I'd gone to his apartment and that it looked like it had been searched.

"Did you tell any of this to police?" she asked.

"Not yet."

There was another silence. She didn't urge me to come forward, drive to Barrington and spill it all to police, though she must have thought about it. There was calculation, an exhale, and a swift change of tack. "I hate to wait a day on this counterfeit-ticket story. How sure are you that there's a connection?"

"I know there's a connection," I said.

"Jesus. You think there's a copy of that tape anywhere? Any other place it could be?"

I thought suddenly of the brown cardboard box in Leonard's studio, his archive. "Maybe."

"What exactly did Leonard say was on this tape?"

"He said that the tape explained the real reason Barry was murdered. He said the cops knew all along it wasn't an armed robbery."

"All right. Be careful. I mean, don't do anything stupid. Don't put yourself in any danger. But if you think you can get your hands on this tape fairly easily, if you can verify any of that, this would be huge. Christ, this could bump the goddamn referendum coverage off the front page."

It was almost seven o'clock when I got to the radio station. The wind howled with dry, frigid air from Canada that whistled right through the Honda as if there were no windows. There were only three other cars in the parking lot. I hoped one of them was Robin's.

I fought the wind to the lobby entrance, feeling tired and numb by the time I got to the door. It was open and all the lights to the FM station upstairs were on, but there were no signs of anyone downstairs. A couple of half-empty coffee cups littered the table and the day's *Chronicle* was spread open on the couch. I yelled a "hello," but got no response. I walked slowly through the long, narrow hallway that led to Leonard's studio and the production booth. I found Robin at the desk, her face red with tears.

"You know?" she asked.

I nodded. We hardly knew each other, but she stood and we embraced. The chill in my limbs had moved to my heart and I felt as if I were somewhere in the distance, listening to myself as I told her about stumbling upon the accident scene, seeing the mangled bike. It sounded like a story I was writing about someone else, not about Leonard, not about someone I knew.

She told me that he'd had a previous heart problem and had gone into cardiac arrest. That his skull had been badly fractured, and even if he'd lived, he'd never have been the same. I kept thinking that she was talking about someone else, someone older, or weaker, or living in a different state.

I looked past her, through the glass window and into the studio. I had a sudden image of Leonard, standing with his headphones on, refusing to sit down, the way he'd flailed his arms with impatience and cut off the callers. And then I saw his headphones, casually discarded on the desk. Through the numbness, I felt a stab. He'd been trying so hard to get me to forgive him, trying so hard to make amends.

We sat down, Robin at her desk and me in a chair I pulled in from the office. She had overheard Leonard calling me about the sedan in the parking lot, but she said strange cars showed up in the parking lot all the time. "Teenagers smoking pot and making out," she said. She kept repeating that she couldn't believe Leonard was dead and eventually lapsed back into tears. "At least he died doing what he loved to do," she finally said.

"Right." I wanted to offer comfort, but the blade twisted again. All I could think was that there was no possible upside to getting murdered. It seemed especially cruel to me that anyone should get murdered doing what he loved to do.

It was freezing in here. I walked back to the little kitchen area to make us both a cup of tea. When I came back with the mugs in my hands, I glanced inside Leonard's studio again and caught sight of the brown box on the floor, Leonard's archive.

I gave Robin her tea and asked if it was okay to look for

something Leonard was supposed to give me. "Go ahead. He wanted to talk to you last night in the worst way," she said. "He seemed frantic about it."

Leaving my tea on the desk, I moved to the studio, trying to fight through the numbness. Kneeling on the floor, I thumbed through the box. Leonard wanted me to find the tape. *He seemed frantic about it.* This was something he wanted, I told myself, something I could do for him. I began diving through stacks of tapes, carefully reading each label. They were each meticulously dated and detailed with the subject of the show. I found a dub of the show I was on. Thinking the man who threatened me might have been recorded even though he was cut from the air, I put the tape in my knapsack.

I was going through the box a second time—I couldn't find anything that wasn't clearly marked as a dub from his show— when I noticed a man at the end of the hall, watching me.

I froze.

Robin's chair was on rollers. She rolled out of her office and into the hall. "Oh," she said, "I forgot to call you."

I stood and walked closer. The man in the hallway was Gregory Ayers. He wore a business suit and tie, and he carried a briefcase that made him look official. Robin had jumped up from her chair and now stood between us.

"I'm so sorry, I should have called you to cancel," she said, "I forgot you were supposed to be our guest tonight. I . . ." She looked back at me, helplessly.

I moved down the hall, beside her. "You haven't heard?" I asked Ayers.

He shook his head.

"There's been an accident," Robin began.

His face grew very still, but he did not register shock. At his age, Ayers was no longer surprised by people's deaths. Robin had started crying again, so he reached into his jacket and offered her a handkerchief. It was neatly pressed, old-fashioned, possibly monogrammed. She held it in her hand, not knowing what to do with it.

Ayers gestured for her to keep it. Reaching for my hand, he told me how very sorry he was about Leonard. I thought about the night at Raphael's when we'd all been in the bar together, the night that I'd rubbed Gregory Ayers's arm for luck. How full of life Leonard had been that night. How full of persuasion. No one that young should die that abruptly. Not Leonard. Not my brother, Sean. A blade twisted inside me and tears began to burn behind my eyes. I blinked them back and quickly left the station.

CHAPTER
20

I PULLED INTO my parking space, turned off the ignition, and stared squarely out the window at my apartment building.

I thought about climbing those dark stairs to my empty apartment to spend the night awake, listening for sounds. I turned the key in the ignition and started the car again. More than anything, I wanted to go to a casino, where it would be bright and loud and crowded all through the night.

I glanced at my fuel gauge, which was nearing empty again. What was I thinking? I didn't have enough money for gas, let alone the blackjack table. I shut the engine off and opened the car door. A sudden image of the mangled bike broke into my head and I slammed the door shut again.

Reaching into my pants pocket, I pulled out the crumpled note I'd found on Leonard's floor. "Hallie, listen to this carefully. You'll forgive me. . . . If this doesn't nail"

Whoever had found the tape must have read the note, must have known Leonard had been trying to get it to me. They had to wonder how much I already knew. How much Leonard had already told me.

I might have stayed in the car longer except that the temperature had dropped at least ten degrees, and it occurred to me that breaking into my car was a lot easier than breaking into my apartment. I took several steps on the asphalt, toward my front door. The light above the door illuminated the entryway.

My brain jumped into video mode, projecting a male form into the hallway. The man was huge, wearing a parka and pressing himself against the wall, waiting. I could almost feel the huge arm grab me around my neck, the metal gun barrel at the back of my head. I shook my head, trying to shut off the picture machine. Something large snapped behind me. I whirled around. In the dark, I saw a branch hanging like a broken arm from a tree.

Past the tree, a man was turning the corner. He was running a slow jog, an end-of-the-workout pace, past Starbucks and onto Elmgrove. He wore a familiar-looking hooded sweatshirt and had a very long stride.

"Matt!" I screamed across the street.

He stopped, looked back over his shoulder toward Starbucks. I shouted a second time and he finally turned my way.

Before I'd worked out what I was doing, I was across the street, meeting him on the sidewalk. He was panting from his run, rubbing sweat from his forehead with the back of his hand and regarding me with curiosity. "What's going on?"

I stood there shivering from both cold and fear. I glanced back at the hanging tree limb, not knowing how to explain.

"You all right?" Matt asked, taking a step closer.

"You heard about Leonard Marianni?" I asked.

"The bike accident?"

I was watching Matt's reaction carefully, looking for some flash of understanding, but he gave nothing away. "Yeah."

"Was he a friend of yours?" The question sounded sincere and just a little surprised.

"Sort of," I said, realizing that there were things I couldn't tell Matt, that I'd have to adapt the story. "I was supposed to meet him today," I heard myself lie, "to get the follow on a vote-no rally I covered yesterday. I got stuck in the traffic holdup—you know, because of the ambulance. I had to identify him for police." My voice broke off.

"You want to go for a drink somewhere?" he asked softly.

I nodded.

"I've got to change; you want me to meet you at your apartment?"

"No!"

He looked across the street at my apartment building and then swiftly up and down the street. "Why?"

I didn't answer.

"Someone come after you?"

I shook my head. "I heard a noise, probably just a branch snapping in the wind. I'm just a little spooked . . . after all that's gone on today." I saw the mangled bicycle again and closed my eyes.

"All right. All right." His voice was his best feature, warm like a blanket. "Why don't you come upstairs and wait for me while I change? Or better yet, I think I have beer in the fridge."

His apartment smelled of pizza. It looked messier than last time, as if way too many meals had been eaten while watching television on the corduroy couch. The number of files had multiplied on the dining-room table, and there was now also a laptop and a printer, with several extension cords plugged awkwardly into the wall.

Matt guided me to the couch in the living room and cleared

a pizza box from the coffee table. He left with the box and re-turned with two beers and a take-out coffee cup filled with brown liquid. He put both a beer and the take-out cup in front of me. "I'm out of mugs. But it's brandy, warmed in the microwave. If I were you, I'd drink that first."

He might have ridiculed all my false bravery earlier that day on the ride from the state police barracks, but he didn't. Instead, he dragged the corduroy La-Z-Boy chair close to the couch and sat opposite me, leaning forward, elbows on his knees while he studied me. I realized then that his sarcasm was a veneer.

The take-out coffee cup had been rinsed, but I still inhaled the leftover scent of coffee with my swallow of hard alcohol. The burning in my throat was comforting.

"All right. What exactly has you so freaked out?" he finally asked.

I tried to think of what I could say that wouldn't say it all. I took another sip of the brandy and told him about the silver sedan. How Leonard had called me at the bureau and told me that he thought he was being followed.

"Why did he think someone was following him?" Matt asked.

I studied his face. There was nothing artificial in his ex-pression, nothing brimming in his eyes. If Matt was searching for the same audiotape, he had no clue Leonard had gotten hold of it. I did not offer to make the connection. "He didn't say," I lied.

Suddenly, his expression changed. Leaning so far forward in his chair that our knees practically touched, he grabbed my shoulders and searched my eyes. "What do you know that you're not telling me?"

"Nothing. I don't know anything."

"But you suspect something; what is it?"

I looked away.

"You think he was *murdered,* don't you?"

"I'm . . . I'm not sure."

He let go of my shoulders and leaned back in the chair, looking at me as if he needed perspective. "You went to his apartment to interview him for a story, a follow-up on *yester-day's* rally? What happened to the counterfeit-scratch-ticket story? To all your theories about the Mazursky murder? You just put those aside?"

I ignored the tone and nodded. He folded his arms and stared at me, his eyes darting between thoughts. Then something else lit in his eyes. "You must have gone to Leonard's right after I dropped you off at the lottery."

I might have said I stopped at the newspaper first, but I didn't think that would gain me anything. I took another sip of brandy and felt it in the pit of my stomach. Vaguely, I remembered that I hadn't eaten lunch.

"To work on a story about *yesterday's* rally?" His sarcasm was getting a little thick, so I didn't respond.

"And Leonard Marianni called you afterward to tell you he was being followed, but not why? But somehow you are now convinced he was murdered—and that the murderer was coming after you next?"

"I never said that."

"If you told me what really happened, why you were going to meet Leonard and what he had to do with these dirtbags who are after you, maybe we could actually catch these people and put them behind bars. You know, *before* they got a chance to kill you."

I was tired and hungry and sick of being scared. I thought about laying it all out: from the audiotape I couldn't find to the note on the floor of Leonard's ransacked apartment. But I remembered the conversation I'd had with Dorothy. The long and pointed silence. The part where she deliberately did not advise me to go to the police with my suspicions. I stalled by taking another sip of the brandy, swallowing. Then, I spotted the logo on the side of the take-out cup: the Mazursky Market. I thought suddenly of Drew. Wouldn't he have made a copy of the tape before he gave it to Leonard?

"It was just all the wind howling outside," I said, standing up. "And all your warnings. I let it get to me, but I'm okay now."

He stood up, too. "No, you're not okay. You're incredibly stubborn and blindly ambitious."

On an empty stomach, the brandy had done its job. I felt steadier, bolder. "I'm sorry I bothered you. I don't know what I was thinking, really. I should probably be getting back to my apartment." I was halfway to the door when I felt his arm on mine again, wheeling me around.

"Hallie, you're going to get yourself killed. Please, tell me you're smart enough to lay off this story—"

I didn't answer.

He shook his head at me and let my arm go. For a minute, I thought he was going to let me out the door, but then he changed his mind again. This time, he put a hand on each of my shoulders with a firm grip.

"Listen, whatever instinct told you not to go back to your apartment tonight was the right one. You look pretty wobbly. If I let you go back to your apartment and something happened . . ." He stopped, left the possibility unsaid.

"I'll be okay."

"Maybe you will, but I won't. I'll be awake all night. Have you even had dinner yet?"

I shook my head.

"I can offer you leftover pizza. Just humor me. Stay here."

Our eyes met. He deliberately held my gaze. A current

flowed between us. I felt it in the grip he had on my shoulders, the warmth of his hands, and the flow of blood in my arms. For a brief moment, I hoped he would kiss me. I could forget about Leonard, about Barry, about the investigative team. The brandy in my stomach made me think it might happen. But Matt, always the professional, knew how to restrain himself. Instead of kissing me, he turned me in the direction of a short hallway.

"I'll warm up the pizza and get you some clean sheets. You can sleep in the bedroom," he said, sounding matter-of-fact. "It has a lock on the door. I fall asleep on the couch half the time anyway."

When I awoke the next morning, there was a clean, folded towel, a toothbrush, and a newspaper at the end of my bed. Underneath the newspaper was a note:

"Orange juice and English muffins in fridge. Don't go anywhere. Be back by eleven."

I snorted at the *Chronicle*'s front-page story about Leonard's death. It quoted the Barrington police about the bike accident as if all their theories were so logical: severe winds, crevice in the winding road, a squirrel that ran out into the bike's path.

Suddenly, I felt anxious. It was already ten-thirty. I couldn't waste time hanging around Matt's apartment. I left him a note thanking him for letting me stay the night and promising to call him later. Then, I headed directly across the square to the Mazursky Market.

It was packed with people. A woman I'd never seen was working the cash register, so I headed through the throng to the back of the store, hoping Drew was behind the counter at the deli. A young man in his early twenties was making sandwiches. I asked him where Drew was and he told me that he'd had to go home, but would be back in a half hour to relieve him. I ordered coffee, drank it, ordered another, and wandered around the store. Drew didn't come back. After the rush cleared out, I finally approached the woman at the register. She was heavyset and sweating profusely in a sleeveless, silky kimono as she reached on her tiptoes to get the man in front of me a pack of Marlboro Lights.

"You know when Drew's going to come back?"

She took a moment to catch her breath, and then she threw her arms up as if to say, who could tell?

"He *is* coming back this afternoon, right?"

"If they don't keep him all day."

I gave her a puzzled look.

"That poor family, it never ends."

"Is his mother okay?" I asked. "No emergency, I hope?"

"Violated is what she is. Husband dead. Murdered in broad daylight." The clerk caught herself, then amended, "Well, not broad daylight, but right here, right in his own store. Shot to death. And what do the cops do? They search the victim's house. Can you believe that? Last week they searched poor Nadine's house, this morning she called here all upset. Now they're searching her son's apartment. Can you believe the nerve?"

I shook my head.

No, I couldn't believe the nerve, the audacity of Matt Cavanaugh, who'd outsmarted me this morning, left me sleeping in his apartment as he searched for the tape I wanted so badly.

A part of me understood that Matt had a job to do, but the other part, the part that had felt so responsive to his concern the night before, was furious. I sure as hell wasn't going to go back to his apartment, and I desperately needed a shower.

I opened the outer door of my building and stood listening for sounds on the staircase. In the bright light of a sunny November day, it was a little easier to be brave. It was a little easier to believe that if I stood there long enough, confirming the absence of shifting feet, of movement in the hall, that I could make it upstairs, lock the door behind me, and be safe.

My mailbox was overflowing with several days' worth of mail. I couldn't deal with all the bills—the mounting debt I'd never be able to repay—so I left it in the box. Upstairs, I checked the apartment thoroughly, triple-locked the door behind me, and headed for the shower. Under the hot steam, I allowed myself a few blank moments before I turned my thoughts to the *Chronicle* and whether I'd ever be able to convince the editors to believe there had actually been an audiotape.

I stepped out of the shower and into a puddle of lukewarm water that had leaked onto the floor. Dorothy had gone out on a limb trusting me with my story about Barry's compulsive gambling, and where had it gotten her? Without the tape to back up my claims, no one was ever going to believe that Leonard's death was murder.

I stood in the bathroom after I'd dried off and listened through the door before I opened it. From the bathroom, I could see no signs of entry. I stepped far enough into the living room to get an angle on the door; it was still triple bolted. My running shoes were where I'd left them on top of the coffee table. I picked them up, ran to the bedroom, and locked the door behind me to change.

I put on a turtleneck and squeezed into blue jeans in record time, but by the time I'd laced up the running shoes, I began to relax a little. I made a quick bowl of tomato soup and grilled cheese and actually finished it. My mother called and I forced myself to sound calm, collected, as if this was just another Saturday afternoon, listening patiently to the update of my cousin Susan's wedding plans. It was almost three o'clock when Matt called. I let the machine pick it up. He apologized for getting "delayed at the office," and not calling sooner. "Don't go to work before I get a chance to talk to you," he said. "I need to talk to you."

To gloat? To keep tabs on me to make sure I couldn't get anything about his search in tomorrow's paper? I grabbed my yellow running jacket from the closet and decided I should get out of the apartment before Matt decided to make a personal visit.

Downstairs, as I was headed out of the hallway, my gaze caught the mailbox again. It was so completely crammed with uncollected mail, I wondered if the postman might refuse further delivery.

I stopped, wrestled with the envelopes, twisting the paper to extricate it from the box. As I expected, they were all bills, four from credit card companies, one from the phone company with the red-warning delinquency band across the top, and a handwritten envelope that no doubt had been left by Hal the landlord.

If only I'd actually won $10,000, all these problems would be gone. If only the big winner of my life hadn't been a freaking counterfeit. I didn't want to think about my luck or my finances, so I stuffed the mail under my arm and headed outside to my car.

As I threw the pile onto the passenger seat, it scattered, several envelopes falling to the floor to reveal the larger, thicker, hand-addressed envelope on the bottom. Familiar handwriting. Not my landlord's.

I locked the car doors and ripped open the envelope.

Hallie,

*Nail him to the wall. Page one. Call me and tell me you forgive
me. ASAP.*

Leonard

Inside, wrapped in a single sheath of bubble packing, was a
tiny microcassette.

CHAPTER
21

I CHECKED TO make sure my microcassette recorder was inside my knapsack, and then quickly pulled out of the parking space before Matt could look across Elmgrove and spot me inside my car.

I fumbled with the tape at the first red light, twice popping it into the recorder backward before settling it into the machine. And then suddenly, Barry's voice, eerily alive, filled the car, as if he were in the passenger seat beside me. "Jesus, this is a lot of inventory."

I felt the shock of his voice. My lungs got tight trying to draw air and my eyes began to get blurry. The road dissolved. A horn behind me honked and I snapped off the machine, letting it fall off my lap and onto the seat. I'd get killed if I tried to listen to this while driving.

The car honked a second time and I put the car into gear, following a Volvo station wagon carefully down Angell Street, trying to pay attention to my driving so I wouldn't sideswipe anyone. But I was wild inside, a frantic mess, trying to keep it together until I was downtown, safely parked, where I could listen, rewind. Listen again.

The *Chronicle* had no parking lot. I drove around the building three times looking for a space, my heart pumping louder and more recklessly each time. It was Saturday, for Christ's sake. Saturday, and no street parking? Finally, I began to see beyond my windshield and noticed the people walking together in clusters on the sidewalks. And then I remembered WaterFire. Tourists were already beginning to gather for the evening's event.

I couldn't think about WaterFire now. All I could think about was listening to the tape. I turned and began heading away from the river and the tourists to what was sometimes called the DownCity section. It was only five or six blocks from WaterPlace Park, but it might have been on a different planet. This old commercial district was still in transition. Abandoned department-store buildings, only partially restored, housed funky nightclubs and the kind of social-service agencies that were closed on the weekend. The streets would be empty at this hour.

There were plenty of spaces on Westminster Street and I parked in front of Lupo's Heartbreak Hotel, a nightclub that was especially dark and barren in daylight. I locked my car doors and grabbed the tape recorder from the seat and re-wound the tape, starting all over again.

"Jesus, this is a lot of inventory," Barry began.

I didn't go cold this time, didn't give way to chills from the dead. Instead, I turned up the volume and closed my eyes to listen.

"Your sales slacking off?" another male voice responded. It was a mature bass that sounded seriously concerned.

"No. Just . . . you know . . . well, maybe a little," Barry replied.

There was a long silence. "The fifty-dollar winners in the same place in the book?" Barry asked. There was a shuffling sound.

"Yeah," the other male voice replied.

"You sure these were checked?"

"We had one bad print run. Don't worry. We threw the entire batch out. The problem's been fixed," the man said, sounding annoyed.

There was a skeptical chortle from Barry. A horn honked in the background and I realized they must be in a car driving somewhere. And then it got quiet, as if the car had entered a garage. I heard something mechanical and then the sound of something being tossed on a dashboard. "Fucking rates in here," the other man said. A couple of seconds of silence and then: "There's a space."

I couldn't tell who was driving, but I imagined Barry parking the car. The car engine was shut off. The other man spoke in a harsh, accusatory whisper: "There's a lot more money to be made on this. You losing your nerve?"

"I'm not losing my nerve," Barry whispered back. "Just make sure there are no more screwups."

There was a click and then empty tape. I found myself marveling at Barry. Not his criminality, but his acting ability. If he was making this tape, he was already in league with Matt, wired for the attorney general's prosecution, but he sounded like a crook with legitimate crook concerns, pissed off rather than defensive.

There was another click and then a different voice thanked Barry. After a minute, I heard the sound of coins hitting the dashboard. The engine noise grew louder and I heard traffic sounds again. "Did you see that article in the *Chronicle*? Business section. It was about this high-tech scanning equipment you guys just bought," Barry said after a bit.

You guys. I stopped the tape, rewound it, and played it again. I remembered a story about some Rhode Island technology company leading the Sunday business section not that long ago. The company that made all sorts of lottery equipment. *You guys.* Did that mean the unidentified male voice actually worked for the lottery?

The buttons on this machine were so tiny that I always worried about hitting the wrong button and recording over the tape by mistake. I checked three times before hitting play.

"That scanning equipment isn't going to affect these tickets. No one is going to scan a losing ticket," the male voice said. "I'm telling you, we got rid of the bad batch. Stop being a pussy."

"I'm not worried about the Smith Hill or South Providence stores. But I'm not gonna sell any more of these in the square. There's a reporter for the *Chronicle* lives across the street, she's buying more and more tickets here all the time."

Shit. That was me.

"The fucking president of the printing company that makes the legit tickets couldn't tell the difference. These are exact copies. And the focus group went wild for this game. This fucking little green leprechaun. I'm telling you, there's money to be made."

There was a shuffling sound, the rustling of paper, followed by more empty seconds on the tape. "Okay. This looks good. I gotta get back to the office; drop me off at my car," the man said.

Then I heard the first note of strain in Barry's questioning. "Hey, how about copying that new ten-dollar game that's coming out? All that radio advertising you been doing, I got customers already asking for that one."

Either I imagined the strain in Barry's tone or the lottery guy was too distracted by his envelope of cash to notice it, because he answered this one directly, with the same slightly smug tone. "You kidding? That's the fucking point of all that advertising."

*   *   *

I listened to the tape three times before I fully grasped it. Before I realized all the implications, and understood. The lottery agent. The focus groups. The advertising. This guy was able to get the counterfeit production ramped up so that it was timed to lottery advertising. This was an inside scam.

I popped the tape out of my microcassette recorder and held it in my hands. It was so small, so valuable, so vulnerable to damage; I was suddenly afraid to put it in my knapsack, where it could get lost among the notebooks, tampons, and twisted papers. I had to get it to the newsroom quickly, safely, this audio proof, this explanation of not one, but two murders. I found a box of Altoids in my purse, poured out the mints, and tucked the tape inside the small metal box. Stuffing it into the front pocket of my blue jeans, I looked up and down the street to make sure no one was around.

The only human forms were the angular-looking people drawn on the window front of Lupo's Heartbreak Hotel. They were life-size sketches pasted to the glass where retail mannequins had once roamed. They were supposed to be hip, colorful partygoers, but the artwork had a harsh, menacing feel. I got out of the car, trying not to look at them as I turned the corner.

I headed down Union, a narrow street between tall, empty buildings. Two drunks stood together midway down the block and held their palms up for money as I passed. I shook my head, walking briskly, as if they weren't there. "Bitch!" one of them shouted.

Scanning doorways nervously, I picked up my pace. The *Chronicle* building was only a couple of blocks away. On Washington, the cross street, I halted. It was bumper to bumper with traffic; WaterFire tourists searched the streets, desperate to park. I wove my way between cars to the other side.

As I was passing Murphy's, a local pub and deli, someone knocked on the window, startling me. I turned around and saw Gregory Ayers at the door, waving. He was dressed in the kind of tweedy sports coat he wore on television, a pair of pressed corduroy pants, and thick-soled shoes. His face looked younger, brighter than it had just last night. Was he here alone? With his wife?

"I just left a message for you at the paper," he said.

At first, I thought it might be about Leonard's death, but his tone sounded businesslike. I gave him a blank look, but inwardly my mind began to rev. As head of the lottery, Ayers *had* to have been informed about my counterfeit scratch tickets by now. I glanced at "The Lot" emblem on the window. Murphy's sold tickets; maybe Ayers was here on business, or as part of an investigation into the counterfeits.

"I need to talk to you," he said, lowering his voice so that it was almost a whisper in my ear. "We'd like to track down the people responsible as quickly as possible."

His breath smelled just slightly sour, as if he'd had a beer, but his eyes were sharp, focused, waiting for my response.

"Right," I said, trying to sound calm, but my heart was beating a million miles a minute. Did he suspect that the counterfeiting was an inside job? If he needed my help, maybe we'd be able to bargain, maybe I'd get information out of him.

"You got a minute?" Ayers gestured toward the innards of the restaurant. It was a favorite lunch spot of reporters during the week, but on Saturday, at this hour, the only people inside would be at the bar.

I didn't *have* a minute. I had a tape in my pocket, evidence of incredible magnitude and a lead on the biggest story in Rhode Island. My feet twitched to get out of here, run, not walk, to the newsroom. I wanted to play the tape for Dorothy before it somehow dissolved. I wanted her to call Nathan on his day off. I wanted editors to huddle together over possible headlines. I wanted to shout "Stop the presses!" at the top of my lungs, the way they did in the movies.

But I was torn. I knew that in another hour, after I'd calmed down and fashioned a rudimentary draft of a story, I'd be on the phone trying to hunt Ayers down. What was the name of the lottery agent who had the Wayland Square territory? I'd have to ask him. Which lottery employees had access to focus-group reports?

"Just a minute of your time," he pressed.

A black Cadillac was waiting on the other side of the street. It was a new, small model and gleamed in an official way. A driver sat behind the wheel, and it occurred to me that it was waiting for Ayers. Who knew where he would go from here, if I'd be able to catch him later tonight?

I followed Ayers inside, past the deli, to a table in back near the bar. Half the bar stools were still upside down on the bar from last night's cleaning. Two men sat at a table, eyes upward, fixed on the keno screen. We took a table near the window, overlooking Union Street. Ayers sat in front of a nearly full beer glass and a half-eaten corned-beef sandwich and pushed both away. Behind him, not one, but two enormous vending machines offered scratch tickets instead of candy.

"I'm so sorry you had to go through all this," he said when I was seated. "You want anything to eat? A beer?" His eyes scanned past me for a waitress.

I shook my head. "Please, I don't have a lot of time."

"Okay. Okay, I understand. Just tell me this. I hear you bought the tickets at the Mazursky Market in Wayland Square. When?" he asked. "Recently?"

I'd answered this question for the state police, nailing the exact day, underscoring that it was the night of Barry Mazursky's murder. Surely they'd communicated the information to Ayers. I wondered if he was doing what I often did, asking questions to which I already had the answers—an introductory softening up. "Two weeks ago. The night Barry Mazursky was murdered."

He looked over his shoulder; I wasn't sure at what. The empty bar stools? The keno screen? When his eyes returned to mine, he nodded, a deliberate and solemn register of a terrible tragedy, but it seemed false somehow. There was something missing from his eyes, some depth he couldn't achieve. I realized why his face looked younger today. There was a layer of orangey makeup on his cheeks and a dusting of powder. He must have been shooting a commercial today or made some other kind of lottery television appearance.

"I'm so sorry you were cheated by this scheme." When he frowned, a deep vertical line in his forehead created a sudden rut in the pancake makeup. He looked old again and asymmetrical.

The door opened and two men entered the restaurant and walked past the deli and tables, straight to the bar. I heard the sound of stools being pulled off the bar and righted on the floor.

"Any idea how the counterfeiters were able to produce such good copies?" I asked.

Ayers ignored my question. "It must have been a terrible disappointment for you."

He gazed at me in a way that was supposed to have meaning, but again, the depth was missing and I had trouble understanding what it was he was trying to convey. Compassion? Sympathy?

"It had to be a crushing blow when they told you it was a fake," he continued.

"Yeah," I said, "that's one way to describe it."

"I'm sorry about that," Ayers said. The rut in his forehead deepened.

I shrugged.

"You know, a counterfeit operation of this kind could really hurt lottery revenues—at a time when the state really needs the money," Ayers said.

I gave him a look. Was there a point to his reiterating the obvious? I got the feeling he was still acting for the commercial, as if he were under a bright light. I glanced over my shoulder, almost expecting a camera, a crew. I didn't have time for this. I needed to take control of the interview. Get the hell out of here. "Who is the lottery agent in that territory?"

Did I imagine that his eyes narrowed? "I'm not sure," he said, slowly. "I'll have to look that up."

He hadn't done that already? Hadn't looked up the agent's name first thing after he got word of the scam from the state police? "I was thinking that the agents were in the best position to know that something was up. Wouldn't sales of legitimate lottery scratch tickets have suffered in those stores?" I asked.

His expression changed, so swiftly, so artificially, it was as if the makeup artist had been in, the face redrawn. "Well, you're right about the effect on state ticket sales. But the state suffers in other ways. Not just past sales, but publicity about this could hurt revenues horribly in the future, affect the programs we finance." His eyes sparkled significantly, and I knew suddenly that all questions up until now had been filler. The point of this interview wasn't to get information out of me. The point was to try to get me not to write the first-person counterfeit-ticket story.

"Premature publicity wreaks havoc on an investigation at this stage," he continued. "I was hoping that you and I could reach some kind of agreement."

Postponing the counterfeit story another day in exchange for giving me the exclusive? Under ordinary circumstances, it was not an unrealistic offer, but not when the counterfeiting could be connected to two murders. "I don't think I can make that kind of agreement."

He frowned and the rut in his forehead returned. There was a long silence. I started to get up. Clearly, our meeting was over. But he gestured for me to sit down. "Please, just a minute more of your time." Reluctantly, I dropped to my seat.

And then, reaching into his jacket pocket, he pulled out something and slipped it across the table. It was a scratch ticket. "Frankly, I think the lottery has a responsibility to you. It owes you—"

This threw me. "It owes me?"

"The counterfeit ticket. You bought it in good faith."

My mouth must have dropped open. Was he saying that the lottery owed *me* money?

"You had a winning ticket. You couldn't have known you were buying a counterfeit."

Ten thousand dollars. My heart began to race. Ten thousand dollars. Was he saying he'd give me that much money?

He studied the ticket on the table. He didn't say a word, but he didn't need to.

I lowered my voice. "Are you telling me that's a ten-thousand-dollar ticket?"

"I have no way of knowing," he said. "Any genuine ticket has the same chance of winning as any other. It could be the two-hundred-fifty-thousand-dollar ticket."

He picked up the ticket from the table, held it to the light of the window, and chuckled. It was the same laugh he used on television after he announced a lottery winner, just before he clapped the winner on the back. His eyes gleamed with his trademark grandfatherly generosity. And I realized two things:

one, that Ayers was holding a ticket worth a quarter of a million dollars, and, two, that he'd never say it out loud.

I stared at the bright bit of paper in his hands. He intended to give it to me. But clearly not just for a one-day postponement on a story. His eyes met mine, a moment passed. One of the men at the bar coughed. From the deli in front, a cash register jingled open. Ayers withdrew the ticket a half inch. "I've seen you, you know, at Mohegan Sun, the blackjack tables. I know you've had a few setbacks."

Stunned, I stared at him. How could he know all this unless someone had been following me? My heart stopped in its cavity. The chambers did not beat. The world did not spin and time moved backward instead of forward. If he'd been following me, he knew I had Leonard's tape.

"I saw you at Leonard's studio, remember?" he said, as if echoing my thoughts. And then, in a very low voice, a barely audible whisper, he added, "We found the only other copy."

The search of Leonard's apartment. Our eyes met. Now his were full of depth, full of intent.

"You saw me pick up a dub from the show I did last week. That's all."

"Right," he said, smiling. "A dub." There was another silence, and then he pushed the ticket toward me. "I'd like to replace your counterfeit ticket as a gesture of goodwill."

Two hundred and fifty thousand dollars. I could pay off all my father's medical bills. My mother wouldn't have to sell her house. My rent would be paid, my debts obliterated. My palms tingled, and I felt the same kind of excitement I felt at the blackjack table when I sensed that the deck had turned in my direction. Two hundred fifty thousand dollars. It wouldn't matter if I didn't make the investigative team. I could quit the bureau job. Freelance. Move back to Boston. Write a freaking book.

Through the window, I saw the black Cadillac waiting outside on Union Street. Besides the driver, I noticed another form, a man, sitting in the backseat.

In front of me, the vending machines displayed the full variety of scratch tickets and my gaze landed on the latest version of the Green Poker Game and its lucky leprechaun. You had to be pretty high up at the lottery to have the focus-group report. *"I wouldn't stand on the same podium as Gregory Ayers,"* Leonard had said the night of the rally.

Gregory Ayers, head of the lottery, was a small-time crook who had risked his position, his state celebrity, for a penny-ante counterfeit scheme? It seemed too bizarre to believe, but Leonard had obviously known about it. That's why he'd attacked him on the air—even though Ayers had been his only ally. Ayers reached into his pocket, pulled out a quarter, and handed both the quarter and the ticket to me. "See if you've won, Hallie."

Despite my intention, my fingers twitched to take the ticket. I was desperate to scratch off the silvery latex, to see the boxes unveiled in my favor. I told myself that I wasn't committing to anything. I was just agreeing to scratch the card.

It was a Caesar's Palace game. The one Barry had been so keen on my buying. I took the ticket and the quarter and scraped off the first box on the roulette side. The winning number was 4. I scraped the first of the played numbers and matched. The price read: $50,000. Another rush of adrenaline moved from my chest in upward spirals till I felt it in my nose.

"Keep scratching," Ayers said.

There was another $50,000 in each of the next four boxes.

"Congratulations," Ayers said.

I held the ticket tightly. All those matching numbers in my hand. A voice inside pointed out that no one else knew I had this tape. Not Dorothy. Not Drew. Not Matt. I could give it to Ayers and no one would ever know.

My fingers trembled so that the scratch ticket actually shook. I gripped one hand over the other. Two hundred fifty thousand dollars. How badly, really, did I want to try to resurrect a failing journalism career?

I met Ayers's eyes levelly. "How do I know this one isn't counterfeit?"

He turned over the ticket and pointed to scan lines. "You want to come back to headquarters with me right now and we can validate it? Write you the check?"

I glanced at the Cadillac waiting outside. "Right now?"

He nodded and I turned the ticket over. Caesar's Palace was the game Barry had wanted me to buy because it *wasn't* one of the counterfeits. I could feel its authenticity in my palms. And how the hell was I going to get out of here if I didn't take the deal? Two people had already been murdered because of this tape. If I didn't give it to Ayers, he wasn't just going to say: *Hey, at least I tried.*

"If I give you this tape, and I leave Rhode Island, I'll never hear from you again?"

He offered a reassuring smile. Two hundred and fifty thousand dollars. I could pay off all my father's medical bills.

Yes, but what would your father say about your taking a bribe? a little voice asked.

I couldn't hear my own answer. It was drowned out by a marching band that beat out the figure on the drums. Two hundred and fifty thousand dollars. A nice apartment right in Back Bay. I could run on the Esplanade each morning. Freelance for magazines and write arty essays in the afternoon. How could I turn down this kind of offer? This kind of life?

I nodded and reached for my knapsack, tucking the ticket

inside. As I zipped closed the inner pocket, I spotted my microcassette recorder inside my purse. The silver metal glinted within a fold of paper.

Ayers smiled that same grandfatherly smile, but behind it I saw the growing impatience. He wanted this deal concluded and was getting anxious. Wiping his forehead with the back of his hand, he created a smear in the oily makeup. "You make your own luck, don't you?" he said, pointedly looking at my knapsack, as if he'd summed up my greed the day I'd rubbed his arm for good luck.

Was I really the kind of person who could take a bribe? The voice inside was back. The voice that had been raised in a good home in Worcester and had gone to Mass on Sundays so as not to accrue any mortal sins.

I thought of Leonard that night in the bar, Leonard who had his own greed for fame and ratings, but who could not have been bribed with money. Leonard had already conquered that demon. *"Gambling changes people,"* Leonard had said that night with a personal knowledge I had not understood. *"They get themselves into all sorts of trouble."*

Like me, $2,000 in debt and desperate. Driven low enough to consider taking a bribe.

Leonard was dead because of this man in television makeup, this despicable, corrupt grandpa smiling for the camera and cheating every desperate schnook in the state. I had the sudden urge to tear up the ticket and throw it in Ayers's face. But with a new shudder, a new spiral of excitement, I understood the real value of that scratch ticket. It was ironclad documentation that Ayers had been trying to bribe me, cover up the counterfeiting scheme, and grab the tape Leonard had dropped off at my apartment on the day he had died. Already I could see the ticket as a fabulous graphic, enlarged in a box on the *Chronicle*'s front page.

Instead of reaching into my pocket for the tape of Barry's conversation, I began scrounging inside my knapsack, fingers raking through papers and pens, bits of lint and grit collecting underneath my nails. I found it deep in the corner of my knapsack: the tape I'd pulled out of the machine earlier, the one I'd used to record my conversation with Nadine Mazursky two weeks ago.

I handed it to Ayers, one counterfeiter to another.

I forced myself to walk slowly out of the restaurant, as if I were a woman who'd made peace with her compromise. But I knew that as soon as Ayers heard my voice on the tape, heard me ask Nadine the first question, he'd know what had happened. Outside, on the sidewalk, I glanced back and saw that the black Cadillac was still parked on Union Street.

I picked up my pace, heading toward the newspaper, praying to God that it would take Ayers a couple of minutes to find a microcassette recorder to play the tape. I was forced to stop at Fountain Street, a one-way street filled with tourist traffic racing at full speed toward the green light. Across the street, I noticed that none of the *Chronicle* employees who usually gathered underneath the canopy to smoke cigarettes were there and realized that on Saturday, the front door would be locked. I'd have to run around the building to the employee entrance on Sabin Street and hope my card key was somewhere in my knapsack.

Traffic whizzed by on Fountain Street at a pace that kicked wind and grit into the air. I had to wait for the light to turn red and bring the cars to a halt. Glancing back again, I saw the door to Murphy's open and Gregory Ayers walk hurriedly across the street to the Cadillac. The car window lowered, Ayers handed the driver something and leaned into the car.

The enormity of what I'd just done hit me. Ayers had already had Barry and Leonard killed; what were the odds he'd let me get away? I stepped off the curb and onto the road, ready to make a run for it, but traffic continued to fly down Fountain, trying to beat the light, which had now turned yellow. I looked over my shoulder again. Ayers was still leaning into the car, a huddle of some sort. Suddenly, he backed away and began gesturing angrily with one hand and pointing toward me with the other.

The driver got out of the car. He was over six feet tall and all in khaki, a hulk of shoulders starting after me. The traffic light turned red, but even if I made it across Fountain, I'd never make it to the *Chronicle*'s back door, never find my card key and get the door unlocked in time.

I scanned the streets, looking for help, and saw a police cruiser in front of Union Station, waiting for the light. Tucking my knapsack under my arm, I ran down Fountain Street and across Dorrance. On the other side of Dorrance, I came to a stop. The sidewalk was filled with pedestrians headed toward WaterFire, a clog of slow-moving tourists taking in the sights. By the time I got to Union Station, the light had changed. The police cruiser was already a dozen car lengths away, turning left onto the highway.

Over my shoulder, I saw the man in khaki crossing Dorrance Street. The world flashed around me in bright, moving bits. Nerve impulses replaced thoughts. My legs took orders from adrenaline. I raced toward WaterPlace Park. It had to be teeming with police assigned to crowd control. There had to be cops there I could call for help.

On the other side of the Wall of Hope underpass, walking paths lined both sides of the river. Turning left would bring me to a dead halt of people gathered around the water basin waiting for the procession of boats to begin the lighting. I headed down the right side of the river, toward the East Side.

The sky was growing dim and the sheer volume of people in the park narrowed the already narrow walkway. I looked nervously behind me. The man was just coming out of the tunnel, scanning the crowd. Almost instantly, he spotted me. My jacket, I realized, was neon yellow, designed to alert cars that a runner was crossing the road. I began pulling it off.

Five teenagers stood together, blocking one side of the path. Coming toward me, on the other side, a young mother pushed a double stroller, creating gridlock. "I need to get by!" I shouted at the teenagers. They looked up sharply, angrily, but did not budge.

"Please, it's an emergency, I need to get by!" I shouted again. The jacket was almost off, twisted around one arm. I turned around again. The man was close enough now that I could begin to make out his features. Even from this distance, I recognized him, the hulk of the shoulders, the one drooped eyelid thickened by the sty. The man I'd seen at Barry's in front of the dairy case. The Parka.

Shit! I blasted between the teenagers, knocking one in the shoulder. A new surge of fear pumped through my heart and into my legs. I heard swearing, shouting, but kept running. The Parka. The Parka was going to kill me. Some Beethoven symphony was piped into the air, pounding to its crescendo. I tried to outrun the pounding and the fear, outpace the nightmare that had been lying in wait.

With each stride, I could feel the metal Altoids box in my pocket digging into my leg, a little stab, a reminder of what was at stake. Nerve impulses connected. A thought. A strategy. I realized that the tape was my only real protection. The Parka wouldn't kill me until *after* he'd secured the tape.

I tried to concentrate on getting a level step on each cobblestone. There was some kind of ramp or stairway to Memorial Boulevard on the other side of the footbridge. If I could get to it quickly enough, escape from the path without the Parka seeing me, maybe he'd get caught up in the crowd and keep running beyond Steeple Street, toward the East Side.

Underneath the footbridge, it was completely black except for a faint light from a strange, formal chandelier suspended over the water. I flung my jacket into the river and saw it begin to float away. Strong urine fumes wrestled with the pinewood smoke of the braziers. I coughed and my foot landed badly on a cobblestone. My ankle twisted and I tumbled to the ground.

Instinctively, I broke my fall with my arms, landing on the path to the side of the footbridge. The skin at my elbows burned and I felt a shock of pain in my ankle. The crowd parted around me, murmuring concern. As I pulled myself to my knees, I spotted some dense ground cover along the river—just within reach. Quickly, I grabbed the Altoids box out of my pocket and threw it into the foliage.

I pulled myself to my feet and winced through the next few steps. To the right were stairs to Memorial Boulevard. I took three steps forward, feeling the pain of my bruised ankle all the way up my leg. The Parka was gaining on me, but I couldn't move any faster.

"Do you need help?" a woman asked. She was in her mid-forties, standing with a group of about five other women, all dolled up in cocktail dresses, high heels, and full-face makeup.

"Yes, I need help!" I gestured behind me. "A man is chasing me."

I struggled up the stairs, crouching low, trying to pretend I was at the end of a road race, gutting through the pain. Behind me, I saw women teetering on high heels, closing in around the stairs, blocking the exit. I hobbled across Memorial, searching for a cop or a cruiser.

I made it to the entrance to Union Station, stopped for

breath, and allowed myself to turn and look. Two college-age boys were standing beside a parked car. A mother with a baby on her hip and a father carrying a toddler in a backpack walked toward me. No Parka.

I slid around the building and leaned against the wall to get a couple more breaths. Could those women really have blocked him from the stairs? Could he not have seen the stairs or figured I'd kept running along the river? I had to get out of here before he figured out his mistake.

I checked up and down the sidewalk. No cops anywhere, but no Parka either. The newspaper was only a couple of blocks away. At the corner, I didn't wait for the light to change. At the first break in traffic, I limped across Dorrance, angling my path so that I crossed onto Sabin Street. I was so dizzy with pain that the painted-tile display on the *Chronicle* building wavered like a flag in a storm.

At the employee door, I pulled my card key out of my knapsack and flailed it under the reader. A red light blinked at me. I heard the sound of a car driving up Sabin Street, waved the card key into the reader a second time, and pulled the door. Nothing.

Slower, I told myself, slower so the code could be read. But my hand wouldn't obey. It shook uncontrollably. A car door shut. Over my shoulder, I saw a black car stopped at the curb. I waved the card into the reader again and saw the light blink green. I could hear the click of the lock giving way, feel the security of the door opening.

Something hard was thrust into my back and a large hand clenched over my mouth. A male voice ordered, "Get into the fucking car."

CHAPTER
22

THE BACK OF the Cadillac smelled of leather, smoke, and a heavy male cologne that made me want to vomit.

The world outside the car spun past, as if I were on some kind of screeching roller-coaster ride that you prayed would end. Only this was never going to end. Gregory Ayers sat behind the wheel, driving the Cadillac, and there was a man next to me, sticking the nose of a gun into the base of my neck.

The man next to me had the same kind of hard, uncompromising features as the man who'd been chasing me, but he was smaller, with thick, dark hair on his head, his arms, and where his shirt was open at the chest. I shivered remembering this man's hair from the night Barry was murdered. He was the man who'd been wearing the gray cap.

He didn't introduce himself, but Ayers called him Reuben. When the car stopped at a corner, the Parka got in beside Ayers. Ayers told him he was an "idiot," and Reuben upbraided him in some sort of Eastern European language. The Parka answered in English. "Fuck both of youse. You try to get through that crowd. And fuck you!" he added, twisting in the front passenger seat to glare at me.

"You don't look so good," Ayers said, looking at me in the rearview mirror. He put his finger on a button and rolled down my window. "If you're going to puke, puke on other cars. Not in here."

"I'm not going to puke," I said, wishing I had a full stomach to retch all over them, or at least the courage to jump through the window. But we were going too fast, weaving through lanes, cutting off cars on the highway. Reuben closed the window when we slowed down to get off the ramp and turn into a part of Providence I'd never seen before. It was a neighborhood of old, listing buildings with boarded-up windows and few streetlights.

Ten minutes later, we pulled into a parking lot behind a narrow two-story building on a corner, a faded sign on the front saying BOOTSIE'S ROAST BEEF. Reuben hauled me out of the car, pushing me toward the building. I tried to picture where we were. Somewhere south of the hospitals, but I wasn't even sure if we were still in Providence.

Ayers and the Parka got out of the front of the car and I was marched to a back door. We climbed a dark staircase, my ankle aching with each step. I was desperate for the sound of customers or of cooking smells, any sign of life, someone to call for help. But Bootsie's looked like it hadn't served roast beef in years. There was no one besides Ayers, the hairy little man with the gun, and the enormous refrigerator shoulders of the Parka.

Upstairs, we passed through a narrow hallway into an apartment that looked like someone had pounded their fists into the walls. Linoleum curled up from the plywood and there were stacks of sealed boxes all over the floor. I was shoved into the center of the living room, where there was a card table with torn plastic matting and two shaky-looking folding chairs. A shade with a water stain was pulled partway down a window streaked with bird droppings.

The only light came from a shadeless floor lamp that was plugged into a wall outlet near the back of the apartment, where there was a hallway and a kitchen with stacks of sealed boxes on the floor. The bald, high-wattage bulb cast a harsh light in the middle of the apartment and left the corners in darkness.

My ankle ached, but I was too afraid to sit down, so I stood at the table while Ayers yelled at the two men for almost losing me. The Parka folded his arms and looked sheepish as Reuben echoed a browbeating in that other language and held the gun.

Much of Ayers's makeup had worn off, but he still looked surreal. He'd changed his jacket for the cardigan sweater he'd been wearing that night at Raphael's. He looked like Mr. Rogers. Only not so nice. He grabbed my knapsack from my shoulder and turned the contents onto the card table. My wallet, tape recorder, dead cell phone, keys, supermarket receipts, brush, notebook, and several crumpled-up papers landed in a heap. Two pens and a lipstick rolled off the end of the table and onto the floor.

"Where is it?" he shouted. "Where's the tape?"

I didn't answer.

Holding the knapsack upside down, he beat it like a rug against the wall. Eraser crumbs, Tic-Tacs, Post-it notes, and the winning scratch ticket rained to the floor. He picked up the scratch ticket, put it into his pocket, and beat the knapsack against the wall again until it was clear nothing else was coming out. Frustrated, he threw the knapsack and it skidded across the linoleum. "Tell us what you did with the tape!"

My brain tried, but failed, to direct thought. I opened my

mouth, but couldn't speak. Ayers gestured to the Parka, who suddenly stepped behind me, imprisoning me with his loglike arms, pulling my back into his chest. His hot breath was in my ear. "I wonder where it could be."

Ayers cackled. Stepping in front of me, he leaned his back against the wall, beside Reuben, who had let his gun drop to his side. Reuben looked away, but Ayers's eyes glinted with anticipation. As if this was the fun part, as if he couldn't wait to see what the Parka would do next.

"Lots of places to look," the Parka said, lowering his voice to a whisper. His breath smelled of raw onion. With his left arm, he put me in a neck lock. Then he reached around me and stuck his right hand into my front pants pocket, his thick fingers stabbing the skin just above my crotch.

I tried to pull away, but he held me in his grip. "Where the fuck is it?" he asked, jamming his hand so deep into the pocket that I felt the fabric tear.

"It's not there!" I shouted.

He took his hand out of my pocket and slowly pulled it up my body, an inch at a time, spreading his fingers as he traveled from my waist to my breast. He was sweating heavily and his body had that same onion smell. He let his hand linger on my breast, drawing another dry laugh from Ayers.

Then suddenly, the hand was cupping my right ear. His fingers grasped the stud of my half-moon earring and twisted it sharply. "Nice jewelry. You think this is worth anything?"

Reuben shook his head. "Silver. Is shit."

"Junk," Ayers said.

With one jerk, the Parka ripped the stud through my earlobe. A bolt flashed behind my eyes. Pain seared through my ear and into my temple. I put my hand to my earlobe and felt a quarter inch of skin hanging from a thread. My fingers were wet with blood.

Ayers chuckled this time. Encouraged, the Parka jammed one hand into my back pocket now, pulling the jeans away from my body. "Let's take these off," he said to Ayers. "Don't worry, I know where I'll find it."

I stared at the blood on my hand. "It's not on me!"

The walls began to swerve. When I inhaled, I was overwhelmed with the onion smell, which was now behind my eyes. I was going to be sick. I was going to puke out the contents of an empty stomach. Then the throbbing in my ear turned into a pounding and I realized that Gregory Ayers was pounding on the table.

"You idiot. Look at all the blood!" His cardigan sweater had splatters of red all over it. And then to Reuben: "Get a paper towel or something from the kitchen, she's bleeding all over my sweater."

"And my cell phone," the Parka noted.

"Do something, clean her up!" Ayers ordered.

Reuben came back from the kitchen with a stack of Dunkin' Donuts napkins, which he shoved in my hand. I sat on the folding chair and wrapped a paper napkin around my severed earlobe, trying to push the skin back together. I winced with new pain.

The Parka removed his cell phone from his belt and began cleaning it with a paper napkin. Ayers walked to the kitchen sink, turned on the water, and dabbed at the blood. "This sweater is ruined. Completely ruined," he moaned.

Returning to the room, he averted his eyes from the bloody napkin I held to my ear. "You should have just given me the real tape. Why? Why would you want to make this so hard on yourself?" Deliberately, he looked from me to the Parka and Reuben and back again, as if he, himself, wouldn't want to spend too much time with them.

I had to think fast, turn fear and nerve impulses into a plan, into some kind of escape. Words sputtered out. "It was in my jacket pocket. I threw it off when he was chasing me." I gestured to the Parka, who was still cleaning his cell phone. "You know. To lose him."

Ayers looked at him and he explained that I'd been wearing this bright-yellow jacket and that the jacket had disappeared and he'd lost sight of me in the crowd.

"Where did you throw the jacket?" Reuben asked.

"In the river." I heard my own voice waver. Ayers's face brightened, and I realized that if he thought the tape was destroyed, the evidence gone, he would be free to kill me. The only reason to keep me alive was to find the tape. If I offered to guide them to it, maybe I could get the hell out of here. Maybe I'd have a chance to get away. "I . . . I . . . took the tape out of the pocket first and threw it into the bushes. Near the footbridge. We could go back there. I could find it for you."

The Parka's eyes began darting, scanning his memory, trying to remember bushes. Were there bushes along the path? By the wall? I wasn't completely sure.

"Do you know what she's talking about?" Ayers asked him.

"Maybe I saw a few bushes," he said, slowly. "Along that wall."

My stomach was tight. I *had* to convince them to take me back. Get me out of this horrible room. "I could show you exactly where I threw it."

Ayers gestured to Reuben and the three men walked past the kitchen and toward the shadowed hallway. They stopped in front of a door, heads together in conference. I couldn't make out what they were saying, but Ayers's voice kept rising in pitch until finally the Parka kicked his foot into the wall in frustration. Then Reuben said something to the Parka in whatever language they spoke. Ayers interrupted and there was more argument.

The Parka had left his cell phone amid the clutter of my knapsack contents on the table. I might be able to pull it onto my lap without them noticing. I leaned across the table and slowly reached for the phone, which was beside one of my notebooks. I managed to sweep it into my lap.

Punching in 911, I waited what seemed like forever until I heard a distant official-sounding female voice. Then I called out down the hall. "Don't hurt me . . . please . . . If you take me back to WaterPlace Park, I promise, I can find the tape."

All three of them shut up at once. My fingers froze on the phone. All three men turned and stared at me. "I know if I re-trace my steps . . . ," I offered.

Reuben started walking toward me and my hands shook in my lap. I was terrified he'd notice that the cell phone was gone from the table, but he stopped midway and turned back to Ayers. "How I keep gun on her with peoples there?" he asked in his halting English.

"The tourists will be gone in another hour or two," I said.

"Oh fuck, we're not going back there, are we?" the Parka asked.

I held the end button down long enough on the cell phone to make sure the service was turned off and cops couldn't call back. Then I snapped it shut. As if he heard, the Parka emerged from the shadows, walking toward me. He stopped and stared at me long and hard to let me know he considered this all my fault. My throat tightened, a vein in my neck feed-ing new blood into my fear. I waited for a suspicious glance at the table, a sudden move toward me and the cell phone on my lap.

But instead, he scratched his crotch and announced that he had to take a leak. Ayers pointed him to the bathroom. When the Parka turned away, I slipped the cell phone back on the table.

Hope beat in my chest for about thirty seconds.

Ayers returned to the table, scrutinizing my ear. "She's bleeding too much," he said. He waited until the Parka walked out of the bathroom, and then began barking new orders. "You'll go alone—when the tourists have cleared. We'll wait here."

I prayed for an argument. Or at least a demand that Reuben go with him. I might stand a chance against Ayers alone. But the Parka only glared at me with his lopsided eyes, as if he'd like to rip the other earring off.

Ayers found some duct tape in a drawer in the kitchen and taped my hands together in front of me, twisting it tight enough so that my wrists burned. He taped my sore ankle to the other one in the same way and used his belt to secure my waist to the chair. Then he handed Reuben the tape and ordered him to tape up my earlobe so he didn't have to look at the bloody napkins.

Reuben wound a piece of duct tape over my ear before grabbing a beer from the refrigerator in the kitchen. Then he relaxed on the floor with some sort of foreign-language magazine.

Ayers dragged the other folding chair across the room, putting it next to Reuben, and sat down. Minutes passed in silence. My temples throbbed in pain. The duct tape fell off my earlobe and drops of blood began to spatter my shoulder. I twisted my wrists in my lap, trying to loosen the tape, but only managed to rub the skin raw. The blood spatters began to dry on my shoulder, and finally the Parka left to search for the tape I had thrown into the bushes.

After what seemed like hours, my head jerked up at the sound of a door slamming. Reuben and Ayers had risen to their feet and the Parka was standing in the doorway. "I couldn't fucking find it anywhere," he said, glaring at me. "There aren't any fucking bushes."

"Right outside the footbridge? Right by the stairs, where I told you?" I tried to sound surprised.

The Parka exploded in frustration, shaking his hand at Ayers, bellowing with fury. "Fuck the tape. I don't give a shit. Let's just fucking get rid of her!"

I held my breath waiting for Ayers's reply. He walked to the streaked window and snapped the shade completely open. Outside, it was still night, but judging by the shade of gray, maybe only another hour or two of darkness remained. He turned back to us. "I can't take the risk that someone else stumbles across it," he said to the Parka. "Go find a Band-Aid or something to put on that ear and take her back to the river. If she can't find the tape, you can do whatever you want to her."

The night sky held thick clouds that made it hard to believe there would ever be a sunrise. My wrists and ankles were raw from where Reuben had ripped off the tape, my ear throbbed and my ankle was weak, but I didn't care. Even flanked by both Reuben and the Parka, with a gun pointed to my ribs, I felt better now that I was out of that horrible apartment. At least outside, there was air to breathe. And a chance.

A chance that the dispatcher had figured out I needed help. A chance that the police would come. A chance that I could get away.

It was a bitter November night. I had no jacket, but the Parka had me clenched in his arm with a gun now pointed at my abdomen. Reuben was close behind us. The onion-tainted body heat was like a furnace. Within minutes, I felt like I was suffocating again.

As we came out of the tunnel into the park, I scanned the terrain, trying to peer through the dim street light and shadows. It had been many hours since my phone call, but surely the cops wouldn't have given up already. Surely they'd still be patrolling the park, looking for anyone suspicious.

Ayers had stayed behind, but he'd demanded to be updated by cell phone. He wanted to know the minute the tape was secured and had called once already while we were still in the parking lot. That had started Reuben and the Parka grumbling in their native tongue.

We took a right and followed the river, toward the first footbridge. Most of the river was black at this hour, the extinguished braziers creating unattractive lumps in the darkness, but there were lights above and under the bridges. I searched desperately, hoping for a cop to emerge from the shadow into the light.

Contained by the river on one side and a stone wall on the other, the path was painfully narrow. I eyed the stone wall, which was ten to twelve feet high and made of blocks that created natural footholds. But even if I could get out of the Parka's grip, there wasn't enough distance. Even if I got to the wall, he'd shoot me like a fish in a barrel.

"Can we slow down?" I asked, shifting my weight and exaggerating my limp. "I can't keep up."

"After you find the fucking tape, we'll slow down," the Parka responded.

Emerging from the second footbridge, the path widened, with enough room for a few trees along the river and near the wall. The Parka gripped me tighter as we passed the stairway to Memorial Drive, hurrying me past my chance for escape, but ahead, at the Steeple Street bridge, there was another stairway, another street exit.

I peered up at the footbridges for a sign of a uniform. Even a maintenance man cleaning up the last of the WaterFire litter. Anyone to call for help. But there was no one.

"Somewhere in there," I said, pointing to ground cover just beyond where I'd actually tossed the tape in the narrow ribbon of green along the river.

"Those aren't fucking bushes. That's fucking ivy," the Parka said.

But he must have seen my darting eyes. He told Reuben to wait at the entrance to the stairway. My heart fell. There was no way to get past him. The Parka stood over me, the gun pointed as I bent to my knees, only a few feet from the river's edge. I glanced up again, trying to will a cop to appear on the bridge. But no one came. I groped through the ivy, flailing through the foliage, knowing I'd dropped the Altoids box at least five feet away.

I glanced at the bridge. Anyone, a jogger, a bum, someone I could call for help. But it was still too early. At least twenty minutes or more until dawn. My fingers dug at the earth, around roots, futilely. No one came. No one was going to come. I moved a few feet forward, closer to the stairway. "Maybe up this way," I said, pointing to another clump of ivy.

The Parka remained standing over me, watching me forage. Wordlessly, I moved on to the next clump and the next. Finally, he began to tire. He kept his gun pointed at me, but backed up across the path to where Reuben was now sitting on the bench.

As I moved past a tree to a clump of ivy at the river's edge, my gaze caught a piece of wood floating in the murky, brown water. It looked like a log from last night's WaterFire that must have fallen off a fuel boat or broken free from the burning pile at the brazier. I considered trying to grab it as a weapon. But then I had another thought.

The river was less than thirty feet wide, with a gondola

platform diagonally across from me, on the other side. Directly in front of me, about halfway across the river, there was one of the braziers from WaterFire. I'd swum in high school and my lungs were in good shape from running. If I took a long, shallow dive, I might be able to stay underwater until I could hide behind the brazier. The water was dark and I'd be hard to see. There was a chance I could make it.

I made a decision: I was not going to go back with these men. I was not getting back in the Cadillac no matter what. I'd rather get shot here trying to escape than let the Parka take me back to Bootsie's Roast Beef, where he could rape me first, where it would take weeks for anyone to find my rotting corpse.

It must have been like the process of drowning, the part where you stop flailing wildly and gulping for air, because the last of my fear dissipated. I no longer felt the pain in my ankle or in my ear. I didn't care how cold the night was, or how cold the water might be.

I noticed that the Parka was no longer actually aiming the gun at me. He was sitting on the bench next to Reuben with the gun hanging from his hand as he watched me. I took a breath and moved to the clump of ivy closest to the water. The Parka stretched his legs in front of him and leaned toward Reuben, saying something.

And then I heard the cell phone ring: Ayers calling for an update. The distraction I needed. My chance. When the Parka reached for the phone on his belt, I pushed off my good ankle and dove into the river.

A shock of water, so cold it was like diving into slush. My chest tightened. I opened my eyes underwater, but couldn't see anything. I had to hope like hell I was going in the right direction, hope I was swimming in a straight line, hope I could hold my breath long enough to make it to the brazier.

I heard someone shouting and then, through the water, a gunshot. I swam like mad through the cold, brown water. My hand whacked something thick and globular that felt like a jellyfish. Only no kind of fish could survive in this river. I couldn't think about what it might actually be. I was running out of air. Had to find the brazier. Had to surface.

I knocked into something hard and lifted my head. I heard another gunshot and a splash of water. I'd hit another log, a floating piece of cedar. I couldn't see the brazier anywhere. And then I realized that I must have bypassed it—and had swum toward the gondola platform because it was now only a couple of feet away.

I heard another splash and looked back. Shit, Reuben was coming after me. My arms were cold, frozen under me as I pulled myself onto the gondola platform. I had no choice but to make a run for it on my bad ankle. I had no choice but to hope the Parka was a really shitty shot.

Pain began to spiral from my ankle to my hip. It was getting harder to ignore it. It was getting hard to take each step. I reached a stairway that led to the Citizens Bank building and heard another gunshot. Something burned into the back of my calf and my ankle buckled. My knee hit the cement. I tried to push myself up, but my leg was too weak and my arms were shivering with cold. I heard the sound of a car somewhere in the distance; I looked up and saw a police cruiser in the parking lot. Two cops jumped out.

I screamed for help. Within a minute, someone was lifting me up by the arms. "You're bleeding," the cop said. "She's been shot!" he called to someone else. And then the black river began to stream behind my eyes, and my body wavered as if swimming through some new medium. The first light of sunrise dissolved and the sky was darker than ever.

*   *   *

I must have passed out, because I woke up on an examination bed in the emergency room at Rhode Island Hospital, covered in blankets, my leg burning.

My wet jeans had been cut off and thrown on a chair. I was wearing a johnny and a nurse was cleaning up the back of my calf. "Saline first. Then a little Betadine," she said.

I winced. The pain of my leg cut through the momentary confusion. I'd been shot.

"The bullet just grazed you. The doctor says you'll only need about eight stitches in your leg and probably four in your earlobe."

I put my hand to my ear and fingered the bandage. My fingers smelled of something dark and sour. River water.

"You lost quite a bit of blood last night. You need to replenish your fluids," the nurse continued. She gestured to a tall plastic cup on a table beside the bed.

I took a sip. Apple juice. I closed my eyes, savoring its ordinariness. It was all over. I was in the hospital, safe.

When I opened my eyes, I saw Matt Cavanaugh standing in the doorway. His eyes were especially dark and ringed, as if he was worried. And then I realized, he was worried about me.

He was completely rumpled, in blue jeans and a sweatshirt, and his hair was still mussed up on one side. He was studying me intently, taking in the bandaged ear and leg, shaking his head. "Are you all right?"

For a moment, he sounded sweet and familiar, like someone I'd known for a long time. Like someone I'd expect to worry about me. Then, he combed his hair with his fingers and stood straight, squaring his shoulders. A prosecutor again. He lifted himself from the door frame and crossed his arms, waiting.

It took me a moment to realize what he was waiting for. "Obviously, I should have listened to you," I said.

He smiled, but without too much triumph.

The nurse dabbed my leg a second time and my eyes opened wide with pain. Matt moved beside the bed and squeezed my hand. And then he said to the nurse, "Can't you give her something for the pain?"

"I'm fine," I said. "Really. It was just the antiseptic."

This reminded the nurse that I needed antibiotics and she set off down the hall. When she'd gone, Matt sat down on the chair beside the bed and, still holding my hand, told me that the Providence police had tipped him off about my distress call. "I've been at the station all night, waiting to hear."

Then he lowered his voice. "We got those assholes," he said. "The guy who shot you and the other guy he was with. They're in custody."

A wave of relief. "They were working for Gregory Ayers," I said.

Matt didn't say he knew that already, but the lack of surprise or indignation told me he'd been trying to prove Ayers's involvement in the ring for some time.

I thought about the tape, the microcassette in the ivy. It was critical evidence that never should have been in my pocket. That never rightly belonged to me. "The tape . . ."

Matt was suddenly at attention, listening carefully.

"Leonard put a copy in my mailbox. It's in the ivy along the river, inside an Altoids box, just past the footbridge, the one right before Steeple Street."

"On the opposite side from the gondola platform?"

I nodded.

A sheen of something came over his eyes. Gratitude, maybe? It almost looked like real affection. Then he offered another squeeze of my hand and was gone.

CHAPTER
23

CHRONICLE REPORTER ABDUCTED." Written by
Jonathan Frizell, the story ran in Monday's paper, the day
after I came home from the hospital. The 24-point headline
was placed above the fold along with an atrocious photograph
of me in a johnny while I was still in the emergency room.

That whole next week I was besieged by requests for interviews from television, radio, and even my old newspaper, the
Boston Ledger. I granted these interviews sparingly after consulting Dorothy first to make sure I said nothing that scooped
our own investigative team.

Gregory A. Ayers was picked up at home, charged in federal court as a coconspirator in the murder of Barry
Mazursky, and held without bail in the ACI, which was
within view of his old lottery headquarters. Ayers was also
charged with kidnapping, felony assault, conspiracy to de-
fraud the state lottery system, and misappropriation of state
funds. He was going to be prosecuted under the federal RICO
act, which meant that Matt Cavanaugh would have to turn
his case over to the feds.

It was strange to be the subject of a news event, instead of the reporter, and I had new sympathy, new understanding for the people I'd quoted in the past. Had I gotten it right? Or altered it just slightly to smooth a transition in the writing? I hoped it was the former, because now I could see that people do remember exactly what they said, how that differed from what was in the paper, and what kind of phrase they would never in their life have uttered.

And the questions were always the same: How did it feel to be abducted? Was I afraid for my life? Was I shocked to discover the evil side of kindly old Gregory Ayers?

I gave reporters the glaringly obvious answers I knew they needed for their stories and tried my best to be quotable, but privately, I was frustrated. I didn't want to be the subject of this story, I wanted to be the byline behind it. State corruption of this magnitude was natural fodder for a Pulitzer and here I was forcibly sidelined by my editors, who insisted I take time off to recover.

And sure, I was lying on my futon with my leg elevated, my sprained ankle still swollen, and both the back of my leg and earlobe sore. And sure, I was still having dreams of the Parka chasing me through orangey smoke so thick I couldn't breathe or see. But the best way for me to get over the violence and ache of seared flesh was to get back to work. Get on with it.

Compulsively, I listened to round-the-clock television and radio coverage of the scandal and reread the week's *Chronicle*. Nearly all of the stories were written, at least in part, by Frizell, who was a shoo-in for the job on the investigative team.

Now, after almost a week of forced recovery, I sat restlessly on the futon with Frizell's latest story on my lap, staring at the art department's rendition of the $250,000 scratch ticket I'd been offered. The graphic had become a logo for the series.

"It was probably counterfeit," Walter said. My mother, who'd spent the first several days with me, had called him and he'd come down from Boston after his shift this afternoon. He was standing at the stove heating up the quart of curried zucchini soup Geralyn had made for me.

"No. Frizell's story today said it was legit," I corrected him. "The governor is launching an investigation into lottery procedures to figure out how Ayers could have identified a winner like that from the inventory."

The way a lot of the reporters, especially the television people, covered the bribe made me sound like a hero for not taking it. But not Frizell. His story pointed out that even if I'd made the exchange, given him the real tape, Ayers would likely have tried to kill me anyway.

I hated to admit it, but Frizell was a good reporter, digging into the details of the story with a thoroughness I had to admire. I began flipping through the rest of the paper to the jump pages to see how many sidebars he'd written, how many stories in today's paper had his byline on them.

"You're pathological. You know that, right?" Walter said. He put a bowl of soup on the coffee table and took the newspaper out of my hands, tapping the inner sections into line and folding it in half.

Walter was laying the folded paper on the bar when the phone rang. Grabbing the cordless from its cradle, he walked it over to me, on the futon.

It was Dorothy. "You feeling better?" she asked.

"Antsy," I replied. "Very antsy."

She wanted me to report to her in the newsroom on Monday instead of returning to the South County bureau. "If you're up to it, both Nathan and I want you to get started on an in-depth story on how the counterfeiting ring operated. You know, why they went to Barry, where they got the technology, that kind of thing. Apparently, the attorney general's office has some background info they want to release only to you."

"Sure," I said, trying to sound cool, but my mind was already beginning to whir. If the AG's office had details it would release only to me, that meant an exclusive. "I'll be there at eight."

There was a pause and then: "Nathan decided that there was going to be such a high volume of investigative stories coming out of this scandal, there may be room for both you and Frizell on the team. He's willing to try you for a probationary period."

As soon as I put the phone down, I jumped up from the futon, oblivious to my ankle sprain, and began hugging Walter.

It was a long and completely silent hug, a communication that covered years of mistakes, of Chris Tejian and my Boston newspaper career. When I stepped away, I felt incredibly light, as if the bandages on my leg and ankle were off and all my stitches were removed. A penance had been paid, an absolution granted. Walter and I stared at each other, not needing to say a word because we both knew that the burden had lifted. That now, I could take his advice. In this small and crazy state, I could finally start anew.

There was a stack of fresh notebooks in my bedroom and I had a desperate urge to outline my plan of attack on the story. As I walked into my room, Walter yelled out that I might want to take it easy on my ankle. "Moderation, ever heard of it, Hallie? Moderation and balance?"

Two weeks later, my story was the lead on Sunday's front page.

The Providence Morning Chronicle

The Mazursky Murder: Corruption from the Casino to the Lottery

First in a series

By Hallie A. Ahern
Chronicle Investigative Team

He sold his convenience-store chain, tapped out every line of credit he'd ever had, and had been in and out of Gamblers Anonymous meetings for three years. Still, Barry Mazursky could not beat his gambling demons.

The manager of the Mazursky Markets in Providence who was shot to death last month in the Wayland Square store had accrued more than $150,000 in debts to loan sharks and was a desperate man, his wife, Nadine Mazursky, said in a recent interview.

That's how he got mixed up with the state lottery counterfeiting scheme that prosecutors say cost the state $2.5 million in lost revenue and allowed him to pay off all his street loans. And according to the state's argument, that's why he was murdered.

The scheme was fairly simple. Using breakthrough technology from an underground printing firm, a ring of men counterfeited $5 scratch-ticket games. Sale of the tickets was 100 percent profit, and since only losing tickets would be printed, there was little risk. "Who pays attention to a losing scratch ticket? You toss them in the trash or on the ground," said Assistant RI Attorney General Matthew P. Cavanaugh, who initiated the state's three-month investigation into the scheme.

See Mazursky, page B-14

"So I can't believe they actually threw in a few fake winners," Frizell said. It was the Monday after my story ran and he was sitting alone in the Fishbowl with the newspaper spread on the conference table in front of him when I walked in. Dorothy and Nathan hadn't yet arrived for our meeting.

"The idea was to increase sales in the Wayland store," I said. "They were small, ten- or fifty-dollar winners that Barry sold only to regular players like me, who he knew would cash them at his store. The ten-thousand-dollar winner I got was a printing error."

"Some error," Frizell said. He flipped to the jump page and pointed to a sidebar I'd written. "And you really believe this crap? That the mayor knew all about the investigation and that's why he lied to you about the memo?" Frizell had already written so many negative stories about the mayor's administration that he couldn't believe that anything Billy Lopresti said was ever true.

I tried nonetheless. "The AG's office confirmed that Providence police had been informed about the counterfeiting investigation and were told to keep a lid on the Mazursky murder probe until prosecutors could get all their ducks in a row. They give high praise to Billy for his cooperation."

Jonathan's expression remained unconvinced. He flipped the newspaper closed to cut off further discussion of my story and launched into an explanation of the piece *he* was writing for tomorrow: a restaurant owner who made a payoff to a health department lackey who threatened to close him down on trumped-up code violations. More proof that the mayor was unredeemable scum.

But I didn't really care about the mayor. Voters had defeated his referendum to legalize gambling by a landslide. Spillover disgust at the corruption of the lottery, most likely, but I preferred to think of it as Leonard's victory: a memorial and a final tribute.

Nathan and Dorothy walked in and cut Jonathan off by dropping a bound folder onto the middle of the table. It was an independent audit of the state lottery dating back five years. Messengered over in advance of the press conference, it revealed "irregular practices" and nearly half a million dollars in unaccountable funds.

In other words, Gregory Ayers had been stealing from the till long before he began counterfeiting. Apparently, his wife, Marge, had both an alcohol and a shopping problem. Whenever she'd succumb to Ayers's pressure to go on the wagon, she'd punish him for her sobriety by going on a buying binge. Furs, jewelry, handbags, and even a marble fireplace mantel that she had imported from Rome.

It looked like Ayers had pilfered from the lottery funds to pay his mounting personal debt. As long as he could hire his friendly accounting firm to rubber-stamp the audits, he was safe from exposure, but the referendum to legalize gambling threatened all that. As part of the bill, a new independent gambling commission, which was to include a member of the Narragansett tribe, would conduct annual audits of both casino gambling and the lottery.

"Ayers had been running the lottery for so long that he started to think that money he gave away was really his," Nathan said.

For next Sunday's segment, he wanted me to explore the theory that Ayers had turned to counterfeiting to try to replace the embezzled money in case the gambling referendum passed. I was to try to reconstruct the whole thing, portray the deterioration of a successful man and the desperation that followed.

Dorothy pushed the audit across the table to me. "Federal prosecutors have scheduled a new press conference for four o'clock. I think they're probably going to announce additional charges against Ayers."

No one mentioned that covering a four o'clock press conference on a Friday meant that I'd be working until nine o'clock, but it hung in the air. Dorothy knew that I'd started work at seven this morning, but also that I wasn't likely to complain. Besides being hired on to the investigative team on a probationary basis, I still had mountains of debt to pay and I needed the overtime.

"About twenty-five inches for tomorrow, then?" Dorothy said. "And maybe a news analysis for Sunday?"

Jonathan, who was rumored to own a ski condominium in New Hampshire, was already packing up his things, eyeing the door. For a moment, the vision of the $250,000 scratch ticket dangled before me. All that money. The apartment in Back Bay. The arty essays that I could have written in the early afternoon.

Dorothy was looking at me with an apologetic expression, as if she felt she might have pushed too far. "The news analysis can wait until Monday, if you want . . ."

I'd had a full week of forced rest and idle time. And it wasn't as if I had any other plans. This was my fresh start, my emotional freedom. I realized Dorothy was waiting for an answer. "Don't worry. I'll be able to manage."

It was almost ten o'clock and I was standing in the last aisle of the Mazursky Market, a salad in one hand and a quart of milk in the other. I was tired from putting in a long day, but still wound up. The stitches in my calf were out, but because of the sprain, I had to wait one more week before I could start running. So I was still working off excess energy and knew that I'd never be able to sleep.

"I had a problem with your story today." Matt Cavanaugh's voice boomed in the quiet aisle.

I let the door of the dairy case swing shut and turned around.

He was standing at the end of the aisle, one hand in his pocket, the other carrying a briefcase. The first snow was falling outside and there were snowflakes melting in his hair and on the shoulders of his camel-hair coat. He was still in a suit and tie, dressed for the office, which he must have just left. "You misquoted me."

I felt alarm begin to rise. I'd spent two weeks researching that story and had been meticulous in transcribing my notes, especially the notes from my interviews with Matt. I'd double-checked every fact, every quote, three times. "What? What did I get wrong?"

"I'd never advocate throwing scratch tickets on the ground," he said, walking toward me. "That's littering."

Now I saw the sardonic smile, the mischief glinting in the dark eyes. I felt such relief that I realized how much I'd wanted his approval on the story—as much as I'd wanted Dorothy's or Nathan's. It had been important to me that Matt saw I could get it right.

Striking a similar tone, I reached into my knapsack and pulled out my silver tape recorder. "I believe I have that in-terview on tape. I can play it back for you if you want."

"Here?" He looked up and down the empty aisle, as if it were full of people who would overhear.

"I can turn the volume low."

He reached over and I thought he might take the tape recorder from me, but instead it was the salad he removed from my hand. Grimacing at the plastic container, he said, "Do you eat this rabbit food every night?"

"Almost."

He shook his head at my dining habits. And then: "How about we listen to the tape over dinner?" And in case I mis-understood: "A dinner that comes from somewhere else."

"Now?"

"You don't appear to have other plans."

He was grinning. I might have taken offense if it weren't so painfully true. Or if it weren't so obvious that he was in the same boat. Just out of work. Alone on a Friday night with nothing to do. I shrugged, nonchalantly, as if to say oh-what-the-hell, hoping he couldn't read me too well, or hear too much enthusiasm in my footsteps. I put the milk back in the dairy case and slowly, as if it were a sacrifice, returned the salad to the deli.

Matt waited for me at the register, where the overweight woman from YourCorner Corporation was ringing up a liter of soda and a pack of cigarettes for a boy who might or might not have been eighteen years of age. But Matt wasn't paying attention; he was peering out the window at the snow falling on Wayland Square, waiting for me. Outside, the snowflakes were enormous, the kind that melted into the pavement and left only the lightest frosting on the grass.

"You ready?" he asked, turning from the window as I arrived. And then, with a glance at the register and that wicked grin: "No scratch tickets tonight?"

"You know," I felt compelled to remind him, "I could have practically been a millionaire."

He sighed. "I think you mentioned that in your statement."

"So it *is* possible to get rich."

He narrowed his eyes at the books of scratch tickets hanging from plastic cases behind the clerk, the wall of bright-colored tickets overstating their promise. "But unlikely," he said, "very, very unlikely."

"Somebody, somewhere, hits a winner," the clerk offered. She used a phlegmy smoker's voice to mimic the lottery's latest radio ad campaign launched to try to rebuild business. "Can't win if you don't play the game."

"That's what they say," I agreed.

Maybe Matt was afraid that I was going to reach for my wallet because he took my hand and tugged me toward the door. And we walked out of the Mazursky Market together without buying anything.